THE KILLING OF CINDERELLA

CHRISTOPHER LEE

The Killing of Cinderella

A Bath Detective Mystery

faber and faber

This edition first published in 2011
by Faber and Faber Ltd
Bloomsbury House, 74–77 Great Russell Street
London WC1B 3DA

Printed by CPI Antony Rowe, Eastbourne

A CIP record for this book is available from the British Library

ISBN 978-0-571-27741-4

One

On the night Lynda Elström was murdered, James Boswell Hodge Leonard was sitting in a basement wine bar listening to Cornelius Cobb telling the story of a budgerigar who could whistle in the key of D minor.

'There's this fella in Gortnamona. In a pub, you know. And he does the singing. And in his pocket, with the gold watch that was his old fella's, (though you daresn't suspect where that one came by such a watch, for he had a way of paying not with the coins but the contents of his fist, if you'll understand my meaning), he keeps the budgerigar.'

'The father?'

'The fella. The old fella's dead.'

'Oh.'

'And when the fella gets to the chorus, well, the little bird, he pops out of the pocket and he does the whistling as bright as if he had the knowledge of the musicals. Now then, isn't that a thing?'

Leonard looked into his glass. Certainly a thing. Had been the first time. And the time after that. And after whenever that was. One, two years ago? The years had made them both word perfect. Leonard put the glass carefully on the fresh bar mat, wiped his mouth with the back of his hand.

'And he's still doing it?'

This wasn't in the script. The other man leaned back, scarlet tie tugged away from his collar and held his half-empty beer glass to the light. Squinting. Seeing it all for the first time and wondering what it was he'd been drinking.

'Now what's that you say?'

Leonard could hardly bother.

'I said, is he still doing it?'

5

The Irishman stared at Leonard's freckled face. Now wasn't that the daftest question? The daftest of the night? The week? The decade? The century? The daftest in the whole history of the human race? Wasn't it so? How could it be that such a fella with all the brains in the world could ask such a daft question? Was he still doing it indeed? Not a human could know. Couldn't the budgerigar itself be long dead? Not even ones with the gift lived for ever. How the hell was he expected to know? He hadn't been home to Gortnamona in twenty years. He cleared his throat with some authority.

'Sure he is. Just the other week . . .'

But for a moment, he'd lost Leonard. The mirror, with its tinsel bow and plastic mistletoe and holly crown, gave him an uninterrupted view of the couple in the corner. Not local. Not Bath. But he knew the man. But from where? It had to be the face. A long, straight nose that slightly curled under at the point. A line of prickly whiskers along the line of high cheek bones and strong, heavy dark hair resting on the blue velvet collar of his grey herringbone overcoat.

The man looked up. Caught Leonard's image in the decorated mirror and discarded it. The ginger curly-haired figure blinking through steel-rimmed spectacles was a nobody. Like the Irishman from central casting. Nothing more than local colour. Fingering his heavy gold cuff links, the man returned his attention to the woman. So did Leonard. The hair dark, thin, beautifully cut to the nape of her neck. The mustard cashmere sweater casually, yet perfectly, thrown about her shoulders, the long slim sleeves of the dark green silk dress slightly ruffled above more gold. Indiscreet bangles from a discreet shop. Not high street. Not high street people. He wondered what they were doing in Shades. At that time of night, mostly regulars found their way down the stone steps from George Street. Leonard returned to his near empty glass and a satisfied chuckle from Michael, the part-time barman who had perfected the very private laugh that all are supposed to hear. He was hunched over the *Chronicle* spread open on the bar.

'I like it. I like it.'

Leonard delayed his order. Cornelius abandoned whistling budgerigars. Michael nudged his audience once more.

'Listen to this.'

They did. The barman smoothed the newspaper's front page and cleared his throat.

'"Cinders Misses The Ball". I like it. I like it. Here we go. "Bond girl Lynda Elström went missing today when Theatre Royal chiefs staged a meet-the-press ball for this year's panto."'

The barman rustled the newspaper with all the style of a seasoned thespian.

'"The whole cast was on stage, including pop star Jason Williams, alias Prince Charming, but the Swedish beauty failed to show.

'"Director, Maurice Poulson, said Miss Elström's where-abouts were a complete mystery and he denied rumours of a rift between him and this year's Cinderella.

'"There have been reports that blonde Lynda, famous for her low-cut dresses, had refused to wear her costume because it was too revealing for a family audience."'

Cornelius's mouth had closed. Now he licked his lips. Cornelius always had something to say on any subject.

'It's what is known as the publicity stunt. In my opinion, the lady was sitting in the dressing room and taking something to dissipate the damp.'

On cue, he finished his beer and plonked his glass on the bar. Leonard nodded at the landlord who filled his glass with cold white wine and flipped the top from a cold bottle of high-priced lager and placed it in front of Cornelius, who, by way of thanks, offered a fresh opinion.

'You see the pantomime is not what it was, you know . . .'

Again Leonard lost interest. He nodded in time to the Irishman's cadence as it floated like some idling broad-winged buzzard without seemingly reaching its goal. The couple had his attention once more. Not their conversation, but their silence. As Michael the barman had started to read the news-paper story, they had stopped their conversation. Now they looked at each other. Intense. Absorbed. Yet by their manner they were not lovers. It was as if they were speaking to each

7

other through silence and deep understanding. Then, with telepathic agreement, they gathered themselves, rose and left the bar and climbed the stone stairs as quietly as they had descended them.

Cornelius watched through the large window as their legs disappeared to the surface then nodded at the half-full wine bottle with all the wisdom of a penitent philosopher.

'Now there's a shame.'

With similar gravity, Leonard eyed the abandoned glasses.

Michael sniffed from behind his bar.

'Waste of splosh, that.'

The angle of Cornelius's tie would now have drawn the admiration of a public hangman. Closer to the Irishman's ear than his chin. He studied the wallboard of wine prices.

'That's a terrible bit of money for just the one bottle. Has a taste of its own, it must.'

'Try it for size. Plenty left.'

Cornelius was hurt. There were those who would volunteer to drain the very devil's dregs. But not Cornelius. Supping unfinished drinks was the step before the detailed learning of shop doorways and railway arches. Cornelius Cobb, sometime actor, writer, poet and careful spender of a little piece of fortune that had come his way twenty years before had a code of his own, mainly made up for the occasion, but loyal to instincts nevertheless. A great observer of people, his often-blurred vision registered faces close up, across streets, peering from the ill-lit ends of alleyways, magazines, newspapers, newsreels and in his imagination. Sometimes, especially towards closing time, the jumble of truth and imagination was confusing. But days, weeks, months later, Cornelius's identikit mind would be triggered. It was a useful faculty and one Detective Inspector Leonard had appreciated from time to time. Which was why they were on first names and why Leonard played the whistling budgerigar from Gortnamona.

'The most expensive you say, Michael?'

'The very most, Con my son. It hurt to take the money.'

'There's a thing. More money than the sense of it. And him

such a man of distinction. A fine reputation he has. But not for the drink of course.'

They both looked at Cornelius. He knew it. He took a long sup of his bottled beer. The handkerchief was as big as his imagination and just as brightly coloured. But this time he had them. Yes he knew it. And wouldn't you know that Michael hadn't the patience.

'You know him then, Con?'

Now what had he just said? He eyed them across the rim of his glass. Supped some more for his moment of theatre and then carefully set the glass on the bar.

'Not as a personal matter, you understand.'

'Who was he, then?'

'The surgeon. The one who does the transplanting.'

Leonard nodded. Dawning. A long time ago. The pictures had been everywhere. A kaleidoscope of such brilliant techniques that it was as if no one else operated on diseased hearts.

'Ross.'

Cornelius was much obliged to Leonard's memory. For his own part, he'd clean forgotten the man's name.

'The same.'

Michael looked at the nicotine-stained ceiling for inspiration. There was something in the back of his mind. Something itching to make its contribution to the gossip. Something that was now rising to the shiny, pink surface of his pointed, hairless skull.

'That's odd. I got it. Yes, I like it. I do. I like it. Wasn't he, um, years ago, um, wasn't he—?'

Leonard nodded.

'Yes, he was, wasn't he?'

Michael took up the nod.

'Yes, so he was. Married to . . .'

He looked down at his newspaper and tapped the front-page picture.

'. . . married to this Lynda Elström.'

Leonard blinked. Cornelius nodded, but of course with some authority.

'Now there we have a coincidence. Isn't that the very situation?'

Leonard for one did not believe in coincidence.

Two

In the restaurant beneath the theatre, the last of the diners had gone. That night there hadn't been many. Hardly worth opening. But it was unusual. The days when cast and staff drank through to the early hours were no more. Business plans, franchising and a fashion for fizzy water had changed all that. But on occasions it was still the best place to flop after the show, especially when the punters had gone. Especially tonight. It was Simone's birthday. It didn't really matter. There hadn't been any cards. Her father would have sent one, but her father was long dead. She missed him, desperately. He was her only true friend, the only person she'd ever believed. The only truthful person she'd ever known. Now she had to make do with Ike. And even that was a cock-up. Ordering someone out is very much a truth. Like another year gone. Best to have a good time now before it was too late. Hell, she was thirty. It was significant. Wasn't it? Must be. She felt lousy and low. Perhaps it was missing her father. Perhaps it was the big scene with Ike that morning. Something about attitude, he'd said. Trust. Trust! From him that was serious crap. Maybe too much in his head kicked in too late for her sympathies. She'd got up. Dressed. Said she wanted him out by the time she got back. So maybe it was nerve. Maybe she didn't have the guts to go back to the flat and find him still there. So the birthday party. It started with all the atmosphere of chairs stacked on tables and 'One For My Baby'. There was Simone thinking about Ike, hating being thirty and wishing to God she'd bought herself the far-too-short skirt she'd seen that morning. And there was Josie, the over-sexed waitress with thick ankles and outsize T-shirt, who now sat with one brawny arm across Simone's slim shoulders telling her the world was a great place. They'd both cheered up when Joanna, the theatre administrator, had come in with the two residents, the director Maurice Poulson and the cuddly stage manager, Tiggy Jones. The kitchen leftovers had soon gone, so had a couple of bottles of wine. Then more wine. Then it got into the great debate. Where was Cinders? Tiggy Jones had his Worried of Bath look. A frown that puffed his dimpled cheeks and sent his Celtic hooded eyes into long slits.

'She's the not the first. She won't be the last. But it lets us down. Bad, bad, bad news.'

Joanna Cunliffe twitched her bent nose and let her fingers trace imaginary furrows along her long thighs. She was in what Tiggy called her 'Executive Think Mode'. When she was like this he imagined her reaching for her mobile to send the Dow tumbling and the Footsie diving for cover. Another twitch. Then a neat smile that spread without feeling almost as far as her anonymous eyes.

'Good story, though. Already had the nationals on. Good PR.'

Tiggy Jones shrugged and brushed flakes of a vol-au-vent from his glorious Technicolor Peruvian jumper.

'We don't need it. We're already booked out, always are.'

'Not the point. Gets people talking.'

Simone and the chubby waitress looked at each other. Shrugged like a well-rehearsed chorus line. Simone raised her hand in mock surprise as she leaned over to refill their wine-glasses.

'You telling us you set this up?'

Joanna shook her short blond curls at them.

'Christ, no. Didn't need to. All I'm saying is that it keeps the story running – and tell me, which other panto's going to get national coverage? Yes? Go on, tell me.'

'If she returns.'

The voice was gritty. East Fifteen, but not cockney. Maurice Poulson. For the past five years, the resident Theatre Royal director. Tall. Gaunt. Black, unblinking eyes. Slate grey short hair combed forward.

Tiggy Jones hugged his roly-polyness.

'A runner? What makes you think that, m'lud?'

Poulson stared into the shadows of the vaulted restaurant. Said nothing. Had nothing more to say. Joanna sipped at the red wine. But not much of it.

'Not nice, Morry. Not nice at all. I've never thought of that. Shit! We could do without that. Do you really think so?'

Maurice shrugged.

Joanna Cunliffe looked at her watch. A quarter to. Call a cab and there'd be plenty of time to warm herself at Nathan's.

Josie, eager to say something and now thinking she had something to say coughed her nervousness away. But then decided not to say anything at all. Not her problem.

Simone thought it was a pretty shitty birthday.

The night porter of the Avon Bridge Hotel looked up from his mini TV set to see one of them disappearing out of the front door. Which one of them, he wasn't sure. Even when they stood together, he couldn't tell. Both five two, five three. Both dumpy. Both the same jet black sculptured curls. The same podgy fingers. The same silver rings. The same flouncy floral frocks. The same cackling laughs which one started and the other finished. The same bouncy walk. The same everything. But then twins were supposed to be the same everything, weren't they? He looked at the gilt sunbeam wall clock as its second hand jerked round to line up with the others. Midnight precisely. Late for her. One of them was in bed for sure. Absolutely streaming. Rang down for a hot toddy at ten. Temperature of 102, said her sister. But the show must go on and all that crap. An understudy didn't exactly fit into a twin act. He went back to the film. The reception wasn't very good on the tiny screen and he could hardly read the subtitles. But it was French and there was always the chance one of them would get her kit off. Fifteen minutes on and just when there looked a reasonable chance of Parisian action, the front door opened and she returned. She gave a very good shiver as she went by.

'Fancied a walk. But too cold for me. Nighty night.'

'Right. Night.'

The porter didn't look up. The shoulder straps were coming down.

Rudi Sharpe was alone in his nylon and candlewick digs. The radiator was hot. He was cold. His pasty, grey face was long with gloom as he turned the stiff page of the worn photograph album. Once he could never have looked at the black and white images without tears. He turned another page. Stared without really seeing the features of the beautiful woman and then carefully laid the album to one side. He held the pillow to his chest and gently stroked the smooth folds of nylon until he was nearly asleep. The plastic tingling of the bedside alarm made him jump. He lay there trying to shut out the cheap noise. When the clockwork spring had spent itself with a final click he opened his eyes and slid from the high bedstead. He leaned wearily with both hands on the edge of the white basin staring into the flat mirror as water gushed from the chrome mixer tap.

'Mirror, mirror, mirror, on the wall
Who, who then is the prettiest bastard of them all?'

The voice was sharp, schooled across a whole continent to overcome chattering and screaming of ill-schooled children. Prettiest? The bevelled mirror laughed at him. Not thee, my darling. Not thee. The years were there still. He saw a face too old for his. The face he remembered as his father's. The exaggerated features. The too-large nose. The sunken sallow cheeks and the full, wet, lips. The hair was all but gone, just as his father's had and, just as his father had done, he'd slicked it with water until the few strands lay like inked isobars across his ivory skull. He drew a deep breath and moved his shoulders to get his blood circulating. Fleshy shoulders patched with black tight curls of moth-eaten astrakhan. He looked at the clock once more, cupped a handful of water to his dry mouth, spat and reached for his sweatshirt.

Outside, he hunched deep into his brown overcoat against the December wind that threatened to leave a skim of ice on the deserted Avon. He paused at the bridge and stared down at the black water. He saw nothing but the images of the tiny, smiling child, her face full of mischief beneath the tumble of brown curls. The sigh he'd intended never came. Instead he broke into a fit of coughing and, wary that he might be noticed, he tugged the chunky mottled scarf about his chin and head down, trudged towards the theatre.

The old lady came courtesy of Norman Rockwell. The white hair, parted in the middle and scraped back over her ringless, dainty ears. The eyes small, clear, shrewd behind rimless reading spectacles. Her shawl she'd knitted herself from the softest slate blue wool and the crisp high pillows she'd washed, then slightly starched, as always. Now she lay deep into the pillows and smiled with delight and deep loving for her son who sat on the edge of her bed. He really was a good boy. And so like his father, even down to the boyish looks her late husband had kept well into his seventies. Jason was fifty but looked ten, maybe fifteen years younger. He'd looked after himself, never drank, never smoked, ate his greens. He was devoted to her and never left her but to return. Even in his private moments she knew he never kept bad company and she saw it as her duty that he should not. She sipped at the malted milk he'd brought her and listened while he talked about all the people he was working with. She loved the gossip, although he never told her really juicy things. Dear Jason simply wasn't that sort of boy. 'Only good words bring the Good News,' he would say. But sometimes she would have loved to hear just the teeniest piece of scandal. Even today and the local radio talking about the Swedish whatshername, all Jason would say was that he hoped she was all right. She finished the last of her warm drink and he took the thick china mug that he'd brought her all the way from New York. A long time ago that. He didn't travel as much as he used to. She thought that was very good for him. Time to settle down. Perhaps . . . No, she mustn't even think about it. Mustn't even hope. But it would have been nice to think that he could have found someone. It wasn't as if he was, well, you know. Not her Jason. A mother would

14

know. Sometimes the papers said nasty things. But she knew. He leaned over and kissed her forehead and she snuggled down with her romantic novel, feeling for the fur-covered hot water bottle he'd bought her that morning. He whispered goodnight and she promised to 'see him in the morning'. As he quietly left the room and the door ajar so that he could easily hear if she called, her mind had already wandered from her page and was drifting to her cosy, harmless, childhood in the Wiltshire countryside. What woke her from broad-leaved trees and meadows of sheep she wasn't sure. But she heard then the backdoor and his footsteps on the crisp path. It was, by the dressing table clock nearly midnight. She tried to stay awake, but was really too tired and slipped in and out of sleep until she was aware that he was back. She could hear him in the kitchen and she smiled, reassured. So typical of darling Jason to play the wireless so very low so as not to wake her.

The balding cab driver wanted to talk. The lady did not.

Three

Norman Philips wasn't much to look at. As a kid his short trousers had always been too long. His long trousers too short. He'd been beaten up on his first day at secondary school because he stammered and had big ears. His mum had 'gone up' the school to complain. The next evening he'd been beaten up again for sneaking. He'd joined the army because they'd have him. He left because they proved he wasn't good enough. He got a trade. Bikes. He'd fix them. Make them go faster. Then he rode them to show they could go faster still. He'd become something of a local hero, but not for long. One mighty crash had made the headlines and that was that. In a year he was all but forgotten. He wasn't the sort of person to be remembered. Until the bikes, he'd been insignificant. He knew that. So did his wife and she'd told him so. On the day she left, he'd asked why. Whatever happens, he'd said, everyone has a right, a need, to know why. Simple, she'd said, he was too short in every department from head to toe, except his ears, of course, which still stuck out. And then there was the limp. She hadn't mentioned the limp, but she might just as well have done. He'd heard her telling her sister that it made her feel sick when she rubbed against the dead leg in the night. He was, as far as she was concerned, a freak – and a short one at that. It was no consolation when the brewery rep she went off with was done for drink driving, lost his driving licence and his job and went back to his wife. Norman Philips still loved his wife, but she found someone else. She'd been a stripper. Nothing high class. Lunchtime pubs then small-time clubs. But she knew how to turn on punters paying twenty pounds for a Crème de Coke. Finding a meal ticket wasn't difficult. Last time he'd heard of her, she was living in the north somewhere with a fat guy who sold pool tables. Philips had stayed in the one-bedroom flat in the not yet smart part of Camden. It wasn't so bad. The view of Bath was fine, if you went outside. There was a pub which didn't have music. When it was very late, he could afford the cab fare home – if that's what it was. And when she'd gone he'd put his memories on the walls. Cheap, loose frames. Good pictures. He'd been good. But as she'd told him, no one catches a falling star. What she didn't understand was that there was nothing to catch. They were like that. Bitches. The lot of them. He'd got his other pictures. The Bitch Gallery he called it. But even that didn't work because there was no one to show it to.

Norman Philips shoved his hands deeper into his blue anorak pockets and limped at a stiff angle across the road and along the side of the closed theatre. He paused in front of the billboards, clear beneath the street lamp. She looked good. Could have still played the Bond movies as long as there weren't any close-ups. He'd seen her close up. He didn't want to look. But he had to. He knew it was all different now. They knew and he knew and he had to walk on, just like an actor, he supposed. Philips reckoned they were like children. Always wanting someone to tell them how good they were and always scrapping. An edgy lot, that's how his mum would have described them. Edgy.

This lot were the same, especially in rehearsal. Telling each other what to do then telling each other not to tell them what to do. Even old Rudi was screwed up. That had to be something different because Rudi was one of the old school. He'd done it all before. But something was getting at him. Then there were those Rostows. Oh, they did all the darling stuff but they were nasty bitches. He knew a bitch when he saw one. This time it was double vision. As for the kid – the little nymphos had already started waiting for him. He played the cool one, but he wasn't. He loved it. But he'd got something else going. Norman Philips knew that for sure. He looked up at another bill. Her and that Jason. He was all right. Really nice. Always stopped for a chat, and he meant it. Jason reckoned he'd seen him in the old days. He talked about Belle Vue. The Hammers. Knew the business. Not like her. She wasn't one of them and they let her know. Just a name. Had never served her time. Never been a spear-carrier.

He peered at his rubber-cased watch. Eight sharp. An early morning drunk, leaning against the dress-hire window, eyed him without humour from the alleyway. The man leaned forward at ninety degrees and swayed, searching the pavement for fresh balance. Norman ignored him and let himself in through the stage door, quickly closing it behind him. He limped up the quarry-tiled steps to the inner door and the long thin stage door office. Bugger it! He was sweating. He could smell himself. He took a big breath and looked through the glass door panel. Empty. A promise was a promise. He flicked a switch and went in. The burglar alarm was set. The place was cold. He picked up a notice that had fallen from the notice-board. Fifteen per cent off meals in the Vaults. He blew on the dirty sheet and pinned it back alongside the Bath Tourist brochure. Never seen anyone reading it, but if it weren't there some bugger'd ask for it.

On the other wall, the staff photographs were square behind the polished glass and he took out a handkerchief to rub a smudge away from the centre lock. He flicked the handkerchief along the arm of the burgundy settle on the opposite wall and threw a couple of newspapers that had been there since last evening into the waste bin behind the counter. The telephone was at an angle. He straightened and recoiled the extension lead. Clean counter policy, he called it. The flap was up. Clean underneath as well as shiny on top. Behind the counter, he checked the close circuit TV monitor. Switched to outside view. The drunk was being sick. Or trying to. Another flick. The screen quartered. The foyer was empty. Thank Christ for that. He always dreaded spotting burglars. He knew that he'd do nothing but call the police and stay where he was with the inner door locked. There were a couple of lights on the switchboard. He ignored them. Box Office could handle that when they came in. He took off his anorak and slipped it over the back of the chair. The movement wafted her scent. He looked about him. The sweat was pouring down. He was shaking now. He put a hand on the counter to steady himself. He'd done everything in slow motion. He'd dusted, checked and re-checked for all he was worth. He couldn't put it off.

He looked at his watch. Three minutes after eight. Time to do it. He picked up the large flashlight, leaned over the counter, pressed another switch to unlock the door through to the theatre. The counter was wet where he'd held on. Inside, a polystyrene cup with coffee dregs was on the upright piano just inside the passageway. He'd have to put up another notice. He started up the stairway to the right. The notice was big enough. THE STAGE. Philips ignored it and turned left down the narrow steps into the theatre's bowels. He was now under the stage, a magical, subterranean world lit by low glows of emergency lanterns. As he went he kept his powerful flashlight swinging in a wide beam. Checking switches and trip boxes. Throwing more light. And then he was through and up to stage left and leaning to one side favouring his good leg. He hated steps. They made his good knee hurt. Made his hip and back muscles ache with that one swinging action. And he needed more space than anyone else which made him look awkward. Made him look a cripple. That's what they thought and he knew it. He stopped at the top and ran the flats of his hands down the backstage switches and then the blue and white working light switch. Backstage was lit by highlights and shafts.

Enough to fool and flatter. Enough to see by. Now he could look. Now he could step on the stage. He turned from behind a long black hanging flat.

You couldn't miss her. He looked away. Then up again. Christ, she was beautiful. But not like that. No, not like that.

Four

At three thirty that morning an unidentified man, apparently in his late seventies, was operated on at the Royal United Hospital for internal injuries. The operation lasted four hours. At nine thirty the consultant noted that his surgical registrar had done a good sewing job inside but that the collar bone was going to be awkward. He added that the torn knee ligaments would take the longest to heal. The police Road Traffic Accident report recorded that the man was the victim of a hit and run incident, DU – Driver Unknown. In the 'Additional Remarks' column, the duty officer had noted that the RUH casualty officer had offered the opinion that the victim had some old dental work, perhaps East European.

At nine o'clock, Mrs Williams took her son Jason a cup of tea. She tapped on the door of his bedroom and waited. It was always better to wait. But when she tapped a second time without an answer, she went in. Jason was fast asleep beneath the great fluffy blue eiderdown she had bought him last birthday. As he stirred to wake himself, she made soft clucking noises and picked up his clothes from the floor. So unlike him. But after last night he must have been very, very tired. She really was a lucky mother.

At nine fifteen, the waitress in the Avon Bridge Hotel served a double Country Style breakfast grill on table nine and asked the Rostow twin if she'd like more toast. The twin beamed. The eyelashes flickered. 'Yes, oh yes please, my luv' then, after a one-second pause, 'Please, if that's all right, dear, yes please, oh wouldn't that be loverleee.'

The other guests laughed and the politely smiling waitress remarked in the kitchen that it was odd how ordinary she was when the other one wasn't there. Chef said twins were like that. Out of water without the other half. The waitress thought that was probably true.

At about nine thirty, Chris Ross fed another pound coin into the public telephone. Cornelius Cobb, who never forgot a face even if it took him a while to remember it, wondered what a nice man like that would be doing in a telephone box.

At nine thirty-five, for the fourth time since seven o'clock that morning, the hotel receptionist told Curly Weekes that he hadn't missed any messages. There hadn't been any. Weekes zipped his flying jacket to the chin, pulled the peak of his Breton cap further down his forehead and went out into the street. He turned right, then left, crossed the road by the gardens and walked past the abbey, up the hill and through the small streets to Catherine Place. As he walked, he looked either straight ahead or at the pavement and ignored those who thought they recognized his face. When he saw the police car outside the flat he carried on walking along the bottom of the square and hurried away.

Five

Leonard arrived at the Theatre Royal at five and twenty past ten. The doctor had finished, the body of Lynda Elström was gone. The house lights and a hundred and more lanterns blazed. The illusion that separated the auditorium from the players was dissolved in a thousand-watt glare. And now the stage was blocked for a very different gig. White-overalled mummers crawled about the tall flat black boards of scenery. Every so often, one would pause and carefully drop even the tiniest find into a clear plastic bag. Below them, in the blood red stalls and side aisles, plain-clothed officers moved quietly among groups of stage hands, actors and staff. All standing. No one sitting. No one abandoning respect for the comfort of the expensive seats. A company of men and women governed by insecurities, superstition and the rules of masquerade, now lost in unspeakable melodrama.

He could see Jack. She was in the side aisle beneath the green EXIT sign briefing one of the Scene Of Crime Officers. The young DC, tall, gangly, ruffled black hair, must have said something because she turned. She was relieved to see him. She'd wondered where the hell he was. She'd called his flat and even his mobile although she guessed he'd have left it in his dresser drawer as he always did. By nine fifteen, Detective Sergeant Jack guessed where he might be, but hadn't said so to a seething superintendent. Now she knew she'd been right. She could see the brown paper bag sticking out of Leonard's duffle coat pocket. She wanted to smile but didn't. No one smiled at a Scene Of Crime particularly when it was murder.

His voice was gentle. Not cultured. Not police issue.

'Sorry. I was er . . .'

She looked at the brown bag.

'Thought you might, sir. Do you want me to put it somewhere?'

He looked uncomprehendingly at her. Daft question, she thought. Leonard was never parted from a freshly baked gingerbread man – until he'd eaten it. Always head last.

'What have we got?'

'From the top, sir?'

'Mm. Mm.'

As she spoke he stared, unblinking, into her eyes. She'd never got used to this. It was as if he were registering not the accuracy but the truth of what she said.

'Lynda Elström, forty something – we're checking – actress. Playing Cinderella—'

'—Playing?'

'Sorry, sir. Right. Rehearsing.'

It was the damned staring that made her make simple mistakes that didn't matter to anyone but him. Her voice soft. Not the briefing tones used on the DC who had difficulty not looking at her warm terracotta sweater. Confidential. An understanding of four years.

'Found at about five past eight this morning, hanging from the wire about ten foot above the middle of the stage.'

'Who found?'

'Stage-door keeper. His name's Norman Philips.'

She glanced down at her tiny notebook.

'Philips with one L and one P. He opened up at eight—'

'—Alone?'

'Eh, yes, sir.'

She'd double check before he did.

'He walked up the steps to the bit behind the set itself – that's where all the switches and ropes are – switched on the lights and found her. Simple as that, sir.'

'Dead?'

Madelaine Jack thought before she answered. What an odd question.

'Yes, sir. As far as I know.'

'What does he say?'

'That he took one look and went back to the stage door and dialled treble-nine.'

'Why?'

'Why what, sir?'

'Why did he go back to the stage door?'

'That was the nearest telephone, I suppose.'

'And that was the first thing he did?'

'As far as I know. Yes. That's the first thing he did.'

Leonard was looking over her shoulder at the stage. The low buzzing came from somewhere below his diaphragm. His eyes came back to hers.

'Isn't that odd?'

'Natural reaction, sir.'

He shook his head.

'No. Natural reaction would be to get hold of the rope or whatever it is and get her down.'

'Frightened?'

Yes. He could understand that. Fear. Fear of touching something as grotesque as a strangled body. Strangled?

'What killed her?'

'Looked like wire round the throat. It was pretty horrid.'

She wished she hadn't said that. He'd be wondering how something could be pretty as well as horrid.

'Medic?'

'Nothing, sir. Cert dead. That's it. Something by two o'clock he said. It's Benson, he's usually quick.'

'Was she warm?'

She shook her head.

'Bowels?'

She looked back to the stage. There was a chalk circle below where Lynda Elström had dangled.

'Not much.'

'Could be either way then?'

'Could be. Benson will know.'

Benson, like all medical examiners, would know. What he would tell was something else.

'Who else did he call?'

'Who, sir?'

He sucked air.

'The door keeper.'

'No one, or at least I don't think he did.'

'But you don't know?'

'No.'

'So who called the theatre boss, or whatever he's called?'

'She.'

'Mm?'

'The administrator is a she, sir, not a he. DI Lane was in. He called them.'

Leonard walked a couple of paces. Turned. It was hard to pace on the slope of the theatre. He needed to walk.

'Anyone see anything?'

'Not yet.'

'Security camera?'

'We think the recorder may be duff.'

He sucked. His expression made her feel it was her fault.

'We've got someone coming in to look at it, sir.'

He said nothing. More buzzing under his breath.

'What was that in the papers about her?'

'Yesterday, sir. She disappeared. Or rather, she didn't show up for the press conference. The photo call thing.'

The buzzing became a low hum.

'Her ex-husband's in Bath.'

He started to walk away. Sergeant Jack followed like a hassled secretary.

'What ex-husband?'

Leonard turned. No smile.

'The surgeon. Ross. Thought everyone knew that. Check the—'

'—Hotels, sir?'

'Mm.'

His eyes wandered the auditorium. Maybe something, or someone, somewhere. The maroon wallpapered boxes with their tasselled wall lights and secret doors. To where? Didn't know. Never been in a theatre box. Dukes and good-time girls and the suitor standing behind in sparkling white shirt front and emerald studs. The two tiers of circles. Marble pillars and brass rails. All empty now. The performance done.

'Who they?'

She followed his look to the back of the stalls. An odd-ball group. Casually dressed. At all angles. People used to waiting around.

'Most of the cast and some of the staff. We've been through the routine with them. Who are you? What are you? When did you last see her? Did you see anything? That sort of thing.'

He nodded at four people sat apart from the main group, talking but with the air of not wishing to be overheard.

'What about them?'

'The one in black with his back to us, is the director. Name's Maurice Poulson. Bit spooky. The one in the fluffy colours is the stage manager, Trevor Jones, although it seems everyone calls him Tiggy.'

'Bouncy?'

'Not at the moment. The blond curly one is the sort of general manager. Her name's Joanna Cunliffe. The one DI Lane called? The redhead is Simone Simons. She runs the restaurant here. They were here quite late last night.'

'What do they call late?'

'About midnight.'

'And she was found shortly after eight. So seven hours. We could do with that time of death. Quickly.'

'Unless she wasn't murdered here.'

Leonard had wondered about that. But carting even the slimmest body about Bath in the middle of the night and then getting it into the theatre and on to the stage was hardly a casual operation. Anyway, passers-by didn't dress stages with corpses. So who?

'We've got her and we've got the stage-door keeper. We'd better get a who's who of the place.'

Detective Sergeant Jack took a folded A4 sheet from a deep pocket of her dark blue sailor's jacket.

'Staff list, sir. Picked it up from the office. Six front-of-house staff including manager, box office and secretary. There's the administrator. Maintenance man. Six part timers – ice-creams, programmes, et cetera. Then three permanent people in the Vaults restaurant. That's what I think they call front-of-house. Then there's the director, stage manager, a deputy, stage hands, stage-door keeper and two assistants. Both of those are knocked out with flu.'

'That it?'

'More or less. There's the cast, but they don't belong here. They only come for the production.'

'What do we know about the guy who found her?'

'Philips? He's been here some time. Came in eighty-nine. I've asked for a check. But as far as I can make out there's nothing special about him.'

'His mother thought so. Where is he?'

She nodded in the direction of the corner of the stage.

'Through there. In one of the dressing rooms. He's in shock.'

'Still?'

She paused. Sometimes she could hit him.

'Yes, sir. Finding women hanging by their necks ten feet above a dimly lit stage first thing in the morning is not his regular work.'

'What if he put her there?'

She didn't know. Hadn't thought of it. She kicked herself. Time and again she'd heard him say it: death is about the obvious. Nine times out of ten murders are social, domestic and pleasure. Most people kept murder in the family. When there was no family you looked at the neighbour – either the one next door or the one on the next pillow.

Six

Three of the small bulbs in the dressing room mirror were dud. Norman Philips hadn't noticed. Norman Philips had drunk six brandies. Maybe he'd drunk seven. He wasn't sure. He hadn't counted. Could have been eight and he was still waiting for breakfast. Leonard looked at the open bottle on the white-topped make-up table then at the uniformed constable.

'Where that come from?'

The constable looked embarrassed. Shrugged.

'Don't rightly know, sir.'

It would wait.

'Detective Inspector Leonard, Mr Philips. I'd like to go over a few points with you.'

'I told her everything I can remember.'

'That's the point isn't it, Mr Philips?'

He didn't like that Mister bit. He knew this guy was trying it on.

'What's that meant to mean?'

'Well, as you say, you've told the officer all you can remember. That means you've told only that which you can remember and therefore there may be more to tell. Yes?'

'For fuck's sake, mate. She's dead. I found her. What more do you want?'

As he said it, he wished he hadn't. He didn't like swearing. They'd think it was the brandy. No. They'd think that he was a foul-mouthed bastard. Just like she'd said he was. He hadn't sworn since the day she'd walked out.

Leonard looked at the ceiling. He wondered why it was black. Sergeant Jack took her cue. The voice was easy. Slight west country burr somewhere.

'Let's start again shall we, Mr Philips?'

What was all this Mister thing?

'What time did you arrive?'

'Eight.'

'Which way did you come?'

'Walked.'

Jack sighed.

'Okay. Which way did you come into Sawclose?'

'Top end. From the precinct. Same as always.'

'Anyone about?'

Why make it easy for them? He said nothing.

'I said anyone about?'

'Maybe.'

'Maybe yes? Maybe no?'

'Maybe.'

Leonard pulled a small chair forward and sat astride, leaning on its tubular steel back. His face was two feet from Norman Philips's. He could smell the brandy. He took off his spectacles and polished them on his pocket handkerchief. Philips focused on the naked eyes. They were cruel eyes. The glasses went back on. That was better.

'Tell me, Mr Philips, you say you came from the front of the theatre and walked down the side to the stage door. Yes?'

Philips nodded.

'Good. Close your eyes.'

Philips stared at him.

'Go on, Mr Philips, close your eyes.'

'What for?'

'Please?'

Philips closed his eyes. He wanted to open them immediately. Didn't.

'Now, try to picture exactly what you saw when you reached the theatre. You're approaching the stage door. What do you see?'

'Still dark, sort of.'

'Good. What do you see?'

'Her.'

'Who?'

'Lynda.'

'Where?'

'On the wall. Bills.'

The sigh came from Madelaine Jack. Leonard tried to sound pleased.

'Okay. Now can you see anyone else?'

Philips was now in a fuzz. Maybe the shock was real. The brandy was.

'No.'

Leonard waited.

'Well, just a piss-head.'

'Where?'

'Opposite.'

'Opposite what?'

Philips opened his eyes.

'Opposite the stage door, of course. Where d'you think?'

He turned his head to where Madelaine Jack was leaning against the wall. She was a bit of all right, this one. Didn't look like a copper. But they didn't nowadays. He blamed television. Leonard was still talking. Listen. Get it right. One word at a time, Lord, one word at a time.

'Did you talk to him?'

'Think I'm daft?'

'Did you?'

He shook his head.

'Then what?'

'Unlocked and came in and – and – and, then I found her.'

His head went into his hands. He wanted to weep. But he wouldn't. Not for her he wouldn't. All her fault. Not his. No crying. Not for that bitch. Not for any of them. Sod them all.

Sod all bitches. And they were all bitches. Leonard leaned forward, his voice above Norman Philips' bowed head.

'Not immediately you didn't.'

Philips thought about it.

'No.'

'Tell us what you did.'

The voice was tired. Tell it again, tell it again.

'Switched off the alarm—'

'Definitely on?'

'Yes. Switched on the lights. Tidied up.'

'Tidied what up?'

'Just things.'

Leonard let go.

'Okay, so you then what?'

'Went up.'

'Up where?'

'You know.'

'Tell me.'

'Stage.'

'Why?'

Why was this bastard making him say it? They knew what he'd seen.

'Why?'

'Yes. Why?'

'Routine. That's why. It's up to me or the first one in to switch on. The lights.'

'All the lights?'

'No. Just enough.'

'And?'

Philips said nothing. He was staring at the floor. Leonard wondered. Just the floor? He nudged him.

'And?'

'Went on to the stage.'

'And?'

The head came up. The eyes were those of someone who hadn't touched a drop for seven years. Until now.

'There she was. Hanging there.'

'And what did you do?'

'You know what I sodding did. I called you lot.'

'Is that all?'

'Of course it is. What else is there?'

'Why didn't you try to get Miss Elström down?'

Philips looked terrified.

'But she was dead.'

Leonard's face was within twelve inches of Philips's.

'How did you know Mr Philips? How did you know?'

The other man began to stumble. To stutter.

'W-Well, sh-she was.'

'How did you know?'

'She had to be, didn't she? I mean, hanging there. Just, hanging there. Listen, mate, you didn't fucking see her. I did. She was fucking dead, all right. Hey, what is this? What, what you saying? What's fucking going on?'

'You sure that's how it was, Norman?'

The voice was soft. Gentle. Friendly.

'What you s-s-saying? Go on. T-t-tell me. What y-y-you s-saying?'

He hadn't done that since he was twelve. Now it started. Now he couldn't stop. He wanted to hear himself get it right. Couldn't.

'What th-th-the f-ff-ff-fu . . . you saying? Eh?'

For a full half minute both men stared at each. Both sensing fear. Neither knowing what the other knew. And then Norman Philips slowly went white, his eyes rolled upwards and as Leonard reached to catch him, slipped to the ground.

Seven

Leonard sat in the administrator's office drinking not very good coffee. He thought Joanna Cunliffe ridiculously young. Short fair curls. The face long, boyish, clear. But it was the eyes that disturbed him. They were almost colourless. No expression. No hints. They'd tell nothing. He hoped he'd got it wrong.

'There's not much more I can tell you. I had very little to do with her. We fixed the apartment for her, got a car organized. That sort of thing.'

Leonard blinked. She didn't.

'When did you last see her?'

'Sunday? Five, six o'clock. They were blocking the show. I was in.'

'Who was the last person to see her?'

Joanna Cunliffe scratched at her thigh tops. She could guess. 'Haven't a clue.'

'And then she disappeared.'

'She didn't show for the Monday photo call if that's what you mean.'

'That's what I mean. Do you know why?'

She shook her head, slowly. Taking her time.

'Not sure anyone does.'

'Someone does.'

'You think it has something to do with –'

She waved a bony hand towards the door.

'– with this?'

'Do you, Miss Cunliffe?'

'We were talking about it last night. None of us knew what the hell was going on.'

'We?'

'Mm. Me, Maurice Poulson, the director, and the SM, Tiggy Jones. You'd have thought that between us we'd have had some sort of idea. But we didn't. Simone, she's—'

'—Catering?'

For a split second she appeared surprised that he knew.

'Right. The Vaults. Anyway, as I was saying, Simone thought that it was maybe a PR gimmick.'

'Was it?'

'Not that we knew about.'

'Would she have done it off her own bat?'

'Doubt it. She could have done, but it wasn't her style. She's more old style. You know, bending extra low for the cameras getting out of limos at first nights. That sort of thing.'

'Not subtle.'

'She didn't earn a living being subtle.'

'Did you like her?'

'Yes. She was very nice. Much nicer than some of them are. They get a rep then the papers keep it going. Doesn't actually matter who you are. They'll decide that. I liked her. She was chatty.'

'Chatty? Or did you talk?'

'You mean did she just pass the time of day or did she talk about herself?'

He nodded.

'Maybe the former. Yes, maybe that. Just chatty.'

'She was in no sort of trouble?'

Joanna shrugged.

'Must have been. But it didn't pass across this desk. Not until now.'

Leonard's eyebrows asked the question. If there was an expression in her flat, cheekboned face, it was one of frustration.

'We're about to get the wrong publicity.'

'There's such a thing in this business?'

'Hell, yes. Especially the tabloids. They've already found out where she was staying. There's a convoy of cameras and crews burning down the M4. There are about thirty hacks outside now and they'll stay there. Then we'll get the shroud anoraks. For months, for years. They'll sit there in the gallery ghouling at the blood stains.'

'There weren't any.'

'They'll see them.'

Leonard placed an ankle across his knee. She wondered about the lime green socks. The brown boots.

'You've had no sign of trouble? No letters, telephone calls?'

'I haven't. She may have, but nothing I've heard.'

'Who would know?'

'Calls? The obvious place would be the stage door. Apart from tickets, most, if not all, calls go through that board. Messages are left there. Mail goes into the pigeon holes. So, if anyone wanted to get in touch, that's more or less how they'd do it.'

He blinked. She noticed that he did that a lot. Perhaps it was the glasses. She didn't know policemen wore glasses. But then she didn't know any policemen. She wondered if he had a private life.

'Tell me, how easy would it be to get in here at night?'

'Well . . .'

She stood and turned to a wall with unfinished wooden shelves and box files. She didn't need any effort. Joanna Cunliffe was six feet tall. Most of it skinny legs. She was flipping through loose sheets in a box file.

'Here you go. I'll copy it for you. It's on the screen but the printer's playing up.'

She handed him a single sheet of white paper. Keyholders. The first one, Administrator.

'That's you?'

'Right. Then Theatre Director, that's Maurice Poulson. Stage Manager, that's Tiggy Jones. Then, let me see, Stage-Door Keeper.'

'Norman Philips.'

She looked annoyed.

'When do I get him back?'

Leonard didn't know. Said so with a quick down turn of his mouth.

'That's all we needed. You sure he'll be okay?'

'I'm not a doctor.'

'But I trust you.'

'Don't. They'll check him over. It's up to you and him.'

He looked back at the list. Tapped the paper. She took her cue.

'Right. Then you've got Front-of-House Manager, Catering Person, and then there's maintenance.'

'All with keys.'

'Mm. Mm.'

'What about alarm codes? How many?'

'Each person has his or her own code. I suspect most of them are birthdays. Complicated, isn't it?'

'So any of them could have got in without the help of, say, you or the director, or anyone else for that matter.'

'Yes. But unlikely. Most people leave the theatre and don't come back until they need to.'

'Unless . . .?'

She said nothing. He tried again.

'Unless they had a special reason.'

She shrugged. That was his business not hers.

'When you saw her on Sunday, anything strike you that was different?'

Joanna Cunliffe ran five-finger exercises up and down her desk top. She took a deep breath. Blew out from her bottom lip into her nose.

'Nothing to do with me. I looked in just to see how it was going. It's useful to know. Local press tend to ask. Well, as I say, I'm big in spreadsheets, nothing else. But in non-theatre terms I'd say she was somewhere between a dog and a lemon.'

'Bad acting may close shows, but not lives. Yes?'

'That's supposed to be my line, Inspector, not yours. But don't get the wrong idea. We're all devastated. Truly, madly and deeply. Real tears. She may not have been a regular trooper or any of that old shit, but she was still one of the family. Don't underestimate that family.'

'Even if one of them is a murderer.'

She shook her head. Shook it furiously.

'No way José. If you think that then you think wrong. For a start no one knew her – not that well, anyway.'

'What's not that well?'

'Pretty obvious isn't it? Not well enough to kill her. These people are actors, not contract killers.'

'But someone killed her. And, that someone knew how to get in and knew how the hoist thing works.'

'I don't.'

'Is that an alibi?'

'Do I need one?'

'Probably. At this stage all we know is that she's dead and that it looks as if someone, or some people, murdered her. So yes. All alibis will be gratefully received.'

'Then do I get my theatre back?'

'The more we can cover, the more you and your staff can tell me, the quicker it'll be. The sort of thing I need to know follows a sequence. Who saw her last? Where? When? How did she get in here? And when? Who else could and did get in here? When was the stage last checked? By whom and—'

'And when. Okay. I get the picture but I can't give you any answers. I don't know who last saw her. I'm amazed she was here, and I don't mean hanging up there like that. As to who could get in here. You've got the list, but do you mind if I offer you a thought?'

'Please do.'

'You're assuming that she came in.'

'She didn't?'

'What makes you know that she left?'

'That's an elaborate idea, Miss Cunliffe.'

'Is it? Really? Aren't you supposed to be telling me that murder is an elaborate business?'

Leonard looked into the colourless eyes. Nothing.

'No, Miss Cunliffe, it is not. Except, of course, in the theatre when it has to survive four acts and two intervals.'

She smiled. But this was hardly a fun day and Leonard soon reminded her.

'Tell me Miss Cunliffe . . .'

She wished he wouldn't say that.

'. . . Your gathering . . .'

Why so pompous?

'. . . Last night. Went on for some time?'

'Not late. We stayed on after the show, yes. But not too late. It was just a one-nighter and cleared early.'

'In the – the, um, the restaurant.'

'The Vaults.'

'Did you all get there at the same time?'

Joanna Cunliffe scratched through her curls with a pencil. Not thinking about it but giving him the impression that she was. She was going at her pace, not his.

'Morry, Tiggy and I did. Simone and Josie were there already. Obviously.'

'Why obviously?'

'Well, like, Simone runs the place and Josie is the waitress when she's not chatting up the clientele or nipping out for a cigarette.'

She sighed. A jerky venting of nervous energy, delayed shock, tiredness, anger and frustration. Leonard knew what it was. He didn't say so but left her to answer even though his question had not been asked.

'We came in and Simone and Josie were sitting at the table just inside the first vault. They'd put a few bits on plates and there was some pasta salad and wine. It was Simone's birthday.'

'Nice.'

She was getting annoyed with this fraud. Okay one minute. Shitty the next. Who the hell did he think he was?

'Yes. It was . . . nice as you call it. Nice people doing a nice thing like celebrating a birthday with a nice girl who is having a shitty time.'

'In what way?'

'The usual way. She's got a man at home who's a designer shit. A photographer who forgets to stay his side of the lens. As per normal, you know? She was feeling lousy. Not exactly aching to go clubbing all night. Yes, very nice. Thank you for asking.'

Leonard paused. He was surprised she'd fallen for it. But it was best to get the smart ones wound up.

'And you arrived at what time?'

'I don't remember. Just before eleven.'

'So you do remember?'

'If you wish.'

'And you all stayed there all the time?'

'Yes. Why?'

'It is normal, Miss Cunliffe, to establish where everyone was.'

'What are you saying?'

36

'Nothing more than that. For example, if you left at, say, midnight and, let us say, that at midnight something suspicious was happening in the vicinity of the theatre, then you might have seen something. Now, just to make sure I've understood. You, Mr Poulson and Mr Jones arrived at about eleven. Two, Miss Simons and, um –'

'Josie. Josie Lucas.'

'Miss Lucas—'

'—Mrs Lucas.'

'Thank you. Mrs Lucas and Miss Simons were already there. None of you left the Vaults until – until?'

'Until about twelve.'

'When you left the building.'

It was her turn to nod. Leonard looked at his finger nails. Kept looking as he spoke.

'And before that none of you left the restaurant.'

'Why should we?'

'You tell me.'

She wasn't going to. Leonard reckoned he'd got enough from her for one day. He pushed back his chair and got up.

'Just one point, Miss Cunliffe: the burglar alarm code. There are seven keyholders, seven codes and presumably this is a modern alarm system.'

Her lips were tighter than a Christmas walnut.

'Yes, Inspector.'

'So presumably it records which code is used to open and close the alarm.'

'Yes, Inspector.'

'Thank you.'

He closed the door quietly behind him. Joanna Cunliffe wondered why he hadn't asked the most obvious question. She wished she'd gone straight home.

Eight

There were still plenty of staff and cast hanging about the stalls. Occasionally a voice was raised. Then laughter, though little of it sounded real. None knew what they waited for, but actors were used to waiting. The man who stopped Leonard in the aisle was tall and plump, looked in his early fifties and not given to waiting. Josie the waitress said he was cuddly. Leonard would have said portly, but he'd seemed agile enough as he hopped from the edge of the stage on to one of the front row seats and then to the aisle. He slipped a spiral notebook into a large cardigan pocket and smiled.

'Are you the wise one?'

The voice was soft. It matched the grey silk of his shirt and the gently baggy jade cardigan. Leonard nodded. He didn't want to talk to anyone until he'd spoken to Madelaine Jack. He wanted her to set up a print out of the burglar alarm. Where she was, he didn't know. The stage search continued. Two white-clothed figures were checking the soft gauze of the painted scenery.

'Good. I'm the SM. Tiggy Jones. We have to talk.'

Leonard looked back at the man. The face was open. The brown hooded eyes as gentle as the voice.

'Sure.'

Leonard dropped into the third seat along and looked up at the stage. It was the only time he'd ever sat so close and he wondered why people would pay so much to look at the actors' knees. Still no Sergeant Jack. The new DC was pulling back the curtains that dropped from the stage to cover the orchestra pit. Leonard thought of using him as a messenger. Jones lowered himself gently into the aisle seat.

'Not callous or anything, but we've got a show that's supposed to open tonight. Presumably it can't.'

'That's right.'

'It can't?'

'That's right.'

'When can it?'

Leonard didn't know. He wanted to put his feet up on the back of the seat in front. Hadn't done that since he was twelve. Now he didn't think his knees would bend that much. He shook his head. He was distracted. The door code thing was bothering him.

'Maybe tomorrow.'

'That's a little vague.'

Leonard turned and blinked at him.

'Your leading lady's been murdered, Mr Jones. Nothing vague about that.'

'Hanky's out. Cue tears. Look, m'lud, I need to know. We've got our pre-panto tour in. Two nights only. Today and tomorrow. We're sold out and the lorry's parked somewhere the other side of town waiting for the signal to come in.'

'In where?'

'The dock at the back of the stage. They need to unload all their gear.'

'They can't.'

'Tomorrow first thing?'

'I said maybe.'

'Do we cancel?'

'What's the tour?'

'The Bay Leaves. You know? The sixties band?'

'Just a band? And they need a lorry?'

Jones chuckled. A warm sound. Properly amused.

'That's thirty years ago, m'lud. There's more to it today than three Fenders and a drum kit. Takes six men just to lift their sound board.'

Leonard hummed his surprise and waved a hand at the Georgian elegance.

'But here?'

'Don't knock it, Inspector. Nothing wrong with middle-aged bums on seats.'

Leonard blinked. Cleaned his spectacles. Squinted into them for smudges.

'I'll get someone to tell you later this afternoon.'

Jones heaved himself from the cramped plush seat.

'I'm obliged, m'lud. I'm obliged.'

'How did she get in?'

Tiggy Jones paused and rested a chubby hand on the back of the seat. He looked down at the sprawling figure of the detective.

'Isn't that your job?'

'She didn't have a key. No alarm code.'

'Maybe she didn't need one.'

'The door would be open?'

'Inspector, Inspector, Inspector. Please come not the innocent. You well know what I mean. But—'

'That someone here with a key and a door code brought her in?'

'Mm. Or she never left.'

'She hid.'

'Or was hidden.'

'Doesn't that make you nervous?'

Tiggy Jones shrugged. Leonard leaned forward. Hands clasped, arms on the row in front like some casual Christian at his devotions. He squinted up at the stage manager.

'What time did the theatre close last night?'

'Don't know. Didn't anticipate being asked. But it was a quick clear. It was a one-nighter. One-man show. Dead simple. One white cane-back chair and the rest was masking. Almost an empty stage. Theatre people don't hang around. It's no different from Fords. The whistle blows. End of shift. The work force is swarming through the factory gates within five minutes.'

'No adrenaline?'

'Oh, plenty. But the symbiosis between end of the show and closing time in the Griffin is clearly understood. Adrenaline needs quenching, not pampering.'

'Talk me through what happened last night.'

'I can tell you what I think probably happened.'

'Let's try it.'

Tiggy Jones took out his note book but didn't open it. He held it across his chest, perhaps for comfort. Leonard wondered whether he would clasp it tightly and cry 'So help me'. He didn't. The soft eyes never left Leonard's.

'There were two curtain calls.'

'Not good?'

'Oh, my word, Julian Glover he was wonderful. Gave his *Beowulf*. Does it all over the world. Marvellous stuff. But he wanted to get away, so told us just the two curtains then he was off.'

'Last train?'

'Him? Oh no. Big Honda. Leathers and bone dome, the lot. Very Buck Rogers. Inside ten minutes he's heading for the M4 and Blighty. Better him than me in this weather.'

'So what time was this?'

'Ten fifteen?'

'So he wouldn't have seen anything.'

'I'll give you his agent's number, but I wouldn't have thought so. Knowing him he wouldn't have even noticed a traffic light.'

'Then what happened?'

'Let me see. Well, curtain down. Then we drop the iron.'

'The—?'

'The iron. The, um, the safety curtain.'

'Go on.'

'The house electrician powers down. That all takes just a few minutes, really. The front of house takes a bit of time clearing. Dawdlers and the cloak room always takes longer in winter. Then when we've more or less cleared, it's up to the SDK. I'm afraid it's all poor old Norman at the moment. Everyone's down with flu.'

'What does he do?'

'Vitamin C. Never seen him with so much as a sneeze.'

Leonard sighed. Jones flicked his eyebrows.

'Sorry. I suppose sense of humour failures are quite common in your trade.'

Leonard blinked. No one remembered having heard him laugh – ever.

'Then what does he do?'

'He walks through, checks for smouldering cigarettes, smelly electric wires, locks, pass door—'

'Which is what?'

Jones nodded above them to the box overlooking the stage.

'Behind there. It connects the front with stage left.'

'That's the right.'

'No. Left as you look at the audience. The door's the way into the auditorium. So it has a door code which means people can't get from front of house to back stage without knowing it.'

'And he'd check that was closed?'

'It always is. Sprung. Never left open. Well, once he's happy that all's well, no one left in the dressing rooms, that sort of thing, then he can lock up.'

'How long does that take?'

'Normally about twenty-five minutes to do the rounds. He could be all locked up in forty, maybe forty-five minutes.'

'So if the show's finished at ten fifteen, the place would have been shut up by eleven.'

'Last night by a quarter to at the latest. But then there's the Vaults.'

'That wasn't closed.'

'Not exactly. Jonah was here and Maurice.'

'Jonah?'

'Joanna Cunliffe, the administrator.'

On the stage, the overalled searchers were starting again. This time, they would swap tracks. A fresh pair of eyes over each part of the stage. Leonard looked back to where the SM was now leaning against the back of the seat.

'I heard there was a party.'

Tiggy Jones shook his head.

'Hardly a ceilidh. A few leftovers and a couple of bottles of wine. Me, Maurice, Jonah, Simone and the new waitress who is, I think, Joan? Joanie? Josie? Anyway, just the five of us.'

He ticked the partygoers off with his fanned fingers.

'And this was in the Vaults?'

'Amen.'

'And you never left the restaurant?'

'Only to go home.'

'Did any of the others leave the restaurant?'

'No. We all left together.'

'So what time was that?'

'Twelvish.'

'Sure there were five of you?'

'Mm. I locked us out. Or at least I think I did. It might have been Jonah.'

'And you saw nothing unusual?'

'Certainly not.'

'Or nothing usual that might help?'

'That I don't know. I don't know what might help. Do you?'

Leonard rocked his clasped hands. But if he were clutching a dice, then there were no sixes to be thrown.

'After you left, did you come back?'

'No, m'lud.'

'Do you know if anyone did?'

Tiggy Jones shook his head.

'No.'

'Did you see anyone hanging about the theatre?'

'Nobody I noticed.'

'Tell me, Mr Jones, how well did you know her?'

'Biblically, not at all. Socially, hardly at all. Never met her until she arrived here.'

'But didn't you book her?'

'Oh, that's not my job. I just hammer them together. Make sure the gear's in place. Maurice, Maurice Poulson the director, would have. This is a rare occasion. Our own production. Mostly we just provide the stage.'

'Why would he have booked her?'

'She's a good crowd-puller.'

'Hardly a leading lady.'

'Come on, Inspector. The only theatrical dame we need is an ugly sister or two.'

'I simply thought—'

'Let's not be naive. This is panto. Strictly he's-behind-you stuff. We've had cricketers, boxers and, God forgive us, rugby players. We didn't ask Lynda here to give her Cinderella. We asked her to give her name and as much of her bosoms as we could get away with in a family show. Although in these days with the kids on whatever they want while the parents shove pornography into the video, who the hell really cares?'

43

'Okay, okay. What I'm asking is why her in particular?'

'I'm not sure there was a particular. Maurice had worked with her before and they were sort of friends, so why not?

'They knew each other?'

'Of course. Maurice knows everyone.'

'So he would have just telephoned and that would have been that?'

'Most likely he called her agent first. Availability? That sort of thing? He –'

Tiggy Jones paused and looked into the distance. A thought written across his rounded face.

'Oh, poops. Her agent. I don't think anyone's told her agent.'

'Is that so odd?'

'Oh yes, in this business it's very odd. First thing you do when you wake up in the morning is to call your agent. If you don't make it through the night, well you get someone else to call.'

Leonard wasn't impressed.

'Oh.'

'More than "Oh", m'lud. Much more. Especially now. After all, someone's just lost at least ten per cent of a nice little earner. Won't like that at all.'

Nine

Madelaine Jack handed him a large beaker of coffee. She'd got it from somewhere other than the corridor machine. Leonard nodded his thanks and leaned back against the thin marble column at the side of the dress circle. They'd come up for another view of the stage. The search team had nearly finished its second rummage. The sergeant in charge was ordering his men to drop their overshoes into the brown paper sack.

'Will he live?'

Jack paused in between sips.

'Philips? Oh he'll be okay, sir. Hospital says no damage other than *le petit bermp* on his head. We'll have to do a PA on that by the way.'

'You can. You're good at forms. We got someone with him?'

'Outside the ward. Think he's a candidate?'

Leonard shrugged. Turned to face the stalls.

'He's odd. He's obvious.'

'We'd need more than that, sir.'

'Comes in, switches off the alarm and then what was it?'

'Went up on to the stage.'

'No, no. Before that.'

From a reefer jacket pocket, she took a tiny notebook and without thinking held out the cup which Leonard took as she flipped back through her notes.

'Here we are. You ask him what he did and he says he "Switched on the lights. Tidied up". You ask him, "Tidied what up?" and he says, "Just things." And that was about it, sir. We didn't go any further.'

Leonard sipped at her coffee.

'Did he strike you as a neat and tidy freak?'

She took her cup.

'Not exactly. Cheap clothes. Very clean. Pressed jeans. But not a freak. Methodical, maybe. The stage door office is like a barrack room. Everything's squared away. But he's not the only one in there. Could be the assistant.'

'But is that the sort of man who doesn't instinctively try to get her down?'

'He's like the rest of us. Goes to pieces in the right circumstances. I mean, sir, that's exactly what he did. Incidentally, it seems that he's teetotal. The brandy that someone gave him could have had a lot to do with it.'

'Who was that?'

Jack shook her head.

'Don't know. I'll check.'

Leonard was leaning over the velvet balcony edge. Hands deep in pockets. Head down. Buzzing. There was something else, something that Philips had said.

'Go through that again?'

This time she drained her coffee.

'Okay. He comes in, switches off the alarm, switches on the lights and tidies up. You say what did you tidy up and he says—'

'Okay. Got that. Is that odd? He comes in, switches off the alarm and then switches on the lights. Wouldn't he have done it the other way round?'

'The lights first, then the alarm? Maybe sir, but don't forget there was probably enough light from the bit between the outer door and the inner door.'

It was still wrong. Something so obvious. Such a perfect routine that on this occasion was wrong. Or, if it were right? He didn't get any further.

From a dark door Leonard had thought locked, a tall man appeared with all the anticipation of The Orator. Very tall. Angular. Black shirt buttoned to the wrists. Black trousers. Black shoes. Coal-black eyes. Unblinking. Jack turned. Started a duty Hearts & Minds smile.

'Hello, sir, this is Detective Inspector Leonard. Sir, Mr Poulson the director here.'

Maurice Poulson said nothing. He didn't quite believe Leonard. The green thornproof. Yellow tie. Brown boots. No. This couldn't really be an inspector calling. Leonard took off his steel-rimmed spectacles and polished them on a green silk handkerchief and smiled at the blurred figure.

'What'll you do now?'

'How's that?'

'What'll you do about Cinders?'

'Aren't you supposed to ask me things like when did I last see her and do I know anyone who wanted to kill her?'

Leonard shrugged. Replaced his spectacles.

'Okay. When?'

'Did I last see her? Night before last. We drank water together.'

'Is that code?'

'No. She only drank water. Her complexion, you know.'

Leonard didn't.

'Where did you go?'

'Her flat.'

'Whose idea?'

'No one's. She was already there. I knocked. She opened. We drank water.'

'She lived here?'

'A winter let. Part of her contract. Lynda could no more have lived outside a capital city than—'

'Mm?'

Poulson sighed.

'I was going to say she could no more have lived here than, fly, but that . . .'

Poulson's words were sharp.

'The wire. It's called the high fly.'

'In the circumstances, an unfortunate expression.'

'Circumstances often are.'

'What time did you leave her on Sunday?'

'Ten eighteen.'

'Precisely?'

'Ten eighteen is precisely, Inspector.'

'Why did you leave?'

'We had finished talking and it was her bedtime. Lynda needed ten hours a night. Woman often do.'

Sergeant Jack ignored his look.

'What did you talk about?'

Was there hesitation? Leonard waited, refusing to prompt.

'Her.'

'Why?'

'She had no other conversation.'

'You knew her well.'

'Hardly.'

'But you'd met before.'

'Had we?'

'Hadn't you?'

Poulson looked at his watch. It was an exaggerated motion. Leonard ignored it. Poulson went on.

'Not really. Couple of London parties. But she always left immediately the photographers had gone. I was there to

47

network. I needed to be noticed. She was noticed. But she never noticed. Not much more to say about her. She had nothing really, apart from her looks – just. The conversation of a fossil. One could only gaze on the outline and imagine what might have been.'

Leonard looked at the floor. His boots. Tapped his toes together. There was no sound on the thick carpet.

'Tell me, Mr Poulson, what else did you talk about?'

'Small problems. Lynda had views.'

'About?'

'Insecurities. They're all the same. For example, she had a big thing about singing. Thought it was too much for her.'

'Was it?'

'Probably. She'd had coaching but she couldn't even hum Eurotrash. So I told her okay, we'd drop it.'

'Very generous.'

'Better than bad notices.'

'Tell me, Mr Poulson, did she have personal problems?'

'Ask her.'

Poulson displayed no worldly arrogance. It was simply a response, built on a line from a half-forgotten script. He had a mental clipboard of them. Leonard buzzed.

'Are you sorry she's dead?'

'I don't get sorry.'

'Not even about death?'

'Especially about death.'

Poulson looked at his watch. A thin piece of square black plastic with a purple face.

'Anything else?'

'My first question.'

Poulson sniffed in contemplation.

'What will I do? This late in the season we're left with jugglers who drop things and Equity-registered drunks. Know any good-time Cinders big in tits and television, and dying – or hopefully not – to work Boxing Day?'

He turned to Madelaine Jack.

'Your big break, darlink. Hand in your helmet. Take to the

boards. Hundred and fifty a day and a chance to sing "Only Make Believe" in public with the great Jason Williams.'

Poulson looked at his watch again.

'Look, I've got to talk to the rest of the cast in an hour. And—'

Jack's words came softly and stopped Maurice Poulson in mid-sentence.

'One of whom may be a murderer.'

Poulson stared through her. Said nothing. Never got a chance. Jack, with the timing of the best in the theatre that day, made excuses and left them in search of the alarm engineer.

'Tell me, do you know anyone who would have wanted to kill her?'

Poulson breathed deeply through his sharp nostrils. So deeply, they nipped together.

'To tell you the truth, Inspector, I wouldn't have thought she had enough depth to be murdered. No. Sorry, can't help. As your trade would say, I haven't a clue.'

Leonard wondered how good an actor a director had to be.

Ten

The entrance was dramatic and off stage. The voice too high-pitched to be identifiable, but the tones familiar. The lawful protests from a gruff and older voice were all but muffled. A town's amateur dramatic society may well, with not much rehearsal, have done better. This was a live, unscripted perform-ance and was good enough to grab Leonard's interest. The youth who then appeared at the edge of the stage wore a long green overcoat flared like a friar's habit about his ankles. His hair, parted in the middle, tossed like two blond tidal waves as he searched this and that way for some unseen heroine. For a moment, Poulson watched in silence. Then he leaned from the shadow of the dress circle.

'Jason.'

It wasn't a greeting but a command. The youth looked up. It was not the face Leonard had imagined he'd seen on posters and screens. The youth was a man. Older than the billboards outside. Leonard followed Poulson through the coded locked door to the tight stairway down to the stage.

'Maurice. It's dreadful. I've just heard. Dreadful. What shall we do? Poor Lynda, poor, poor girl.'

The face may have changed but the voice was still that of the youngster who'd first knocked them out in the sixties. He had a wall of gold and platinum discs with tunes people recognized even though they were too young to have heard them first time round. He had a face that didn't need a caption and an image that frustrated the best efforts of the tabloids. Jason Williams had built his own wall of recording industry fame and his mum a nice and not-so-little bungalow.

Poulson put an unfatherly arm across the flimsy shoulders.

'Sure, Jay, sure. We're all really beat up. Really. Now why don't you get some coffee and we'll all talk later. Yes?'

'Tea.'

'What?'

'Tea. I never drink coffee.'

'Right. Get some tea. And I promise—'

'Mr Williams?'

What Poulson was about to promise never emerged. But Leonard did.

'Detective Inspector Leonard. Mind a few questions?'

Poulson patted the shoulders and pulled his arm away. Williams swung towards him. Pleading.

'Maurice, please. Please stay. I'm not sure if—'

He tailed off. Poulson had gone. Cue star for solo.

'Tell me, Mr Williams—'

'Sorry. Who did you say you are?'

Leonard didn't mind. He fished for his identity badge. The other officers wore them on jacket pockets. Leonard's rarely appeared.

'Detective Inspector Leonard, Avon and Somerset Police.'

Jason Williams peered at the ID card. Smiled. Leonard started again.

'You say you've just heard. How?'

'Right. Well, I just got here, right? The police. Everything. And Curly? You know? Curly?'

He pointed, almost accusingly, to the back of the stalls where a teenager in a leather flying jacket was in deep conversation with the new detective constable.

'Well, he told me. My God, this is dreadful. Poor, poor Lynda. Who could have done such a thing? I mean, it's so, so sick.'

'It is?'

'My God, Inspector, of course it is. I mean the high fly? Like that? Of course it's sick. Don't you think so? Poor, poor girl. Such a beautiful and wonderful person.'

'She was a friend?'

'Of course she was. She was wonderful.'

'How long had you known her?'

The barely furrowed brows creased. The head bobbed and the famous twin blond waves flopped. The intense expression suggested Jason Williams was consulting a deep archive of diaries.

'How long? I'm not sure. Three, four weeks?'

Leonard counted to five.

'And she was your friend?'

'Of course. I said she was. My God, we were working with each other every day. Poor, poor Lynda.'

'You must forgive me, Mr Williams, but three or four weeks doesn't seem long to establish a friendship.'

Williams looked genuinely surprised.

'If it's long enough to break a friendship why shouldn't it be long enough to make one?'

'So you knew Miss Elström quite well?'

Jason Williams was recovering.

'Oh no.'

'But you said you were friends.'

'That doesn't mean I knew her. In fact I hardly knew her at

all. I knew about her, of course – my God the whole business knew about her, but no, I didn't know her. You don't have to know someone to be friends, do you? I mean, well, my God, it's when you know someone really well, that – well, that's what breaks friendships. I mean, my God, isn't it?'

He looked truly perplexed at Leonard's *naiveté*. Leonard moved on. Quickly.

'Did Miss Elström mention any problems, anything that she seemed uneasy about?'

'There were the usual crazy letters and postcards. But mostly she didn't see them anyway.'

'How crazy?'

'She was something of what the tabloids call a sex symbol. You know? She had this title, Bond Girl. Only she wasn't, of course.'

'No?'

'My God. No way. It wasn't official Bond, just a cover. Never really made it artistically, so to speak, but God did it make her or did it make her. I mean, everyone but everyone saw it. And that meant everyone saw her. I mean, saw every-thing. No wonder she started getting letters. Still getting them – and that's got to be twenty-five years ago. Maybe from the same people. Everytime it gets a show on TV, well, more letters. My God, it's terrible.'

'Is it?'

'My God, yes. We all get them. I'm still getting letters from women who were writing when they were teenies.'

'What happens to the letters?'

'The office handles them but a lot get through. They soon find out where to send them and how to.'

'Did you see Lynda's?'

'No, she mentioned them.'

'She was upset, then.'

'I guess so, but everyone gets them. That's part of the deal, Inspector. You get famous, people want to tell you so but sometimes they have a sick way of doing it. Still, when they stop writing, maybe that hurts even more.'

Jason Williams had relaxed. He was now talking about

something he knew. The business. It was as if he'd forgotten the day's agenda. Leonard brought him back.

'And now she won't know, Mr Williams.'

Jason Williams looked at the floor. The misery was back on his face. Leonard wondered how real it was.

'Did she ever tell you anything that suggested that she was being threatened, or that she was in danger?'

'No. She was really very private. No regular man in her life or anything like that.'

'She say so?'

'No. But the gossips would. They'd know. They know everything. If they don't they make it up.'

'When did you last talk to her?'

The hands went into the deep pockets. The green habit swayed.

'You got a mobile, Inspector?'

Leonard looked surprised. Williams explained.

'My mum. I need to call her. She'll have seen it on the telly.'

'At this time of the day?'

'Mum watches all day. Have you?'

Leonard shook his head and carried on.

'When?'

'Did we last talk? I suppose Sunday. Rehearsals.'

'What about?'

'Mainly the singing bit. We were supposed to do a couple of songs. She didn't want to. She thought she had a bad voice.'

'Had she?'

'Oh yes. Lot of them do. But that's no big deal. I tried to convince her she could talk in tune, you know? Rex Harrison went through the whole of *My Fair Lady* like that. Made an album. It's still on the play lists. She wasn't convinced, so I left it to Maurice. I didn't hang around, I had to pick up my mum. Last Advent service in the abbey, you know.'

Leonard supposed he did, but he would check. Jason Williams in church would be noticed.

'Just a routine thought, Mr Williams, were you in Bath last night?'

The relaxed Williams hugged himself in his huge green overcoat and shivered.

'Oh, the poor girl.'

'Were you?'

'Oh, yes. I always stay with my mum. At the bungalow, you know. Home-cooking and a cup of tea in bed. Loves to make a fuss of me and I like to make a fuss of her. You know?'

'You were there all night?'

'Of course. We had our tea, that's what mum calls dinner. She did toad-in-the-hole. I love it. Love it to bits. Then we watched telly.'

'Anything in particular?'

The singer was rubbing his temples with thumb and little finger. Massaging his memory, or pretending to.

'To tell the truth, I wasn't actually watching. Mum was. Of course she watches everything. In the old days she'd look at the test card. And she'd make a great Test Match commentator. She just keeps going. So she was watching and I was, now let me see, right, I was signing pictures. Maybe two hundred or so. Completely knackered, I was. That okay? Helpful?'

Leonard said nothing. How was it that a singer, someone who had to get up and go through maybe a dozen songs every night, could have a lousy memory? Maybe they had the same words. Leonard didn't know.

'Okay, Inspector?'

Leonard buzzed. Hands in pockets. Head bent. Scuffing the carpet.

'Mr Williams, did you leave the house last night at all, for any reason?'

'No. I've just told you.'

'Did you talk to anyone, say, on the phone, or have visitors?'

'Who?'

'Friends?'

'She's the only one, you know.'

'Miss Elström?'

That laugh. Leonard remembered it from the TV shows and countless interviews. Head back in joy. Then forward in modesty. The hair flopping. To Leonard, it was all an act. Maybe that's all these people ever did – perform. If so, he was in for a long, hard case.

'My God no, Inspector. My mum. May not sound very romantic to you. But she's my girlfriend, you know? Sure you haven't a mobile? So convenient, you know. Must call her.'

The new detective constable was hovering. Red and white stripe shirt and a well-pressed dark blue suit. Leonard wondered if he wore red braces. The youth with him most certainly didn't. Leonard recognized him from his pictures on the bills outside. Every child and mini teen knew every detail about him. Curly Weekes. The new face of the new era. The nice quiet one with the widest smile on the noisiest of weekend morning television kids' shows, Saturday Sensation. He'd look good as Buttons. The kids would love him. So would the mums. Now he looked wretched. So sad, but real. The young face with the big brown very red-rimmed eyes.

''Scuse me, sir. Thought you'd want to have a word with Mr Weekes. He says he had a call from Miss Elström last night and she was upset.'

Eleven

Jason Williams had made something of a fuss. He wanted to stay. He wanted to be with his 'dear friend Curly at this time'. Curly had no feelings either way. But Leonard did. He nodded at the constable who shepherded Williams away. Gently but firmly. Constables were better at that sort of thing than inspectors.

When they'd gone, Leonard sat in the nearest aisle seat. Curly sat on the floor with his back against the wall and knees drawn up to his chin. A slim youth in a standard uniform of sheepskin jacket, brilliantly white T-shirt, 501s and Pumas.

'Well?'

For some moments, Curly Weekes said nothing. Seemingly focused on a point beneath the front seat. He began in simple monotones as if he were in a trance.

'She called me last night.'

'Called you where?'

'Hotel.'

'What time was this?'

'Nine then eleven something.'

'She called twice?'

The black tight curly head moved up and down. Slowly. Remotely controlled. Leonard wanted to ask the obvious. Stopped himself. Curly Weekes was in some sort of mental pain. Leonard needed to take him step by step, otherwise he could lose him.

'Were you expecting Miss Elström to call?'

'Yeh.'

'Both times?'

More nodding.

'She said she would.'

'When?'

'Nine.'

'No. When did she say that she would call at nine?'

Weekes, hands clasped around his legs, rubbed his chin across his knees.

'I saw her in the afternoon. She said then.'

'That was after she'd disappeared. You're sure?'

Wrong wording. Leonard had broken the spell. Weekes looked up. The eyes were very red rimmed. No sparkle. He rubbed his forehead with the back of his hand. The palm looked pale enough to be ill.

'She didn't disappear. She had things to do.'

'She went missing.'

'Okay. But that's not disappearing.'

'Is that what she told you?'

'Right.'

'When?'

'In the afternoon. When else? Isn't that obvious? Weren't you hearing me? Isn't that plain enough?'

It was. But Leonard had to hear it. The spell was long gone. Time for answers and no questions. For the moment anyway.

'Okay, Mr Weekes, how about you telling me what happened in the afternoon. Okay?'

Leonard dropped one leg over the seat in front. Curly Weekes stretched his legs in front of him. Long legs. Right across the side aisle. Tiny feet. Narrow feet. Stuck his hands into the jacket's slanted pockets. In another setting, two friends shooting the breeze. It wasn't another setting.

'We went for a drive. Wanted to get somewhere quiet.'

'What time was this?'

'About four until about six thirty.'

'So it was almost dark when you met?'

'Yeh, it was. That's why. Easy to get recognized. You know?'

Leonard could imagine. They were hardly obscure. The very blond and very obvious Lynda Elström and Curly Weekes, the star of teenage Saturday television with his smiling ebony face postered on more bedroom walls than the hottest footballer.

'Where did you go?'

'Up the top somewhere. I dunno. There's a race track or something? It was pretty quiet.'

'Why did you have to go there? Why not go to her flat?'

'You crazy? People would know.'

'So what? Members of the same show. Friends. You may have a secret, but no one knows that you do.'

Curly chewed at his nails.

'You don't understand. She'd got grief. She didn't know who was watching the flat. Maybe nobody. But she didn't know that. We had to handle it her way.'

'Okay. How did she know where to go? Neither of you know the city.'

'We just drove.'

To Leonard that didn't make sense. But he wanted more of Curly Weekes before he clammed.

'What did she tell you?'

'Said there'd been some letters. Then calls and she said – that – that there were things.'

'What things?'

'Something about a lot of pressure and she might go away for a couple of days but she would keep in touch.'

'Did she say what the pressures were?'

Curly's head shook.

'Did you ask?'

'Course I did. But she just said she had something to sort. Something big and I had to wait. There was some guy she had to talk to.'

'Who?'

'She wouldn't say. She just said that I should stay cool and that she knew someone here—'

'In the theatre?'

'No. In Bath. She said I'd get a number where I could call.'

'But she must have said something, anything, that gave you some idea. I mean, why drive all the way out to the race course to tell you something that she could have said on the telephone?'

Leonard had been right about coaxing Curly Weekes. The youth was back to staring, but this time his head nodded in agreement. There was more.

'She said she knew some things about some people.'

'Which people?'

Curly Weekes looked about him like some street urchin about to deal.

'Here.'

'In the theatre?'

Weekes nodded.

'Yes.'

It came as a whisper.

'Okay. What sort of things?'

'She wouldn't say.'

He looked up quickly.

'Honest.'

'Go on.'

'That's it. That's all she said.'

'Anyone else know?'

Curly looked the other way.

'Mr Weekes?'

'Right. Maybe someone else.'

'Male? Female?'

The shrug was hardly seen.

Leonard sucked in a stream of stale theatre air. This was hard work. Weekes wanted to tell him something but didn't want to say anything and Leonard didn't understand why.

'And what happened after that?'

'I went back to the hotel and, well, I waited? Like she'd said to do?'

'For the telephone calls?'

'Right.'

'Tell me about the first one.'

'She just said everything was going to be okay. Told me to forget what I'd seen in the car—'

'She showed you something?'

'No. She meant – I meant – I dunno what I meant. She meant that I should forget what we'd talked about.

Curly Weekes looked hard. Leonard waved a hand.

'What happened at the second call?'

'She said she had to meet someone and maybe get things straightened out. Then she'd call again.'

'Did she?'

Another shake of the curly head.

The head was moving. Side to side to side to side. The big round brown eyes now closed. Soft ribbed slits through which awful tears seeped. The voice now gone. Just a whisper. He was back to the monotones. Back to the staring.

'No. No she didn't. Never.'

To Leonard, something about the whole story had been wrong from the beginning.

'Tell me, Mr Weekes, I still can't grip why Miss Elström chose you to talk to about her – her problems?'

Silence. The mouth was turned down so much that it crossed the harsh line of ugliness to the dreadful curve of utter misery.

'Mr Weekes?'

'Because . . . because . . .'

The head dropped forward into soft-fingered hands. And the

sobs that had sent trembles through lips and cheeks now sent uncontrolled heaves through shoulders to neck until the whole body of the teenager shook. Throughout it all the voice was thick and stifled, yet clear.

'Because . . . because . . . she loved me. We loved each other. We were going to be married.'

Twelve

As Leonard ducked into the biting wind along Manvers Street, he thought of the huge, swirling, snug green overcoat and wondered what Jason Williams had lied to him about. He wondered about the tears, all real enough, but how much had Curly Weekes hidden?

Leonard had never got used to being a policeman. There were times when he wanted to walk away from the whole thing. It wasn't something as simple as being fed up. That would have been easy. Leonard spent much of his life giving the impression that nothing touched him. Some said he was cold. Some who knew him a little better said it was because he was an orphan and that he'd grown a shell and that everything about him was contrived. Even his name had been given him by the visiting chaplain. No one remembered, if they'd ever known, whether the chaplain had a sense of humour or really did believe that a memorable name was about the only reasonable advantage they could offer the quiet, freckled child. The one or two who had become very close to Leonard knew about his moods and the recurring bouts of morbid contemplation of death – his own. Whatever world Leonard visited, he had made sure no one else lived there. Madelaine Jack believed that the problem with Leonard's private life was that he was the only one in it. But she didn't say so.

Beneath the routine of police investigation, Leonard could burn enormous energies, go for long periods without sleep and keep his team guessing as to what next he might ask of them.

And then, Leonard would slump, despondently. Murder cases, and there were far more than the public ever realized, drew him deeper into his shell just at the time when he should have been open with his colleagues. Instead, he wanted to walk away and think about what he'd seen, heard, been told, wondered, believed, disbelieved. In theory they all did that – but they did it together. It was called Routine. But to work it had to keep to the same routine. In the old days they called it team work. Now at Manvers Street police station they heard senior officers speaking not of team work but interpersonal sequences. Whatever the jargon, Leonard simply carried on being Leonard. In modern police routine, Leonard didn't belong and perhaps he'd never belonged just as he'd never been popular enough to have a nickname. He'd stayed because very simply he hadn't left. Jack knew the problem. Leonard was never a policeman. Criminologist maybe. But she didn't say so.

They'd once talked. Late, late into the night, about right and wrong, justice and injustice, excess and revenge. Leonard had talked about crime as something anyone had a right to turn to. He saw it as a perfectly natural form in society. He regarded evil as a convenient definition necessary to put the rest of law abiding society in perspective. He regarded it as a human right to commit crime, even the worst kind, even murder. But he believed that rest of society therefore had a right to demand whatever punishment they liked. To him, neither was right nor wrong except in pure majority terms. After they'd talked it was daylight and she'd gone home and had not slept. The next morning in the characterless surroundings of Manvers Street police station, neither mentioned the conversation of the night before. There was no embarrassment, they simply didn't mention it. They were both proper keepers of secrets, each understanding the other's tacit laws of privacy. What, if anything, he had understood of Madelaine Jack, she didn't know. But she'd long understood that beneath Leonard's code, there was fear of betrayal, of intrusion and most of all, fear of disappointment. She knew this after the time she had asked him why he always went on holiday by himself. Simple, he had said, travel by yourself and you can always go back again. No memories but your own. That night she had been allowed a peep into Leonard's world, but not asked in. Better that way.

Now as she watched him approaching the police station, head bent, hands deep in the old duffle coat that came out every December, twenty-eight-year-old Detective Sergeant Madelaine Jack knew him well enough to see his mood change. His walk had become a trudge as he lost himself in a barely tolerable agony of a murder investigation. She understood why it was better not to get too close. Always better to call him sir.

Leonard looked up. She was on the steps.

'You coming or going?'

'Coming. Just got back, sir.'

'Good. Curly Weekes reckons he was with Lynda Elström between fourish and six thirty yesterday afternoon. He says she was in some sort of trouble, but he doesn't know what. Reckons she had something on someone in that place. And . . .'

He held the door for her. She didn't mind.

'. . . as a bonus, he claims they were about to be married.'

He looked at her for reaction. She raised her eyebrows and pressed the inner-door buzzer. The outer lobby felt damp. Welcome to Manvers Street nick. The civilian in the station office pressed the inner-door release and in silence they mounted the biscuit and marbled stairway to the first floor and the tiny room jammed between the chief inspector's and the patrol inspector's. Leonard didn't complain. Some did. He saw no point. All the offices were too small. Even the district commander's corner suite with its private bathroom was an unmodernised 1960s cubbyhole. The window in Leonard's room was cracked and sticky-taped. He kept snagging trouser legs on the splintered underside of his desk. The black plastic protection ends had long gone from the coat stand. There'd been a mirror, but that had been lost when the place was painted three years ago for a Royal visit. He wondered if it was worth mentioning his office to a friendly ram-raider. Maybe the insurance would be worthwhile. Why not? That's what the rest of the city did.

Jack was waiting. He drifted back.

'And he claims she was going away for a few days to sort

things, as he put it, and she'd be in touch. She called him, he says, at nine last night and some time after eleven. And she then said she would call him later because first she was meeting someone. Last night, that is.'

He leaned back in his chair and rested his boot on the open bottom drawer. He'd found the remains of a gingerbread man's leg. He tapped at an empty pad top with a stainless steel paper knife. She was taking off her coat. Hadn't said a word.

'Well?'

'Classic stuff isn't it, sir? Murderer claims the victim said she was going away. Six months later we dig up the back garden. There's his wife.'

'So we should have Curly at the top of the list?'

'Could be, sir, could be.'

'Real tears.'

'Remorse?'

He tapped some more. Picked up a paper clip and flicked it across the room at the filing cabinet.

'Wedding bells? Is that likely?'

Madelaine Jack shrugged.

'According to everything we know about her, she's been on her own for a long time. On the other hand, even if she had said they were getting married, there's no telling that she meant it.'

Leonard was now bent over the desk drawer looking for gingerbread leftovers.

'Women are like that, aren't they?'

'People are, sir.'

'Tell me something, what if it's all wotsit? Suppose the whole thing's a fantasy?'

She nodded. He dropped the paper knife on the blotter.

'Right, let's start checking him. What's that new D.C. called?'

'Leweson, sir.'

'Get master Leverson—'

'—Leweson, sir.'

'Right. Get him to go through the whole routine. Check the itemized calls from the theatre and look out for calls to her number. When and how many. Then check out this car thing. Check her car. Something's odd about it. Like . . .'

'Like, where is it now, sir?'

'Right. Maybe hired. Check the firms. Check the model. Tell him to see if it was noticed up by the race course between four and six thirty. Then see who she'd been phoning. If she set up a meeting, she probably did it by phone. Get an itemized bill on the number and see if she's got a mobile. Same thing.'

'Her telephone probably won't have been itemized. It's a theatre rental.'

'That administrator is as hard as nails. She'd want a complete list of what she's paying for. Also check Weekes's hotel. Incoming calls might be registered somewhere. They'd certainly know if he made any out even if they didn't connect. Get Lawson to check them against her flat and mobile numbers. Got it?'

'Leweson, sir.'

She needed the smile. They both did. She was halfway along the corridor on her way in search of Leweson, when he called her. He was still sitting there.

'What did you say when I met you downstairs?'

'I've just got back. I was about to tell you and you started.'

'Right. And?

He brushed the gingerbread crumbs from his trousers.

'Ross? I found his hotel. He's staying at the Rivers.'

'Where is he?'

'According to the manager, he went out this morning, shortly after eight and hasn't been back. No messages.'

'Mm?'

'He hasn't any messages. I thought that was odd, sir. I mean, a man like him gets messages all the time. And anyway, his ex-wife gets murdered, it's already on the news and the billboards, you'd think someone would have phoned him. Wouldn't you?'

'Assuming anyone knew where he was staying.'

'The woman you saw him with? Surely she must have known.'

Leonard was doodling.

'Single or double?'

The lip was bit. She hadn't asked.

'The manger didn't mention a partner.'

'And you didn't.'

'No, sir.'

'But you will.'

'Yes, sir.'

Strictly Detective Inspector. Strictly Detective Sergeant.

'Okay.'

She was dismissed. As she headed for. the corner stairs and the Major Incident Room she quietly cursed James Boswell Hodge Leonard. By the time she reached the stairs, she was quietly cursing herself for such a simple mistake. Leweson, who was about to tuck into pie and chips in the canteen next to the MIR, got the full no-nonsense briefing from her. If DC Leweson cocked up on this, it was Madelaine Jack and not Bernard Leweson who would feel the sting from the mildest mannered detective inspector in the whole of the district.

When she got back, that same officer was sitting side on to his desk and gazing at the cracked ceiling, his hands clasped behind his neck. Stretched. The crackling made her wince.

'Curious, really.'

'Sir?'

'Why hang her?'

'Someone's sense of the macabre?'

He hunched.

'Could be. Or?'

'Something that went wrong sir?'

'You mean sexual? Miss Whiplash? Not her style. Or so they say.'

Jack looked a little sceptical.

'So they do.'

He was buzzing again. Vespers composed by a tone deaf atheist to be sung at one decibel. She didn't say so.

'What about a public execution? It's a pretty impressive scaffold.'

'More Tyburn than Newgate.'

He didn't understand. He laced his fingers tighter behind his neck, crackled again and squinted at Jack through the crook of his arm.

'What?'

'Well, sir, at Tyburn all they did was to hoist the prisoner up. So it was, well, slow strangulation – dancing at the end of a rope. Well, when they invented the trap door at Newgate instead of, well, just hanging about until dead, the door opened and you were, as they used to say, for the big drop. If you were lucky it was quick.'

'Which was this?'

'Tyburn. But why? Why so sadistic?'

He got up and went to the window. Across the way, the discount store was offering big credit deals. But you had to answer a lot of questions. Bit like this. He dropped into the creaking chair. Too many questions.

He touched the tip of his right thumb.

'One. Her ex was in a pub last night. Coincidence? Where is he now?'

Then the index finger.

'Two. Who was the woman with him? Three. Why did they leave the pub so quickly? And – and four, where did they go?'

The little finger.

'Five. The security camera is buggered. How so? Or . . . who so?'

'You think it could be sabotage, sir?'

'What's the engineer say?'

She chewed at the corner of her mouth.

'I'm sorry, sir. Haven't had time to check.'

'But you will.'

'Yes, sir. I will.'

He tapped his left thumb.

'Seven—'

'Six, sir.'

'Six. We still haven't the print out of the burglar alarm. Seven. Who filled Philips up with brandy?'

'Most likely he did, sir.'

'But we don't know. Okay—'

He paused.

'Eight, sir.'

'Eight. Was this Jason Williams really home? Nine. Did Poulson really leave her flat when he said he did and ten, where are the sick letters she was sent? And –'

He changed hands again.

'Eleven, did she really meet Curly Weekes, tell him she had dirt on someone and did they really talk as late as eleven o'clock on the telephone? Not bad for a morning's work with no answers.'

The telephone stopped her from saying anything. She made quick notes on her tiny pocket pad. Leonard was off again as soon as she'd put down the phone. He was tapping his left index finger.

'And another thing, twelve—'

'And twelve sir, that was Benson.'

Looked up at the wall clock. Gone two. She'd said it would be.

'And?'

'She was strangled.'

Leonard nodded. Obvious really. Jack hadn't finished.

'But not by the wire, sir. Bruising's all wrong. Timing's wrong. Throat's ruptured in wrong place. He reckons she was strangled and *then* strung up on the wire.'

'Dead?'

'Very, sir.'

'Tyburn then Newgate. Strangulation then the big drop. Hands about the throat then the wire. Maybe someone with a sense of history.'

'Or a sense of drama, sir. Right place for it.'

Thirteen

They sat or sprawled in the back stalls. Some wore coats, one a hat, some sweaters. Poulson surveyed the gathering with some contempt. To him, the stage staff were okay. Regular guys. The front-of-house staff he didn't really know. The actors? He knew them all right. There wasn't one of them with any balls. A thespian dairy herd never really happy unless they were chewing the cud or being milked. They lived on anecdotes and draining performance. Bad actors dressed up. Good actors stripped. This year there wasn't one who didn't need the big dressing-up box. So best get on with it.

'Okay. These are the facts. The police are going to be here for the next twenty-four hours. Until they've gone, stage and understage are out of bounds. Use the side door into Beauford Square. There's a policeman on it. You'll have seen we're surrounded by policemen and the press. Now for sake of Moses, for once in your lives, don't smile at the camera. Don't gossip to the press. Look suitably sober and say nothing more than we're all devastated. If you like you can be really pukey and say that the show goes on. Nothing more. I've spoken to all your agents. Same applies to them and, of course, to staff here. Questions?'

Jason Williams had all but disappeared. The enormous bottle-green coat looked as if someone had thrown it, casually, into a pile on the chair. The bundle moved. The voice from behind the great unflappable collars was tight. Nervous. Anxious.

'Maurice, eh, I mean, eh, well, Maurice, do you think we should call it a day? You know? A wrap or whatever it's called? I mean, well, my God, I for one don't feel like Prince Charming. What you say? Mark of respect and all that? Finito?'

Poulson stared at him. Williams looked away. He'd got his answer. Poulson scanned the rest of the cast. Hilda Rostow fed herself purple cachous and, baubles clinking, nodded every time someone said anything. She was lost without her sister. Angela Billings was famous as being everyone's friend. Aunty Ange, they called her. Now she abandoned *The Times* crossword and propped her over-large glasses into her swirl of grey-streaked hair and looked up.

'Actually, darling, it would be nice to know where we go from here. I assume we haven't, eh, lost another of our number to the Bath Strangler?'

Jason Williams screwed his young-old face in anguish. Hilda Rostow giggled in G sharp. Joanna Cunliffe sighed her distaste. Simone and Josie looked at each other, perplexed and feeling outside the group. A couple of the stage hands slumped deeper into the seats and said nothing. Angela Billings hitched the decorated Russian shawl about her large comfy bosom and waited for an answer. She'd touched a nerve end. Poulson raised an eyebrow at Tiggy Jones who looked at his notebook even though he knew the answer. Tiggy, by habit, always consulted his notebook – about everything.

'Sorry. Nothing. If he hasn't heard, then he's the only person in Christ's kingdom. But I suppose, well, we do have all-day opening hours in Bath. Sorry to be so cruel, m'lud, but it does seem a day for it. Mm?'

Angela Billings propped her blue-rimmed spectacles on the very tip of her designer nose and went back to nine across. Without looking up, she said what the rest had not.

'Are we all suspects in the grand inquisition? After all, the dear girl was a coincidence of our lives and as far as one, or rather this one, can tell, we're the most likely people to have known how to, how shall we say, hang her out to dry?'

She took her time looking up. The smile came as she perfectly focused on Maurice Poulson's black eyes. Angela Billings was celebrated for her timing.

'What do we think, darling?'

Poulson was expressionless. His black humour had deserted him.

'We think we all stay cool. The guy running things will be back inside an hour. He wants to go over the where were you on the night bit. Okay? Any problems with that?'

There were a few shrugs. A few grimaces. A few nods. No one, not even Miss Billings, said anything. Poulson delivered his health warning.

'So a little advice. This Leonard's not the schlemiel he appears. Don't fall for the tweeds and brown boots. This one doesn't knit yogurt on his day off. And his tart's twice as clever. They're a good act. So no up-cocks.'

Angela Billings had not finished.

'Are you tell us, darling, that we shouldn't co-operate with the police?'

'I'm telling you that police don't co-operate with anyone. They believe there's a secret here. They want it. So watch it.'

'Don't we want them to have it? The little secret?'

The conversation was too much for Jason Williams who was giving more and more the impression that he wanted his mummy or the lavatory. He wriggled further into his great coat.

'For God's sake! What are we talking about? You telling us that one of us killed Lynda? You out of your tree? None of us knows anything about it. My God, until she arrived here, we hadn't even met her.'

Angela Billings filled in nine across and laid the half-completed puzzle aside. The warm voice was satisfied. She didn't bother to turn. Just smiled sweetly.

'Really darling? You *do* surprise.'

Fourteen

The briefing hadn't gone too well. Detective Chief Superintendent Marsh, as ever, wanted to make sure the right procedures were followed. This, he said, would be extra sensitive. The whole nation was tuning in. The head of the press office had come over from Portishead. Lynda Elström was, within the space of two hours, a national heroine. Just one film and a decade of first-night and television appearances which may not have inspired serious acting offers, had most certainly done something for a whole generation of acne-suffering teenagers. The tall, scrubbed, bony, dark suited and white-cuffed Marsh was brought up with a Nonconformist view that actresses were ill-disguised prostitutes. There were moments that for this son of that church, nothing had changed. This, he feared, was one of them.

'Devious practices. Mm?'

Leonard shrugged.

'Nothing says that. No bits of string. No plastic bags. Clothing straightforward.'

Marsh did not blink.

'What was she wearing?'

Leonard wasn't sure. Jack was.

'Black silk leggings. Black cashmere sweater. Knee length. Black fur-lined boots.'

Marsh stared at Jack. She felt uncomfortable. Not professionally so. He sucked sharp breath through thin sharp yellow teeth.

'Undergarments?'

'A body, sir.'

'An unfortunate phrase.'

'It's a sort of, well, a sort of swim thing, a one-piece – well, sort of things dancers wear.'

'Colour?'

'Black, sir.'

He was staring at her again.

'Black silk leggings. Black body. Black jumper. Black boots. That's a lot of black.'

Jack said nothing. Leonard shrugged.

'Fashion. Casual. Late at—'

He stopped. The man from the press office looked over his shoulder, following Leonard's line of sight. A cartoon of an old district commander. Leonard was blinking. Sergeant Jack skimmed his words. Fashion. Casual. Late at night. Late at night. Late. Night. Of course! How on earth could she have missed it? Tired? They all were. She didn't say a word. Marsh sensed but couldn't see.

'What is it, man? Come on. What is it?'

Leonard had turned his head. Held his bottom lip between thumb and forefinger.

'Silk leggings. Cashmere sweater. Leather boots.'

Marsh waited. Leonard double checked his memory.

71

'December. Night. No coat.'

Jack closed her eyes. Whispered.

'Thirteen.'

The man from the press office scribbled in his spiral bound notebook.

'How's that?'

She said nothing. Marsh ignored him. He was tapping the point of his crossed knee with a long thin silver pencil.

'Midnight. Below zero temperature. And she wasn't wearing a coat.'

'No, sir.'

'And as far as you know, none has been found?'

Leonard looked at Jack. She shook her head.

'Nothing obvious, sir. Odd clothing in some of the rooms, but nothing out of place. Nothing, well, sir, which screamed designer money at us, which I imagine she'd have been wearing.'

Marsh's black eyebrows twitched in Leonard's direction. The answer was obvious, but Leonard went through the routine.

'She either goes out without a coat. So why? Or, she goes out with a coat but takes it off. So why?'

'Or?'

'Or so?'

'Why yes, man. Or, she doesn't go out, but she is taken out.'

There was a gap. Jack eased in.

'Excuse me, sir. I've read the prelim on the flat search. No signs of violence.'

Marsh wasn't impressed.

'Miss Elström, or at least as I'm given to understand, was hardly an Amazon. A strong man could simply overpower such a lady. And, even if she struggled, then any disturbance could be tidied easily enough. After all, there's no blood in a strangling.'

Leonard anticipated the next question. Got in first.

'Haven't had a chance to look myself. I'll get up there later this afternoon. First we need to know if, where and when she made a telephone call to Curly Weekes, then we may have a better idea about a lot of things.'

'You've not much now, have you?'

'No, sir.'

There was a pause. A pause with the weight of silence that follows the gospel reading. The elder spoke.

'Then we won't be keeping you, Leonard. You have your work to do.'

Fifteen

The flat was quietly furnished. The furniture was good reproduction from a workshop of craftsmen in Bruton. The bookcases filled mostly with ornaments. A blue goose with a golden egg. A small soldier with a large musket. An impossibly thin dancer. A sturdy peddler with a glorious bunch of shiny balloons. An empty Irish decanter surrounded by six matching glasses, each with the blower's label still stuck to the base. An ebony cigarette box from another age. Three books. An actor's autobiography. Keble Martin. A dictionary of quotations. A mantle mirror was perfectly polished and made the room twice its size. The flame-effect fire was unlit and sullen. In front of it, the sofa was big and blue. Laying over one end, a full length black astrakhan coat with a collar big enough to hide a full grown Cossack.

'That it?'

Sergeant Jack raised her eyebrows. Bent and sniffed the collar.

'Could be, sir. Pretty expensive pong.'

'Check the bedroom.'

Leonard opened the two draws of the sofa table. Empty except for blank postcards with the flat address and matching blue envelopes. The leather cornered blotter pad was clean. The nasty brass letter knife abandoned as an ornament. He opened a heavily panelled corner cabinet. The television. Had to be. Jack returned with two bottles of perfume.

'Looks like it. Charlie for the daytime and *L'air du temps* for whenever. Couple of things in the wardrobe with the same smells.'

Leonard picked up the coat. Put his nose close to the collar. It smelled clean. The sort of smell he imagined he'd known as a child – but hadn't.

'But would she have gone out at that time of night in something as elaborate as this?'

'Not exactly an anorak girl, was she? I mean, sir, something like this is, well just something like this. I bet there isn't a non-designer label in the place.'

Leonard let the black coat fall gently back to the arm of the sofa. The coat slid open. The label said Roma. So did his coffee bag.

'This place is empty. Perfect. She wasn't even here.'

'According to Poulson, sir, that would have suited her just fine.'

'What about in there?'

He headed for the bedroom. Champagne and greys. An incongruous jangle of crystal chandelier. Ceiling-to-floor silk curtains tied back with pink piped belts on to brass hooks. Greys and creams in the almost plain silk wallpapers. Cream dressing table with powder colours of nymphs. No shepherds. Neat pots and bottles. Designer porcelain and glass courtiers ranged in deferential and essential attendance. Heavy brocade quilt across the queen-sized bed. A soft cream silk kimono. No teddy bear. The white telephone, a sliver of Swedish plastic with its blinking red pinprick of light advertising its voice-activated dial. Wardrobes double and mirror doored. Shelves of soft sweaters. Drawers of silk lingerie. Stockings. No tights. Two racks of hardly worn shoes and boots. On the floor and at the back of the second wardrobe, a light brown calf attaché case. It was easy to open. The locks had been forced. It was a very expensive case and very empty.

Sixteen

Tiggy Jones had cleared a room for Leonard to see the rest of the cast. With its cream-glossed brick walls, odd chairs, a pretend mahogany desk on bright chrome legs, it was more a cell than an interview room.

Jack had given him a folder for each of the cast. The one on the desk was marked in black felt-tip. The Rostows. Inside the publicity still showed the twin turned up noses, same tiny ears peeping from the same sticky sprayed black curls. The rosebud mouths pouted the same kisses and the small eyes disappeared into tight crevices of powdered and puffed flesh. Big ladies. Size sixteens and climbing dressed in billowing high-necked frocks like two shimmering spinnakers.

The door was opened by a slim WPC and one of the twins, which one he didn't know, hove to in the exact centre of the square room. Tiggy Jones had said she was Hilda.

'Miss Rostow?'

A chubby right hand flopped from the wrist. The round voice giggled at him.

'Oh please don't get up. Unless you want the little boys' room.'

She turned to the WPC, whom she'd flattened against the doorpost. Giggled. Another routine delivered. Turned back. Leonard was not impressed. Showed it. No expression. No impression. He pointed to the chair. Leonard leaned against the opposite wall. Hands in jacket pockets. Ankles crossed.

'I'm Detective Inspector Leonard, Avon and Somerset police.'

'Of course you are. Love the tie.'

'You are?'

'Hilda. The good-looking one. Unless of course, my dear, you think she's better looking, then I'm Rose.'

She held out a silver tin of cachous. He shook his head.

'Oh please do, they're bad for me.'

More giggles. More cachous. More jangling baubles. Lips pursed, more to come. He cut her short. Leonard was his own straight man. Scratched the side of his nose. Shifted against the wall. Looked at the floor as he spoke.

'This is a murder inquiry. I'm asking routine questions of everyone. I'd appreciate your co-operation. Will you please give me your movements last night.'

Even as he spoke, he knew the phrasing was lousy.

'Well, Inspector, giving in to our fetishes, are we?'

'Miss Rostow, last night, a colleague of yours was strangled until dead or, left hanging to die in her own time. Shall we proceed?'

Hilda Rostow's expression did not change. The piggy eyes did not flicker. She popped another tiny purple cachou between her crimson rosebuds and made tiny, childlike crunchings with her tiny, even, childlike teeth.

'Tell me Miss Rostow, your movements last night?'

'Oh dear, we seem to have made an itsy boo-boo. Well my dear luvver, we're afraid you'll think this enormously boring. Poor Rosie by any other name has the most dreadful stinker, and we don't mean Roger the Lodger or Souther the Border who expects to pay the rent in kind. Oh no. Temperature of hundreds and simply hundreds. So last night we played Miss Nightingale Pulls It Off. Our bedside manner from heaven was perfected. The patient lives. We're now expecting something from the Palace.'

Leonard flipped a page in his mental notebook.

'You're staying at the Avon Bridge?'

'We always do. So we do. They know our ways and we get a good price.'

'Did anyone . . .?'

'The night porter. Such a dear. Made sure we had a little soup and pinctus linctus. Wally. Such a dear. A terrible pervert. But a dear one.'

'And you were there all evening and all night?'

'We tucked darling Rosie in at seven and apart from tinkles, there she reclined, I with her.'

'All the time?'

Another cachou. More crunching.

'Are you asking us if we did the dastard deed, Inspector?'

'I'm asking where you were. I'm asking everyone where they were.'

'Gracious dearie me. So you think we all did it. How muffin.'

'You don't seem shocked.'

'We're not dead, my luvver. Not us. So why should we be shocked?'

'I imagined that a murder in the company would be shocking in itself.'

'You find death shocking, Inspector.'

He nodded. 'The manner of death shocks.'

'You poor lamb.'

'But someone you knew? A violent death? In this theatre?'

Hilda Rostow pinched another cachou from the tin. Then, with an obvious second thought popped it back in the tin and snapped shut the lid. She slapped herself on the wrist and dropped the tin into a vast pocket. She smiled. Then didn't. Leonard was running his finger through the thin layer of dust on top of the grey filing cabinet. He turned back to her, assuming the sketch was done. Yes it was. She gave a big but bad RADA sigh and much heaved inside the spinnaker's folds.

'If you think for one moment that we should be shedding into the little lace hanky, then we beg your pudding, petal. Hardly knew her. Didn't think much of what we did know. But, lo she cries, pulling herself up to her full Abraham, if you think we did for her, then think again. Think again. We do good dames, but bad Pierpoints. Okey doo-doos?'

Leonard wondered if she were like this all the time. Promised himself to ask. If she were, then life could be hell. If she weren't, then why now?

'What didn't you care for?'

'She was great. Wonderful. Warm.'

'You said just now that you didn't think much of her.'

Hilda felt for her tin. Left it where it was.

'So we did. So we did.'

'Well?'

'Well we can't all be the same can we?'

'That's not an answer.'

'No. But then there's not much more. We met. We didn't like her.'

Leonard polished his spectacles on his tie. Held them up to the light and squinted through the immaculate lenses as he spoke.

'Both of you? You always say "we"?'

'We love nominatives.'

'Aren't we being too clever?'

'We do our bestest dearest.'

She was laughing at him. He waited before he put his spectacles on.

'When did you first meet her?'

'When we came here.'

'Not before?'

'Listen, we get some good giggy wigs, but not her sort. We're very big in Weston. She's very big in *Playboy*, or was. But you're wee-weeing against the wrong lampposts. Without us telling you your job, Dickie Darling, you could do with a good strong man. Nothing personal, of course.'

'Did she have man trouble?'

The wrists flapped about. She really should have had a boá to fling across a shoulder. A bare dressing room was hardly the setting for the grand gesture.

'My dearie deariest, did she have man trouble? That woman *was* man trouble. Surely you've worked that out for yourself?'

'Which man?'

'Mm – Mm. Naughty, naughty, no catchee monkee. That would be telling, darling. But have a little think in your bath. There's one who thinks it's his right. There's one scorned and we all know how that little sting sings, don't we? There's one who thinks she just wanted to be understood. One who thinks she was laughing at him. One who simply wanted to touch. And that, my sweetness and light, is just the matinée crowd.'

'Go on.'

'Oh no, no, no, Nanette. Save it for your bath. Just think about them, and her. And do do keep your hands on the sponge otherwise you'll have to get stronger glasses.'

'Someone special in the cast?'

'We're each someone special.'

'You know what I mean.'

'Yes sweetness, I know what all men mean. So did she. She made a specialty of it.'

'That's very bitter.'

'Don't you mean sour? Yes of course it is. She was a lovely girl, only five years younger than us and as far as anyone else was concerned, she could have been twenty years younger. Sourness comes with the damson, darling boy. But we earn a living and don't have to protect ourselves from silly men, though it must be nice. That's what we think, anyway. Don't we, Rosie darling? Yes Hilda, my dear, of course we do, There you are, Inspector. Satisfied?'

'Was she seeing anyone in the cast?'

The tin was out. The lid back and the podgy fingers popped the tiny cachou into the sweet-smelling too-pink-gummed mouth. Then another. She hunched up in naughty girlish delight.

'Don't look. Don't look. Eating for two, you know. Anyone? Maybe. But you'll have to ask them yourself. After all it shouldn't be hard to cross most of them off your list. When it comes to the trouser department, most of them can't, won't or don't. But if I were you, I'd start at the bottom and work up. Figuratively, of course.'

'Have you ever been blackmailed Miss Rostow?'

Leonard's hypothesis was that there never is a pause when there appears to be. But too quick an answer is a pause. It gives the victim breathing and thinking space to anticipate the follow-up question. Hilda Rostow's answer came back without a breath.

'Of course, dearie. We all have.'

'By whom?'

'Gracious me my loverlee. Gracious me. Productions make us work for peanuts. We do it instead of doing door-to-door brushes. Isn't that blackmail?'

'You know it isn't and you know what I mean.'

The eyes were the piggiest he'd seen. They were nasty,

spiteful, hating eyes. The mouth smiled. The eyes spat malice. Was answer enough for the moment. Had to be. Later, he doubted that he'd have got much further. But at that point, he silently cursed Detective Sergeant Jack. There was a sharp knock at the door and she beckoned him from the corridor. As he closed the door behind him, she caught his expression. Wished she hadn't.

'Sorry, sir.'

'Better be brilliant.'

'DC Leweson has got the printout from Curly Weekes's hotel. He got three calls last night but because in-coming calls don't register, we don't know where from. But more interestingly, our bright little Buttons made fourteen calls between midnight and nine fifteen this morning. All to the same number. The one in Lynda Elström's flat.'

'So at nine fifteen this morning, Curly Weekes thought she was alive.'

'Not quite, sir – he *hoped* she was.'

'That it?'

He turned back to the door.

'Not quite, sir. I've got the fairy godmother down the corridor. She says darling Cinders didn't deserve to go to the ball.'

Seventeen

The hit and run victim was moved from general surgical to the Intensive Care Unit at three o'clock that afternoon.

Eighteen

Angela Billings had been in most things. It started at RADA and, some said, finished there. She'd been one to watch. Rep at Farnham. Rep at Nottingham. Then Norwich. Then Birmingham. Then Salisbury. Then the RSC but never much more than the nurse. Aunty Ange was a good jobbing actress who'd never been out of work for more than six weeks since she left RADA. Once married to a very ordinary but kind surveyor, she now had a big flat in Bath and a small cottage in Suffolk. She cared for a selfish life rather than one that always had to be explained. So, she was a contented working widow in her sixties with plenty of time to think for herself and she was quite looking forward to Leonard's questions.

Angela Billings loved crime. She thought it exciting. Protected by a little money and a reasonable address, she saw crime as some predatory crab in a murky rockpool. She liked seeing society nipped and pinched. Her sense of social history explained that crime was a legitimate trade with its own unofficial guilds and conventions. She detested the hideous, especially the violent, aspects of crime. But regular crime she saw as a not unreasonable fact of everyday life and rated most grand and respectable institutions as inhabitants of a similar underworld. She felt as much outrage when an insurance company invoked an obscure clause in order not to pay out as she did when her shoulder bag had been snatched in broad daylight.

And Angela Billings had once benefited from crime. A year ago, she had tackled a burglar in the early hours. For her action she received a black eye from the villain, a commendation for bravery from the chief constable and, more important, a two-column picture of herself in all the national newspapers and as a result, six months in a television soap. It was that character Leonard recognized when he entered the dressing room. He'd never seen the programme, but he hadn't escaped the publicity campaign.

Angela Billings thought Leonard more interesting than his

partner. He didn't look part of the institution. His sergeant did, in a very modern way. She was very courteous and clearly intelligent. But there was no sense of risk, therefore Madelaine Jack did not interest Angela Billings. The man who now cleaned his steel-framed spectacles on a green silk handkerchief spoke with a soft voice. Apologetic. She'd once played a 1930s country doctor's wife. He'd have got the part of the doctor.

'My name's James Leonard Miss Billings. Detective Inspector Leonard. Sergeant Jack tells me you have your own thoughts on Miss Elström's death.'

Angela Billings stroked the soft black wool of her Russian shawl and smiled contentedly. The grey streaked hair perfectly done for a Knightsbridge shopping expedition.

'Not thoughts, Inspector, observations. All very simple. It might help you to know that on Monday morning, poor Lynda, as now we must call her, told me she was leaving the show. Now, you might imagine this was something of a surprise, especially as we hadn't even opened.'

'When on Monday?'

'Nine o'clock? That's right. Just before the photo call.'

Leonard buzzed. Jack flipped a fresh page of her notebook.

'She say why?'

'A big problem she said. Then she said she was feeling ill. Certainly sounded it, but not flu-ill. Stressed. She said something about being under a lot of pressure and needing space.'

'You say sounded it? Does that mean you didn't actually see her?'

'How clever. Exactly that. She telephoned. In fact, at first she didn't tell me anything.'

'Then why telephone? Are you – were you particular friends?'

Angela Billings peered over the top of her outsize glasses.

'Isn't the standard reply something along the lines, "never laid eyes on 'er in me life, guv" or something similar?'

Leonard didn't reply. The actress took deep breaths. So did her flowing smock.

'No. We most certainly were not friends. But we'd met. Years ago on location in a couple of rather bad films. Then again at a little BAFTA award. The judges were very generous that year. I was very gracious. Poor Lynda was the prize-giver. Given the cut of her frock, it was, I remember, appropriate that the award was for best supporting actress.'

'A friendly face anyway.'

'Certainly not unfriendly. But no darling, there was something else. As you've probably discovered, I actually live in Bath. The are a lot of us in the profession. In fact I live just round the corner from Catherine Place. She'd been for tea, although she didn't drink any.'

'Water.'

'Absolutely. And my dear, not too hot if you don't mind. A slice of lemon, but not too thick. So, where am I? Right. She telephoned on Monday morning and wanted to know if I had a bank in Bath. Oh no, I thought. Here's trouble. How much? But not a bit of it. She said she had something that she wanted to put in a bank deposit box and would I do it for her.'

'Did you?'

'I said I would. But I didn't. She said she would meet me at the bank. But she didn't. And that was the last time I heard from her.'

'Did she say what it was?'

'No. She said it was an envelope. Something she didn't want lying about.'

'But not what was in it.'

'But not what was in it.'

Leonard rubbed his nose with a thin forefinger.

'Did she say she was going to pull out of the show before or after she asked you about your bank?'

'After. Why?'

He sucked his teeth. Shook his head.

'I'm not sure. But it's best to get things in order.'

He was buzzing again. Thinking there was something wrong with what he'd heard. Again, he didn't know what, or even if he were right. Sergeant Jack watched Angela Billings watching him. Cut into the pause.

'Miss Billings, I know you've already told me the brief detail of what she said, but do you mind telling us again?'

'I'm word-perfect, you know, darling.'

Jack smiled. A bright, friendly smile.

'I'm sure you are, Miss Billings. You always are.'

Angela Billings chuckled. It was something she did rather well and rehearsed rather often.

'How charming. Very well.'

She dismissed Jack and turned back to Leonard and fixed him with her grey-brown flecked eyes. He guessed her spectacles were readers and that he was probably out of focus. But the style was fine. And the voice.

'As I said, she sounded stressed. I asked if everything were all right. At first she said fine. Then as we talked, I could hear in her voice that whatever it was was real. So I pressed her. Very gently. Didn't want to frighten the poor lamb. And then she told me. Said she had problems. I asked if there was anything I could do. She said it wasn't the panto. Yes, there were problems there but nothing she couldn't handle – which I have to say I doubted, after all I probably knew more about her than she did, although I didn't tell her that. So, a little more sympathy and then she said that people were getting nasty and she was going to pull out.'

'People were? Not a person?'

'No darling, people plural. But, don't ask me what she meant, or who they were or are. Haven't a clue. I asked her if she'd talked to her agent, or to Maurice and . . .'

Angela Billings paused. Leonard didn't know if the pause were scripted or not, but it was dramatic enough.

'And . . .?'

She took another breath as if re-starting her voice box. The first words came with the breath.

'Very odd. I've only just remembered. I said something like "Have you talked to Maurice about this?" and she said . . .'

'She said?'

'She said, "You've got to be joking."'

'Any idea what she meant?'

Angela Billings shook her head. Very slowly. Her mouth rounded and silently became a 'No'. Leonard looked at her without seeing her. Was he being set up? Why?

'Tell me, Miss Billings, when she didn't show up for the photo call, why didn't you tell anyone what she'd told you, that she was going to pull out?'

'But I did, Inspector.'

'Who did you tell?'

'Why, Maurice, of course. Who else?'

'But I thought her disappearance was a big mystery to him.'

'Goodness gracious, darling, I know you did. Why do you think I'm telling you?'

Nineteen

It was gone midnight and felt gone midnight. Everyone was tired. The stage search hadn't finished until eight thirty. Tiggy Jones had loitered. Notebook in one hand, he wanted the all-clear. The vans would be in the following morning at eight sharp for the band fit up. Leonard had said okay as long as forensic cleared. That didn't happen until eleven that night. Forensic were the only ones on overtime and there were patio doors to be paid for. Meanwhile, all but four people on Sergeant Jack's list had been interviewed. Rosie Rostow and the two assistant stage-door managers were still down with influenza and had been for the past forty-eight hours. The fourth was the other ugly sister, Rudi Sharpe. He'd gone missing and not for the first time according to Tiggy Jones, who'd called the usual pubs but without any joy. Jack had put a constable outside Sharpe's digs and told him to wait and not come back without the dame.

On the top floor of Manvers Street Police Station a quiet, spartan training office, had become an overcrowded major incident room. Forty officers, a third of the station's already stretched working strength, had been detached to find Lynda Elström's killer. Files were filling, pads of forms ticked off in triplicate. Flights of jerkily entered digits, had arranged themselves in neat groups on desktop screens. Books and reports, schedules and lists fought for space among neglected felt-tips and abandoned and stained mugs that had held too much instant coffee. Now the lull. Investigations were nowadays full of lulls. Partly procedures, but mostly it was all about money. Overtime for police officers was about as likely as Thankyou For Smoking notices. Not that the investigation could go very far in the middle of the night. Godly or godless, witnesses were left to sleep while clues festered or vanished. Officers whose daily routine it was to probe the abnormal went to their homes, to their clubs, to their children, to their beds and did normal things. Or tried to. A policeman at a dinner party could still be expected to make a fellow diner nervous. A policewoman was still seen as feminist, not feminine. And did their children defy discipline to prove something to their peers? Artificial presumptions about people investigating the real world of make-believe. For the duty sergeant the make-believe was trying to find enough officers for an already over-stuffed duty rota. For Leonard, at a time of night when coughs reached right along corridors, it was the one moment of peace to go through the increasing pile of paper for the third time.

As he ran an index finger down the rows of already carefully written up initial statements, Leonard would occasionally glance up and check a detail against the chalk board that was almost the whole of the right-hand end wall. On the left-hand side, nominal numbers of people interviewed. In the middle, telephone numbers, theatre, hotels, digs, bleepers, mobiles, officers' names, messages. There was no joke, no cartoon, no graffito.

He hunched forward over three piles of information, finger tips supporting his aching head.

'Going-home time, sir?'

He hadn't heard her come in, but Leonard knew Jack had been there. They'd been together for five years. People talked about instincts in CID teams. Leonard had little time for labels. Whatever it was, it worked. Not for the first time, Leonard wondered whether he'd want to work with another sergeant. He'd have to get used to the idea. She was very good, she'd already got through her inspector's exams and she'd be promoted soon. Then what? Somewhere he knew that if he'd been a better policeman then he wouldn't even have to think about such things. Stared at the pile of paper.

'Time you were in bed.'

The duty sergeant looked up. The snigger that started came to nothing. He was like most of the other officers. Wondered about these two. Some reckoned there must be something going on. The way they spoke to each other. Sometimes they seemed to know what the other was thinking. Had to be something there, or so it was said. But then you looked at Leonard and wondered. There was a view in the basement locker room that the only thing he'd got his leg over was his pushbike. Always got a laugh that one, partly because there were plenty who thought it probably true. But then no one really knew. No one knew Leonard. Years ago, a senior officer had noted that Leonard had never been popular enough to have a nickname. As for Madelaine Jack, most of them had the hots for her. Most of them, especially the noisy ones, were more than a little frightened of her. She was good-looking all right. Sporty looking. Knew how to smile. Knew how to put someone in their place without a word. And Jack was a fast-tracker. Most policemen were never promoted, that was the simple nature of any large organization. She'd get there. Maybe the top. They all knew that. The difference was that Madelaine Jack didn't know that. She had yet to decide where she was going. And when. But at far gone midnight on the first day of an investigation, there were more immediate matters. Madelaine Jack dropped into the chair across from Leonard. She was holding an initial report. Waved it.

'DC Leweson, sir. Lynda Elström's car?'

He nodded.

'Or rather, the non-car. He's checked Swansea and the Met. No car registered. He had a word with the neighbours in Catherine Place. They didn't know anything about a car. Joanna Cunliffe didn't know. She thinks she would have. For example, she was never asked to fix Residence Parking.'

'Someone else's name. Company name?'

'Could be. I'll get him to check her agent. They'll know if she was a company or not.'

'Car hire?'

'Not here, anyway. None of the local rental firms has any record of a car going out in the name of Elström. They'd have a credit or charge card record and they haven't. Also, there's no rental car on the non-return list and nothing parked locally. We'll check the car parks in the morning. I suppose it's that important, sir?'

Leonard wasn't sure. But he said yes.

'What does the kid say?'

'Says it's true and that's that.'

'Glib.'

'Elaborate.'

'Okay, but why the car drive? He says because they didn't want to be seen. Why not her flat? Once in, they wouldn't be seen. Once it was dark, there'd be just as little chance of being seen arriving at the flat as making a rendezvous in town.'

'Unless she expected someone else to arrive at the flat?'

Leonard took off his glasses and dropped them on the pile of papers in front of him. Tilted his head back and blew out a gentle stream of very old and late-night breath at the out-of-focus ceiling.

'Seems as if someone did. That briefcase was forced.'

'She could have done that herself. Forgot the combination or something.'

'It was empty.'

'So she was keen to get whatever was in it.'

'Which was what?'

'The envelope for the bank?'

'If Billings isn't lying.'

'If Lynda wasn't.'

'Suppose she wasn't. That means someone must have known the briefcase existed. Either someone had seen her with it—'

'Hardly a briefcase-toting lady—'

'Right. Or it was someone who knew her well enough to know she had one. Who? Someone from the theatre? The husband? We got anywhere with him?'

'Mm.'

He rubbed at his spectacles and hooked the steel arms over his large ears.

'And?'

'I re-checked the hotel. Mr and Mrs Ross of 14, Singleton Terrace Mews, London, W1.'

Leonard made a squiggle on one of the reports.

'Smith? Or real?'

'I looked him up in *Who's Who*. There is a Mrs Ross, née Makins, Cassandra Makins. In fact she's Mrs Ross the Third. Two dissolved – legally, not acid.'

'Obviously they're not there?'

The duty sergeant's telephone rang. He picked it up, making a note of the time on his logbook as he did. Jack was shaking her head.

'Not since after breakfast. Said they'd be back very late. Their cases are still in the room. I was looking for someone to put over there. We haven't a spare body. I said I'd call later. Didn't want to put any pressure on him.'

The duty sergeant was holding his hand over the receiver and looking expectantly across at Leonard.

'A Mr Cobb? Says he knows you, sir?'

Leonard leaned over for the extension. Looked at the wall clock.

'At this time of night? Okay.'

He listened without interrupting Cobb. This time no budgerigar. Three minutes and there was some mention of a lady pianist who left her teeth in the area of top G. Still Leonard listened, especially when Cobb reached the point about Ross, the telephone box and then the lady in the sporting vehicle. Leonard promised them both a heart starter in Shades shortly before noon and quietly replaced the receiver. He leaned back in the steel-framed chair.

'The husband and the third Mrs Ross were seen driving in Bath at nine thirtyish this morning.'

He looked again at the clock. Twelve forty-five.

'Sorry. Yesterday morning.'

'If they were leaving the city it would explain why he hasn't contacted anyone. Maybe he doesn't know.'

The duty sergeant flipped a couple of pages back in his official black pocketbook.

'Press desk says it's been on the BBC since ten this morning, sir. Chronicle had it in their final edition. Billboards by twelve. So I reckon only the blind would have missed it and the deaf, of course, sir. Chances are if this Ross is cruising about in a car, then he's going to have the radio on.'

Jack stuck to the devil's advocate.

'He still might not know.'

Leonard tapped his teeth with a pencil. Dropped it on the pad in front of him.

'Or?'

'Or, sir, he might have good reason to know.'

Leonard stretched and struggled into his duffle coat.

'Ask the hotel to call us soon as he gets back. Don't scare them. Our duty to inform and all that stuff.'

Jack nodded. What was that about going-home time?

'Yes, sir.'

'And let me know when you get something. Okay. I'm off.'

'Oh yes?'

The voice was deep. Croaky. From behind him Detective Inspector Ray Lane, who was supposed to have taken early retirement on health grounds, but hadn't, and should have by the look of him, was leaning against the door frame. A cross between a nonchalant matinée idol and a drunk clutching a late-night lamppost.

'Scusa dottore, scusa. Got an interesting one downstairs for you.'

'Now?'

'Prego, sunshine. Taxi driver and guess what? He reckoned he had that Cinderella in the back of his cab last night. Interested?'

Twenty

The taxi driver did nights. Ten 'til six. Lane had heard the whole story. Not hard luck, just hard listening. Graveyard shift? Apart from the clubs, it wasn't bad. Until five years ago he'd been a London cabbie. Second divorce did for that. Then married a widow from Bath. Third divorce had hardly seemed worth it. But he had. Now he was on his own, self-employed, in his fifties, a driver's paunch, most of his sandy hair gone but none of his confidence.

'No one indoors to bother me.'

Leonard, blood-hurting tired, didn't care a fig. He simply wanted to hear what had happened to Cinders twenty-four hours earlier.

'Got this call just after midnight. Natural for me. I won't do the clubs and they knows it. So through it comes. Cash. Catherine Place. Out comes this party soon as I pulls up. Reckons she'd been watching. All in black, she is. Black hat, black trousers, black boots and black bins.'

'Bins?'

'You know, sunglasses. In December. Midnight. Still that's nothing today, is it? I mean, everyone does their own wotsit. You know? Anyway I clocks her, don't I. Had her in the back before. Ten years ago in London. But I could be wrong. I could be wrong. And she don't say nothing. I tries a couple of times. Weather. Christmas shopping. Usual stuff. But she keeps shtum. Not even a yes, no, shut yer face. Then we gets there and I knows for sure.'

'Get where?'

'Down by the theatre. Right?'

'Why then?'

'Obvious. I mean I makes the connection. Theatre. Her. Her. Theatre. Anyway the big give-away is the face. It's dark, right? She can't see her money. So she has to take the bins off. Course, I didn't say nothing. I mean, you don't. Fare wants privacy, then fare gets privacy. Know what I mean?'

Leonard had been standing with his back to the darkened

window of the interview room. He glanced about. The cheap animal posters and thin chrome hat stand were supposed to make the place relaxing. The taxi driver didn't need pictures and nasty vinyl seats. He was enjoying himself.

'But you got to give it a go, haven't you? So I says to her, "How's the old glass slipper business then?" Still says nothing. Doesn't even look. Puts on the bins and she's out. Doesn't even say goodbye. Still none of my business, until tonight. I reckons I sees this car again, you know the one she met?'

Leonard shook his head. Lane had given him an outline, but that was all. The cabbie had picked up Lynda Elström shortly before midnight and dropped her near the theatre shortly after midnight. Hadn't been asked to wait.

'At the Theatre Royal.'

The taxi driver looked at Leonard as if he were thick.

'Not the theatre as such. Behind. Kingsmead Square. Know where I mean?'

The expression on the taxi driver's round, pasty, nightshift face said that policemen were no longer expected to know the time nor street names. Leonard knew, but why would Lynda Elström?'

'She ask for Kingsmead Square, specifically?'

'Course.'

'Didn't just ask to be dropped by the theatre? The back of the theatre?'

'No way. The call was Catherine Place to Kingsmead Square.'

'From your office?'

'Right. Listen, mate. You want the full nause or not?'

Leonard was silent. Thought it through. Nodded.

'Tell me about the car. What sort of car?'

'Blue Beamer. Soft top.'

'Beamer?'

'BMW.'

'Where was it?'

'Which time?'

Leonard stuck his hands hard into his jacket pockets. Jack made a cosmetic tick in her tiny notebook.

'When you got to Kingsmead Square, what happened?'

'Well she pays me. And that was that. But I was a bit curious.'

'Why?'

'Nosey, I suppose. You know, *the* Lynda Elström. That time of the night. Well, you got to be a bit curious, haven't you?'

'What did you do?'

'Well, I leaves the inside light on for a bit. Makes a bit of a thing about logging the fare. Then I takes me time and swings round the one way. All legal. I sees her. She gets into this Beamer and she's just sitting there.'

'Could you see the driver?'

'Not really. The light was all wrong. You know?'

'Then what?'

'Well, mate, then nothing. I could hardly lift the bonnet and do a ten-thousand-mile service on her, could I? So that was it. But I thought about it. Then when I knocks off this morning I goes home and gets me head down. Didn't surface until gone four. Wasn't until I gets on the rank tonight that I hears about her. You could have done me with a feather, you could, and that's a fact.'

'Okay. But I'm still not clear about the car.'

'Yes, well, that was it, wasn't it? I'd been wondering about her and whether I should say anything, you know, official like, when there it is.'

'There what is?'

The driver took a deep breath. Looked from side to side. Coppers! Where did they get them from? Obvious, wasn't it?

'I'm in the line, you know at the station, when into the picking up point comes the same car.'

'You're sure?'

'Good as. There can't be many of them in this place. Light metallic blue, two seater. Dark blue hood. T-reg. Well I never seen many round here before – not blue and T-reg. Have you?'

'What time was this?'

'Couple of hours ago? Half ten?'

'What happened?'

'Well it goes straight to the end and there's this guy. In the crowd, just come off the London train by the looks of the queue. It was late. Anyway, in he gets and they're away like a flash of pigshit. Right little tearaway.'

'Did you see the driver this time?'

'Not really. But I reckon it was a woman. Lot of hair. Maybe. But I couldn't swear to it, I mean they didn't actually hang about posing for pictures did they now? Anyway, I was three or four back and had to be watching the pick-up point not them. I moved up, got a fare for Bear Flat and that was it. But when I got back, I got to thinking about it and thought I better come in here.'

'Car number?'

The driver looked at Leonard with some amazement.

'Knock it off. I'm a cabbie, coppering's your job.'

Twenty-One

Leonard sat with a glass bowl of Calvados, his legs stretched out and contemplated the rich greens, browns and burgundies of his thick wool socks.

'Tell me, why does an attractive blonde with a life apparently uncomplicated by money shortages, exotic substances, tangles of lovers or ill health get herself murdered?'

Johnson really had no interest. Such a list of possibilities suggested that any one might be reason enough for almost anything. Far less exciting complications had produced violence. Why, crossing the road with good purpose and not even capriciously, had claimed so many of one's kind. Not even Johnson's innate sense of superiority could be protection enough from all sorts of perils in the ancient city.

'You see every murderer must have a motive, even if that motive is short-lived.'

Johnson stirred. The pun had passed by.

'Most of the time we look for a motive. In other words, we're looking to see who *might* have been the murderer. Process of elimination. Yes?'

Johnson blinked. Why was it that experts always asked others to agree? Basic insecurities? Probably. Please go on. Leonard had only paused to collect thoughts, not agreement, and did so.

'But in this case, we have to go back to basics. Which means? We don't look for the murderer. We look for the one person who can lead us to the murderer. And who's that?'

How tiresome. If one knew then one should say so. Johnson did not bother to respond.

'It's obvious.'

Naturally.

'The one person who can lead us to the murderer is Lynda Elström.'

Too deep. Too deep. When a mouse is dead simply look for the cat's whiskers. After all, a funeral you've got. It's a hanging you want. Clearly, this one did not know his Mehitabel, yet.

'If we know enough about her, we may find what she did or threatened to do that made someone kill her. How does that sound?'

Less than elegant.

'She made a living from being famous. But how much of a living? She was single. But how single? She had an ex-husband. But how ex? She was not admired professionally. But did that worry her? Did it worry someone else? Something worried her. Ask the lady with the blue spectacles and rinse. Which of these would arouse enough passion for murder? Money? Yes. It often does, but only if someone were murdering for her money. So who gets it? Check.'

Johnson purred in the comfort of having few ambitions apart from a recent bit of fish that money need buy.

'What about this so-called engagement? Could she have met Curly Weekes to tell him the joke's off? Possible. And the spurned lover turns murderer. Very possible. Check.

'The husband? Straightforward. No third person. Not triangle, just a straight line. To what?

'Money. Was she milking his bank balance? Was he broke? Going broke? Into debt? So one and two would tie in. Motive enough? Check. Which leaves professional jealousies?'

Ah, the haunting of failure and escaped success. Too tiresome, especially when one is so successful.

'Cinderella was hardly a part to die for.'

Puss in Boots, on the other hand . . . So, my friend, you are left with nothing. No hypothesis from which to contrive your theory.

'Which leads to the conclusion . . .'

What that conclusion might have been, Johnson was spared. Leonard's thoughts continued, but not aloud. Leonard dozed. Images of Cinders in Disney simplicity chased by grotesque goblins each with green and scarlet painted face and nails to scratch at eyes. Poulson, sneering. Jones chuckling but with the smile upside down. The Rostow twins gripping Lynda Elström's arms and twisting them into plaits of white slim flesh. Curly Weekes, crying and tearing at her clothes with long, pink-palmed hands. In a corner Con Cobb crouched, his scarlet tie a blindfold about his thin shaven head, rolling budgerigars into tight balls which he flicked to a sightless executioner. Norman Philips, a bent, crazy figure on a wooden heaving deck, shouted soundless obscenities as he hauled on a great ship's halyard. High above them all, Madelaine Jack dangled and jerked from a great black, charred gibbet.

Johnson blinked slowly and admired the fortune that balanced the glass bowl of barely touched liquid on a rising and falling stomach. Far in the dream a bell rang. Short rings. Then again. Pause. Nothing. Johnson waited. Then when the soft noise came she turned her gaze to the small hallway and the softer call of The Other One. This pleased Johnson who plopped to the floor and stalked to the living room doorway where The Other One stood, uncertainly but ready to scratch at Johnson's ear.

'Sir?'

The glass rose and fell. Johnson rubbed against The Other One's leg.

'Sir?'

That's right. A little louder.

'Sir?'

Leonard came out of his dream. At first out of vision, then very clearly, he saw the figure in the doorway.

'I'm sorry, sir. I rang and saw the light and . . .'

He was still there somewhere. The Tyburn silhouette.

'Must have dozed. What time is it?'

'Three, sir.'

'Bugger.'

'Yes, sir. But you said you wanted to know, and, well, as your phone was engaged . . .'

She looked to the dresser where, as ever, Leonard had left the receiver on the surface to escape for an hour into his privacy. Johnson was back on the arm of the deep chair. Waiting. Courtesies?

'Oh right. I'm sorry. Have a seat. Um. Drink?'

'No thank you, sir.'

Johnson twitched. The Other One sat. Johnson purred.

'How odd.'

'Sir?'

'Nothing. Go on.'

'They're back.'

He'd forgotten.

'They? Who they?'

'The hotel. Mr and *Mrs* Ross, or so the register says.'

Madelaine Jack yawned. Wished she hadn't sat down. The day was already twenty-one hours long.

'They've been divorced ages.'

'Money. Jealousies.'

'Motives.'

He shrugged and swung his feet on to the floor. His gums tasted of yesterday's gingerbread. Calvados was a lousy mouthwash.

'We need motives. One would do. Tell me, do you believe Philips?'

'I believe he found her. It had crossed my mind whether or not he'd discovered her.'

'You mean he found her where he'd left her.'

'Mm. Exactly.'

'Motive?'

'Panic? Made a pass at her? It all went wrong.'

'Opportunity?'

She rubbed her itching nose with the heel of her hand.

'None, unless he happened to meet her after her mysterious rendezvous in the BMW. Just supposing, sir, Philips hadn't gone straight back to his flat after the theatre closed. Just supposing he'd hung around for, well, for any reason – that bit's not important at the moment. Then he went back to the theatre for something. Again that's not important now. But then supposing he met her near the theatre and she was upset and he said come in and have a coffee, talk, call a cab. Anything. But, supposing that were all true, then there's opportunity.'

'Lot of supposing.'

'The whole case is. We've no sign of a motive other than this story of Angela Billings'. And less sign of an opportunity. If she'd been killed in the park, in her flat, in the street, even, then opportunity would not be a problem. But in an apparently locked theatre when we know that it was all shut up and empty before she was killed . . .'

Leonard drained the glass. It tasted awful.

'Supposing it wasn't empty. Supposing whoever she met in that BMW had keys.'

'And a door code.'

'The two go together, sir. And we know who had both.'

'Okay. Then we need that printout. As soon as we get the door codes used, we can start on the names again.'

'Which cuts out the actors. They don't have keys or codes. Only the regular staff do. Unless of course we're looking for more than one person.'

Johnson stretched then hooked one very white paw and groomed its stubborn end. Rather obvious, she thought. Rather obvious.

Twenty-Two

The morning briefing was like most second-day briefings. It was what Madelaine Jack called a Now-We-Know session. Unless there were eye-witnesses or confessions, day one of a murder usually followed a pattern. The victim was found and more often than not, easily identified. Then came the obvious connections: family conflict, drugs and spontaneous reaction. Most murders were family affairs. Husbands, wives, mistresses, lovers, cruelties. Drugs could be anything from territorial disputes to violence brought about by crazed minds. Spontaneous crimes were rarer. A fight over an insult came close to the top of this list and often the root cause would be found in the first two categories. Leonard hated briefing. He was tired, looked it and wanted to get away. Instead, he stood in front of the chalk board. The whole team was in, most of them standing and leaning. It wasn't a big room. This wasn't HQ where there always seemed to be enough of everything – including space. But the coffee was just the same. Most of them had mugs of it. Leonard had been gazing at the board. Still not enough. But it was day two. His quiet cough summoned their attention.

'Murder it is. Medic says strangled, probably hands. Probably conscious during the attack. Stretches and strains in other parts of the body suggest rupturing due to resistance. The wire came later.'

'Sir?'

Leweson was going to be one of those officers who liked everything a step at a time. Leonard nodded for him to carry on.

'Do we know how much later?'

'Good point. Not sure. The cutting into the neck suggests pretty soon. But we don't yet know for sure.'

Everyone looked ahead. But Leweson had scored. Leonard rarely congratulated. He looked back to the board.

'Time of death, you can see, is somewhere between twelve thirty and two a.m. Maybe. Curly Weekes says she telephoned him at his hotel at about eleven that night. His hotel telephone printout shows he did receive a call at eleven fourteen. But we don't know from whom and we don't know from which number it was made. BT doesn't show any calls from Lynda Elström's flat at around that time. We haven't found a mobile phone in her flat.'

Leonard nodded at the ever-attentive Leweson.

'Get the mobile company to give you a printout. Weekes may be telling the truth.'

'Sir?'

Leweson was pushing luck.

'Does that mean we think Curly Weekes could be lying, sir?'

'We think everyone's lying.'

It was Bernard Leweson's turn to look straight ahead. He'd just lost his brownie. The whole room knew so. Leonard didn't wait.

'We know she was picked up by cab shortly after midnight and dropped in Kingsmead Square five minutes later. The cab dispatch office confirms. Let's say a quarter past twelve at the latest. She may or may not have been meeting someone in a blue BMW two-seater soft top. This year's registration. That's the last sighting we have of her. But a similar car was seen last night at about ten thirty, driven perhaps by a woman, and picking up a man who may or may not have been a passenger on the London train. We don't have a number. Someone check the traffic wardens' office. There can't be too many light blue T-registered BMW two-seater soft tops. Not even in Bath.'

He paused. There wasn't much to go on.

'So we think we know where she was shortly before she died. But we don't know *why* she was there. People like her don't up and go. What happened just before midnight? What happened earlier in the evening, earlier in the day or maybe last week, that decided her to go to Kingsmead Square at about midnight? And, don't forget, she didn't show at the panto photo call. Why? This woman Billings claims Elström says she was pulling out. We'll be asking Poulson true or false. But where was she? We need to know. She was out of sight for at least twelve hours. But not out of sound. Billings and Weekes had calls. And don't forget, according to Weekes, she had a friend in the city who was going to pass on messages. Ask around at the theatre, the local rag, in the better restaurants – she probably didn't know many greasy spoons. We need to know who she knew in this city.

'Right. Anything else?'

A short constable with big brown eyes and very white teeth raised a very long arm.

'Avon Bridge Hotel, sir?'

'Go on.'

'I checked with the night porter there. Had to get him out of his pit. Pretty confident. He says one of the Rostows went to bed that night with flu. Hadn't been down all evening.'

'Which one?'

'He didn't know, sir. As he said, they're identical. Anyway, about midnight the one without the flu went out for a breath of air. No more than ten minutes. Too cold. Too wet. Too tired. Or something like that.'

'Certain of the time?'

'Reasonably, sir. I checked the TV listings. He was watching one of those old French films and it was just finishing. I asked him if he could remember the bit he was watching when she came in. Thought I'd check with the channel, maybe they could ID the scene and give us the running time.'

'Right. Where was their room?'

The constable looked pleased with himself.

'Just along the corridor from the main hall. Ground floor? She couldn't have gone out again without him seeing.'

'Unless?'

'Sir?'

'Unless?'

'Unless what, sir?'

'Think about it, then check.'

The short constable looked blank. They all did. They couldn't see. Leonard could, but he was moving on.

'SOCO? Anything?'

The senior Scene Of Crime Officer picked up his clipboard and started a classic situation report.

'Stage swept fore and aft and diagonally, sir. Nothing exceptional. We have nine hairs. Two may match Elström. The others are over at Chepstow. We should get something on them later today. We may need a couple of swabs.'

'Long? Short?'

The searcher shrugged.

'Something in between. But Chepstow may give us something. Always hope, sir.'

There were a few tired laughs. The forensic laboratory at Chepstow could usually do nothing more than match something, not provide an exclusive clue. It was up to the Bath team to find a suspect to match and take DNA swabs.

'Go over the statements again. Look for anything that ties in with this story the taxi driver's telling. And someone check the taxi driver.'

Blank looks.

'The driver was the last person that we know saw her alive, or said he did. It is a fact of death that the last person who *did* see Lynda Elström alive was the person who murdered her. So check him. Then double check him. Anyone anything?'

A constable with a soft Bristol accent coughed, half raised a hand.

'Brad?'

'Seems to me, sir, well, we need a bit of a steer. We don't know for certain that she was actually murdered in the theatre and, at that time of night at this time of year –'

'Go on.'

'I suppose it depends where she was murdered, but might body temperature change and therefore our time of death. If that were so, sir –'

'It widens the field. Right. Ask the doc. Okay?'

'Sir.'

Leonard was about to get up, but Constable Bradley hadn't finished.

'The second point, begging your pardon, sir, is these locks and codes. Who should we be, well, sir, concentrating on?'

'Likely suspects?'

'Yes, sir.'

Leonard took off his spectacles, pinched the bridge of his nose. He'd been asking that one himself. He held his spectacles up to the strip light and polished at them with a green silk handkerchief.

'The ones in the Vaults alibi each other. The actors seem a regular bunch, apart from Curly, that is, and he could be just wishful thinking. Which may just leave, Philips. Then we've got the wire, the high fly, as they call it. Not everyone would know how to operate it. Not even the actors.'

'Rehearsals, sir?'

Leonard was about to shake his head. Didn't. He didn't know the answer. Instead he nodded.

'Why not? But the short answer to your original question is that not one of them has even the smell of a motive and none has an easy opportunity.'

Constable Bradley almost apologetically slipped in his third question.

'That's what I was getting at, sir. No one in the place seems to have been likely for the frame so that would leave us with someone outside who knew how to get in or, begging your pardon, sir, someone who had someone on the inside.'

'A conspiracy?'

Constable Bradley had gone as far as his hypothesis would take him. He didn't think he'd been foolish. Leonard was certain he hadn't. Bradley had summed up neatly. They knew nothing. They were tourists in this one.

Jack was in the corridor. She'd got her blue reefer jacket on and sheepskin gloves sticking out of the slanting pockets. Over her arm was Leonard's duffle coat.

'Thought you'd want to get on, sir. I got the traffic warden supervisor to give his people a burst. Eyes peeled for a blue BMW et cetera?'

He took his coat as they walked to the corner stairs.

'And?'

'One of them's just called in. It was, and apparently is, parked round the corner from the Rivers Hotel, in which . . .'

He held the door for her.

'Mr Chris Ross and his dame dosseth. The surprises of life doth spice our ordinariness.'

'Talking of which, sir, I've got a preliminary backgrounder on Philips.'

'Don't tell me. Ex-SAS. Royal Protection Duties and chairman of Bath NSPCC.'

'Boring! Better than that. I'll tell you on the way.'

Manvers Street was wet-cold. The electrical discount store windows were covered in mock snow swirls of Christmas bells and white holly. Almost lost behind the spray-on sparkle, huge Santa red posters promised even bigger percentages. Buy Now, Pay Easter. As they bent into the wind and walked towards the abbey, Leonard wondered what he would be doing on Christmas Day, or even at this rate, Good Friday. A Salvation Army Band stood in a circle spitting 'The First Noel' into their cornets, tenors and tubas. Leonard glared at the Sister rattling her collecting box. He detested her contented smile.

Twenty-Three

The surgeon was dressed for a smart morning in Bath, but not one which would be threatened by blustery showers, splashing cars and umbrellas with an inside-out tendency. The gold-buckled black shoes were shined but not shiny. The three-button suit was dark but not sombre. The primrose shirt pretty but not effeminate. The cuffs long enough to show off jade links, but not to hide the elegant, precious hands. The green polka-dot tie had freshness that suggested it had been knotted for the first time. The thick hair was brushed back from the great man's high-boned face. Leonard thought Chris Ross shifty.

'We'd half expected you to get in touch, sir.'

They were sitting in the sitting room of the Regency Hotel's only suite. No reproductions here. Ross steepled his fingers, tilted his head and smiled first at Jack, then at Leonard. The two police officers were being given an audience.

'Of course, of course. I wasn't quite certain what to do. You see, I only heard about this dreadful moment when I was in London yesterday. I think perhaps I would have telephoned as a matter of duty this morning.'

He'd seen this duffle-coated policeman somewhere. Where? It would come.

'Duty, sir?'

'Well, yes?'

'But your ex-wife? Duty?'

'My dear man, there's nothing so ex as an ex and it was twenty years ago.'

'But you were married to her.'

'At the time.'

There was something between bitterness and annoyance in his voice. Leonard was careful.

'I'm sorry, sir, celebrated marriages aren't something I know about. There were problems?'

Where? The quiet voice, young for his lined and freckled face, was unfamiliar. But the man. Where had he seen him?

'Look here, Inspector, is this necessary?'

To Leonard it was. The one person who knew Lynda Elström when she wasn't being Lynda Elström was in front of him. Everyone else claimed they hadn't know her. But someone had. Someone had known her well enough to kill her. The one person who could tell him something that might have aroused a killer, was Chris Ross.

'I'm sorry, sir. I think the answer is yes. You're the person who can tell me something about her. Something about her is what I need to know if we're going to get the person who killed her. Murdered her.'

Ross let his patrician's steeple collapse and stroked the velour arms of the high-backed morning chair. He glanced at both of them in turn. At their hands. No rings.

'I'm afraid there isn't much. You see, she wasn't much. The perfect blow-up doll. Tall, blessed with a wonderful physique and only a little intelligence.'

'But enough to look after that, um, physique?'

Ross shook his head. Such a weary shake of the fine head.

'No. No. No. You see Lynda adored her body. Adored her looks. I said she was a perfect doll. Lynda looked after her own body as she looked after her dolls. She loved her hair, loved her skin, loved the way she smiled and moved. Let me give you an example. Lynda did not get dressed. She dressed herself up. Just like a doll and, just like a doll, she would bend and dress herself to perfection and remain that way until it was time to change into another outfit or another pose.'

Leonard was gazing at the elaborate ceiling cornices and buzzing. Jack's cue.

'But in spite of this you married her?'

'No, sergeant. In spite of all that, she married me. Perhaps I was part of the dressing up. I was, although modestly, something of a celebrity in my field. The youngest heart transplanter in Europe. New techniques. Magazine interviews. The world was going through one of its phases of creating spectacular things for personalities to do. So I did spectacular things. I jumped out of aeroplanes for charity and the newspapers wondered about the insurance on my limbs. I did the Matterhorn, the tourist route of course, but the television and tabloids didn't mention that. I swam in a shark cage – my God I was petrified – for heart foundation funds and of course I did the usual pro-am tennis and golf appearances. Apart from the 007 badge, I was her real life Bond.'

'And she?'

Oh dear. Did he detect a hint of disapproval, sergeant? Then how about this?

'And she? We met at a charity film show, more heart money of course. She was wearing a dress that couldn't have taken more than two medium sized silk-worms and a single mulberry leaf to produce. She was the sexiest thing I had ever seen. And I told her so. There and then. And do you know? That was it. No one had ever bothered to talk to her like that. She was a goddess. Untouchable and untouched. The cameras clicked and so did we. My God she was untouched. The next morning I was still shaking. I couldn't think, never mind work. We were married in a month. There now sergeant, now you know as much as I do. I hope *you're* satisfied.'

His insinuation was so obvious that Jack nearly laughed. But she didn't. Not even a smile. This man would assume anything but deadpan as a sign of pleasure and that he had given it. Leonard was back from his cornices.

'But it didn't last.'

'Nor could it. Living with the media was difficult. We couldn't go to a party, or a theatre without some photographer aiming his lens down the front of her dress. But why not? That's what she did for a living. But who was I to complain? After all, I suppose I only married her for her body.'

He turned to Madelaine Jack and smiled.

'It was a difficult time, sir?'

'I suppose. To know that every hot-blooded male is lusting after one's wife is, as you call it, difficult. For the first couple of months it was wonderful. My needs were similar to her needs and none of them was very complicated. But our marriage had given her career a boost. The beauty and brains captions were a doddle for picture editors. I remember one time when Lynda was filming in Spain and there was some unfortunate photograph of her with one of the actors and as far as I remember, some complete nobody, a best boy or a third grip or whatever they call them, which I suppose on reflection might have been appropriate. A disco. She wasn't wearing much. When did she? Nor were they for that matter. Anyway, they had their arms around her. All a bit of a tangle, really. Hardly intimate. But it looked very shabby. So what did we get? One of the Sunday tabloids carried the picture with a small one of me at the side – taken ages before, off guard of course, completely unawares and looking tired and therefore Worried of Harley Street – and the headline was, wait for it: 'His Wife in Their Hands'. Underneath was the entirely spurious suggestion that all three had ended up in same bed.'

He paused, his eyes on the moss green carpet. Perhaps counting the grey *fleur de lis* for breath. He looked up and give his once famous half smile. The teeth were still good. The dimple still in place.

'Yes, I'm afraid it was sometimes very difficult. I suppose looking back it's surprising it lasted as long as it did.'

Ross had said his piece. Leonard had let him go on. He thought he knew more about Lynda Elström, he certainly knew more about Ross.

'Tell me, sir, since your marriage, eh, finished, what sort of relationship have you had with your former wife?'

'I'm not sure I like what you're suggesting, *Inspector*.'

He hit the title with enough emphasis to remind Leonard how far he would be allowed to go.

'I'm only suggesting, sir that, well, if you'd remained in touch, then you might have been able to help us with some of the blank spots in her recent life. Who she was friendly with. Who she wasn't friendly with. That sort of . . .'

Leonard tailed off. Ross was nodding, sagely. As if remembering.

'We were still very good friends. But I knew few of her's. I'm not sure she had many.'

'Do you mind telling me when you last saw her?'

'A couple of months ago. Perhaps three. We lunched at the Ritz. It was a Friday.'

'That's quite accurate, sir, especially as you can't remember when.'

'We only ever lunched on Fridays and only at the Ritz. It was where I asked her to marry me. And before you begin to wonder, yes it was fun to have a date like that. But that was it.'

Leonard was looking at his boots. He shifted in the chair. The Georgians must have been well padded. Madelaine Jack crossed her legs, but Ross's head turn was too late. Her voice was official but soft. He wanted to call it husky, but it wasn't. He wondered if she smoked. It was that sort of sound. He hoped not. He hated cigarette breath.

'Do you mind telling us what sort of car you drive, sir?'

He rather liked the sergeant. Forgotten her name, but wouldn't forget the eyes. Very round. Very brown. And the legs. Surely too slim for a policewoman, especially with those sensible shoes. Why didn't she take off that awful coat? He wanted to see the rest. He gave her a half smile. 'Mm? Oh sorry, Inspector, I mean Sergeant. Do you mind telling me why you want to know?'

She'd heard it before. There was a standard answer. It always worked.

'I'm sorry sir, it would be helpful in elimination.'

'Oh well, why not? Yes. As a mater of fact, I drive a Bentley. A Continental.'

She supposed the matter of fact was an apology for such luxury.

'And where is it now?'

'At home I imagine.'

'Thank you, sir. Is that your only car?'

'Yes. My wife has her own. Little BMW. It's outside some-where. Or at least it was. Come on, Sergeant, what is this? You must know perfectly well what can we own. It's all on computer nowadays. Inspector?'

Leonard got up and stretched.

'You see, sir, shortly before she was killed, your ex-wife was seen getting into a BMW, one just like your wife's. Same colour. Same year.'

'Really? My goodness, if you think it was Cassie's car then think again. I mean we weren't even here when poor Lynda was murdered.'

'You were, sir.'

'Nonsense.'

'I saw you. Saw you both.'

Ross stared at Leonard. Then he remembered. His arm came up in slow motion like the dawning in his eyes. His hand stretched out and he clicked his fingers.

'Of course. That's it. I knew I'd seen you. In the mirror. In—'

'Shades, sir.'

'What?'

'Shades sir. The wine bar.'

'Right! You were sitting with that – that – Irish fellow and the barman was reading out about Lynda missing the press conference or whatever.'

'That's right. So you see, I do happen to know that you were both here the night Miss Elström was murdered. In fact—'

The door opened and a thin blonde with a nervous pinched face darted in. Then stopped, one hand on the door knob in surprise.

Leonard turned from the window. Looked expectantly at Ross who rose and held out his arm to the woman.

'Come in, my dear, come in. This lady and, ah, gentlemen are from the local police. You can imagine why.'

He turned to Leonard, head inclined.

'Inspector, I don't think you've met my wife, have you? Darling, this is inspector Leonard and his – ah – his sergeant lady.'

There was a long silence. Ross, now in full smooth flow, broke it.

'If you really want to know about Lynda, then Cassie is the person to talk to.'

'I'm sorry, sir. I'm not sure I follow you.'

'I too am sorry, Inspector. I thought you knew. Cassie is, or rather, I suppose, was, Lynda's agent.'

Mrs Ross was certainly not the woman Leonard had seen in the wine bar.

Twenty-Four

As her husband poured coffee, Cassie Ross, or Cassie Makins as she continued to be, explained in her short, sharp, jerky speech.

'I've been down to theatre. Christ, this is bad news. Didn't hear until yesterday evening.'

'It was on the news and in the papers.'

She looked at Leonard.

'Coming back from Penzance, we've got a cottage. God knows why. Sodding long way and wet when you get there.'

'Your office didn't call?'

'Apparently. By the time they knew, I was on my way.'

'Mobile?'

'In Cornwall? You tried it? There's no footprint. Anyway, I switched off. Thinking time.'

Leonard was jiggling coins in his duffle coat pocket. Jack tried her own question.

'Tell me, madam . . .'

As she said it she wondered why. She'd even started to use his language. Cassie Makins squinted in her direction.

'Where were you at about midnight the night before last night?'

'I've just told you. Penzance. Why?'

Her husband cut in.

'Well, darling, it seems that these people have a notion that poor Lynda was seen getting into your car at about that time.'

'Rubbish.'

'We have a witness, madam.'

'You can have thousands of them for all I care. Anyway, why would she do that for Chrissake? For a start, she couldn't drive.'

'I meant into the passenger seat.'

'Did you? So what?'

Madelaine Jack decided that if she ever gave up Manvers Street for the boards, she'd hire Cassie Makins as her agent. Such abrasiveness was worth ten per cent.

'You see, madam, the taxi driver who dropped Miss Elström in Kingsmead Square saw her get into your car. And I have to tell you that he recognized your car again last night at Bath Spa station.'

Somewhere deep inside, Leonard groaned as he polished his spectacles. Sergeant Jack was about to be clobbered.

'Connection?'

'The connection, madam, is the witness.'

'Nonsense. Last night I met the London train. Ten thirty. It was late – again. The night before I was in Penzance. Thought you'd understood that.'

Leonard blew into a green handkerchief. It was a loud noise. Not tenor horn, but impressive. The complication had dawned on him, but not on Jack. And Cassie Makins was not about to make it easy for her, nor anyone else. Cassie Makins had never made anything easy. Leonard tried a smile. Like most of his smiles, it came to nothing much, but it surfaced somewhere in his voice.

'Tell me, how did you get from Penzance?'

'Same way as I went. Train.'

'Which would explain why you missed the radio news bulletins.'

She didn't bother to answer. Instead, she finished her coffee with a gurgling, sucking sound. Without taking her eyes from Leonard, she held out the cup. Ross took it with the deftness of a flunky, and much of the servility. He poured more and handed it to his wife. She ignored him. He replaced the cup and saucer on the silver-plated tray and smiled the smile of a Victorian parson in debt to his patron.

'Would anyone else have used your car?'

'No.'

'You're sure?'

'That's what no means.'

'And you, sir?'

Ross used the same be-nice smile. With a crooked forefinger, he stroked at the small whiskers on his high cheekbone as a Rajput caresses his moustaches. Perfectly in control. Understood the question. Understood what his answer should be.

'Absolutely, Inspector. Absolutely.'

Something one of them had said had jarred. But Leonard couldn't remember what it was. He was confused. Someone had driven the BMW, or could it be that there were two? Unlikely, but not impossible. He wanted to ask about the woman in the pub. The woman Con had seen next morning.

'Had you come to Bath just to see Miss Elström?'

'Yes. No. I also handle Jason Williams. Don't look so surprised. Nothing strange. More actors than agents. Think about it.'

It was an order. Leonard obeyed.

'More ten per cents.'

'Fifteen.'

Leonard nodded as if impressed.

'What sort of trouble was Miss Elström in?'

'Who says she was?'

'She was murdered, Mrs Ross. People about to be murdered are invariably in trouble.'

'A certain kind of trouble.'

'We think Miss Elström may have been threatened. Letters. Telephone calls.'

'Course she was. Lynda's looks got all the macs and hand-shakers coming on. She was probably in the Good Nutters and Stalkers Guide. But it never came to anything.'

'We have reason to believe that this might have involved someone in the theatre. Maybe a member of the cast.'

'Might and maybe. Sounds like a doll act.'

'So you've never heard anything of this?'

'No way. I would have known.'

'Why so?'

'Actors tell their agents everything. It's part of the percentage.'

'Then you'll know that she planned to quit.'

The pause was long enough to look at a small, smart gold wrist watch, spin a signet ring and pick up, open and snap close a thin black leather diary on the table at her side.

'Not so.'

'She told at least one member of the cast.'

'Rocks.'

'We have a statement.'

'She couldn't walk out without telling me first.'

'We understood that she told at least one person on Monday morning and that was probably why she didn't show at the photo call. She implied that she was under some stress, was being threatened and even knew something about at least one other member of the cast that contributed to this stress. She planned to go.'

Cassie Makins screwed her eyes and twitched her lips into a bloodless line. Her husband held his smile and seemed of little help. She held out her hand and he quickly reached for her coffee. She sipped. Made a face. Gave it back. He replaced it. She'd had enough time to think through her answer.

'Okay, Inspector. Hear this. Lynda was ill. Or thought she

was. Whatever the yes or no, she displayed the symptoms of the illness.'

'Which was?'

'She was losing her memory. She was convinced she was in the not-so-early stages of some fatal disease. Actors all go through insecurity crises. Most of them have one a week, but this was serious, or at least she was convinced it was. For example, she couldn't remember her lines for more than a day at a time.'

'And was she right?'

Cassie Makins looked through him. It was her husband who answered in a solemn voice trained long ago on the wards.

'We think so, although we needed more time to find out the extent of her illness. For example, was it, well, in layman's terms, real or imagined?'

Leonard took his time. The sadness in the surgeon's eyes was real enough.

'Which is why you were both in Bath to see her?'

Ross continued with practised smoothness.

'You see, Inspector, in spite of her celebrity, she had almost no friends, not close friends.'

Leonard wondered if they knew about Curly Weekes. Cassie Makins cut across her husband.

'And you've got to remember that any friends she did have tended to be in the business. Lovely people. Supportive. But the last people she was going to tell. In spite of what you might imagine, we were among her few friends.'

'But you say you never saw her. You were in Penzance and you, sir, were where?'

Ross neatly adjusted the perfect creases of his trousers and crossed his right leg over his left knee. The socks were silk.

'That is not entirely true. I saw her in the morning.'

'The morning she was killed?'

'Yes. For about five minutes. Let me explain a little. You have been very gallant, Inspector, for not raising the identity of my companion in Shades.'

Leonard said nothing. Jack turned another page in her notebook. Cassie Makins looked across to her husband. He waved a hand at her.

'Isabel.'

She shrugged.

'She is a colleague at my clinic. Dr Isabel Feira. She is a psychiatrist, although poor Lynda did not know that. I asked Dr Feira to see her. We thought it better informally rather than at the clinic. That morning, I saw Lynda at her flat. Two, three minutes, no more. We arranged that Dr Feira and I should go to the flat at six thirty. We did. She wasn't there. We never did see her and Dr Feira went back to London that evening shortly after you saw us.'

'Why six thirty?'

'It was the earliest she would make it. She said she had a photo call at the theatre and then rehearsals. As we know, she didn't show up for us nor for the photo call. In fact the first we knew that she'd gone missing was when the barman in the wine bar read it out. Remember?'

Leonard nodded. Jack turned another page in her small notebook.

'We went back to the flat. She still wasn't there and I took Dr Feira to the train. And I'm afraid that's all I know.'

'You stayed in Bath?'

'Until the next day. I had to go up to town.'

'I should tell you, sir, that you were seen making a call from a public telephone box in the morning.'

'Should you?'

'Like to tell me about that?'

'Little to say. We're thinking of buying a house here. I'd seen one first thing and called the estate agent to pick me up. Which she very kindly did. Is that a mystery?'

'At about that time, your former wife had just been lowered on the wire that was used to murder her, sir. That's my mystery.'

Twenty-Five

Con Cobb was trying to tell the story of his uncle who had the association with the Troubles and had gone to live in Dundalk but had taken the drink seriously instead of the Troubles. On the day the fellas with the balaclavas had come to him and asked about driving the vehicle, he had been perfectly sober. On the evening he'd got behind the wheel, he'd been perfectly drunk and, there was another complication. No one had thought to ask the uncle if he knew the way of driving. Into the gear it went. Up came the left foot, down went the right foot and when the wall came straight at him, the uncle put his right foot down with considerable vigour and a deal of mistaken self-preservation. A fine accelerator it was on the Ford van that night. So the uncle, fearing that Eamon of the Garda at any moment might be surrounding him from behind, decided that it was the time to leave Dundalk.

Michael the barman leaned over the counter.

'I like it. I like it. What happened to him?'

'He secured a position in a drapers and haberdashers, so he did.'

'Where?'

Cornelius Cobb looked at Michael with some amazement. The man was clearly insane.

'And don't you think that a matter of high security?'

He turned to Leonard who'd been sipping and looking into the distance.

'Of course the uncle was—'

'Tell me about Ross in the phone box again.'

Some men would have looked hurt to be cut in full flow. Not Cobb. Any story was as good as the next one.

'Your heart, man? Well, wasn't I on me way when I sees him? Bright as day, which it was, in the telephone box. I thought to myself that would be strange. A man of his distinction reporting to the public telephone. But I'm thinking that your man is far too grand to be carrying one of those little things.'

'Mobile?'

'So they are. But all the tarts and the low life have themselves two and three, so they do. You could see he was a gentleman enough. So would he be needing one of those things? Of course he wouldn't. Just like the uncle you. He was a gentleman whatever—'

'Where was this?'

'Dublin.'

'No. Where was Ross?'

'At the end of the crescent.'

'Royal Crescent?'

'That's what I said.'

'What time?'

'I'd been for me shave. Nine thirty it would have been.'

'Sure?'

'No. But you'll not be calling for the hurry-up wagon if I'm wrong a couple of minutes or ten.'

'And then the woman that was in here with him arrived.'

Cobb looked at the ceiling. At his empty glass. At the ceiling again. Leonard waved a hand at Michael. Cobb held up his own.

'Not for me, sir. I've a day's work to do.'

'And when's that?'

Cobb thought about it.

'You're right. Maybe I'll be doing it tomorrow. Okay. Just the one.'

It took five minutes and neither spoke. When he'd taken his first sip of the bottled beer, Cobb rubbed his lips and glanced at Leonard from the corner of his eye.

'You mention the woman. Well, I've been thinking. I couldn't say for certain. It's been so long, you understand.'

'Go on.'

'The car. Oh yes, sir. The car was there. As clean as the day it was born. But I saw only the back. A wonderful and expensive sight it was too. What they call the haute couture, but then you'll be knowing that.'

'How do you know if you couldn't see her?'

Cobb nodded. Thought about it again. Nodded again.

'And that's where you're right. Perfectly right. You having the analytical mind. I have the confession. I made the connection. It being a vehicle for the ladies and that.'

'Is it?'

'Such a pretty little thing. Now could you imagine a man in such a thing? You could not. I know that. You could not. Not even the uncle in his sensible moment would have attempted such a vehicle, him not fully conversant with the mechanical arrangements. I was telling young Michael—'

'Your uncle.'

'That's exactly it. Circumstances combining against the poor fella.'

'And he crashed into the wall.'

'An unfortunate state of affairs.'

Leonard slipped off the stool and headed for the stairs. Stopped. Turned and came back. He dropped a five pound note on the bar.

'Should you give the day job a miss, it's my round.'

Cornelius Cobb who'd had no intention of turning his hand to anything that day, looked pleased with his morning's work and had the dignity not to let his twitching fingers close over the legal tender. Leonard was buzzing as he all but skipped up the stairs to the street. He too looked pleased. He now knew what was odd about Cassie Makins's story.

Twenty-Six

Norman Philips was back on the stage door. He had a plaster on his temple and some bruising which made him look more colourless than usual. All morning he'd been telling caring inquirers that he was feeling okay but managing to look quite ill when he told them and so had encouraged grateful sympathy and plaudits about his bravery. In theatrical terms, Philips had been wounded. Therefore his playground stature had grown and it was acceptable form to milk the performance for all it was worth. In the increasing tension, the company had drawn closer and the stage-door keeper was now very much among their number.

Leonard was surprised to see Philips. No one had told him that the stage-door keeper was out of hospital. Leonard's simple approach to investigations meant that he never lost sight of his fundamental belief that the villain was usually the most obvious suspect. The problem was that modern policing was complicated by procedures and bolt-on departments. The need to gather evidence that would convince, not the courts, but the increasingly reluctant Crown Prosecution Service, led investigations towards complex explanations of motive and opportunity. Now, as Leonard looked at the sweating Philips, he was close to being convinced that the door keeper was the most obvious suspect. But for the moment, Philips could wait. He wasn't going anywhere.

'Where's Mr Poulson?'

Philips did not answer but picked up a telephone and looking straight ahead at the blank wall, waited for someone to answer the director's phone.

'M-m-Maurice? Oh – When? – Oh. The co— policeman. The insp-p-pector wants him. Okay?'

He replaced the receiver with a crash, missed the hook and had to do it again. He didn't look at Leonard and instead made a big thing of ticking an already ticked list.

'He's in a meeting. They'll tell him directly.'

Leonard said nothing. As he watched the other man, Leonard remembered Madelaine Jack's observation that Philips, an ordinary not very bright man, doing an ordinary not very bright job, comes in one morning for an ordinary not very bright day's work and discovers a woman hanging by the throat from a wire on a half-dark stage. As Jack had said, these were hardly the circumstances to bring out the best in someone. He supposed she was right. And yet, he also remembered her surprise on Philips's background and the newspaper cuttings. He watched as Philips sorted late mail and cards. Messages. While-U-Were-Out notes. Watched as he stuffed them in pigeon holes behind the counter.

'Like this job?'

Philips put down the small pile of letters, but didn't look up. He nodded.

'Nice people.'

'Let's hope so.'

As he said it, Leonard wished that he hadn't.

'I like them.'

'Good. Bit different from what you're used to.'

'I'm used to this.'

Leonard pulled at his tie and used the end to wipe his spectacles.

'I read somewhere you were pretty good.'

Philips stopped fiddling with the clipboard of lists.

'There's not much to be good at. Long as you keep a note, keep the place tidy, go through the routine when you have to and mind your own business, it's pretty straightforward.'

'I didn't mean this. The bikes.'

Philips licked his very dry lips and looked up.

'Who said?'

'I checked. It's part of the deal. Someone gets murdered, everyone gets checked.'

Two stagehands came in from the street door, laughing. They stopped when they saw Leonard. The eyes changed. The cheeks stretched. Just like choir boys emerging from the vestry into the solemn aisles. One raised a hand at Philips who pressed a button beneath the counter to let them into the theatre. Philips had acknowledged their greeting without any enthusiasm. Leonard was now leaning against the counter. He didn't want to lose Philips.

'I didn't know speedway was still popular.'

'Hardly the Bath scene, is it? Southerners.'

'But you were at the top.'

'Sure. Big hero. On the track. Autographs. Photographs. Bits in the paper. Didn't mean much down the M1, did it? Local boy makes local good. That's about it. Big name in the Indian. Big tandoori eater. You know? Big deal, eh? Villa reserve goalkeeper earns more a week than I did a year. Your computer tell you that?'

'Still bitter.'

'Lemons are.'

'You weren't a lemon. Just bad luck.'

'That what your secret files say?'

'Not secret. Newspaper cuttings.'

'You believe what you read if you like. I believe what I know.'

'It says you fell off too many times.'

'We all did.'

'Which is why you gave it up.'

'I got more pins in my legs than the bike had.'

'Not worth it?'

'Nobody was paying the bills when I was lying in hospital. Nobody gives you insurance. Nobody reckons you unless you're winning.'

'Including Mrs Philips?'

Norman Philips considered Leonard for half a minute or so. His lips moved. Nothing came out.

'There is no Mrs Philips.'

'There was.'

'Was a lot of fucking things.'

'And she left you.'

'Good riddance.'

'You mean that?'

Philips moved his lips but there was no sound except his sharp, short breaths. He was blinking and clenching and unclenching his fists like a child trying not to cry. When it came out, it was bitter. Fury.

'Fucking trash. Stinking, lousy, two-timing trash. They're all trash. Every one of them. I hate them. I do. I hate them. God fuck them to hell. That's all they want. That and money. All of them. All women. They're all whores. All of them. I hate them all.'

'Including Lynda?'

Leonard didn't get his answer. Behind him, the electric lock clicked and Maurice Poulson, head to toe in black, held open the door leading into the theatre. Leonard gave Philips another look. He was shuffling letters.

*

Poulson led Leonard by the covered piano and up the right-hand staircase and out on to the stage. The policeman's eye saw chaos and the puzzler's mind saw the beginnings of order. Men in jeans and sweatshirts, ponytails and rings and boots, short back and sides and spotless trainers were heaving, rolling, roping and directing. Black mini pyramids, planished silver trunks and matt-dark blocks were all being rolled in from the back of the stage. The great doors into the bay were open and the van that had loitered for two days on the outskirts of the tinsel and holly-dressed city was being unloaded in double-quick time. One of the stagehands was demanding a tea break, but an Earl Grey tea break. Another said to ignore him, he was always like this after eighteen pints of cider. A thin man in pressed jeans and lamb's wool was chalking the stage. The band would know where to stand. Tiggy Jones, still with that notebook was waving at a small figure high above the stage.

'Go back up stage to full tab – drop split in – okay, Gonzo – lose that then.'

Just behind the footlights, a galvanized box gantry, the full width of the stage, was gently rising on clinking chains, its rows of black-cowled lanterns being returned like dull souls to the theatre's heavens. This was the fit up. The band was in. The stage was returning to its living, for the moment ignoring its dead.

Poulson waited as the gantry continued to rise. Leonard looked about him. Lines and wires. Hooks and levers. The narrow space behind the curtains was crammed with every device for making the scenery appear and disappear, the curtains rise and drop, for entrances and exits, for flying fairies. For swinging Cinderella.

'Which one controls the wire?'

Poulson, concentrating on the rising gantry, ignored him. Tiggy Jones, shaggy rainbow jumper bigger than before, was standing on the other side. Poulson's call was quiet but everyone heard.

'That going to be too close to the iron?'

The gantry stopped rising. Tiggy Jones came to the footlights and craned upwards. Shook his head. Waved a hand. The gantry continued its journey. There was a clunking and clicking. The gantry was home. The souls at rest. Poulson turned.

'The high fly?'

'What?'

'You were asking about the wire. The high fly.'

'Right. Which rope controls it? This side of the stage or the other?'

Poulson pointed. A straight, black-shirted arm. Leonard wasn't sure which rope. Who would be? Only someone who knew the routine. Who knew the ropes.

'Can I see how it works?'

'Too dangerous now. I'll get Tiggy to show you once this lot's done. Come on.'

He stepped easily from the corner of the stage on to the arm of the nearest front seat. Leonard, whose instincts were to keep his feet, if not on the ground, then off the furniture, jumped and landed clumsily in the front aisle. Poulson was sprawled in the middle seat. Leonard leaned against the pit rail. His back hurt. Poulson waited. Leonard had wanted to see him. He was seeing him.

'Tell me, why do you think Miss Elström would have come to this theatre at about midnight on the night she was killed?'

'To get killed?'

The voice was bored. Leonard didn't believe it and he couldn't understand why Poulson was giving this performance. It was more than bitterness and, anyway, why should Poulson be bitter when he wasn't even saddened by Cinderella's death? His reputation was that of a cynical man who, with just a little more luck, one major production, might have been where he really wanted to be – Hollywood and the biggest stage. But he wasn't lucky enough and he wasn't unique. To Leonard's mind, Poulson was just another act.

Lynda Elström had been killed, perhaps sometime after midnight according to the medical evidence. Therefore if Lynda Elström had come to the theatre at shortly before that time, she had come to be killed, whether or not it was her intention or suspicion. The Poulson philosophy of logic held. Next question.

'She was seen in the square just behind here. Kingsmead?'

Poulson had nothing to say, so said nothing.

'Getting into a car.'

Still nothing.

'A blue BMW sports convertible.'

'Ah.'

'Ah?'

'Yes.'

'Why?'

'The answer, you know. And, Inspector, I assume you know the lady.'

'We met this morning. She said she'd been here.'

Again no answer.

'Was she?'

'I don't know.'

'You didn't see her?'

'Should I have done I would know.'

Four stagehands were manhandling a large and clearly heavy control board down from the stage. They were big men, but could barely keep the flat bed of electronic buttons, knobs and faders at the shoulder height needed to lift it above the rows of seats to the sound set up at the back of the theatre. Poulson took no notice.

'Tell me, Mr Poulson, it would seem that when you, Mr Jones, Miss Cunliffe and the others were in the Vaults restaurant, Lynda Elström was outside this theatre, meeting someone. That someone might have been her killer.'

'Good.'

'How so?'

'It narrows your investigation, and most importantly, it clears our little birthday group.'

'Had you wondered?'

'No.'

'Why?'

'I don't mind who killed that night as long as he or she does not do it again.'

'You don't mind murder?'

'Oh, yes. But I don't mind who does it. There is a difference.'

'Would you do it?'

'I think so.'

'Under what circumstances?'

'Anger. Remorse. Jealousy. I don't think I would be any more original than that.'

'And did you?'

'No.'

The gang was now trying to lift the control panel over the lower balcony. Tiggy Jones had followed them. Now he took one end and with no great effort raised it above his head until the others had scrambled over and could take the weight. As he walked back to the stage, he smiled across at Leonard and Poulson.

'The Georgians hadn't thought about 622s being lugged about. Bad design. No foresight, the Georgians, m'lud.'

'622s?'

Poulson was looking at the stage as if he'd lost interest in Leonard.

'It's the thing they were shifting. The sound desk. It controls all backing, effects and the amps.'

He started to rise.

'Am I excused, Inspector?'

'You say you were in that restaurant from elevenish to gone twelve.'

Poulson sat down again. Sighed. Not the sigh of a weary English master at his marking. A sharp sound. A hiss.

'I said I was.'

'All the time?'

'Yes.'

'Every minute?'

Poulson thought.

'More or less.'

'More or less what, Mr Poulson?'

For the first time, the director looked interested.

'I made a couple of telephone calls.'

'A couple?'

'Maybe four. Maybe five.'

'In the restaurant?

Poulson started to shake his head, and then paused. The implication of Leonard's question was greater than its innocence.

'No. Not in the restaurant. I was trying to find Lynda and it was best not to do so in public.'

'You were in public?'

'Simone and Josie. Yes, of course.'

'Where was the telephone?'

'Box office.'

'Can you tell me what time this was?'

Poulson was quicker this time.

'Not really. Didn't really look.'

'Were you the only one to leave the Vaults?'

'Yes. Apart from loo calls, I suppose I was, although the box office is hardly far away.'

'Loo calls?'

'A lot of wine, Inspector. A lot of wine.'

'Let's go back to those calls. Why then? Bit late for calls.'

'No. I'd tried all day. I imagined if she'd stayed in Bath, then by midnight or so it would have been time for bed – her sort of bed. Remember? Ten hours? So if she were anywhere, she'd be at the flat.'

'But my sergeant tells me you didn't believe Lynda when she said she'd quit.'

'She didn't say she had, she said she would.'

'An empty threat.'

'No. Lynda believed every word she ever said. Compulsive liars often do. She believed she was going to quit. She didn't. Well, not in the way she'd planned.'

Leonard ran his hands through his hair and closed his eyes. Clasped his hands behind his neck.

'You know, Mr Poulson, you had such contempt for her that I'm surprised that you hired her.'

'I hired her image.'

'So you keep saying. But why hers? Surely there are masses of women like her. It's almost as if you got her down here to – to humiliate her. She couldn't sing and yet you wrote songs into the show. Everyone knew that she couldn't do it, but she went through the humiliation of having to say she couldn't. She had trouble learning her lines. You knew that. But you still chose her. You enjoyed her suffering.'

'It didn't delight me.'

'You didn't feel for her.'

'I'd done that.'

'When?'

'Mm?'

'When? You said you'd felt for her. When?'

'A figure of speech.'

'You never use them, Mr Poulson. When?'

'I didn't murder her.'

'But you'd known her more than you've suggested.'

'Had I?'

From behind them came a strong voice. A female voice. Full of urgency.

'Morry! There you are.'

They turned. A bigger woman would have bustled. Instead, the tall, skinny figure of Joanna Cunliffe loped down the side aisle.

'Morry. They've found Rudi.'

'Oh dear. And which barman do we owe a taxi fare this time?'

'Shut up, you fool. He's in hospital and they think he's dying. Someone's tried to kill him.'

Twenty-Seven

The surgical registrar usually saw uniformed constables, maybe sergeants. That was the rating for most RTAs. The idea of a detective inspector, even if he didn't much look like a detective inspector, was novel. But then she supposed the connection *was* unusual. Even the registrar had heard about Lynda Elström's death.

'He was admitted at twelve fifteen a.m. yesterday. Initial

examination revealed multiple fractures. Clavicle. Left and right fibula. Left tibia.'

'From top to bottom.'

The registrar, a slight, dark-haired woman in her thirties, paused. She did not care for interruptions. She said nothing. Continued when the class of Leonard and Jack had settled.

'I happened to be in. Another patient. The casualty officer asked me to have a look at him. Internal haemorrhaging. He went down to theatre at three ten a.m. Surgery started at three thirty a.m. Patient was transferred to the ITU at seven thirty a.m.'

'Complicated.'

'More than we had imagined when we started. As you know, he'd been hit by a car, or so we believe. The injuries were consistent with being struck by a vehicle and, I would suggest, at some speed. But I'm not an expert.'

'Not an expert witness?'

'Not an expert witness, although I've cut and stitched more than my share of RTAs.'

'Fast motorcycle?'

'This was some impact. I'd have thought if it had been a motorcycle, then we'd have had two admissions.'

'Bikers are great survivors, especially in this weather. Well protected.'

'Surely there must be bits and pieces lying around. Headlights and things.'

'There's enough "bits and pieces" as you call them to start a scrap yard. The average on that corner is nine minor shunts a week. The road gets swept once every eight days.'

'Then it'll be still there, won't it?'

'Depends.'

The surgeon shrugged. She'd said her piece. She twitched her nose and looked at Sergeant Jack. Jack felt she was expected to ask a question.

'Which injuries caused the decline?'

'Good question. He's not a young man. Do we know how old?'

Jack shook her head.

'Seventies, certainly.'

'Well, the trauma is serious enough. The fractures are difficult. The internal injuries include rupturing. Kidneys. So you could say that was enough for most people his age. Then come the complications – and here I'm speaking in very broad terms, not offering a clinical opinion.'

This time the nod came from Leonard. This was the medical generation brought up on fears of litigation and trusts and administrators only too careful to nurture that fear. Opinions and detail prognoses were couched with codicils more complex than the medical terminology they protected.

'I understand, Doctor, but tell me, what's peculiar? What complications?'

'In general terms you know that shock and trauma play odd tricks on the body and the mind. A simple example is the number of people who suffer a complication that has no direct connection to the injury.'

'Lie in bed, lie in danger.'

The surgeon was halted by Jack's intervention.

'What?'

'Sorry. Something my father's always said. He, um, he's a GP.'

The registrar looked at the policewoman with interest. So did Leonard. He hadn't known. He'd known about her stepfather. But not her father. He wondered why. The registrar took a breath and carried on.

'But this one's more complicated. He's still in ITU, but by now should be out on the ward. He's not. Why? Because, and in strictly non-medical jargon, your actor friend is fighting us.

Leonard wasn't certain he understood.

'Are you saying the patient doesn't want to live?'

The doctor stuck her hands in her pockets. Shrugged. She was saying that, but she wasn't going to spell it out.

'I'm saying he's fighting our best efforts to make sure that he does.'

Leonard rocked on his heels. Without looking up, he asked the obvious.

'Will he win?'

The registrar didn't answer. Not even a shrug.

In the waiting room, Joanna Cunliffe sat huddled in a quilted coat. Her hands were somewhere deep in the sleeves, her long legs tucked beneath the uncomfortable but practical chair. She looked tired and miserable.

'What's going on, Mr Leonard? What's this all about?'

She looked up, peering at him through one eye.

'We're trying.'

'But Rudi! Another one.'

Jack sat down beside her. Touched her shoulder.

'We don't know that. All we know is that he was hit by a car. The driver didn't stop. Maybe coincidence.'

'Really?'

Madelaine Jack shrugged.

'We have to work on what we know, not what might be. All we know is that Lynda was murdered and that Rudi was hit by a car.'

'Then what's next?'

'Should there be a next?'

'It goes in threes.'

Leonard was leaning against the opposite wall. A poster asked him if he was thirsty and tired. Shouldn't he have a diabetes test? He was thirsty and he was tired. Maybe he would. Or maybe he'd get a drink, a good night's sleep and a nine-to-five job.

'Tell me about Rudi Sharpe, Miss Cunliffe.'

'Tell you what? He's just a nice guy. Does the show every year. Here. Bristol. Cardiff. Does a great dame. Everyone knows that. Been doing it for years. He's kind, he gets on with everyone, he helps the youngsters . . .'

'He gives to the Red Cross.'

She nodded.

'Probably. And to everything else. Don't knock him.'

'I'm not. I'm wondering how such a warm and wonderful human being who owes his success to his kindness and his agent manages to get himself in here right in the middle of a murder inquiry and, or so the quack says, doesn't want to come out. Any takers?'

He looked at both women. Joanna Cunliffe looked at the floor. Jack was looking out of the window. She turned to the other woman. Her voice was softer than Leonard's.

'You see, Joanna, there may be a connection. For example, did Rudi know Lynda before he came here?'

Joanna Cunliffe shook her head.

'You need to talk to someone who really knew him, someone like Angela, Angela Billings. She's been around for years. She knows everyone.'

'But did you ever see Lynda and Rudi together? Take messages from one to the other? Did they talk? Did they have mutual friends?'

'Or enemies.'

Leonard's voice from across the room was dry. Cynical. Jack looked at him, sharply. There was something nagging him. This was the Leonard she never quite understood. This was the man who would change mood on a single trigger word without really knowing what he was shooting at.

'Everyone loves him.'

'Except him.'

'Who?'

'Himself, Miss Cunliffe. Rudi himself. He's lying there, apparently, willing himself to die. Doesn't that strike you as odd?'

She was scratching at the tops of her thighs, creating long tram lines on the soft denim.

'I don't know. It's all right for you, you're used to this sort of thing.'

Leonard stared at her in silence until she looked up.

'Let me explain something, Miss Cunliffe. We get reasonably well paid for being ordinary people trained to do an extraordinary job. That's all. Nothing else. Nothing magical. So we need help. Go back to your palace of magic, Miss Cunliffe, and get that bunch of oversensitive and insecure magicians you employ to start telling us what they know. Because if they don't, maybe you'll be proved right. Maybe everything will start going in threes.'

Twenty-Eight

Rudi Sharpe's digs were just ten minutes' walk from the hospital. A three-storey Bathstone terraced house with big square bay windows. There was clean white paint on the open front door before which Leonard and Jack now stood. The landlady may not have been in the great tradition of theatrical landladies, but she'd have got a speaking part in a plonky television soap. The hair was ash blond curls and perfectly groomed. Wigs usually were. The turquoise, crushed-velvet jumpsuit matched the fluffy cerise mules. The earrings dangled with hooks strong enough for drawing-room curtains. The whole effect matched the white toy poodle which the landlady held under one arm while she wiped its snout with a pink tissue. The dog yapped at a passing neighbour, who eyed Jack and Leonard with open interest. The landlady stepped back into the hallway.

'You best come in. Letting the heat out. Don't want my heating bill up.'

Leonard wiped his feet with one eye on the notice telling him to do so.

'We'd like to have a look at Mr Sharpe's room. Is that all right, Mrs Potts?'

Mrs Potts sent her eyebrows up-and-down creasing then stretching her heavily powdered forehead.

'I suppose that's all right.'

She looked at Jack, clearly believing she'd get truth from the nice young lady rather than the odd looking man in a soggy duffle coat. Jack put on her most reassuring smile.

'Quite all right, Mrs Potts. It's very usual on these occasions.'

The landlady didn't ask what these occasions were. The up-

and-down eyebrows increased their flicker rate as she led the way up the broad staircase. More white paint on the banisters. Heavily patterned carpet everywhere to cope with the wear and tear of b&b. On the half-landing, Mrs Potts paused, slightly out of breath.

'Quiet, he is. But then I expect you guessed that. Been staying here for donkeys' years, he has. Came first time, let me see now, sixty-four. That the bad winter?'

Leonard didn't know, but he nodded.

'That's right, then. Came that year. Always comes when he's playing Bath. And Bristol, you know. Never stays over there. Always here.'

She pressed on. Along a corridor and then another short flight and another half-landing, this time with a tall, double-glazed window looking down on to a small garden screened from neighbours by neatly barbered Leylandii. Tucking the poodle under her other arm, the landlady searched her slanting pockets for a small bunch of keys and opened the door in front of them. Leonard was quick without alarming her. Before she could enter, he was standing just inside the doorway.

'We'll just have a look round by ourselves if you don't mind, madam, then we'll come and see you.'

'Well . . .'

The eyebrows were working overtime. Jack switched on the smile again.

'Usual, Mrs Potts, you know. Usual way. Won't take a minute.'

The room was just big enough for the high Edwardian bed. On the lilac candlewick bedspread, neatly folded winceyette pyjamas waited to comfort and warm a wickedly hurt body. Jack and Leonard went into their routine. First a quick look about the room. Cheap whitewood wardrobe and dresser. White basin. A crumpled, spotted handkerchief and a half-empty bottle of red wine on a small round stool. On the floor, a thin book of Scottish poetry, a single green sock hanging over the bed end and on the puffed bolster, a scuffed leather photo album with camels embossed on the cover. On the dresser, there was a pretty china ashtray with some loose change in it and a plastic bedside alarm clock that had stopped at six minutes past seven. Leonard wondered which one.

'Not very lived in is it, sir?'

Leonard bent down to look at the bottle. He hadn't heard of the label, but then he wasn't good at Chilean vintages. He straightened and looked about.

'Odd. No wineglasses.'

'Tooth mug?'

He nodded at the cupboard and chest.

'You take the drawers.'

The wardrobe door stuck. Leonard tugged. Still stuck. He tugged harder and the gilt knob came away in his hand. Quietly, Jack took it from him, slipped it back over the thread which had been packed with a thin strip of foil and gently turned.

'Thank you.'

'My pleasure, sir.'

Inside on wire hangers were an expensive but old jacket, three pairs of fashionably cut but cheap trousers and four city-striped shirts. On the floor, two pairs of slim, very shiny shoes each with wooden shoe trees. A third pair of trees lay on their sides. On the single eye-level shelf heavy sweaters. Leonard went through the pockets. A soft blue silk handkerchief and an old silver penknife, but nothing else.

'Suitcase?'

It was under the bed. A grubby shirt and dirty underwear. The chest of drawers was neatly packed. White boxer shorts and T-shirts in the first drawer. Socks in the second. Nothing in the third. Leonard looked about the room.

'Wallet.'

'Sir?'

'According to the accident report, he had no ID, which was why it took so long to know who he was. But there's nothing here, either. No credit cards, money, letters, diary. Come on, start again.'

Old-timers would have been proud of Rudi Sharpe. Sergeant Jack found the wallet and his money under the mattress. Three hundred pounds in notes in an envelope, two service-till receipts and a mailing counterfoil. The money had been with-drawn six days earlier. The wallet was leather, brown and Dunhill. There was a row for credit cards. Just a green American Express and his banker's card. Behind them, Sharpe's Equity card and a donor's card. Leonard wondered which organs had survived his reputation around the bars. Three ten pound notes and a creased newspaper cutting. Just a paragraph and a picture. It must have been twenty years old. A twenty-years-younger Lynda Elström.

'Well, well. At last. Someone who knew her.'

'Or wanted to, sir.'

He nodded.

'Pass that album thing will you?'

He flipped over the charcoal-grey pages. What he was looking for wasn't there. Just family black-and-white snaps. White crinkly borders. A long time ago. Some of them, judging by their hairstyles and clothes, a very long time ago indeed. He was about to close the book when a picture made him pause. It was a woman in perhaps her late twenties, maybe early thirties. Rich dark hair and high cheekbones. A simple cotton frock with the high, padded shoulders of the 1940s. There was no caption. No legend. Leonard shut his eyes trying to picture the main features. He had a feeling that he'd seen this woman before.

Mrs Potts was waiting with her poodle in the hallway when they came down. She wanted to appear helpful without being nosey. But her nature got the better of her.

'Find anything, then?'

The poodle sneezed and had its snout dabbed for its pains. Jack remembered her duty.

'A very tidy room, Mrs Potts. Very tidy indeed.'

Mrs Potts wasn't born yesterday.

'The answer's no. I haven't been in there since Mr Sharpe left the other night. Nothing's been touched. I knocked yester-day and put me head in. But that's all.'

'It was you who rang the police wasn't it, madam?'

She looked at Leonard with suspicion. If he was an inspector or whatever, surely he knew that. The eyebrows went up and down.

'And the hospital. He had to be somewhere.'

'But why were you so concerned? After all, staying out one night is hardly a cause for alarm at Mr Sharpe's age.'

'Obvious, isn't it? I heard him go out. That was gone midnight. I mean, lots of times he'd come in gone midnight, but not gone out – not without saying, anyway. Not much for the likes of his age to do around Bath at gone midnight, even Christmas time. Well, you two should know that, shouldn't you? As I say, he'd gone out before, but not much and he'd always say something. I mean, he'd been coming here for a long time. One of the family, you know.'

Leonard leaned against a radiator and stood quickly. It was burning hot. Mrs Potts gave good value.

'Tell me, madam, did Mr Sharpe have any visitors?'

'When?'

'During the past week.'

'Might have done.'

'You're not sure?'

'There was a lot of perfume smells in his room one day.'

'Which day?'

'Couldn't say.'

'Recently?'

'No.'

He wasn't going to get any further. He eyed the hooded call box at the far end of the hall, next to the freshly painted door marked W.C.

'Telephone calls?'

'Nothing much. Sometimes his agent would ring. That Mr Wellbeloved over at Bristol.'

'Nothing else?'

''Cept the day, of course.'

'The day?'

''Course. The day the poor man was knocked down. Already told the constable, I have.'

'I'm sorry, Mrs Potts, I wonder if you'd mind going through it again?'

'What for?'

He was hoping she wasn't going to ask that. Jack smiled.

'It's routine, Mrs Potts. Simply routine. Sometimes people remember extra things when they tell us something a couple of times. All right?'

Mrs Potts looked doubtful. The dog struggled a little and she shifted the beast to the other arm.

'Well, he had three calls that afternoon and two that evening. Up and down like a yo-yo, I was. No good calling up, of course. Deaf as a doorpost, he was. Or said he was. Convenient, some people find it. The deaf ear, that is.'

Leonard agreed.

'And?'

'And that's about it.'

'Name? Male? Female?'

'She didn't say who it was, but it was a woman all right.'

'You're sure there wasn't a name?'

Mrs Potts looked at Leonard as if he were simple.

'That's what I said. That's what I said the first time. I'm not daft, you know.'

'Accent?'

'Who?'

'The caller.'

'English, of course. I'd have said something as significant as that, now, wouldn't I?'

'And you don't know what the calls were about?'

'They weren't for me, you know. 'Course I don't. Didn't listen, you know.'

Leonard measured the hallway with his eye. An eavesdropper would be pretty obvious, especially with a snivelling dog under her arm.

'Tell me, just one small thing. If you think back, there's no idea about where the lady was calling from?'

'How could there be?'

'Background noise. Clock chiming. Platform announcement. Television. That sort of thing.'

That was different. The constable hadn't asked her that.

'Don't think so.'

But she didn't sound so sure now.

'Would you do me a favour, Mrs Potts? Would you just

close your eyes for a moment and see if you can remember answering the telephone? Will you?'

She closed her eyes. Opened them again suspiciously, and then closed them once more. Even the dog was still. For a full thirty seconds, there was hardly a sound from the boarding house hallway. Then, slowly, Mrs Potts shook her head.

'No. Nothing. Nothing at all. Sorry.'

He shrugged. Tried the smile again. Failed again.

'Never mind. Worth a try.'

She dabbed at the mutt's nose.

''Cept it must have been local.'

Leonard raised his eyebrows. It was good enough for Mrs Potts.

'Well, one time they got cut off and he rang back straight-away. Well, he was on there quite a time and I don't think he put more than a couple of coins in the box.'

Jack had moved to the door, her warm gloved hand on the latch. Leonard nodded towards the old-fashioned public phone.

'Better have the number, Mrs Potts.'

'Not a secret. 856677. It's in the book. And the tourist guide.'

He edged towards the front door. Mrs Potts hadn't quite finished.

'Listen. I know it's bad and all that. I mean poor old Mr Sharpe getting knocked over. But what's it got to do with this Lynda Elström? I mean it has to have something to do with it, doesn't it? Otherwise you two wouldn't be here.'

Leonard tried the Jack technique. First the professional and reassuring smile, then the textbook reply.

'Just routine, Mrs Potts. Normal in these situations.'

Mrs Potts believed Leonard less than she'd believed Jack, which wasn't much. She reckoned he didn't know. On that point, she was right. He turned on the path and waved. Mrs Potts was wiping the dog's nose.

'So, whoever she was, was English.'

'Might not be, sir. Do we know what Lynda sounded like?'

Leonard shrugged, the movement almost hidden by the

heavy duffle coat. They'd stopped by a fat letter box on the corner of a side road.

'Chadwick Street. We know Chadwick Street. Why?'

'Jason Williams, sir. His mother lives here.'

Leonard stuck his ungloved hands deeper into his coat and turned right, into Chadwick Street.

Twenty-Nine

Mrs Williams slipped a woolly cosy over a large brown teapot and splashed milk into three china cups. They were sitting in the kitchen. Bright. Modern. The latest gadgets. But still no tea bag had ever got in. Still a place for strainers and knitted cosies.

'There. Won't be a sec. Let it brew a bit. Yes?'

Leonard didn't want a cup of tea but had said he did. Jack really wanted a big mug of it and had already judged the teapot big enough for two cups all round.

'Tell me, Mrs Williams . . .'

He paused. He shouldn't have done.

'Tell you what, dear?'

'Do you—'

'Would you like a ginger nut? You look like a ginger nut man.'

Leonard was. He didn't know that it showed. Jack could have told him.

'Thank you.'

'Good. D'you mind getting that tin? The Quality Street one.'

She didn't point. That would have been rude. Leonard looked about. The tin was on the far work surface beneath a photograph of Jason on stage at the Palladium. Jason was everywhere. Mrs Williams's whole life was Jason. He'd done no wrong and could do wrong. It could be tricky.

Leonard put the tin on the table in front of them and eased back the lid. It was full of ginger nuts. She might have shown

Bunter the Remove tuck box. Leonard's eyes grew. Jack wondered if it might be an act. It wasn't.

'Tell me . . .'

Mrs Williams gave the teapot a little shake.

'There. Nearly ready. A minute more. Sorry, dear? What was that?'

'I was wondering if you remember much about the night.'

'That poor girl died?'

'That's right.

'Such a terrible thing. Really terrible. They had a film on. Lovely it was. Not one of those new ones. At least I think it was a film. Might have been a video. I never really know. Jason puts them on for me and I just watch. Awful isn't it? I mean, when he's not here, I watch all day. He doesn't know, of course.'

'So he was here that evening – was he?'

Mrs Williams smiled and gave the teapot a final swirl. Then the strainer. Then the pouring.

'As it comes?'

'Eh. Thank you. He was—'

'And what about you, dear? Like it strong, do you?'

Jack smiled. She'd had to do a lot of that today.

'Thank you. Just as it is. Thank you. No sugar.'

'Oh, you're all the same, you young girls. Watching your figure. You've nothing to watch, I'd say. There's many as would like yours. Isn't that right, Inspector?'

Leonard took refuge in his tea. He waited until the first sips were taken and the biscuits handed around. Then he tried again.

'Your son, Mrs Williams. You see we have to go through the routine. Check everything so that we can, um . . .'

'Eliminate them from your enquiries?'

'Yes, well, I suppose so.'

He was finding this old lady difficult. He didn't believe she was half as daffy as she made out. But that was what they all said when the Police Complaints office wanted to know why an officer had leaned on a perfectly ordinary and innocent member of the tax-and rate-paying public.

'Eliminate. Yes. That's what they do on the television. Still, I suppose it's quite real.'

'Was he, Mrs Williams?'

'Was who what, Inspector?'

'Was your son with you all evening?'

'Course he was. All the lovely pictures to sign.'

'And he never went out?'

Leonard waited.

'No. Course he didn't. Jason brought me a nice hot milk and tucked me up just as I used to tuck him up when he was little and his dad was alive.'

'And he didn't go out again?'

'No. I just said.'

'You would have heard him?'

'Oh, yes.'

'You're sure?'

'Course I am, dear. You see he brought me my drink and we had a little chat. Then we said our prayers. And Jason did some more signing them pictures of his. Then he finished the washing up and then he went to bed. Three minutes before one o'clock, it was then. I could see by the new bedside clock he brought me. Way past my bedtime, you know. But it was a good film.'

Leonard finished his tea and said 'Thank you'.

Outside, it was more of the damp cold he hated. It had started to rain again. Jack threw back her head and gulped in cold air. The central heating had been turned old-people high.

'"Then we had a little chat. Then we said our prayers!" It's almost too good to be true.'

Leonard was head down into the rain, his duffle coat hood up and buttoned across his throat. She could still hear the buzzing. The voice was muffled.

'Anything else strike you as odd?'

She went on her guard. What had she missed this time?

'Only that she was a little uncertain, but then why not? She's in her eighties and the police are scoffing her ginger nuts and

141

asking about her son's connection with a murder case. She's a right to be nervous. And any court would say yea.'

'The clock?'

'Another present from darling Jason. It's probably digital. It's good enough, I suppose. Twelve fifty-seven is a pretty accurate alibi, sir.'

'How would she know?'

'Well, it's common knowledge when Lynda was murdered. We were asking where Jason was. So she'd know he needed an alibi.'

'Didn't mean that. How did she know what time it was? In a dark bedroom.'

'Okay sir, but even if it's set for a twenty-four-hour read out, three minutes to one or double-o fifty-seven is pretty easy to see.'

'For you it is.'

He stopped. Peered out from beneath the wet khaki hood. The rain was spotting on his steel-rimmed spectacles. Even as he spoke it began to click in her mind. The neatly tied-back hair. The smiling eyes. The thick granny glasses. The thick lenses. He was pointing at his own glasses.

'Easy for you. Not for me at night. People don't wear their specs in bed. So how could she know what time it was? She's lying.'

'Or . . .'

Leonard squinted through the rain-dropped lenses.

'Or what?'

'Well, sir, how about it being even more complicated, although the answer's the same. You see, sometimes people do wear their glasses when they're asleep.'

'I don't know anyone who does. You'd break them when you turned over.'

'When I came to your flat last night, or this morning, or whatever it was, you were, if you don't mind my saying so sir, out cold. But—'

'I had glasses because I'd fallen asleep rather than gone to sleep. No. Mrs Williams wasn't reading or watching television.

She was in bed, tucked up not for the calvados but the night. Lights out. She said so.'

'Okay, sir. She's short-sighted, yes?'

'Go on.'

'Supposing she was lying there in the dark, with her glasses on because she didn't intend going to sleep?'

'Why?'

'Because she knew Jason had gone out. Supposing she was doing what all mums do. Supposing she was waiting for her little boy to come home.'

Thirty

Maurice Poulson, Tiggy Jones and Leonard sat in Poulson's office. Poulson was angry, Jones avuncular and Leonard uncomfortable. His chair squeaked. It was an elaborate affair with thin legs abandoned by a Ionesco touring company. Leonard thought it appropriate. He sensed the absurd creeping into the investigation. BMW drivers who were there but not there. Clocks that were on time but could not be seen. A weeping Buttons who needed a mother, not a wife. A neat and tidy dame who played for laughs but wanted to die. A leading lady who could not remember her lines, whom no one knew but who must have known someone enough to be murdered by them.

'I cannot believe this, m'lud. But perhaps we were harsh on the poor girl.'

Poulson looked across at Tiggy Jones.

'Poor girl? Whore.'

'Maurice! Such charity.'

'Crock of shit. She couldn't remember her lines because she wasn't bright enough. Because the only work she'd done was in a studio where she'd been fed them one at a time. I don't buy this memory thing or whatever it's called. No way.'

Tiggy Jones was scribbling a note to himself in his spiral book and did not seem the least put out by this verbal attack. He was used to Poulson. Leonard waited. He wanted to hear flesh tear.

'The point you're missing, Maurice, is that it may explain many things.'

'Like?'

'Like not wanting to sing. Like going off with Jason's mail. Like not remembering her rehearsal schedule. Like me having to take her back to her apartment because she'd forgotten the way. Like not showing for the photocall. Like—'

'Like being good box office and nothing more.'

'You hired her.'

'Not for her acting.'

'*Just* for her box office?'

'What the hell's that mean?'

The scene had gone too far. Both realized it at the same moment. Both remembered the audience. Leonard was sitting in his gilt chair, hands in pockets, legs stretched out, chin on chest and, apparently, preoccupied with the sodden welts of his boots. He looked up at Tiggy Jones and blinked.

'And Rudi Sharpe?'

'Terrible. Absolutely terrible.'

'Yes, Mr Jones, but what's the connection?'

'Does there have to be one?'

'Let's try. What was the connection between Rudi and Lynda?'

The SM pulled at his earlobe. But no inspiration dropped into his palm.

'None – as far as any of us knows. Rudi's been around for years, but not around her side of the profession. Good jobbing dame.'

'Always?'

'No, but at that level.'

'They talk to each other?'

'Only the way everyone does. Not deep meaningful conversations, if that's what you mean?'

'I don't think the inspector knows what he means.'

'Connections, sir. It's like a printed circuit. Everything's on the board but someone has to solder the bits together.'

'This is not the third form.'

'I was just explaining, Mr Poulson. You may have something that makes sense to none of us until it's connected with something else that makes no sense by itself. Assuming, of course, that you want the murderer found.'

'You know my feelings. Couldn't care less. She—'

'Wait a moment, m'lud. Wait a moment.'

Tiggy Jones had been flipping through his fat notebook. He'd got almost to the beginning of pages covered with tiny writing.

'I knew there was something. End of RD-1.'

'R what?'

'Sorry, Inspector. Rehearsal Day One. At the end, I've noted here, Lynda asked me for Rudi's digs. The address.'

'Not telephone?'

'No. Just the address. I said I'd get it for her. I knew where it was. Everyone knows Old Mother Potts, one of the last theatrical landladies. But I didn't know her full address without looking it up in the office.'

'She say why?'

Tiggy Jones looked at the ceiling then back at his book.

'No again. But I guess she wanted to write or send something. She said to make sure I gave her the code.'

'Couldn't she have found it?'

'Inspector, please. This is a star. Ring three times and wipe my arse, I've finished do-doos.'

'Why couldn't she ask Rudi?'

'She could have done, but he'd gone and we didn't call him.'

'Telephone?'

'No. We didn't call him until Day Three.'

'And you gave her the address?'

'Joanna did. Or at least I suppose she did. I mentioned it and she said she'd telephone.'

Leonard cleared his throat.

'Tell me, what was that about Jason's mail?'

Jones huffed his eyebrows and snuggled the back of his neck into the rolled collar of his baggy lilac cardigan.

'Nothing, really. Their pigeon holes are next to each other. Easy mistake.'

'She took Jason Williams's mail by mistake?'

'Absolutely.'

'How long did this go on for?'

'Not sure. Poor Jason had been getting in a bit of a state. No fan mail for days. Times are bad enough, but he expects at least one pair of knickers a day. He wasn't even getting phone messages. Then one afternoon, Norman was on the stage door and he saw her clear Jason's pigeon hole.'

'So she'd taken all the mail?'

'Far as we know. Everything.'

'What did she say?'

'I can't quite remember.'

'But a week's mail?'

'Well we only really knew about that day's letters and messages.'

'Didn't anyone ask about the other days?'

'Don't think so.'

'Why?'

'I suppose because no one was really interested. It hadn't been a big thing. And it wasn't as if Norman came rushing through and said "Guess what Lynda's done?" It only came up in conversation. And Jason didn't say anything, so no one else did.'

'Why didn't he?'

'I don't know. Ask him.'

'But wasn't she embarrassed?'

'It was only a big deal later – when we thought about it. Naturally, no one said anything to her.'

'Why not?'

'We don't do that sort of thing. We avoid offstage problems by pretending they don't exist. Anyway, even if someone had said anything, she'd have laughed it off, just as she laughed off everything that she was wrong about.'

'How could she?'

Tiggy Jones rubbed his full tummy as if conjuring an answer

from a hidden genie. It was Poulson who replied, his voice dry, hazel–twig sharp.

'Lynda was a sly, scheming, lying, manipulative bitch. So the answer is, without a second thought.'

Leonard chewed his bottom lip.

'For someone who says he didn't know Lynda Elström, you have a very clear idea of her character, Mr Poulson.'

'That was not an idea. It was fact.'

'Hearsay?'

'I-say.'

'Based on long observation?'

'On long experience.'

'Of Miss Elström.'

'Of sly, scheming, lying, manipulative bitches.'

'They're everywhere?'

'In the theatre, yes.'

'Women?'

Poulson nodded slowly, his eyes fixed on Leonard's.

'Women? Yes. Of both sexes.'

Tiggy Jones gave his umpire's laugh.

'Come on, Maurice, you're being naughty. Inspector Leonard's making a valid point. Lynda was suffering memory loss. Did we know anything about this? Answer is no, we didn't. Perhaps we should have. I mean, she'd always suffered selective memory loss. My word, who hasn't, m'lud? Who hasn't?'

'Including you two?'

Leonard's voice seemed to come from far away. Thinking aloud. Nothing more than that. Poulson's reaction was much more than that.

'Don't give shit, Inspector. We don't need it.'

'Maurice, easy now. Easy.'

'I'm making an observation, Mr Poulson. Mr Jones says that Miss Elström had always suffered – "selective memory loss", I think you said, sir. That suggests to me that you knew her before she came here. But you said you hadn't.'

Tiggy Jones smiled. Almost beamed.

'A figure of speech.'

Leonard had had enough. He stood. The chair creaked as he did. For a moment he stared at the floor. His hands deep in his jacket pockets.

'See it from my point of view, gentlemen. In your business, you give people things to say. When they're word perfect, you then tell them how you want them to say them. You even tell them when to say them. They're not lying because there was no truth in the first place. That's okay out there on stage left or stage right or whatever you call it.'

He looked up at Poulson, who sat, as ever, rock still.

'You told me not to give you – shit? So don't give me shit. Not even one of your luvvie farts. Okay? You can direct, or whatever it is you do, for all you're worth, but I'm only interested in truth.'

Leonard had said his lines and made his exit. Later he thought it a lousy performance. He didn't look back, which was just as well. The smile had not gone from Tiggy Jones. The sneer had not left Maurice Poulson.

DC Leweson was at the top of theatre lobby stairs chatting to the Vaults manager. It dawned on Leonard that here were too many people in the investigation who might know something. Too many for him to talk to. Too many to rely on other people. He waved a finger at Leweson. Simone Simons smiled at the young constable, gave half a wave and disappeared down to her restaurant.

'Sir?'

'Got a job for you.'

'But sir—'

'Now.'

'Yes, sir.'

'Get a list of the cast and Jones and Poulson. Okay?'

Leweson nodded.

'Get everything you can on them.'

'All of them, sir?'

'All of them. Go through their careers. Newspaper cuttings, social lives, National Insurance records. Call their agents, theatre writers, critics, the editor of the *Stage* and anyone else you can think of who will know anything about them. Stick it on that new cross-match computer thing.'

'X-Ref, sir.'

'Thank you.'

'Sir.'

'Match each and every one of these bastards. Birthdays, dates, shows, interviews, personal appearances, agents, anything that you can think of, with Lynda Elström's career. Oh, and while you're at it . . .'

'Sir?'

'Get the Netcuts on Norman Philips. Ring someone in Birmingham. Someone will know him. This speedway thing. Let's see how good he really was.'

Thirty-One

Bath had been fashionable for two hundred years and more. It thrived on not changing on the surface. The sameness in the fabric disguised little. It had been built by incomers for incomers and it continued that way. It was a friendly city but only for friends. Milsom Street still took half an hour to walk down on Saturday mornings – assuming you were still on speaking terms with everyone you knew. Hanoverian history lessons still appeared screwed to the walls of the city's monotonous build-ings, most of which looked the same. The least inquisitive knew, Wood elder and younger, Pinch and Baldwin, Good-ridge and Palmer, Killigrew, Beau Nash and Lightoler. Great Pulteney was greater than its namesake – as any of the very sniffy estate agents would know (and say). The chain-stored shopping precinct was as anonymous as anything created in every city in the land. You could eat as well as anywhere, drink as finely and get mugged, knifed or raped as well and as randomly as in any celebrated European metropolis of historical and architectural interest. Leonard was tired of it all. He was tired of instant experts and the change they insisted on. He was fed up with having to be part of the change and the influence of those experts who were nothing more than people who looked the part or who could make whatever it was they did, look good enough for a weekend magazine colour spread.

The sinewy redhead at the counter was part of that change. She knew a little about cooking, but mostly she knew about presentation and managing. She knew about business plans and what everyone else was doing. She knew about getting someone on the *Daily Telegraph* to write that the Vaults was the place to see the actors and be seen by people who came to see the actors. She knew about getting people in and getting them back. She knew about reputation.

'Miss Simons? My name's Detective Inspector Leonard.'

She looked stressed. She pulled down the hem of her T-shirt and the electric blue Vaults logo stretched down like the eyes of a wounded Disney character.

'I know. I talked to your friend. Madelaine?'

'Oh yes, Sergeant Jack. She said.'

He'd never heard Jack described as his friend. He supposed that she was.

'Right. Something bothering me about your, eh, birthday party wasn't it?'

'That's what the ad said.'

'And it wasn't as advertised?'

'Never is, is it? Want a coffee?'

He could smell it.

'Please. Black. No sugar.'

'It's decaff.'

'No thanks, then.'

She replaced the glass coffee jug in the filter machine.

'Sorry. No call for anything but nowadays.'

Leonard nodded.

'But as far as you knew, Lynda was still alive. In fact, she probably was.'

'I know. But they were all so serious about her. Maurice was really nasty. Mind you, he's never anything but grim. He makes Lenny Cohen look like Mary Poppins.'

'The others?'

'Joanna's okay. She's had a calculator transplant. As long as the books balance she couldn't care a toss. Mind you, even she was screwed up. Tiggy was okay. Nervous. But then he doesn't have to worry about it. I mean, SMs look after the clockwork stuff. Make sure the scenery's there, the ropes and the lights and everything else.'

'What about the waitress? Josie?'

Simone smiled.

'Oh Josie's okay. Be useful if she could keep her legs together. But yes, she was okay. Mind you, she's quite cute. She knew there was something funny going on.'

'What sort of funny?'

'Oh, not ha-ha. Funny peculiar.'

She poured herself some coffee. Offered Leonard a second chance. He shook his head.

'What did she say?'

'Well, nothing. Not then, anyway. I mean, it wasn't exactly her place. But afterwards she told me that she'd seen Lynda that night. Or thought she had.'

'But she'd been here, hadn't she?'

Simone sipped at the black coffee.

'Right. But she smokes. Smokes a lot. We don't have smoking anywhere in the theatre. Not even in the offices. You can get binned for two things – your hand in the till and smoking. So as soon as we shut down, out she goes for a cigarette.'

'What time was this?'

'Early. One of those nights. One-man show. Not many covers. So eleven fifteenish and, according to her, Lynda went bombing by in the back of a cab.'

'Which direction?'

'She was out the front, so it can only be up towards Queen Square. It's one way.'

'She's sure?'

'Says she is.'

'Where is she now?'

'She said Christmas shopping. Knowing her, that could mean anything that's on special offer in Boots or trousers. She'll be in this evening, about six thirty.'

'Why didn't she tell anyone?'

Simone sipped more coffee and crossed her legs. The black skirt was new. He liked it. She thought through what she was going to say.

'She told me.'

'Only you.'

'Mm.'

'Why? Didn't she realize this was exactly the sort of thing we need?'

'It's complicated.'

Leonard let out steam. Simone ran her hand through her thick dark red hair. He was really quite nice. Pity he was a policeman. Pity about Ike.

'You see, Inspector, not everyone gets A-plus for quick and logical thinking in this life. Not everyone is a star. How old are you, Inspector? Forty something? Then how come you're not a king? Chief Constable or something? Not being rude, but Inspector's no big deal. See what I mean? Josie is a good waitress. When her husband's home from the army, she's a good wife – well, sort of good. I run a good restaurant. That's it. That's all you are. That's all I am. That's all she is. So when Josie sits with the gods – and believe me, to Josie, Maurice is close to sacrifices – then she doesn't offer any advice. Once she hasn't said anything, then it's harder to say. Okay?'

'But she told you.'

'Right. That's where it gets complicated. You see, that morning, I'd split with my partner.'

'What's the connection?'

'Ike, that's my partner—'

'Is or was?'

'Is. We're back.'

'Sorry. Go on.'

'Well, you're not going to believe this, but Ike, well, he had something going with Lynda.'

Leonard leaned back in yet another rickety chair and buzzed.

He stood, clasped his hands behind his neck and clicked his spine. Simone winced.

'Crazy isn't it? But you can see why she told me and didn't tell them.'

He couldn't. But then he didn't know Josie.

'Ike and Lynda Elström?'

Simone had got up and poured more coffee. She came to the table with two cups. He said nothing.

'Okay. Ike's a lensman. Stills photographer. Most of the stuff you see here is his. Foyer, outside, everywhere. He did the publicity pix for the show. She asked him to do some head and shoulders for her. He's got a studio at the top of Walcot. She went there a couple of times. Then, I think, a couple of times more.'

'For head and shoulders?'

'Exactly.'

She was nibbling at her nails. He thought how little time Lynda Elström had been in Bath.

'That was quick.'

'Ike's quicker. She wasn't the first to go in there for a head and shoulders and come out with a full perm. He's a good-looking guy. Knows how to relax them.'

'So that's why you pointed to the door.'

'Right. But there's more to it than that.'

'Sounds enough.'

She shook her head. He really was quite nice.

'This is your bit coming up. I soured him because he couldn't leave her alone. What I didn't know then was that Lynda asked him to do something special for her. I don't mean, well, you know what I don't mean. She was calling two or three times. Twice I picked up messages. Said she needed to see him. Naturally I believed she'd really got the ants. but Ike said it wasn't like that. Then on Monday, my birthday of all days, I pick up the phone and it's her. Eight in the morning. I went ballistic. Told her to screw herself, but she probably was doing that anyway. Then I soured Ike. Told him to wash 'n' go – by the time I got back.'

'That was the night you were all in here?'

'Exactly.'

'And presumably he didn't.'

'Exactly.'

'So what did he do?'

'That day? Apparently he met her. Some time in the evening. Maybe they'd just met when Josie saw her. I don't know. What I do know is that when I got back, he told me that she'd asked him to do a special job for her and it was a scorcher.'

'Drugs?'

She shook her head.

'I don't know. What I do know is that when I called him and said she'd been killed, right here in the theatre, he wobbled, badly. He took off.'

'He left?'

'Straight into orbit.'

'Where? Why?'

'I don't know where. He just said he was going. Said he was in a big fright. He said he would call. But he hasn't. That was, um, that was what I was about to tell that guy, when you came along – the dark-haired one.'

'And you've no idea what it was?'

'Nothing.'

'And you've not heard from him?'

'No. I mean, he could be miles away. I called his mother. She hadn't heard from him.'

'Where is she?'

'Scotland.'

'Not exactly an away-day to the Mendips.'

'That's Ike. Mind you in that crazy car of his he'd be there in six hours. I know. We did it one night. Terrified the life out of me.'

'Car?'

'Crazy.'

'What sort of car?'

'One of those BMW sports things. A dream, until he gets behind the wheel.'

'Blue? Soft top?'

'You've seen it.'

Leonard shook his head.

'No. But I know someone who thinks he has.'

Thirty-Two

Leonard had remembered humming Jason Williams hits. Must have been twenty years ago, or more. Student days. Catchy tunes. Not good enough for classics. Not bad enough for lifts. Good supermarket stuff. Buy the tune. Buy the soap. Williams was still singing them. Leonard now did his own humming. The pop star had the sort of preserved face that one day, and very suddenly, would disappoint. He'd been baby-faced in the early days, but the lines that had never broken through, were now starting to. The creams couldn't be relied upon for much longer. If he'd been humorous enough, then personality would have lifted Jason Williams above the age thing. But Jason Williams had long ago become the image. Now he had no real Jason Williams to fall back on.

The waitress, with what Leonard believed to be Bath's perfect bottom, arrived with their two white plates of monkfish. She smiled and said she hoped everything was fine. Was there anything else? She kept looking at Jason. She was old enough to be his daughter, to have made him a grandfather. But she still looked. Perhaps she too saw the magic flaking. Selsey went flying through to his kitchen. He was smiling and cursing at the same time. He was supposed to be cooking. Woods was packed. All very well, but didn't the world know they were running at Cheltenham? A big winner yesterday and not a glimpse of the beast's tail. A bet wasn't a real bet unless you were there with the card, the book, the pencil and maybe the hipflask with the sweet-smelling neck. A serious-looking and overweight writer, almost hidden by a great green fern, crouched over cutlets at the corner table and wagged a stubby finger at a quiet literary agent blessed with the gift of listening. An aristocratic young man, not long since a youth, with a castle far too big for him and a bride far too clever for him, picked at game and pondered whether the beautiful woman opposite him was having an affair with his youngest brother. Across the way, a gaudy lady of a certain age repaired her lipstick and hoped for a jollier afternoon with her hairdresser lover than she'd had that morning with her lawyer husband.

None of this high and low life came to Jason Williams. He squiggled a fork into the carefully prepared dish. It could have been rice pudding.

'My God, can't you understand? I cannot see the big deal.'

The voice was still very young. He looked about him. Not for praise. For privacy. Leonard said nothing and chewed. The monkfish was very good. Jason Williams leaned forward and lowered his voiced.

'There was nothing in it. She made a mistake. Go look for yourself. My pigeon hole is next to hers. A mistake. I asked her. She said sorry.'

'What happened to the mail?'

'She – she panicked. Threw it away.'

'All of it?'

'Apparently.'

'Every time?'

It was a guess. It worked.

'So she said. I believed her.'

'How many times did she take it?'

'I don't know. Maybe two, maybe three.'

He put down his fork.

'Look, Inspector. If she wanted my mail, fine. Saved me opening it.'

'Maybe she didn't. Maybe she wanted your phone messages.'

'Why would she?'

'You tell me, sir. You tell me.'

Williams had wanted to tell Leonard something. But he wasn't sure it was a good idea. For God's sake, this was what an agent was for wasn't it? Wasn't it? Leonard had met Williams in Milsom Street. Bath was that sort of place. He'd suggested eating and Williams had said why not. He was that sort of person. But Woods was not the most private place in the world, especially for a murder investigation. Especially with one of the most well-known faces in Britain sitting there. Williams looked about casually and smiled at a gawper, who had the decency to blush.

'Okay. Now this is all I know. Lynda was getting heavy breathing calls and suggestive postcards, okay?'

'You told me that.'

'What I didn't tell you is that she suspected that they were coming from someone in the theatre.'

'Why?'

'Because she'd only been getting them since she'd arrived in Bath. And you're right, she was looking for messages, not mail, because she wanted to compare handwriting. See.'

'Couldn't she simply dial back and check the caller's number?'

'She tried. It was a switchboard system. No way into it. Can't you see how she was thinking? Yes? No? The switchboard meant the theatre to her.'

'Could have been anyone in a Bath office who saw that she was in the city.'

'And knew her private number? You got any idea what it means to have a public face, Inspector? It's a wire act, believe me. It is. You want everyone to know you all the time but you don't want any touching. You know my mum gets guys trying to marry her? You know that? My God, it's disgusting. They want to marry my mum. You know why? Yes? No? They want me – me, for Chrissakes – as a son-in-law. And they want the money. That bit I can understand. But not the touchy feely stuff. Okay?'

'So who knew her telephone number?'

'Lynda's?'

Leonard nodded.

'Only Jo-Jo and—'

'Who?'

'Jo-Jo. Joanna. Joanna Cunliffe. Her and Maurice. Then anyone she gave it to.'

'But it would be pretty easy to come by.'

Williams's hair moved gracefully as the singer swayed his head.

'Not so easy as you'd think. I suppose anyone who could look at the accounts would know. But it's harder than you think.'

'But you knew.'

'No.'

'She never gave it to you?'

'Why should she? I never asked. No need. Phone numbers are precious. You don't give them away without reason.'

'Who do you think was making those calls?'

The shoulders that shrugged beneath the soft silk polo neck were narrow. Still boyish.

'Had to be a nutter. How many nutters do we have? Look, Inspector, I'm trying to help, but I can't if I don't know, can I?'

'Depends on what you do know, sir. For example, did Miss Elström ever mention that she might know something about another member of the cast?'

'What sort of thing?'

'Did Miss Elström ever try to blackmail you, sir?'

Williams put a forkful of monkfish into his mouth. Suddenly, he remembered what his mum had told him about talking with his mouth full, and to chew his food forty times. Leonard had learned to wait.

'Listen, Inspector, we're doing the pantomime, not you. Blackmail? You out of your tree? I didn't even know her. Why would she blackmail me – and about what? I think that's seriously sick. I do, I really do.'

'In confidence sir, there's nothing in your past that would . . .?'

Williams put down his fork.

'Let me tell you something that is pure gold. I've been in the business for, well, for more than half my life. There hasn't been a month when some shit-arse tabloid editor hasn't tried to find the dirt on me. I can tell you, one editor offered a ten-grand bonus to the reporter who could find the shit that would stand up in court. Ten grand. You know what they got? Nothing. Sweet FA. You know why? Because in the business, I'm the most boring guy in the world. I do the business and go home. I've got a fan club that runs into millions that says that's not a bad deal. So no, Inspector, nothing to know, nothing to put the arm on. Okay?'

He looked at his watch. Escape time. Leonard put a halter on him.

'I've been talking to Mrs Williams. Your mother.'

'I know who you mean. I did get an A-level.'

'Yes, sir. Anyway—'

'Leave her alone.'

'Routine, sir. Purely routine.'

'Leave her alone.'

'I needed to check a couple of things about your movements that night. As I say, purely routine. Do you mind telling me what—'

Again Williams leaned over. This time it wasn't simply confidential. 'I spend a nice evening with my mum. Not clubbing. Not doing the main drag. Not doing drugs. Not party-partying. A nice quiet, cocoa evening with mum and two hundred photos to sign. Two hundred. You ever had to sign two hundred anything? Mega fart – you can quote me. You know how long it takes? This is no wavy-line stuff. Some of these bastards have dozens. Hundreds. Real anoraks. They make comparisons. Then you get the smart bastards. The sell them at a profit. You know that? But sign, I still do. Why? because it's the image. Because my agent tells me to. Because among those two hundred are some regular people. Real fans. They travel with the tapes. True believers. But two hundred? It takes for ever. So I speak again. Watch the lips, Inspector, watch them. I spent the evening with Mum. I signed, I went to bed, I got up. Not even a pooch for walkies.'

Leonard wiped his mouth with one of the heavy white napkins that cost Selsey a fortune to launder.

'Where are they?'

'What?'

'The photographs?'

'Gone.'

'Where?'

'Posted, of course.'

'You licked two hundred stamps?'

'My God, Inspector. I stopped licking stamps after my first album. I sign. They go to my agent and the office sends them.'

Jason Williams was nervous. He was getting noisy.

'Look, I had a pee before I went to bed. Should I have saved you a sample or something? What is this? Murder One? My God, you know where I was. My mum is hardly likely to lie. She's eighty-odd, for Chrissakes.'

'Hardly doddery.'

'You know what she said, poor luv? She wanted to know if she'd said the right thing. Know what I said? I said, "Look Mum, tell the truth, just as you brought me up to do." Then she says, "Well I did tell the truth, Jason. I did. But I'm worried." That's what my mum said. She said she's worried. Now in my book that's persecution. I'm not even sure what I'm doing here.'

He threw down his own napkin. The drama didn't quite come off as it landed in the middle of his hardly-touched lunch and that embarrassed him.

'Tell me, Mr Williams, does your mother wear her glasses when she goes to sleep at night?'

Jason Williams's mouth turned down at the corners. The shake of his head was a tiny worrying movement. An affliction more than a calculated expression.

'Not as far as I know. Why?'

'She said it was just before one o'clock before you went to bed.'

'So?'

'But if she didn't have her glasses on, how could she see the clock? Could be that she'd been waiting up for you. I was wondering if you'd gone out for a stroll and forgotten to mention it. Unimportant right, then. Easily forgotten. Many do.'

'You saying my mum's a liar?'

'No.'

'Sounds very much like it. And I don't care for this. It's out of order. Okay?'

As Williams's voice went up, so Leonard's lowered into almost a murmur.

'I assure you, Mr Williams—'

Almost a shout.

'Like hell you do. What's going down? My mum's straight. A proper mum. Leave her alone, okay? If you don't, I'll have every newspaper screwing you for harassing a nice old lady.'

'I was simply pointing out that without her glasses and in the dark, your mother would have, to say the least, difficulty in seeing Big Ben, never mind a bedside clock. Perhaps you'd like to reconsider your movements that night.'

Jason Williams was pale. He stood very slowly and with both fists on the table leaned over to Leonard. The restaurant hushed. This was some performance.

'Did you see the clock?'

'No, but—'

'Stuff "No, but", Inspector, stuff it. I spent weeks finding that clock. Had it sent over from New York. If you had bothered to look you would have seen that it's digital. It lights in the dark. And, Inspector Leonard, the flaming numbers are six inches high. Six inches. My God, old Stevie Wonder could have read it. So back off, Mr Policeman. Put your rubber truncheon away. She's my mum, not one of your flaming supergrasses.'

Jason Williams's exit was magnificent. As he reached the door, the waitress with hardly a skirt to her name handed him the long green cashmere overcoat with the huge collar. The admiration in her eyes reached heaven. His shy smile of thanks cut across two generations and into her pit-a-pattering heart.

Leonard did not have to look about him to see the hostility at the other tables. He was beginning to think he might not have got things exactly right.

Thirty-Three

Rudi Sharpe died at six minutes past two. The waiting constable telephoned Detective Sergeant Jack who called Selsey who was sitting in the bar with his hat on, a glass of white wine in his hand and Leonard opposite. Selsey, being Selsey, was suggesting that a public fanging by a popstar in one of the best and most crowded eating houses in Bath was something you dismissed with style. The message from Jack saved further debate.

'Poor old fella.'

Leonard nodded.

'Been around for some time.'

'And a sound racing man. Oh yes. A man with an eye for a loser that one was.'

'You knew him?'

Selsey looked hurt.

'Quarter of a century. Met him the first day I came to Bath. At the other place you know. Liked his veal, but then he would. Viennese.'

'Why Sharpe?'

'Don't know where he got it from, but try putting Shcharansky on the posters. He changed it in forty-six or 'seven.'

'He was that old? We thought he was seventy-ish.'

'Older. His parents were Russian Jews. He came here after the war. He'd been in the state circus or something. He'd done all the touring stuff. Europe. Even America. But he settled here with his hands, knees and boompsy-daisy routine.'

'You must have known him well.'

'No, but we used to talk. He liked a drink.'

'Not just the one.'

'Those Slavonic types are all the same.'

'As what?'

'Sentimentalists. Give them a drink and they're back to the old days. They're pessimists about the future and think the present is a waiting room.'

Leonard looked at him and blinked.

'Who said that?'

'I did.'

'Right.'

'Thank you.'

'He talk about his friends?'

'Not much, except that most of them were dead.'

'Why would he give up like that?'

Selsey shrugged and sipped at the white burgundy which was never far away.

'Just told you.'

'Pessimism?'

'No. Sentimentalism. It rhymes with fatalism.'

'So no future?'

'Not without the past, no.'

Leonard pushed back his chair. A few were left. They looked up. Curiosity. More than one conversation lost its thread, Most had never seen a detective inspector. But they didn't look for long. He tucked two grubby notes under the empty wineglass.

'Too deep for me.'

Selsey grinned. It was his smoked salmon and champagne in the back of a limousine on the way to the Gold Cup look. Anticipation of sheer pleasure.

'When it dawns, drop by, we'll open a bottle of Tat.'

Leonard's favourite waitress made herself busy at the till. He got his own coat from the rack.

It had stopped raining but he felt miserable and damp. His duffle coat was still soggy, the pockets too cold for his bony clenched fingers. On the corner of Bartlett Street, the publicity woman who'd once toyed with his tie in a smart hotel, cut him dead. Why not? Most people he knew for the wrong reasons. Too close meant he'd asked questions and most people he traded with didn't like questions. He bought a *Big Issue* from the street vendor outside the book shop and the man wished him Happy Christmas. The dental nurse who ground her teeth, smiled and said Hello from behind rolls of wrapping paper. He mouthed a reply neither of them heard. It was supposed to be Happy Christmas. In the lanes down to the abbey, Dancer was organizing a couple of shivering girls in different doorways. Begging was good business, especially this close to the Christian festival. Dancer nodded. They'd known each other too long. Too many questions, but Dancer said that he should have a nice time anyway. The irrepressible draper with more heart surgery than any living being raised his trilby and wished him well. Still the smile wouldn't come. Why was everyone so damned nice? By the time he got back to Manvers Street, Leonard was grumpy.

Jack was in the upstairs corridor talking to Marsh who wore his regulation look of a disapproving elder.

'What you make of this, then?'

Leonard was still struggling out of his duffle coat and wasn't quite sure what 'this' was.

'Coincidence, sir?'

'Don't be daft, man.'

Marsh sniffed at the government surplus smell of the sodden coat, turned and stalked off in search of sanity. Leonard raised an eyebrow to Jack.

'He meant the door codes, sir. We've finally got the list. It seems that Norman Philips was the last person to use the stage-door entrance.'

'Right. Exactly as he said he was.'

'Not quite, sir. If you remember he claimed that he closed up and left at about ten forty-five – after the show? The printout shows that's about right.'

'So?'

'It also shows that he came back in at twelve fifteen and didn't leave until two a.m.'

Leonard was nodding as if it all made sense and shrugging back into his duffle coat. He turned in the opposite direction Marsh had taken and headed for the stairs.

'Come on, then. Don't just stand there. Let's—'

As he started, he knew he shouldn't finish. It wasn't the look on her face, he simply knew she would have anticipated what he wanted. She didn't smile.

'Thought you'd want a word with him, sir. I've got him downstairs.'

He loosened the wooden toggles on his coat. Jack took two A4 envelopes from her yellow file.

'DC Leweson, sir, the netcuts on Philips you asked for and a note from a Sergeant Wrightson. Seems he's a big speedway fan up there.'

Leonard only glanced at the newspaper headline cuttings but scanned the local man's remarks. The crash. The bottle. The obscurity. All predictable. He was about to replace the report, when a paragraph caught his eye. The wife. He started reading from the top. Yes, Wrightson had known him well.

'And just another thing, sir. I had a quick look through his flat. He had this lot all over his bedroom walls.'

Leonard took the top brown paper sack and shook out Philips's gallery of photographs. Plenty as the speedway king, but mostly hard porn. All of them poorly lit. Amateur stuff but there was nothing amateur about the models. Three or four he recognized, but from where he didn't remember. Nothing to do with this investigation. Jack gave him the second folder.

'These lot are more us, if you'll excuse the expression, sir.'

Lynda Elström smiling. Lynda Elström pouting. Lynda Elström getting out of a car. Lynda Elström falling out of her wet collarless shirt at a party. Lynda Elström in an almost nothing bikini. Lynda Elström at her most revealing. Then, Lynda Elström staring straight at the camera. The famous garage calendar picture that had started it all thirty years earlier. And in the middle of her naked left breast, a large cigarette burn.

Thirty-Four

Norman Philips believed the world was a bitch. His whole life said so. He sat in the corner of the interview room with his head high against the wall, his eyes closed, the blue plastic mattress damp and sticky through his cotton trousers. He knew what they were thinking. But they weren't that smart. It had taken the bastards long enough to get to him. And he didn't care a monkey's. Never had. If she'd listened to him, it wouldn't have happened. If she'd believed he could help, it wouldn't have happened. He hated her. She hadn't deserved anything better. Only he wished she hadn't died.

The door opened. He knew who it would be without looking. When he did, his eyes had been shut tight too long and he screwed them against the brightness. There he was. Wiping his flaming specs again. She was behind him, like some flaming nurse. Well, they could flaming rot. They'd made up their minds. Why make it flaming easy for them? He couldn't think of a single flaming reason why. Didn't even flaming try. He closed his eyes again.

'Mr Philips?'

Nothing.

'I think you know the problem, Mr Philips.'

Nothing. Leonard sighed.

'Right. We have the door printout and it shows that you returned to the theatre at twelve fifteen and left at two.'

Nothing.

'Is that right?

Nothing.

'Which means you lied to us.'

Nothing.

'You told us that you left after the show and didn't return until the following morning, when you discovered Miss Elström.'

Nothing.

'The medical report puts the time of Miss Elström's death at about the time that you were in the theatre.'

Nothing.

'We have no evidence to suggest that anyone else was in the theatre. Mr Philips, the arithmetic isn't complicated. One plus one. That's all.'

Leonard stuck his thumbs in his waistcoat pockets.

'Fancy her, did you?'

Nothing. It was going to be hard. In Leonard's mind there were set routines for murder suspects. The easiest was the person who simply wanted to tell what had happened. The second group included those who had cast iron alibis and were clever enough to take you on. They were usually calm, apparently imperturbable. Then there was the chatterer who would tell you tell you what he or she thought you wanted to hear. The hardest was the one who didn't conform to any pattern especially those who'd committed a crime without knowing why or even without realizing it. But that didn't mean they were daft. They weren't going to succumb to a cup of milky coffee and a chocolate-biscuit interrogation. The interrogator had to know which one was which. More and more suspects changed pleas. More and more lawyers successfully raised doubts about interrogation techniques and police procedures even when everyone but the jury knew the accused was guilty as charged. Now Leonard tried to assess Philips. The first time he'd met him, Leonard had nothing to go on but instinct. Instinct wouldn't survive cross-examination in a criminal court. This time he had to get it right. He knew Philips had the opportunity to kill Cinderella, but Leonard now had to dig out the motive. There had to be something that hadn't shown up. He tried again.

'Tried to chat her up?'

Keep going. Make friends. That's what the text book said.

'Okay, Norman, let's see what happened. She was friendly with everyone. Chatty. That's what they say. You were the first one she saw when she came in. Always smiling. Sexy. Always saying hello and how are you? Very special, yes? A star. Unattached. Not always accepted by the other members of the cast. Right?'

Philips didn't even look. Leonard didn't expect him to. If it came, it would come like all crashing cymbals – on the crescendo. Leonard had time. Philips may have his eyes closed, but he couldn't shut his ears.

'So she talked to you. You did things for her. Got her mail together. Her messages. Showed where things were. Maybe a few errands? Ordered cars. Taxis. And she was really grateful. You became . . . what did you become Norman? What was it? Fantasies, Norman? Did you go home and have big fantasies? Wake up in the night, did you, Norman? Made you ache, Norman, did she? Pretend she was there. Taking her clothes off for you?'

The head still back against the wall. The eyes still closed.

Leonard paused. He hated this. He hated what he did. It was an act. His voice was different. His language was alien. The persistence was mechanical. The target unobscured. The end premeditated. Thus the curiosity nil. He felt unclean. It would be the last one. He threw away his script. The sigh of exasperation was real enough.

'For heck's sake, Mr Philips, this is stupid. Ghastly. C'mon. Just tell me what happened. If nothing, just tell me and we can all go home. I really don't care.'

He thumped down in the corner seat. Jack's frown didn't quite meet her brow. She'd seen this routine dozens of times from training school to cell. But Leonard was breaking the rules. She was supposed to be the nice guy. He couldn't be both. Could he?

'I mean, I mean, tell me, it simply went wrong, is that it? She just wouldn't conform to your fantasy, or something. I mean, for goodness' sake, it's natural.'

Nothing.

Leonard looked across to Jack. Eyebrows. The hardest interrogation of all. The silent type. Warned of his rights. Offered a solicitor. No reactions. No emotions. No answers. Nowhere. Leonard dropped his head on his chest. Eyes closed. Legs out in front. Hands bunched in jacket pockets.

Jack's voice was firm yet quiet. Detective Staff Nurse Jack.

'You see, Norman, a lot of people here are starting to say that if Lynda was murdered between twelve thirty and two a.m. and, the door codes show that you were the only one there when she was murdered, then you must be the person. But let me tell you something. I'm a woman. I don't buy this idea that she wound you up and that you – well – went mad. You see, as a woman, I can sense there's more to you than that. A woman knows these things. You understand me?'

Nothing.

'And even if you did hurt her, I don't believe you're the sort of person who would do it deliberately. All I'm trying to do, Norman, is see it from your point of view. No one else is,

Norman, and no one else is going to. The evidence is against you. So why don't we start trusting each other? We're not here to simply get a result. We need to know the truth, Norman, and we think you're the only person who can tell us. That's how important you are. Do you understand?'

Leonard only half-listened. The drone of the friendly questioning. Not expecting to get a response. Jack could keep going like this for hours. But Philips wasn't in the text book. Leonard needed something else. The pictures? His ex-wife? There was something Sergeant Wrightson had scribbled. Leonard stirred himself.

'Tell me Norman, when did you lose your nerve? Eighty seven? Eighty?'

Nothing.

'Booze, wasn't it?'

Nothing.

'People said after the last crash. The pins. The screws. Said they didn't blame you. Right? But it wasn't, was it? It was before the crash, wasn't it, Norman? You'd been at the mahogany. Rum and Coke man, weren't you? Big on the rum, easy on the Coke. Got the right coke, I suppose, have I?'

Philips took a deep breath.

'Broken Horse? Ring a bell, does it? Big rep in there you had, Norman. Ten, twelve doubles a session? That's what they say. You were a champion all right, Norman. Rum Rider. Remember the cartoon in the pub?'

Shorter breaths. Much shorter. Eyes still closed. But now screwed up. Leonard leaned very close.

'The big crash, Norman. Into the last bend. Second into that last bend. He was screwing you, wasn't he, Norman? He was screwing your wife, wasn't he? Remember it. Very wide. Too wide. Remember hitting the side, Norman? Remember the wall?'

The sweat was coming. The silence held.

'Spannermen said Rum Rider was pissed. That was it, wasn't it? Big mess. Failure. Lost it on the bend. You in hospital that night, Norman. She didn't even come to see you. Remember why, Norman? He was screwing her. That why?'

The violent shake of the head. The silent scream. The fists bunched to strike out at Leonard.

'You didn't have the guts, Norman, and you haven't got the guts now. You want to hit me, Norman, don't you? You want to hit me because I'm telling you that you lost your nerve and you lost your wife and the spannermen spat on you. No guts. Still no guts. Still Rum Rider.'

'It's not true.'

At last.

'But she didn't come that night did she, Norman. Did she?'

Just the slow shake of the head.

'And everyone knew where she was. In his caravan, wasn't she? The spannermen knew. They saw, didn't they, Norman? The word was round.'

'Lies. They were lying.'

'No, Norman. No. Look at me Norman.'

Philips stared ahead.

'Norman. Look at me.'

Philips turned his head. Slowly. Frightened what he might see. Leonard had taken off his glasses. Those eyes. Philips hated those eyes. They were evil. He wanted to look away, but couldn't.

'That's what started it all, wasn't it, Norman. That was it.'

But Leonard had been too clever. He'd taken Norman Philips too far back and now the stage-door keeper was lost in the tragedy of something that had happened in another place at a time that didn't matter to Leonard. All that came from Philips was a softly and hopelessly whispered memory.

'Bitch.'

Later, Leonard would say to himself that he had no idea what came over him. He knew that it was rage. Rage against a murderer who had the coolness simply to sit there as if he were lost in a sonata. What happened next brought the custodian to the spy hole and Jack to the edge of fright. It brought Norman Philips back to life.

Leonard stomped his brown-booted feet in frustration and swung round, picked up the tubular chair by the legs and hurled it against the steel door. His hands opened slowly and reformed into a cold, bony necklet in front of the other man's face. Philips pushed himself tight into the corner and covered his head with his arms.

'He's mad. He's f-f-fucking mad. Get the bastard. G-g-g-et him.'

Leonard's hands moved closer to Philips's face.

'This how you did it, Philips? This how? Round her lovely neck? Then squeeze? That it?'

'Get him away. He's fucking m-m-mad I t-tell you. F-f-f-fucking mad.'

Leonard's voice rose to a vicious snarl.

'Did she scream, Philips? Wouldn't she shut up? You squeezed harder, Philips, so she couldn't scream. That it? Remember the sound, Philips? The coughing. Did she struggle, Philips? Can you feel her now, Philips? Feel her against you? From behind, was it, Philips? Behind? Behind so you couldn't see her face. Couldn't see her tongue. Her eyes. Feel her lovely bottom against you Philips? Could you? Is that how it was?'

Philips was shaking and sobbing. His head bobbing. Leonard pulled out the pictures Jack had been holding. Held the top one inches from Philips's face. He didn't need to see the naked breasts. Didn't need to see the rest. He knew. The harsh round cigarette burning away the nipple.

'Felt good did it, Philips? Felt good when you did this? Did it?'

'Yes, yes, yes. She's a bitch. A fucking bitch. They all are. She got it. She got it. She deserved it.'

Thirty-Five

It was late the next morning. Everyone had slept. Some for longer than others. Now they sat in Marsh's office. In front of him was a copy of Philips's statement. He'd been in the Griffon with a couple of the stage hands after the show. As usual, he'd drunk nothing but Diet Coke. When the pub closed, he'd dropped into a club to see a friend, but hadn't stayed long, and shortly after midnight he'd gone back to the theatre to pick up his anorak. He'd locked up and was just leaving when he saw Lynda Elström walking up from Kingsmead. He'd been surprised to see her because she was supposed to be missing. He'd asked her where she'd been. Lynda Elström had been friendly and kidded him not to be nosey. She said she'd been to see a friend and now she was looking for a cab. Philips had told Lynda Elström that there were too many bars in the area that needed bouncers for her to be walking about by herself at that time of night and he'd offered to call a cab on the theatre account from the stage-door phone. She'd agreed and they'd gone in. According to Philips's statement, the cab company had been engaged and they'd talked while they waited. He claimed she'd encouraged him and he'd put his arms about her. At first she seemed not to mind, then, he said, she'd struggled and the next thing she was choking and he didn't know what to do. He went outside to see if there was anyone to help. When he came back she was dead. Simple as that. No mysteries. Old-fashioned lust plus panic equals murder, let's go for manslaughter. Philips was charged with murder. They'd got their result.

Marsh's investigation wash-up was succinct. This had been quick. But this wasn't the end. The arrest in a case like this was often the easy part. Now came the long process of double-checking evidence. An arrest was one thing, Crown Prosecution was another – even with a confession. Even an ordinary barrister could easily get Philips to change his mind. All it took was a hint of police duress. And, there had been rumours of an interrogation which stepped outside the Chicksands police interrogation rules. Philips would appear in court that morning and Leonard, as the head of the investigation, would object to bail. Philips would be remanded in custody. All straighforward. But now, Marsh wanted box files of forensic and medical evidence. Then he wanted background statements that would show Philips as the only person who would have had the inclination, motive and opportunity to murder Lynda Elström.

Marsh looked about the room.

'I want more evidence than the CPS can shake a stick at.

This is going to be a big media trial. I don't want us slipping up. I don't want anyone accusing us of getting it wrong. This has go to be open and shut inside a week. Understood?'

They all nodded. There was no need for speeches. Lane was his usual relaxed self. His situation report had been as concise as ever. Shift changes. Evidence teams. Outstanding statements collated. The man from the press office looked a little nervous. Marsh did not like the press office. He didn't like the idea of his officers and his investigations being part of the image thing. But this was not any case. The tabloids had kept it running on their front pages since day one. This morning the arrest story was even mentioned in the *Financial Times*. Quick. Clean. Efficient. Some of the papers were running old pictures of Norman Philips. Action shots of the one-time speedway champion. He was being billed as the star on hard times. A sad, dangerous figure spurned by the sex-goddess. Then, there was Leonard. One of the tabloids had a fuzzy picture. The *Chronicle* would have a better one. Now he slouched in the corner chair. He'd hardly said a word since coming into the meeting. He was back in what Jack called his 'slump mode'. Legs straight out balancing on the heels of his dull-buffed brown boots. Hands deep in jacket pockets. Head on chest.

'You're not happy, James.'

Leonard scratched his not-too-well shaven chin on his tie. Off came the spectacles. Out came the handkerchief.

'No, sir.'

'Are we to be let into the spirit of your unhappiness or must we wait for our own inspiration?'

Leonard slipped his spectacles back on and brought Marsh into focus. For a while he said nothing. For a while Marsh waited. The white shirt, diamond white. The cuffs one inch from the dark-blue suiting. The silver links oval and flat and blank. The tie to suit the city's finest undertaker. The man from the Press Office clicked his ballpoint pen.

'Hey! You're not going to tell us that we've got the wrong guy?'

'James?'

Leonard blew a stream of air over his bottom lip. He began

to tick off his fingers and thumbs as he went through the list of questions he'd scrawled some time during the middle of the night.

'Rudi Sharpe. Accident or deliberate? And why didn't he want to live? Who sent her dirty messages? What happened to them? She told Curly Weekes that she knew things about people in the cast. Did she? If so, what? Did she really want to marry Weekes? Was it important? Curly said she hired a car. No hire company has her name. Also, Cassie Ross, or Cassie Makins as she calls herself, said Lynda couldn't drive. Lies or mistakes? And she says said she was in Cornwall. Was she? Ross says Lynda's memory was going. Important? Poulson says he'd hardly met her. But we think he had. Important? We don't know. We're told she asked this photographer fella, Ike, to do a special job. What was it? Don't know, Ike's disappeared. And we think she may have met Ike. It may have been him she met in Kingsmead. Blue BMW. We've checked out the registration. Could have been. And then we have Angela Billings saying Lynda was about to walk out. Why? That is, why was she going to walk out and why did Angela Billings bother to tell me? And the Williams man. Okay, I know he loves his mother, but why so screwed up? Then there's the briefcase. Empty and forced open. Clean or dirty? We don't know.'

He paused. Marsh blew his nose into a spotless white handkerchief. The noise would not have been out of place at Jericho.

'I see. I see. Is that it?'

Leonard waggled the heels of his boots.

'In Philips's statement he doesn't say why he hoisted her on the high fly, the wire.'

Marsh peered through half-frames at his copy of Philips's statement.

'He admits it here.'

'Yes, sir. But he doesn't say why.'

'Let me refresh your memory, James. "I just wanted to put her up there. Let everyone see her."'

'Yes, sir. But he doesn't say why.'

Marsh swivelled the charcoal-grey seat one way then the other. Looked into the middle distance.

'So, James, back to the earlier question. Have we got the wrong man?'

The man from the press office looked from one to the other. Leonard shook his head.

'That's not what I'm saying, sir. It's a bit like getting the answer to five across but not knowing how you've done it. Yes, I think we've got the right man, but I don't think we know why.'

The Major Incident Room at the Manvers Street police station was quiet for the first time in days. The reduced duty-list of officers was now in the business of collating, re-checking statements, movements and timings. Above all, timings. Legends were born in law courts where cast-iron cases were destroyed by gaps in police evidence. Just two minutes could be turned into an error of probability. Properly exploited that EOP would end up in the judge's summing-up and it was too often the factor that swung the jury towards the all important phrase 'reasonable doubt'. The team had been working on three groups of timings chalked by Leonard on the end board. First, he wanted the period in Norman Philips's statement when he said he'd met Lynda Elström and the time he'd strangled her. What had happened during that time? Then they had to pin down how long Philips had been out 'looking for help', as he claimed. The third point was the macabre moment when he had carried her body up to the stage and hoisted her aloft on the high fly wire. If he'd killed her at twelve thirty, say, why stay until two a.m.?

At about the time Leonard had been wondering aloud in Marsh's meeting, Jack had returned from Horfield Prison where Norman Philips was being held on remand. Leonard walked into the MIR as she was finishing her debrief.

'So, according to him, he was outside for about three minutes. No more. But he doesn't really know. He said he threw up. We've checked the pavements and gutters. We think we've six different vomit traces – remember we've got four clubs within fifty paces. So we're getting a DNA on them all. Shouldn't be difficult, that one. Time checks weren't too high on his list, which is not unreasonable, but doesn't help us. Anyway, that's all we've got. Then we come to the crazy bit. He says he couldn't leave her there. He says, and I quote, "she was all over the place. Untidy".'

A couple of officers sneered. Another snorted his disgust.

'The guy's loopy.'

Jack half smiled, she'd expected something like that.

'Exactly. But either is, or he's woken up to the barking game. I can smell a diminished responsibilities, while the balance of his mind was disturbed and so on coming here.'

Leonard coughed.

'May I?'

'Sir.'

'When we first saw him he talked about the place being neat and tidy or something. Check it. Character stuff. It goes either way in the state-of-mind argument. The CPS may need it. Sorry. Carry on.'

'Well, as I say, we now get to his public hanging.'

She nodded to a constable at the front desk. The Visev tape that now backed all audio recordings in interrogations lit the corner screen. The automatic lighting, focus and directional sound produced perfect recordings. But prisoners didn't always produce perfect answers. The screen showed Jack sitting across from a thin woman in startling green who was Philips's lawyer. Philips sat hunched beside her. Jack's voice was clear. Her questions short, as the training sessions insisted. Short questions were harder to answer because the prisoner didn't have so much time to think of an answer.

'How did you get Lynda to the stage?'

'Carried her.'

'How?'

'What's that flaming mean?'

'In your arms? Over your shoulder?'

'Oh . . . fireman's lift.'

'And you're sure she was dead?'

The thin voice of the thin lawyer cut in before Philips could answer.

'My client doesn't have to answer that.'

'Why?'

'My client is not qualified to give a medical opinion.'

For a full minute nothing was said. Then Philips looked up at Jack.

A whisper of admiration came from one of the older and bolder detective constables.

'Nice one, Jacko. Nice one.'

Make the prisoner look at you whenever possible, said the text book. Then go in with a friendly question.

'Were you frightened, Norman?'

The thin voice cut in.

'My client reserves his right not to be called by his name. That is regarded as coercion.'

Norman Philips carried on as if she weren't there.

'Yes.'

'What frightened you, Norman?'

'My client—'

'The place. You know? It's creepy. Don't like it anyway. Flaming creepy. Even in the daytime, with people about. Bits make you creep? You know?'

'I think so.'

'It's like that people are there. I mean, from before.'

'Ghosts?'

'You think I'm flaming potty, don't you?'

Jack's head shake was exaggerated. She wanted the camera to see it. There was no way she was going to fall into the defence trap of diminished and disturbed responsibilities.

'Certainly not. I don't think you're potty, as you call it. Did you know what you were doing?'

The thin head jerked forward. The flat, skinny palm went up in front of Norman Philips's face

'My client refuses to answer that question.'

'Did you Norman?'

'I repeat, my client refuses to answer.'

'Norman?'

The nod was brief. Hardly noticed. Jack understood that it would be. Came again.

'Norman? Did you know what you were doing?'

'I must object—'

'Course I did. She was dead. I'd killed her. What more d'you want?'

The thin woman stood. Pushed at the table with her hands flat on its dark surface. She turned to Jack and then at both cameras.

'This interview is now at an end. My client wishes to consult on his legal rights – in private.'

'Tell me, Norman, why did you hang her?'

'I repeat—'

'So everyone could see.'

'See what, Norman?'

'See what she was.'

It was all too much for his lawyer. She turned, bent close to his ear. The whispering was picked up by the digital system. But not the words. Whatever was said, the interview was at an end. For the moment it didn't matter. Maybe Philips had got something that he wanted. Madelaine Jack had got some of what she wanted.

She sat back, exhausted. The tension of watching the replay had been as great as the interrogation itself. The old and bold constable nodded.

'Class act, class act.'

Ten minutes later she was back in Leonard's tiny office at the front of the building. He was loading a pile of papers into a cardboard box. One week's routine form filling and reading. What happened to the information revolution? Paper-saving screens had simply created more people with authority to generate paper. He looked up as she came in. Didn't look at all guilty as he shoved the carton into the corner. It could wait until the new year. Even Easter.

'Anything else?'

She nodded. Slid a clear folder from her file.

'This. It arrived this morning. Our Mrs Potts thought it should go with his things, as she calls them. His birthday was day before yesterday.'

The Retained Property officer had spread open the card so it could be read as evidence without removing it from the folder. A bowl of flowers at a window ledge. In the distance, fields of poppies and blue hills beyond. Obvious and big. Leonard turned over the folder. The signature was firm, carefully written and in purple ink.

> *Happy birthday*
> *much love*
> *Lynda*
> *X*

Leonard peered at the envelope. Same handwriting. Posted the previous Saturday in Bath. He looked up, eyebrows raised and tapped the card with a finger.

'Why?'

'Friends?'

'As far as we know, they'd never met before coming here.'

'New friends?'

He remembered Jason Williams's thoughts on making friends. The theatre was that sort of place. Deep and cuddly friendships during the run. Good and bad companions.

'Could be. Could be. But this is the only card. Isn't it?'

'Yes, sir. But isn't that a sort of show-bizzy thing to do? The star sends flowers and cards to the jobbing cast?'

He didn't know.

'Suppose so. Luvvies loving each other to bits. What we do know is that she sent him a birthday card so someone must have told her it was his birthday. So why didn't that someone send a card?'

'Maybe he told her.'

'Important?'

'Well, sir, if she hadn't been murdered and he hadn't been knocked over it would only have been important to them. But as it is . . .'

'But it doesn't tell us anything.'

'And we've got a murderer.'

'Only one.'

'Sir?'

Leonard was scrabbling in his desk drawer. Empty. And the baker was too far away.

'Supposing we have two murderers?'

'Rudi Sharpe was deliberately run down?'

'Why not?'

'Because it would then be a complex conspiracy. Philips kills her in a moment of – of passion, say. Where Rudi Sharpe fits, that is beyond anything we've come across so far.'

'We've got more loose ends than we have evidence for a sure conviction.'

Jack flipped at her bottom lip making blopping noises. Thinking about it. Thinking how to put it.

'But the loose ends don't lead us to another murderer, sir. We've got one already. Even if the whole cast was lying and they're all brothers and sisters and Rudi Sharpe was the daddy of them all, and Curly was really Lynda's love child and Ike did porno pix of the Rostows and Mrs Williams is on the game, even if all that were true, sir, it doesn't alter the simple fact that Norman Philips is a sad character who panicked and killed.'

Leonard steepled his fingers beneath his chin and looked down at his desk. Where was that DC with the cuttings folder?

'And if they are lying? If this thing about hardly knowing her is crap? Then what?'

'All of them?'

He shook his head. He was stuck. He looked back at the card.

'I suppose she did send it. Not a forgery or something?'

Jack flipped back pages in her pocket book and dialled a number. 'Mr Ross, please.'

It took ages. It wasn't him. It was her.

'Mrs Ross? Sergeant Jack here. What colour ink did Lynda use? . . . Yes, it is . . . Thank you. Will you be staying in Bath for the next twenty four hours? . . . Thank you. We'll be in touch. Bye now.'

'And?'

'Well, sir, Lynda used purple ink. So at least we know

whoever sent this used the same colour ink, maybe even the same pen. Maybe it was Lynda.'

'You have doubts.'

'No, sir, actually no. But I was wondering if Mrs Ross knew why.'

Leonard looked down at his list. Sharpe. Weekes. The Rosses. Poulson. Ike. Billings. Williams. He pushed back his chair.

'Okay, we've got to start somewhere. May as well be her.'

It was another trudge in miserable Christmas weather up the hill towards the Rivers. But at least it took them by the gingerbread shop.

Thirty-Six

Leonard couldn't remember if he'd known that Cassie Makins smoked. A dull, stubby odourless cigarette in a long holder. Ross was in London, she said. But he'd be back. She was drinking hot water with lemon.

'Tell me, Mrs Ross, why would Lynda have sent Rudi Sharpe a birthday card?'

'Did she?'

Jack handed her the rice envelope. The card was clear enough to see the signature.

'Oh. How odd.'

'You recognize the signature?'

'Lynda's, of course.'

'You're sure?'

'Naturally. I own fifteen per cent of everything she's ever signed. You bet I do.'

'It couldn't be a forgery?'

Cassie Makins peered closely. Then held the card at a distance.

'If it is, it's very good.'

She handed Jack the envelope without looking at her. Leonard was not done.

'Give me some ideas.'

'About what?'

'Why she would have sent it.'

Cassie Makins's mouth twisted. She seemed to sneer more easily than she smiled.

'Maybe she felt sorry for him.'

'Why so?'

'Sad man with a bottle. They do say.'

'She was a reformer?'

'A soft touch.'

'Think of something else.'

'The newspapers say you've arrested that doorkeeper.'

'Right.'

'Then why the questions? She's dead. You've got your man.'

'How well did she know Rudi Sharpe?'

'Search me. Ask the cast. They ran with them.'

'You're sure they'd never met?'

'Not until this gig.'

'If you don't know how well she knew him, how can you be sure they'd never met?'

'Pardon me?'

Leonard sighed. Ignored it.

'Tell me about Jason Williams. How long have you managed him?'

The eyes flickered.

'Ten years.'

'Why?'

'Because that's how long.'

'No. Why do you manage him? He must have had someone before you.'

'He was being ripped off by his label. It went to law and, surprise, surprise, he won. After that came the mega re-think. He wanted to be something else. Wasn't sure what that else should be. We've got a lot of those people. Big stars, big names, but no longer doing much. We both make a living out of it.

'Okay. Try again. Why you?'

The pause was long and she kept it going while she lit

another cigarette, then took her time twisting into the scarlet holder.

'The connection.'

'Please.'

'Lynda. I remember now. It was her suggestion.'

'To you or to him?'

'To him.'

'They knew each other?'

'It's obvious.'

'Not to me, Mrs Ross.'

'Okay. They'd been paired a couple of times. You know?'

He shook his head.

'Showcasing, premiers, awards. That type of thing. Best be with someone, especially when there wasn't an item. Good for their images. She got a family image out of it. He got the sex thing.'

'But no touching.'

'Shit, no. No touching. Look, Inspector, is this really important?'

'Yes. Oh yes, it is. You see, Mr Williams told us he'd never met Lynda.'

'Dickhead.'

'Mm. I imagine he might be.'

Leonard rose. The nod was near a bow.

'Thank you Mrs Ross. I'd be pleased if—'

He paused. Her blank eyes were on him.

'Tell me, Mrs Ross, did you know that Lynda planned to marry Curly Weekes?'

'Crap.'

'He says so.'

'Crap.'

'He says they loved each other.'

'More crap. Lynda loved Lynda. That was that. So the kid's talking—'

'Crap?'

'At the very least, Inspector, at the very least.'

He turned back to the door, speaking to the solid panels as he left.

'I'd be pleased if you'd make yourself available for a statement some time this evening.'

'Why?'

But Leonard had gone. Jack smiled her best smile.

'Just a formality, Mrs Ross. I'll call you later.'

The taxi was steamed up. The driver had one eye on the rear mirror but not for the traffic. Leonard and Jack said nothing until they stopped outside the theatre. It would have been quicker to walk. But the rain was now heavy. People hunched, shop doorways were crowded, paper bags sodden and umbrellas clashed. Leonard and Jack stood beneath the theatre's canopy before going in.

'She may be right, sir.'

'Why would she have encouraged the kid? Wouldn't be sex. He doesn't.'

'She was pretty quick about it, sir. Stamped on the idea. And the voice – I'd hate to be her dentist.'

'What you make of the Williams thing?'

'She called him a dickhead, sir. Wouldn't mind betting he'll have an explanation by now. Bet she's called him.'

'Hope so. He'd never have told us.'

'Why did she?'

'Maybe she guessed we'd find out. Maybe it wasn't important.'

'Like the birthday card? Maybe it isn't, sir. After all, we're there.'

He shook his head and smeared a discarded cigarette butt across the pavement.

'Philips killed her for his own crude reasons. But I can already hear his counsel stripping her down into something else. He'll probably get off with compensation at this rate.'

'And la Ross?'

'That's what I'm saying. There's a Lynda sub-plot. She's part of it. They're all part of it.'

He squinted at her from the corner of his eye.

'Paranoid enough for you?'

'It'll do for now, sir. So no Jason-baby for the moment. Who then? Short and Curly?'

He nodded and pushed the glass-panelled door for her.

Thirty-Seven

The barely visible netting was dressed. The so-real inglenook with its black range and backlit fire, it's copper pots and giant-size pans held centre stage. The besom propped against the wall. The dresser with its blue and white spotted plates which would never go through the smashing routine perfected by the grande dame of dames. The rocking chair cushion would whoopee for another Rudi, but it would never be the same. All was set for the Boxing Day opening and the mega surprise of all – the new Cinders.

Joanna Cunliffe and Maurice Poulson had worked hard. They'd got their Cinders but they were playing the secrecy game for every penny's worth of publicity. No one would know until she stepped on stage. That was the plan. Every national newspaper, every television show was playing the same ghoulish game. Thousands had been offered to find the name. Big stars had been called to see if they were at home. Some had played it for themselves. Coy, ambiguous remarks. It could be any of them. Hotels had been staked out by journalists who knew it would be the scoop and bonus of the year to be the first to find the new Cinderella. Never before had a panto had television cameras set up ready for the big moment. The grandest entrance of them all. Even the cast had been kept out of it. For the past twenty-four hours, Poulson had rehearsed the new Cinderella without the rest of the company. The first night might turn out to be a farce or a gas. Whichever way, this theatre would be biggest panto news in Britain. They were already booked out, booked to extend. If they'd wanted to, they could have played Cinders until Easter. Joanna Cunliffe had been right. The anoraks had booked for every night.

Curly sat, as he'd sat before, back against the plush siding. Knees up to his chin. Dressed, as he'd been dressed before. The sheepskin jacket, brilliantly white soap-ad T-shirt, 501s and Pumas. Standard cute uniform for the extremely cute. All was as before, except this time there was no dark vision in the carpet. Now his face was open, his eyes bright. Curly Weekes wanted to talk but didn't know what to say. No problem – Leonard was there to help.

'You said Miss Elström drove you up to the race course.'

'She wanted to talk. We both did. Right?'

Leonard stared hard into those bright brown eyes.

'No, not right at all, sir.'

Curly looked back. People didn't call him sir. No one called anyone sir anymore, everyone was first names. Even if you didn't know them. Had been all his remembering life. Not for this guy. He was somewhere else. Leonard's voice was as soft as Curly's eyes. Deep down, just as shifty.

'Tell me, sir, you're sure about this ride?'

Curly nodded.

'And Miss Elström picked you up as you told us?'

'Right. It was dark.'

'You see sir, we have reason to believe that Miss Elström hadn't learned to drive. And I should tell you, sir, that we know she didn't have a driving permit, didn't own a car and didn't hire one in the city.'

Curly shrugged Leonard away.

'Not important. Not now, is it?'

'Need to know her movements that day.'

'But you've got the guy.'

'Still need to know.'

'But this isn't nothing to do with it. I mean, well, nothing to do with it. I mean, I mean he wasn't there or nothing, was he?'

'Someone was.'

'Who says?'

'You drive?'

'No.'

'Miss Elström didn't. Somebody must have. Unless you're not telling us the truth, sir.'

186

Madelaine Jack winced. It was the sort of remark that ended up in court. Litigation had become a joke – until the pink complaint form arrived. Curly Weekes was in the shadow of the half-lit stalls. He rubbed furiously at his eyes and the gold signet ring, heavy and obvious against his black face, moved back and forth like some crafted firefly. He looked up to where Leonard was leaning against the back of one of the stalls. Then to Jack. 'Someone was with us.'

'In the car?'

'Right.'

'Who?'

'Can't say.'

'Why?'

'Confidential.'

'Murder does not keep confidences Mr Weekes – unless of course you happen to be the one that's dead.'

The teenager's eyes showed little. Where was the pain of the confessed love? The agonies of that last moment? Leonard removed his spectacles and rubbed gently at their perfectly clean lenses with a mustard silk handkerchief.

'Tell me, Mr Weekes, do you know much about murder? Mm?'

Curly Weekes knew about being the darling of Saturday kids television, nothing else.

'Well, sir, it's all about facts. Fact one: Miss Elström was killed. Fact two: Norman Philips has said he killed her. Fact three: we don't know Miss Elström's whereabouts before she was murdered. Fact four: you say you do – or at least partly. Fact five: fact four makes you a preliminary witness to facts one, two and three.'

Madelaine Jack did not blink. Facts one to four were fine. Where on earth had he got fact five? Curly Weekes did not see it that way. Leonard did not hurry him. There was no need.

'I had nothing to—'

'To do with it, sir?'

'Right.'

'Then I think we need to know what that car drive was all about. Who was the driver?'

Again the pause. Again the need to talk and the need to keep silence.

'She called me. Said something was singing. Said someone was going to help. Said she was meeting someone. Said she needed me there in case of something.'

'What something?'

'She was just nervous. She trusted me. I told you. Told me where to be and then when they turned up I just got in the front. She was in the little bit at the back.'

'So she wasn't driving.'

'Like you said. She didn't.'

'Did you know the driver?'

'Not then.'

'Who was it?'

'Guy called Ike. He's a stills man.'

Leonard looked at the ornate ceiling.

'His car?'

'Right.'

'A blue one?'

'BMW.'

'Go on.'

'Lynda had this envelope thing? And she said he knew what to do with it. Okay?'

'What was in it?'

'She didn't tell me.'

'You ask her?'

'Right. But she said it was safer if I didn't know.'

'Safer?'

'For me. That's when she said she had this black on someone in the theatre. Ike said it was dangerous and he didn't want anything to do with it.'

'So he knew what was in the envelope.'

'Not everything. He knew what it was but he didn't.'

Leonard thought about it.

'Would you like to explain that for us?'

'Well, it's like knowing that something's a letter but not reading it so you don't know what it says. Okay?'

'So it was a letter?'

'I don't know.'

'How big was the envelope?'

Curly Weekes measured with his hands in an oblong.

'She had it in this bag thing. Brown.'

'Overnight bag? Paper sack? Briefcase?'

'Right.'

'Which?'

'Executive thing. Briefcase.'

'What happened to it?'

He had to think that through.

'Not sure. I think she took it.'

'Tell me, Mr Weekes, anything special about the case?'

Another shake of the head.

'Nothing. It wasn't up to much.'

'Plastic?'

'No deal. Class job, leather. But the locks was hacked.'

'It was hers?'

'Never seen it before.'

Leonard turned over his shoulder to Jack.

'Ask someone to show the case to Philips. See if he recognizes it.'

Jack moved further down the side aisle, speed-dialling her mobile as she went. Leonard returned to Curly Weekes.

'I still don't see why you had to go up to the race course.'

'They were following her.'

'They?'

'Somebody.'

'Who said?'

'She did.'

'How did she know?'

Curly Weekes looked blank. Whatever Lynda Elström had ever said had been okay by him.

'She said we had to get somewhere where no one could see us.'

'In a blue BMW soft top.'

'But they couldn't see inside.'

Leonard paused and stared at Weekes for some seconds. He tried to imagine him as the innocent Buttons, but Perrault's fantasy seemed far removed from this Christmas tragedy.

'Tell me, sir, did she ever say anything about not being able to remember things?'

Now he sat up.

'Who told you that?'

'We understand she was having treatment.'

'You got it wrong. That Cassie wanted her to see some shrink. They thought she didn't know, but she did.'

'Was she having problems?'

The shrug was a street trader's before the final pitch. Full of authority, full of confidence.

'That's why she trusted me. That's why she needed me. We all need someone, you know.'

'Was she frightened?'

'She got mad sometimes. Mad about it. Not me. Then she'd cry.'

'Who else knew about it?'

'Just me and her agent.'

'Nobody in the theatre.'

'No. It weren't that ghoul, you know. Just small things. But she was going to quit anyway.'

'The show?'

'No. Everything.'

'Because of this, I suppose.'

'No, because of everything. She'd had enough. Made plenty. Wanted away. Said we'd go somewhere real bendy, Seychelles? Something like that. Do nothing, maybe write a book about it all.'

'Memoirs?'

'Right. That's when she told me she had this stuff on a lot of them. Not just here. Knew them all, see, knew what they did.'

'And she was going to say so?'

'Right.'

'Where'd she get this – this "stuff"?'

'She just got it. She was well smart, you see.'

Smart enough to get murdered. Curly Weekes let out a long,

low sigh. The eyes were sad again. He didn't really know, he was on his own again.

Thirty-Eight

The coffee was no better. Simone was nervous. She fiddled. Grating and grinding the cup into the saucer.

'He said he'd call and he will, when it's safe.'

'Safe from what?'

'You're the policeman.'

'But I can't know what's frightening him until I talk to him. Where is he?'

She'd washed green gel into her red hair. Leonard thought she looked like a high-class Italian soccer fan. She was nice.

'Ike'll surface when there's air. You'll have to wait.'

'Tell me why he went.'

'I told you.'

'Tell me again.'

'Soon as she was dead. He said it was too dangerous. He said it could be him next.'

'Try and remember the exact words.'

'Well if you really want to know . . .'

'I really want to know.'

'Okay. He said, "Fuck me, this is fly time. I'm out. I'll call."'

'And that was it?'

'Yes. Oh, he kissed me goodbye. But it could have been his arse for all he knew. I tell you, Ike was rolled over.'

'And you've no idea where he went?'

'I said.'

'But you wouldn't necessarily tell me.'

'Right.'

'Maybe he doesn't know he's safe now.'

'Maybe you don't know he is.'

Leonard leaned back in the wooden chair. Rocked against the wall. Did she know more? Did he?

'You think there's someone else?'

'I think it doesn't make sense. So do you or you wouldn't be asking questions still. Why bother? You got old Norman. Okay, the poor bastard may, just may have lost it and put his hands on her.'

'May have?'

'Okay, probably did. Shit, the sad sod spent most of his time dreaming about his hands on something instead of himself.'

'You know that?'

'Come on, Inspector. Give some age. Women know. The weak silent type. Couldn't keep his eyes off her. If she went closer than a metre he had to sit down. And she knew it. But you know as well as I do that this thing Ike's into has nothing to do with Norman. This is something different. Spooky, okay?'

That was what bothered Leonard.

Blackboard one showed that Philips had murdered Lynda Elström.

Blackboard two showed Lynda Elström had been tied into something involving Rudi Sharpe who was now dead and Ike, who'd had a fling with Lynda, had got into something so deep that he feared for his life.

Then there appeared an envelope of information so valuable that someone had tried to steal it by levering off the locks. Leonard stopped. Then why hadn't they succeeded? Somewhere in the back of his mind fingers clicked. Of course! How stupid. Someone had succeeded. But that raised another question. And the answer to that question would tell him why Ike believed the murdering wasn't over. Equally, if Simone were right and there was no connection between Blackboard One and Two, then Ike was right.

Leonard was tired and far away. He heard the greeting before he realized it was real. The figure was real enough. Soft and comfortable, someone had said. Cuddly, someone else said. A cuddly rainbow of soft greens and mauves. And the omnipresent notebook.

'What ho, m'lud.'

He helped himself to coffee. Leonard raised his hand. Tiggy

Jones lowered himself gently on to the nearest chair. He made it look ridiculously small. The atmosphere was thoughtful as a group hangover. Leonard swilled what was left of his coffee. Didn't anyone serve undoctored grains?

'Tell me, Mr Jones, who was sending those sordid notes to Lynda Elström?'

'Was anyone?'

'She told Jason Williams so. And Curly.'

'And you've seen them?'

Leonard hadn't. He'd wondered about that. Jack's hypothesis was that she destroyed them. Nasty spiders.

'Unless a third party is involved, a victim often gets rid of them until we get involved.'

The roly-poly stage manager smiled, indulgently.

'Not Norman. Forget it – not his style.'

'You're certain?'

'I've known him since he came here. Good man. Sad maybe, but then so was the Moor.'

'Who was not a good man. What about the obscene phone calls? Nothing true in that?'

'Who said obscene?'

'She said.'

'To you? Okay, m'lud. You are the wise detective. I am but poor Esdras and you are free to scorn my visions, but here lies my thought for today.'

He opened his open notebook in front of him on the table.

'You interested in telephone calls?'

'We have a printout.'

Tiggy Jones shook his head.

'No you don't. You have calls on the cube system that runs from the main switchboard. They're only itemized over sixty seconds. Don't be surprised. I know these things. And, what you don't have is the old phone board. It's hardly used. Remember the old BT Senator system?'

Leonard nodded. It didn't seem that long ago. In an age of communications, even five years was long ago.

'Okay. When we went to optic fibre, we kept the old board

as back up. We couldn't afford to lose lines. Most bookings come that way. It still works, but you can't run smart phones through it. Still with me?'

Another nod. Jones turned three pages of figures.

'I take the read every week. Maybe twenty or thirty calls out. Its memory holds the last fifty.'

He tapped the notebook.

'All here. Now, if I wanted to make a very private call, I'd do it from a payphone, okay? But in this place, the only pay phone is in a very public place. Has to be. It's for the public. So, if, I repeateth, *if* I knew about it, I'd use the old back-up. Why? Hardly anyone knows the telephones exist. They're down below and in two store rooms.'

Simone put fresh coffee in front of him. She nodded towards the bar.

'And there's one behind there, in the cool room.'

'Used by?'

'Hardly anyone. It's only there in case anyone was daft enough to get shut in.'

Leonard was falling behind. He shifted in his chair.

'Okay, Mr Jones, I'm ready for the arithmetic.'

'On the main board you've hardly any calls to Lynda's apartment. Probably most of them are on the zero one line, which is Joanna's. But on this one –'

Again he tapped his notebook.

'– there are twenty-one calls. The first three are more than a minute each. The next four, each no more than forty seconds. The rest, that is the majority, no more than ten seconds. They're all to Lynda's apartment. Which, m'lud, suggests what?'

'That if they *were* obscene calls, then she soon recognized what they would be and put down the phone.'

'And probably recognized the voice immediately.'

'And therefore it was possibly the same voice.'

'So you *are* a detective.'

Leonard wondered and did the arithmetic again.

'So I am. So I am. But I'm not certain that it tells us anything more, unless you've got times of the calls.'

'A hundred years ago, the great Marshall Hall would hitch his gown, tilt his wig revealing his ginger curls and cry—'

'Norman Birkett.'

'What?'

'It was Birkett who was ginger, not Hall.'

'Then, my dear, the blessed Norman would cry, "If it pleases m'lud, I will call my star witness." Okay?'

'It'll do.'

Jones turned two pages of his book and pushed it across to Leonard.

'The initials against those blocks of times are staff. NP is Norman, MP, Maurice et cetera. Okay? What you have there is the names of people who were in the theatre at the times of those calls.'

'So what?'

'Mostly, Norman Philips was not in the theatre when they were made.'

'So he made them from outside the theatre.'

'Fine. But it still doesn't exclude the fact that someone was calling her from here. And if we go along with the idea that she recognized the voice and that's why she put down the phone, then we can guess it was the same person. It was certainly the same phone.'

'Which is where?'

'I don't know. That's why it is an intrigue.'

'The extensions are logged on here?'

'No, the chip in the machine itself logs the call. I'm saying that somewhere, someone had a handset which he—'

'—or she—'

'—or she plugged in to make the calls and then unplugged.'

'You forget that Philips has confessed.'

Tiggy Jones tugged the wide collar of his purple silk shirt closer to his chin and puffed a dismissal.

'In his present state he would confess to the Crucifixion if you asked him the right question.'

'His door code.'

'And no one else knew it?'

'Did they?'

'I certainly did. I'm sure I'm not the only one.'

Leonard groaned. He could picture defence counsel with that information once Norman Philips decided to change his plea to not guilty and cite dubious interrogation methods. It was almost as if he had to start again. He was convinced Philips had murdered Lynda Elström. The case was that simple. It was beginning to be complicated by side-bars. But Leonard wasn't going to take his eye off the ball. Philips was guilty and he'd said so. But Marsh still needed the basket of evidence that fed the appetite of the CPS.

'Tell me, Mr Jones, if you're so certain about his innocence, then who did kill her?'

Tiggy Jones pulled his notebook back across the table.

'You forget, Inspector, I'm the one with foresight. You're the one with insight.'

He tore four pages from his notebook. Passed them over to Leonard.

'But for what it's worth, I should start here.'

Thirty-Nine

Leonard was munching a gingerbread man. Madelaine Jack was looking at the pages of the stage manager's notebook. She'd been through the lists six times making notes as she went along. She finished and dropped her pencil on the table in front of her. The point snapped. He handed her a fresh one from the Marmite jar he'd kept for most of his plain clothes career. She ticked the last number and looked up. He was watching her with those green eyes that she sometimes thought were hazel, depending on his mood. She'd miss those moods when she went and she supposed that wouldn't be long now. She knew she had to move on – that was what career were about. Headquarters would be different. The dream academy at Portis-head was a place to be noticed. She wondered again, as she'd wondered so many times, if that was what she wanted? Had to be, otherwise why was she doing it? He was waiting.

'Sorry, sir. Miles away.'

'Nice place?'

She looked at him for cynicism. There was none.

'I'm not sure, sir. I'm not sure. Anyway, about these times. They add up to not much more than a big so what? Or have I missed something?'

'Maybe not.'

'Let's accept the Jones version. He suggests that Philips didn't make grubby calls nor send letters.'

'The letters that no one has seen.'

'In the envelope? Obvious place, sir. The one she was going to give to Angela Billings.'

He thought about it. But why give them to Ike or anyone else, for that matter? A big envelope. Briefcase size. Briefcase.

'What did Philips say about the case?'

She closed her eyes. She'd made the call. She'd asked when she'd got back. She'd been told no one had had time to go over there. She'd said not to worry, she'd do it herself when she went to the remand prison. She'd forgotten.

'I'm sorry, sir. It's slipped my mind. I'll make sure. Today.'

'That would be good.'

God, she could do without his moods. She hurried on.

'Right sir. Obscene calls?'

He nodded.

'Different issues, sir. Obscene calls from someone else. Does it matter who?'

Leonard leaned back and hooked his thumbs in his waistcoat armholes.

'Philips's lawyer could easily say that whoever was sending the letters and making the calls was far more likely to have murdered her. Then if we can't pin it on Philips, they come in with the change of plea. Murder by person or persons unknown plus a wrongful arrest claim is all we're left with.'

'Why d'you think Jones is making such a fuss about Philips?'

'Jones is a notebook man. Meticulous. Records every detail. Everything has its place.'

'Including murder.'

'Including murder.'

'Well, according to him, the touring company would be unlikely to know about the telephones. And so if we believe his numbers and initials, then the only constants in the list are JC and MP.'

Leonard got up and took his jacket from the back of the chair. He looked out of the window. Gloomy and glum and still raining. He wanted to go home.

'Okay then, Cunliffe or Poulson. Who first?'

Joanna Cunliffe was in the stage-door office laying down daily orders to a bleary assistant stage-door keeper full of powders, potions and an angry cold sore on her upper lip. The administrator was keeping her distance.

'No one in without an appointment. All calls unless they're for me or front-of-house to be recorded and rung back. Nothing put through at all. Savvy? Nothing at all.'

She looked across to Leonard and Jack.

'Won't be a minute.'

She wagged a finger at the girl.

'And another thing. No parcels accepted. Any doubts whatsoever, call me. Okay?'

The girl nodded, croaked and sneezed. Joanna Cunliffe waved a hand in front of her face. Her exasperated schoolma'am expression stayed in place.

'And use a tissue.'

She turned towards the electronic door which clicked as she reached it and they followed her down the stairs, along cream-bricked underground corridors and the temporary office she was sharing with too many filing cabinets and a recalcitrant laptop computer. She fiddled with the coffee machine. The plug spat and the stainless steel reservoir glugged to no great effect.

'Shitty thing. We've got a twelve-thousand-a-day production coming through and I can't afford a filter that works. Still, that's my problem. What's yours? How's Norman?'

'Sticking to his story.'

'Off his head.'

'He may try to say so.'

'Why not? He is. Sad sod. Good at his job. But too lonely for his own good.'

'He had pictures of Lynda all over his bedroom wall.'

'Twenty-five years ago so did half the spotty males in the country.'

'But they didn't line up to strangle her.'

She swung in her red leather chair and scratched at her thigh top.

'Okay. What can I do for you both?'

'How often did you telephone Lynda at her flat?'

She frowned. Not trying to remember, but not sure of the question.

'Hardly ever. Why?'

'Someone did.'

'Big deal. Not me, José.'

'Why would you have called her?'

'Maybe something to do with phones, lease, that sort of thing. Everything else would go through her agent or Morry.'

'Which telephone would you have used?'

She nodded to the slim black pack-phone with its winking red power light.

'Why?'

'Lynda was getting a lot of calls on the old BT system. We think they were pest-calls.'

'So she claimed.'

'You don't think she was?'

Joanna Cunliffe shook her head.

'Not any more. She probably got a lot at one time. But, well, let's say that she was wearing well but wearing out. Besides, unless she gave out her number, only me, Morry and her agent had the number. It's unlisted and all calls would be on an intercept unless she gave the thro' prefix.'

'Which you, for example, would know to dial before the regular number to get straight through.'

'Right.'

Leonard's head was on his chest. He buzzed. That seemed to

leave only three options for phone calls. Jack picked up his thought.

'On the intercept system, does the operator call every time someone tries to get through?'

'Can do. But Lynda had a collect bank on her number. No calls ever went through to her. She rang the bank every time she wanted to hear the numbers and selected those she wanted to call back. Bit like an answer service without being able to leave messages. The bank has a code, so all she did was dial the code. That way the caller couldn't back trace her number. I had another code and all I did was prefix her home number with that code and I'd get through. It even had a different ring sequence so she'd know it was a friendly call.'

'It seems very elaborate.'

'Being a star is.'

'What about the calls that went straight through? Would Miss Elström have known who had that prefix?'

''Course. She would have chosen the number herself.'

'So every time the phone rang, Miss Elström would have known it was one of three people.'

'Ye – es. Unless of course she'd given it to someone else without telling us.'

'Curly Weekes called her.'

'Then she must have given him the prefix, or someone did. But he's hardly a heavy breather. I mean, the thing about breathers is that you don't know who they are.'

'He or she?'

Joanna Cunliffe scratched at her head with a pencil and said nothing.

On the main stage, the Rostows were going through their routine. No one else. Just the two in baggy trousers and tops. No custard pies. They'd save that for the final dress rehearsal the next day. Leonard imagined the line. What did you do on Christmas Eve? I threw custard pies at my sister. What did you do, Inspector? I wondered who had killed Cinderella. But surely you know that. No harm in wondering.

'Sir?'

He came back.

'Sorry. My turn.'

'Nice place?'

He huffed a great sigh.

'No. I'm afraid not.'

'I was wondering—'

'What are you doing for Christmas?'

She looked surprised. Wished she hadn't. He was immediately embarrassed. He didn't ask questions like that. Never.

'Well, sir, I'm, uh, well, I suppose unless we get this cleared, then it's mince pies in the canteen.'

The head was down again. Studying the strong contract carpet. Above them on the stage, the two women were slapping hands, buttocks and knees. The whole thing was bizarre. He scuffed the carpet, but got no inspiration as he had when a kid. The carpet, like most things in Leonard's life, was worn flat. The Rostows stopped. One of them looked down at the script lying on the floor. One more time. This time faster, slicker, funnier. Hand slap. Spin. Spin. Buttock slap. Spin. Knee slap. Cross knee shuffle. Hand. Buttock. High hands and *bump*! The final clash of bums. Pause. Then turn front. Pause. Coy looks and bows. Even the ad libbing was scripted. The spontaneous applause anticipated.

Leonard clapped. He really had enjoyed it. He'd never seen it before. Never been to a panto. Always imagined that he had. But hadn't. The twins gave him a special bow. He wondered why women always bowed to the audience. Why did they never curtsey? He would ask someone.

The twins were sitting, legs dangling over the footlights and fanning themselves with script pages.

'Hot work if you can get it.'

Unison gags. Unison nudges, winks and nods. He wondered if they liked each other. Or did they simply love each other and leave it at that? The twins weren't really funny. They just did it for a living and he knew he was no different. He didn't even like what he did for a living. Suddenly, his childish enjoyment had gone and the black dog bit. Bit deeply. To hack this case, he had to penetrate the code of this theatre. Leonard's mood had changed and now he felt cheap anger.

'Which one of you met her that night?'

Blank stares. Then heads turning to each other. Mock horror.

'Met who?'

'Which night?'

The lines could have been scripted.

'Don't give me shit.'

'Naughty –'

'– policeman.'

'I said no shit. Which one of you met her?'

'Me?'

'After you, darling. But save some for me. I just love his freckles.'

Two-and-a-half-second bursts of laughter. Then a big breath for Rosie.

'Let us remind your notebook that I was in my beddy-byes with a temperature of 102. My dearest and only nearest gave her Nightingale. That is of Crimea not Berkeley Square.'

'One of you was seen outside this theatre shortly after midnight.'

Madelaine Jack turned away. Where was he going?

'Then my chummy little freckly cherubim, or even sweety seraphim, take your pick I'm sure. It must have been a dream. We must have been sleepwalking. We must all be in vunderlander, darlink. My little heart throbbed not for you but for my darling blister who gently perspired.'

'Sir?'

Leonard turned. Jack was looking to the back of the stalls. On the raised balcony Simone Simons stood with half-raised hand, the other twisting at her T-shirt. Leonard turned back to the twins. He knew something. If only he knew what it was.

'I'll be back in a moment.'

'Can't—'

'Wait.'

Leonard turned and tried to walk with some dignity. He didn't know how to do that, nor why he should be trying. The policeman in him said that he'd touched something. The realist told him that he hadn't a clue what it was. Somewhere inside he knew he hated them.

Forty

The thin young man sat hunched over the corner table beneath the low brick vaulted ceiling. He stroked the wisp of dark soft whisker that hung from his bottom lip pausing only to drag on a crude twist of cannabis. Simone said something none listened to as the two men sized each other up. Simone laid a protective arm across his, Ike's, thin shoulders.

'This is Inspector Leonard and – I'm sorry, I've forgotten your name.'

'Madelaine Jack. Sergeant Jack.'

Ike looked not at her, but into her. A long way in. She knew what Lynda Elström had known.

Simone smiled. Not very strongly. As if for something to do, she went over to the coffee machine, but didn't pour. She was in attendance. Leonard sat opposite Ike. Jack sat at the next table out of his line of sight. His dark eyes behind even darker lashes followed her. She looked obediently at Leonard's profile.

'Where do we start?'

Ike looked at Leonard and sipped from a blue beaker.

'Would you care for some water? It is very good.'

The voice was soft. Irish. Southern Irish. Cobb would have known where. Leonard waved his hand. He could do without the meaningful stuff.

'Simone says Lynda Elström hired you to do a special job. What?'

Ike slowly wagged a finger. The Musketeer sleeve of his white lawn shirt brushed the table.

'Slowly, Inspector. Slowly. First we ask. Then we explain. Maybe. Where's Norman?'

'Prison. Why?'

'You're sure he's your man?'

'Yes. Why?'

'You're sure there's no one else?'

'Why?'

'So many whys, Inspector. So many.'

'You're scared?'

Ike nodded. Slowly.

'Oh yes, very.'

'Why?'

'There you go again.'

Leonard removed his spectacles, laid them on the table and stared at the blurred figure before him. The Irishman stared back, then looked away. Not nice eyes.

'Tell me, Ike, why you here?'

'She said you wanted to talk.'

'She said you'd come when you were ready.'

Ike turned and smiled at Madelaine Jack. Nice eyes. Leonard brought him back.

'I could take you in. Protective custody.'

'I'd like that.'

'Why should I?'

Ike gave a short laugh. The funnel had burned down and Simone leaned over with a saucer. The days of ashtrays were long gone.

'Because I know things.'

'I need what you know.'

'Others already know it.'

'My others or your others?'

'Others here.'

'Danger?'

'Very.'

Ike put his hand on Simone's shoulder. He would always be a bastard. She knew that. He needed her. That was all she wanted.

'You see, Mr Leonard, she trusted me.'

'There was a lot of it about.'

'No. That was it, there wasn't. Just three people. We had something going for a little while, you see.'

He stroked Simone's back. It was all right. All gone now. Not to worry.

'And she needed my help.'

The pause was for another sip from the blue beaker.

'For what?'

'I'm a photographer.'

He waved his free arm about the restaurant. Huge grainy monochromes. The stars. The scenes. The magic. An intimate exhibition of a moment framed in the now-dark proscenium just footsteps away.

'She wanted more pictures? Of herself?'

Again the slow side-to-side movement. The hair long, black and touchable.

'She had all the pictures in the world, very special pictures.'

'Of herself? Your pictures?'

'Oh no. Wrong side of the lens.'

'This is a silly game. You mean she had pictures of other people. Now I get it. The envelope in the car. The briefcase.'

'Curly?'

'He said you were there.'

'A child.'

'She trusted him.'

'Her teddy.'

Leonard hadn't thought of it. Jack understood.

'Tell me, Ike, tell me about the pictures.'

'Easy, boss, easy. First I've got to know how much you know.'

'Nothing. Philip Norman killed Lynda. That's it, except Curly and Jason Williams both claim she was getting nasty mail and phone calls.'

'Williams said that, did he? Well, he should know.'

'His calls?'

'She said so.'

'Why?'

'She had something. He wanted it. She believed he was sending the mail. Threatening to have her wasted unless she destroyed everything.'

'She say anything about looking at his mail?'

Ike nodded his head.

'I heard. Everyone heard. She told me that she, uh, she – how do we say this? She, uh, she sent him some proof in the post. Then she tried to get it back.'

'Why would she send it in the post?'

Another shake of the head.

'Why would that screwball do anything? She had the eyes. You know? The mad ones.'

'What did she have?'

Ike whistled through his teeth, taking his time.

'Okay boss, here we go. Lynda calls me and says we should meet. We do. Easy, like. Very public. You know the coffee place in the RPS?'

Leonard nodded. He bought his postcards there.

'So where better? Great pix. Great pix.'

'Save the commercial. Go on.'

'You're real pushy, you know that?'

'It's a real murder, Ike. You know that?'

'Okay then. We meet. She says she's got some negs. Hot negs.'

'Pornography?'

'That's what I'm thinking. I can handle that. But it's not. Okay, it's porn, but real.'

Another pause. Another sip. Simone was lighting another joint for him. Puffed then handed it over. Leonard wished that he were home. Jack knew that but kept her eyes on Ike. Through thick smoke he blinked slowly and began once more.

'She's got one, just one, in a folder. I get the peep. It's too real. Too real. You follow me?'

Leonard was nearly there.

'Go on.'

'She says she has a lot more. She wants copies made because she wants them put somewhere safe. You know? Maybe one set in the bank?'

Leonard was starting to catch up. He remembered what Angela Billings had told him.

'Tell me, what were the pictures?'

'Stay there, Inspector, stay there. Let me do this, okay?'

Ike turned to Jack, a small, very silly smile on his face. Jack felt nothing.

'Okay then. She says can I do this for her. It has to be very quiet. No one must know. I say maybe. Course I can. Easy. Do it all the time. Scan then straight on to the Mac. Negs then prints. Better quality than the originals. Colour them. Crop them. Move heads on to other bodies. Reverse. Spin. Anything. I don't tell her that, of course. I say it could take time. I then ask her what's in the rest. She won't say. Then I ask why she's doing this. She says pension. I say that's mega-dangerous. She says no one said it was easy. Do I come or do I go? I say I come. She says we meet the next night and I get the pictures.'

'Which was the night you drove her and Curly up to the race course?'

'Which was the night I drove them up to the track? No one follows up there without you knowing.'

Ike's voice had dropped. Just above a whisper. He was reliving the whole scene with Lynda Elström. Leonard felt vulnerable. But he didn't want to stop. Break the circle. Jack was watching him. He held up his hand. Four fingers. Code 4. She went out to the warm red and friendly cream corridor that led from stairs to stalls and tapped into Manvers Street. Spoke quietly, precisely and urgently. It would take a few minutes. She didn't bother to tell him, didn't have to. Instead she remained in the entrance. She hoped no one was going to try the Lars Porsena bit.

'How did you keep in touch?'

'How didn't we? She calls all the time. She wouldn't let me call her. Said the line was fixed or something. So the bell keeps ringing. She comes on at eight in the morning – like it was lazy-time afternoon. You know that?'

Leonard glanced across at the entrance to the restaurant. Jack was standing there, facing along the corridor. He turned back to Ike.

'Go on.'

'Okay, so she says she had more negs. I get the first envelope. I say where's the rest. She says no way. Later. Then she wants to know how long it will take. I tell her depends how many she's got. She says plenty. So I tell her she can have copy prints of the first lot that night. She says she has to have them all by midnight.'

'She say why?'

'Said she was meeting people.'

'She say who?'

'No.'

'But you asked.'

'Not then. Later. But she wouldn't say.'

'But we know it was in the square.'

'Right.'

'Why not her flat?

'Yeah. Good one. Don't know. But she was strange about that flat. Like the Christian Brothers at school. They'd never let each other into their rooms. Maybe the same with her. She never trusted.'

'She did. There was Curly, you and who else?'

Ike paused. He looked down, then sideways at Simone. Her whisper was enough.

'Tell him, Ike, tell him. Can't hurt him now.'

Ike nodded slowly.

'Rudi.'

Leonard tapped the table with an abandoned teaspoon. And Rudi Sharpe was dead. Maybe, just maybe then, not hit and run but aim and run.

'She was meeting him? One of the people that night?'

'Not one of them. You see, I didn't want to get into this. I was scared out of my fucking head. And I told her she should be. I told her that Curly may have the biggest dick in Bath but it wouldn't do her much good if it came to nasties. She said she knew that. She said Rudi would be with her. She said he was okay.'

'Why?'

'She didn't say and I didn't ask her. It had sort of slipped out anyway. None of my business. I'm the picture man, remember. Strictly business.'

He shivered. It wasn't cold in the Vaults.

'But why Rudi? She must have said something, anything, that made you wonder.'

'Okay. I say to her, listen, if there's trouble, what do you expect an old guy like Rudi to do? I mean, he's not too hot at the kick-boxing business. And she says he doesn't have to do anything, just be there. He's my proof, she says. And I say if you're trying to put the arm on these people then they could turn nasty. And she says it won't come to that – not if I'm reasonable and they are.'

'What did she mean by that?'

'Look friend, I don't know. By then, I don't want to know. Why the hell you think I got out when Sy told me she'd been killed? Okay? Big scarebaby, that's me. Specially after what I'd seen.'

'People?'

'The prints. I do the first lot. Eight prints. She calls. We meet.'

'In the square?'

'Right. So I give her the negs and the prints. She gives me the next envelope. Says to be back twelve fifteen. She says not twelve fourteen. Not twelve sixteen. Twelve fifteen.'

'Why?'

'Maybe she's seen too many movies. Maybe this is the meet and she didn't want me to see them.'

'What happened after that?'

'She calls again. Says she wants three prints of each pic'

'Did you?'

'Right. Like she ordered. Twelve fifteen.'

The taxi driver was right.

'Okay, Ike. Now showtime. What was on the prints?'

It was taking time. Leonard counted slowly. The first minute went. Leonard wondered why he was playing the game. Simone's arm was back across Ike's shoulders. Another sip at the water. Another puff. He passed to Simone. There `was a noise in the corridor. Jack said something they didn't hear. Then two uniformed policemen appeared and stood sentry at the entrance. Ike relaxed.

'The first lot were crazy. Sado shit. Chains, whips, the whole dip. Okay?'

'Who?'

Ike puffed. Simone was now standing behind him, working her fingers into his shoulder muscles. He looked up. She bent to kiss his forehead.

'The twins.'

'The Rostows?'

'Right.'

'Who else?'

He didn't want to say. He looked at Simone again. The barest of nods. It would be all right.

'They were beating shit out of him.'

'Who?'

The quiet mumblings at the entrance became booms. Jack was apologizing that the restaurant area was closed. The protestation became louder. Jack half turned to where Leonard watched. The large, colour-coordinated figure at her side took it as an agreement and came down the three steps into the Vaults. Jack was right behind him. Her expression said sorry.

'Ah, there you are, m'lud, there you are. And Ike. What news from the lens, dear boy? My humbleness is yours, Inspector, for this intrusion, but I have a little something as the dear honey eater would have said, and methinks it's best for your ears only.'

Leonard didn't move. Beating shit out of a *him*. Jones? Poulson? Philips? Sharpe? Or someone he'd entirely missed? He waited for Jack to take charge. She knew what to do. With little effort, the recovery was made. Jack was by the table and almost without a word, had ushered Ike and Simone out of the restaurant with the girl grabbing her big hessian shoulderbag as she went. Ninety seconds later the three of them were in the back of a police car and on their way to the sanctuary of Manvers Street.

'Something I said, m'lud?'

Leonard was pouring coffee. He looked across to where Jones had settled in the corner. The notebook was there. The smile was soft, reassuring.

'Coffee?'

'Never during the Christian festivals.'

Leonard supposed that was clever, but really didn't care. Patients and condemned men cracked bad gags. Leonard sat down.

'You were saying?'

'So I was. Most certainly was. We've had three threatening telephone calls. How about that?'

'Who we?'

'Well, I took one, Jonah did, and there's one on the booking line if you want to hear it.'

'Saying what?'

'Rather dramatic, I'm afraid. Something along the lines of "Tell your darling Cinderella that if she sets foot on the stage it'll be the last ball she goes to. If she doesn't believe me, ask Lynda." Not very nice.'

'Nothing else?'

'Wasn't that enough? In fact I found myself saying something really silly like, "who is this?" or something. Really corny, m'lud, and, I'm afraid, wasted. He'd gone.'

'He?'

'Right.'

'Same voice on all three?'

'I think so.'

'When was this?'

'Just now. I immediately tried the recall number, but as you can imagine, it didn't.'

'Who else have you told?'

'No one. I looked for Maurice, but he's out. Then I saw the twinnies and they said you'd come in this direction. So I hotted my little tootsies and here you were, with Betsy's Dreamer.'

'Dreamer?'

'Something Maurice calls him. Sweet Betsy from Pike who crossed the big mountain with her darling Ike. It's very American folksy. Bit like him.'

'You don't like him.'

The sigh was big. Melodramatically big.

Leonard's mobile buzzed from the deep of his green tweed. He ignored it.

'A passable and wonderfully cheap photographer. But his imagination wanders beyond his darkroom.'

'Meaning?'

'Meaning that Ike is a troublemaker. He has a reputation for mixing too freely and feels rejected. He's not one of the company but would like to be. It's a common enough emotion with fringies. So, sometimes he feels extra bitter and he, well, he has been known to spread rather malicious gossip.'

'Lies?'

'Is gossip truthful?'

'To the listener, of course.'

'Not to the victim.'

'Have you been?'

Tiggy Jones wafted a softened arm in the air. His eyes closed.

'Good gracious me, no. Even the mighty Ike passes me by. The SM is worthy of his corn and nothing more. Not even scorn.'

The buzzing continued from Leonard's pocket. He took out the phone.

'Yes?'

Jack's voice sounded relieved. She'd been willing to believe Leonard's phone was where it usually was when he was on duty – in his flat.

'Clear, sir. All comfort and joy. I've got them in your office.'

'Good. I'll be back soon.'

'Quick one, sir?'

'Go on.'

'Ike's other person in the picture—'

'Yes?'

'I think he may be with you right now.'

Tiggy Jones was looking at Leonard with soft brown eyes. Leonard switched off his phone.

'Tell me, Mr Jones, have you plans for the rest of the day?'

'Inspector! Really!'

'Mr Jones.'

'No, sir. I shall be here.'

Leonard got up and leaned across the table. He was close enough to smell the sweet breath of the other man.

'Good. Very good, Mr Jones. Just make sure you are.'

Forty-One

Somewhere in Leonard's head a crime within a crime was taking shape. Yet the police theory of motive and opportunity had been satisfied. They'd got their murderer and, as a bonus, the confession was holding. The CPS lawyers were confident. But what about the pictures?

Maybe the pictures had nothing to do with Philips. This was a private affair and, after all, there was nothing illegal going on. Consenting adults. Nowadays leather, chains and whips were no longer top-shelf. Marriage-guidance counsellors carried discreet pamphlets. Students were doing Ph.D.s in it – liberal thought in social responsibility. This was a private matter between Jones and the Rostow twins. Nothing to do with the murder. So why was he so bothered? Tiredness was the obvious answer. Everyone was tired. Leonard was overstretching his team. It was Christmas on the calendar, but not in Leonard's head. He needed something. He needed to work out how a murder and an apparent attempt at crude blackmail could be connected by something more reliable than coincidence of time and place and, one person. The connection of course, was that one person. Victim and would-be victimizer. Something obvious. It was as he got to his closed office door that a tiny spot of light danced across his brain. He turned the handle and stood in the doorway.

'Where did she get the pictures?'

Ike looked up. Simone was drinking more coffee, this time from Leonard's mug. Jack was sitting in his seat. No one answered. He tried again.

'I said, where did Lynda get the pictures?'

He closed the door behind him and went over to the

window. It had started raining again. Ike pushed long dark hair back over his head and let out a long sigh.

'She wouldn't say.'

Leonard turned, rubbing at his spectacles.

'You asked?'

Ike nodded.

'What she say?'

Another one who shrugged with his mouth.

'Said it didn't matter.'

'But it did. It does.'

'That's what I told her. I said someone would want them back. She said they could have them – at her price.'

Leonard gave a final rub and slipped his spectacles on. He thought for a moment, staring at Jack's black shoulder bag.

'The briefcase. Anything?'

Without a word, Jack left the office and headed for the Major Incident Room. Someone must by now have shown it to Philips. Surely? Please, surely.

'She had a real smart case.'

Ike was nodding in answer to his own statement.

'Mm. Real smart. She had the prints in it.'

'Brown?'

'Right.'

'Someone broke into it.'

'I did.'

'You did what?'

'When we met that night. First time. She had the pix but they were in this case thing. Then she said she couldn't remember the code. She got real mad. Didn't know what to do. Crying all over the place. But it was strange crying. Not because she couldn't open it but, well, because she'd forgotten the fucking numbers.'

'So what did you do?'

Ike gave what went for his modest grin.

'You ever looked at one of those things? Three seconds with a blade and zappo! Open.'

So much for big-time burglary hypotheses. Leonard took off his duffle coat, then his jacket and sat down pulling out his bottom drawer as he did. He propped a booted foot on the edge and leaned back. Simone was still drinking coffee. He thought she must be minus a stomach lining.

'Okay, Ike, let's clear a couple of points. Where do you *think* she got those pictures?'

Shrug.

'Did she take them?'

Shrug.

'Could she have done?'

'It's a point-and-press world . . .'

He tailed off. He wanted a smoke. Simone put down Leonard's mug.

'Nothing to do with me but, um, if she had taken the pictures, who developed and printed them? Not exactly one-hour D and P job, is it?'

Leonard eyed her. She was right. That was even more reason to think that someone else had taken them. But he wasn't going to get anywhere with Ike on that.

'These pictures. The Rostows and Jones?'

'Right.'

'Why should I believe you?'

Ike looked at Simone.

'Okay?'

She nodded and took a large white envelope from her sacking shoulder bag. She tapped the envelope on her upturned fingers, then, the decision taken, leaned over and emptied its contents on to his desk. The Rostow twins, snarling, grotesque, sagging, comical figures in their leather corsetry, boots and gauntlets. Arms outstretched and chained to the iron bedstead, every inch of Jones was presumably enjoying the agony his face expressed.

The door opened without a knock. It was Marsh. He eyed Ike and Simone and beckoned Leonard to the corridor.

'How long is this going to take? You have too many men tied up on this. Christmas you know. People take their time. Overtime is supposed to be a thing of the past. Budgets, you know, James, budgets.'

Leonard buzzed. Looked down and tapped his boot.

'Very soon, sir.'

'That's what they say about the future.'

'Couple of days.'

'There aren't any. Christmas is the day after tomorrow.'

'Tomorrow?'

'Tell me why.'

'Come and have a look at these, sir.'

Leonard led him back into the office. The pictures were spread across the desk. Marsh looked but recognized no one. His face expressed the elder's distaste. The dark eyes turned first to Ike and Simone and then to his inspector.

'The connection?'

'Lynda Elström had these pictures on the day and night she was murdered. The man's the stage manager. The fat ladies are in the cast. We think she may have tried blackmail.'

Marsh picked up a couple of photographs and looked again.

'No Philips.'

'No, sir.'

With the expression of a man who now wanted to wash his hands, Marsh dropped the prints among the others.

'Seemingly you have good reason to think these important. As much as one may personally disapprove, these are the sort of pictures common today in our society.'

Leonard took a breath but the sermon was not done.

'Truly despicable. Utterly sordid. But we live in a society indifferent to, well, to this sort of thing. Hardly, James, I would have thought, the motive for taking another's life.'

The elder's lipped curled. The eyes glinted. The bony white fingers twitched.

'And as we have to accept, none should be surprised that such things occur among theatre folk. It is a profession, after all, that boasts a history of which many respectable folk would feel considerable shame.'

Ike and Simone were one point before open-mouthed surprise. The sermon of the theatrical whore had not been so preached for a hundred years. Certainly not with such feeling. Leonard's sigh punctured their silence.

'Right, sir. Well, I'll get this sorted as soon as I can.'

But Marsh, preaching over, had not finished. He flipped through the scattered prints.

'Two questions, James, two questions.'

'Sir?'

'Who took these pictures?'

'I don't know, sir.'

Marsh eyed Ike.

'And you? You know?'

Ike still wanted a smoke. The head went from side to side.

'No. But they weren't set up. Too many shadows and eye glints. No close-ups. Not a lensman.'

Marsh eyed the photograph then Ike. Who was this person with opinions on such a matter?

'Ike's a photographer, sir.'

'Ike. Ah yes, let me see – Ike – Ike Wilson?'

Ike looked up. So did Leonard. So did Simone.

'Right.'

'Mm. Last August at the RPS. Crypts and Gravestones. Excellent monochrome. Excellent.'

Ike perked up. But if he thought he was going to get a commendation from Bath's senior police officer in the middle of a murder investigation just two days before Christmas with thirty-two officers manoeuvring for double overtime, then he was wrong. Marsh had the other question to ask. The question Leonard should have already asked – and answered.

'Curious there should be so much fuss over these. They are nothing more than common snapshots.'

Marsh's black bushy eyebrow raised in question towards Leonard. Leonard was lost. Marsh returned to Ike.

'One must assume, Mr Wilson, one must assume, that there are some more – shall we say damning – pictures?'

Leonard felt very junior. What an obvious question. Why oh why had it not been his? Simone was back in the sacking shoulder bag. This time the envelope was blue. Shiny, shiny blink blue. Instead of dropping them on the desk, she handed them quietly and solemnly to the elder and then went back to her pew by the radiator. Marsh paused thoughtfully before handing the envelope, unopened, to Leonard, who cleared a space on his desk, unwound the cotton tie and took out a dozen large colour photographs. As Leonard laid them in careful columns, short spits of angry air escaped Marsh's tight lips. The door opened and Jack returned with her news. Without looking at the desk she sensed the disgust in the atmosphere. Ike stared into the ceiling. Simone looked miserable. Leonard looked on in angry disbelief. Small, mostly dark-haired naked children were captured in hideously explicit sexual positions with the same adult.

'My God, I don't believe it.'

The whisper came from Madelaine Jack. Marsh remained impassive. Leonard looked up to where Ike and Simone sat side by side.

'Did you know?'

Simone said nothing. Ike shook his head.

'No one knew.'

'But Lynda did. Where did she get these? You must have some idea.'

'No.'

Simone's voice was small. Quiet. Frightened.

'What will happen?'

Marsh turned to the door.

'We need to talk, James.'

Leonard picked up the top picture and followed him out.

As the door closed behind them, Jack gave Ike and Simone a quiet smile and promised yet more coffee.

'There's lots to do, you know. For the moment I think it's best you stay here.'

'We under arrest or something?'

Simone's voice was quiet. Jack shook her head.

'Certainly not. But there are formalities. We need statements from you both. They have to be recorded. You can ask them to be put on video-tape. It's good if you do. Then everyone can see you. They know you're under no pressure.'

Ike shrugged his indifference. Jack picked up the first picture.

Looked at it, put it down. She picked up another picture, turned it over.

'I've got to number these. Plenty of time. Nothing to worry about. You're safe here.'

She tried to sound reassuring. It only took one or two right words to reassure. They were hard to find. Even when they were found, they didn't last long. Head bent, Jack started marking the back of each picture before dropping them one by one into the fawn Banner evidence sack. The pictures would be individually recorded again. Jack would have to do that downstairs. Highly Confidential. The maroon Detained Property Record would simply give Form 400 picture numbers. The bureaucracy worked. Formal, unbiased and unshakable yet vulnerable to defence lawyers who would jump on any discrepancy in the police handling of evidence. She wrote a number on the corner of the final picture, turned it over, looked at it for a moment before sliding it in with the rest of the now anonymous bundle. She stood. Ike and Simone looked up, two puppies waiting for a walk.

'Stay here for a moment. I'll be back in ten minutes. White with no sugar, right?'

Ike waved fingers at her. Anything was good. A smoke would be fine. Maybe something stronger would be fine.

Jack closed the door, quietly. She walked in silence along the silent corridor, past the empty chief inspector's office, the pigeon holes stuffed with rainbows of notes and reminders. With a mental shake of her head she noticed, for the first time, the week-old sign on the new Child Protection Unit – the door was closed as if business was bad. Her shoes clacked on the normally busy, biscuit stairway and pushed open the swing doors and crossed into the comforting normality of the DPO's office. She signed in the pictures and watched as they were logged In Confidence. The duty officer said something she hardly heard and she remembered nothing of what she said in reply. Her memory was full of the last picture that refused to budge from her head. The silent and motionless tableau. The dark, silk-haired child holding a naked man in her mouth. The ecstasy on Jason William's creased face.

Forty-Two

Marsh was a sombre charcoal sketch in his high-backed chair. Nonconformist anger crackled deep beneath his frost-white shirt. Leonard sat, as he mostly sat, hands deep in jacket pockets, legs stretched out, resting on the thick black heels of his dull buffed brown boots. In the corner blue seat, Lane sucked his teeth and examined his knuckles waiting for the bell to ring on the silence that followed Marsh's last remark. The black eyes of the affronted elder stabbed Leonard for an answer.

'I agree, sir. We can, as you say, "smash him to smithereens". But there's a bigger picture.'

'A filthy picture, James. Filthy. And it's one you and your liberal cronies have yet to cover with your misguided notions of freedom – whatever that may mean in this sad, sad day and age.'

Leonard quietly counted. Let it go. Just as he'd let it go for the ten years he'd been in Bath under Marsh's stern command. He heard the hiss and got in just before Marsh prepared to launch another assagai for the city's moral majority.

'There were three different children in those pictures. Three different occasions? We don't know. But my guess from the background, they were taken in the same place. So, where do the kiddies come from? Who supplies them? Where were the pictures taken? Who took them? In other words, are we talking about a ring or just Williams? Personally, I believe it's organized. Drop on him and we scatter the organization. Put this out to tender—'

'A separate investigation?'

'Yes, sir. If we do, then we'll bust something bigger.'

Marsh rubbed at his bony nose with a bonier forefinger.

'Ray? You look uncertain.'

DI Lane scratched at his oversize belly and a button popped on his striped shirt. He sat up and draped an arm over his gut.

'Well, sir, have we got a murder? Yes. Have we got a result? Yes. Have we got underage sex? Yes. Have we got a result? Yes – if we want one. But we've also got a connection. The

Swedish party had the pictures that led us to Williams. So we now have to ask, did those pictures lead Williams to Lynda?'

'James?'

'She intended them to. She told Curly and Ike that she planned to use them. She was going to blackmail Williams, and for that matter, the twins and Jones.'

Lane shifted, bent down and picked up the offending button. The exertion made him puff.

'We sure about this Ike guy? I mean, here we are wondering who took the pictures and who gave them to her and along the corridor we've got a photographer who knew them all, did their kosher snaps, whose girl tells us that he was always getting into leg-over situations with whoever turned up at his studio and who was running off extra prints to order for her right until the night she was topped. And—'

He stared. Just remembering. Leonard finished it for him.

'And he's got a studio. Very private. Ideal for whip-lash-away pictures and maybe worse. Except the pictures aren't studio quality.'

Lane was nodding, enthusiastically building his own mental picture.

'But what if Ike's been letting out the studio? Maybe it's DIY pictures, but in his studio.'

Marsh curtly coughed them to order.

'Why would he come in with this evidence?'

Ray Lane shrugged.

'Frightened, sir? After all, she was murdered an hour or so after he saw her.'

'But there's no connection.'

They kept returning to something they didn't want to believe. Leonard hurried on his specs.

'Maybe Philips is lying. Maybe he didn't kill her. Maybe it's attention-grabbing. Maybe he's a nutter. Maybe he thinks he did but didn't.'

Marsh tugged at his starched cuffs, twisted towards the back wall and stared thoughtfully at the operational area map. A complex of lines, colours and numbers. All leading from or to Manvers Street. To where he was sitting. To him.

'You see, James, until we know otherwise, all the evidence leads to Philips and Philips has obliged us by raising his hand when asked. This other business is nothing more than a mess of side streets. It simply proves what a dank and dreadful society festers in the theatre of today. But, and having said that, I'm not at all happy. Fresh eyes. That's what we need. Fresh eyes. Ray, get hold of that slip of a girl Philips calls his lawyer and go out and see him again. Go over his statement in detail. Play defence counsel. Trip him up. See if he's telling us the truth.'

Ray Lane liked that. Old coppering. The new breed of senior officers would have a management solution to the problem. Marsh took another breath, this time for Leonard.

'James, my senses tell me that your doubts are well founded. But I see no evidence that convinces me either of us is right. The one thing I do know is that every time we hit a paedophile he's cracked immediately. Wanted to talk. Right?'

'Yes, sir.'

'The worst of them want protecting from themselves. Mm?'

'Maybe, sir. In this case, it's different. This Williams is not your average lonely old child-feeler. This isn't a package tour to Bangkok. High trade sniffs and "unusual practices", as the book calls it, come in very expensive packages and for fun not for comfort.'

'Maybe. Have you seen this man work? Mm?'

Lane and Leonard shook their heads. Jason Williams was to hum to, not to scream at.

'Pity, gentlemen. Pity. You might have learned something. Your initial report on him, James, was interesting. Did you not think your man a little precious? Anyway, not being one to follow these folk, I thought I should acquaint myself with the style of his work, so I sent for some videos of his shows. He strikes me as being a very insecure person. When he sings there's a nervousness that is real. Appealing and real. And the lyrics. Have you noticed his own lyrics? Very insecure. Very mummy's boy. We know about the mummy's boy species don't we, gentlemen? Convention tells us that he loves his mother. But we know the opposite is true. It's the mummy who loves the boy. If he won't let go he begins to resent what he is. He takes it out on mummy, makes more demands. Then punishes. If he's smart he punishes other people. If she's smart she lets him because he'll always come home to suckle. Basic Jester and Tombs. Yes?'

Lane nodded. If he'd paid more attention to the criminal-typing gospel according to J&T; he might have got further. Leonard nodded. He had paid attention, but he was yet to be a believer. He stood and went to the window. Christmas didn't look any better from here than it did down there. Passers-by huddled against the festival. Inside, Leonard wished it didn't matter.

'Tell me, sir, if I'm going after him, supposing he doesn't crack straight away. Supposing he says so what? What if he says the pictures were taken abroad where it was legal?'

Marsh glared. Spiked his completely clear and shiny desk with his middle talon.

'He won't. He can't. His whole career would blow up. His whole life has been built on his clean apple-pie image. He will be destroyed. What was that decoration they gave him? Head bowed over the monarch's hand? Owing all to his loving mother? Ambassador at Large for the United Nations Childrens' Appeal. Childrens' Appeal! No. We have him. The question is, James, did she have him? Did she threaten him?'

'You mean did he kill her to silence her?'

'Don't tell me what I mean, James, and you, Ray, get over there and talk to Philips. I don't like this. I'm not one hundred per cent sure we've sorted it as we should.'

Leonard leaned against the wall. He tapped his bottom lip with a pencil he'd absent mindedly picked out of the superintendent's pewter mug.

'We need rummagers, sir. A full team. If I'm going over there, we need to strip-search his London house at the same time. That means bringing in the Met. Barnes, isn't he? And isn't there some place in Scotland? Better have a word with Grampian. Those pictures could have been anywhere as well as Ike's studio.'

'You'll not be forgetting the pretty little bungalow will you, James?'

'But that's his mother's place.'

'Mummy's boy, James, Mummy's boy. See where he keeps his toys, will you? Mm?'

Forty-Three

The weather had turned from cold and wet to warm and dry. They stood on the steps of the police station and breathed deeply. The community relations officer, a contented man with a bushy black moustache, waved a hand and smiled. Leonard felt the same as he'd done at the crematorium when his only friend had died. Empty and with a deep need to say nothing but to speak. He nodded back, but the constable had already disappeared inside.

'By the way, sir, that case. Philips says it belonged to guess who?'

'Maurice Poulson.'

'No, sir. Rudi Sharpe. Or he thinks so. He says Rudi used to have one like it. Never went anywhere without it. But that was last year's panto. Philips reckons he hasn't seen it this year. Maybe he lost it.'

'So for Kitty Fisher read Lynda Elström.'

Williams was not at the theatre. At the stage door they said he'd not been in all day. Poulson was about but they didn't know where. The Rostows were rehearsing. Tiggy Jones was out but would be back. Dry cleaners, they said. Leonard looked at his watch. Try the bungalow. He turned quickly from the desk and collided with Angela Billings.

'So, we three really do meet again.'

The voice was too rich and too soft for some blasted heath. The blue-framed specs were on a gilt chain and *The Times* was neatly folded at the nearly finished crossword. She was the only one of them clean as far as he could tell. He wondered how good she was with real anagrams. Better, he imagined, than with her pins. Leonard steadied the actress with his hand under her elbow.

'I need a word.'

'You look, Inspector, as if you need a drink. Step this way – and do not do the funny-walk routine.'

They followed the flowing floral figure down the next flight of turning staircase until they found themselves passing through a doorway and under the stage itself. Stores, lights, the musicians' alcove for the orchestra pit, switches, lanterns, pipes and wires. A stagehand was greasing the trap-door lever, an electrician was checking a circuit breaker, a carpenter repaired a box. And then up the other side, by the Stage Left, Wardrobe, Dressing Rooms 1–7, notice, up more steps and eventually along a passageway and into a small room with a big square mirror and blazing bulbs. Angela Billings waved them to a velvet-covered bench and without asking, poured three glasses of cognac. She sat at her dressing-table chair and raised her glass.

'To absent friends.'

Leonard nodded, slowly.

'Cheers.'

'I thought you'd be back.'

'You did?'

'Of course. Finding how was easy. Finding why is not, is it?'

'We think that's pretty straightforward.'

'Oh, we are smug, aren't we? I never thought that, darling. Never at all. You see, I'm simply an old – well, an old most things, actually. It struck me that there are so many noises off that you have a play within a play, if I may use my corny theatrical metaphor. Mm?'

'See how love and murder will out.'

'How clever.'

'Congreve.'

'Then very clever. I only know my own lines and my cues. Don't you think that too awful? But of course you don't. You have so little regard for us.'

'Who says?'

'Why you do, darling. Your whole attitude. Your body language. You think our men pimps, our women whores.'

'Is that what I said?'

'Congreve.'

'How clever.'

'Yes. I suppose so. Cleverer than you think. But you, dear Inspector, you're not as clever as you think. Oh dear, I must not say such things in front of your pretty sergeant. But if you had a little more regard for us, if you weren't so convinced that we were all terrible people, instead of hard-working, and I'm afraid, often non-working folk, then you would not have been blind to so many obvious moments.'

'And you're going to tell me?'

'If you wish. Tell me, as I hear you say to everyone, tell me, Inspector, why do you suppose poor Norman did that dreadful thing to poor Lynda?'

'Panic. He went too far.'

'No, darling, I don't mean why did he kill her, if indeed he really did, I mean why hang her on the high fly?'

'For all to see.'

'To see what? Her beauty destroyed? Her public punishment? Humiliation?'

'Maybe a combination.'

The actress picked up her cognac, smelled it and put it down again.

'No, darling. Dear Norman was hanging us all. You see he hates us. He was once a god. No one knows about it. No one cares about it. We say good morning and goodnight because we all know our lines. That is the nature of our profession. We're a claque for our kind and we let in no one else. We keep the shabby magic for ourselves. We kiss our enemies hello and scratch our friends goodbye. And poor Norman wanted so much to belong. And so when we rejected him, without realizing it of course, he hanged us, publicly. In doing so, again without realizing it, he let in intruders. You, my darling. And yet, because you feel superior, you never touched.'

Leonard stretched his legs and blinked at Angela Billings. She thought him nice. Wondered if he were sleeping with the sergeant. She thought not. He was far too self-centred. Probably had cats but certainly not dogs.

'What didn't I touch?'

'That we're sentimentalists. That we live on the past but not in it because we live in hope, even though our agents treat us like dirt. So you never understood that we gossip all the time. That we all have tales about the mighty and quite a few about the lowly. That we've all been in everything and that we all know each other even when we don't because we learn our gossip as well as we learn our speeches.'

Leonard heard what he had not listened to before.

'So you all knew her.'

'Of course.'

'Even if you'd never met her.'

'Clever boy.'

'Including you.'

'Especially me.'

Leonard cursed inside. She would make him sweat. Drag out each word.

'Okay Miss Billings, tell me, why especially you?'

'Because many, many moons ago, her father was my lover.'

'You're Lynda's mother?'

The chuckle never rose higher than that. Again, the actress sniffed at her cognac. Leonard wondered why, it wasn't special.

'No, my sweet. Heaven forbid. I would, naturally, have been a magnificent mother. But my various amusements were musical rather than dramatic'

'I'm not sure I understand.'

'Of course you don't. Policemen rarely do. All those dreadful criminals you mix with.'

'Please?'

'Many years ago, when Lynda was tiny, tiny in Vienna—'

'—I thought she was Swedish or Norwegian or something.'

'Whoever heard of a blonde saying she was Viennese when she could say she was Swedish? Anyway, darling, as I was saying, a very long time ago, I was in one of the wonderful Trevor Sumner touring companies. You're far too young to remember. And, for two horrid, horrid weeks we did *Misanthrope* in Vienna. A mistake, my darling. A ghastly mistake. As much as I love the Viennese, you have to do so many things with sausages or cream cakes before they see the humour.'

'What's this to do with Lynda?'

'Patience, please. After all you're catching up, not leading the pack. I was a very young actress. This was not only my first tour, but my first time abroad and, well, I became "involved" as we used to say in those days. He was the company fool. Did rather special things with his face that so matched his voice. He could juggle, tumble, could do almost anything dear Trevor asked of him. And I must say, almost anything I asked. It was not love, but it was a marvellous affair. It was what my father would have called "for the duration". We held hands in public. My goodness, we did. But when we got to Vienna he let go. So what did I do? Foolishly, I followed him one day. And yes, he had a wife and a baby.'

'Lynda?'

'Yes, of course.'

She sat back gazing at Leonard. Waiting to see if he were as bright as he pretended to be. He buzzed. The puller of faces. The juggler. The tumbler. All those years ago. And now she was telling him. For only one reason, surely.

'Rudi Sharpe was Lynda's father.'

She didn't answer. The amusement was in her eyes.

'Why didn't you tell me all this before?'

'It seemed irrelevant. You were arrogant. It was up to Rudi to tell you.'

'But he was—'

'No. Not then.'

'Did he say anything about her coming to Bath?'

'Very little. There is little to say about true sadness. You see, Inspector, hardly anyone knew Rudi was her father. Her mother's family had been grand. Rudi was, well, Rudi was rather ungrand. They married rather quickly and divorced rather quickly. But, my darling, she was with child. I'm not even sure she knew so when they parted.'

'Which was when?'

'A year or so before we toured. That was the first time he'd seen her – and the last. So I'm afraid, Lynda grew up believing her father had abandoned them.'

'Had he?'

'Probably. But I didn't know. When I first knew him he was a bastard. It took time to mellow, or in Rudi's case, to marinade.'

'Drink.'

'It passed his lips.'

'What about the time in Vienna? Was she too young to remember?'

'Absolutely. Toddling. No more. He'd keep in touch with her mother, although all in secret. She wouldn't allow anything else in case Lynda or her so-called father found out. Then one day, we were together in rep, Norwich it was, and there she was in the tabloids. Masses of blonde hair everywhere and a darling little frock which must have been run up for a pixie. What they used to call a starlet, complete with publicist's pedigree. Her mother had married a boring physicist from Stockholm and so the Swedish beauty had some truth. But when he saw her, Rudi saw her mother's face.'

As Leonard had in Mrs Potts's top bedroom. The photo-album and the woman he thought he'd recognized. He hadn't. He'd recognized her mother.

Now he understood the birthday card. Understood why she had trusted the old man.

'Tell me, when did she know?'

'Lynda? This time last year.'

'Panto?'

'No, darling. A funeral.'

'Whose?'

'Her mother's. The stepfather had long gone. I think the Scandawegians go in for a lot of suicide, don't they? Something to do with being in the dark. Anyway, last winter her mother had a bad winter or something, and, well, off she popped with her toes in the air.'

'They met at the funeral.'

'Oh no. They met because of the funeral. Lynda went and,

obviously, for the first time, went through her mother's things. Among them was a huge bundle of letters.'

'From him?'

'Absolutely. You see, they'd never stopped loving each other. Rudi was a romantic. A sentimentalist. So was she in her way. They'd loved. They'd never stopped loving. It must have been very deep. Anyway, poor Lynda lost a mother and found a father. She returned to London and, um, well, looked him up.'

Leonard was beginning to get a shape, but he didn't know what it was.

'How do you know all this?'

'I was there.'

'When they met?'

She was smiling at him. Smiling? Laughing. She knew so much. He knew very, very little.

'Mm.'

'I don't understand.'

'Of course you don't, darling. That's why you wrap yourself in those silly clothes. You must really stop creating yourself and be something you are.'

There was a long silence. She wasn't embarrassed. By his side on the hard sofa, Jack kept perfectly still. Leonard was hurt. It was a new emotion. 'Why you?'

'We were very close, very close. Rudi wasn't awfully brave. He needed me. But perhaps you find that less than easy to understand.'

'I didn't see any tears when he died.'

'You didn't look, darling. You simply wanted a reason, not a truth.'

'You were even scathing about him.'

'Scathing? What a lovely old-fashioned word.'

'You were.'

For the first time, Angela Billings looked away. Her voice still warm, now softer.

'Yes, I suppose so. I'm ashamed, but yes. I suppose we all have our tweeds, don't we?'

The story was too involved for it to be this simple. Leonard looked down at his hands. He wanted thinking time. Jack shifted on the bench. Something Angela Billings had said. Deliberately? Teasingly?

'Miss Billings, you said *hardly* anyone knew.'

'You talked to Maurice.'

'He knew?'

'Well, my dear, this is not from me, you understand, but he has known her for donkeys. And of course he knew Rudi.'

'Then?'

'Of course. Don't let Maurice's rugged good looks fool you. A merry little band were we. Maurice was another of darling Trevor's young men. He needed so many, you know. Such an appetite.'

'And he would have known about Lynda?'

'Maurice knew about most things. He made it his business to.'

'I thought Tiggy Jones was the note taker.'

'Tiggy's a pet. But he worries. So everything goes in his book.'

Jack paused. Leonard was still looking at his hands.

'When you say everyone knew about Lynda, does that mean that Lynda would have known about everyone else?'

The actress smiled. A sweet, sticky smile.

'Oh no, dear. She wasn't in the school you see.'

'If I told you that Lynda knew a lot about certain people in the company, things they'd rather she didn't know, would that surprise you?'

Angela Billings took her time. Up came the cognac, but this time she sipped.

'What sort of things?'

'Private things.'

'Gossip.'

'No, Miss Billings. Hard evidence of, well, of very nasty pastimes.'

Angela Billings pulled her Georgian shawl closer to her neck and snuggled into the soft midnight colours.

'And what would that have to do with Norman?'

'We think nothing.'

'Well, well, my dear, then who killed our Caesarene?'

A long silence. Then Leonard looked up.

'So many knives before the emperor had fallen. More hands than Norman Philips rang?'

'But, Inspector, that's for you and your bogus Congreve to decide. You're the thinker in the family, I'm simply the fairy godmother. I do three wishes, slippers and glass coaches. Not murders.'

Forty-Four

In Manvers Street police station DC Leweson tapped at the open door of Detective Inspector Leonard's office. From the inner office the forty-a-day tuned voice of DI Lane called "Gone Fishin". Leweson went in, clutching his deep box file of papers, reports, newspaper cuttings and photographs.

'I think I've got something, sir.'

'You want a doctor, then, not me.'

'Seriously, sir. You know where DI Leonard is?'

Lane had his jacket off and his braces hanging. He looked what he was: a hangover from the old days of the Bath police. He happened to be one of the best officers never promoted beyond inspector. More management style, more attention to detail and less to pints of bitter and short cuts might have got him further. But not much. He was tired and due to go soon. He'd miss it, but he knew it was time. But what wouldn't retire was his nose for the way an investigation was going. This one had confusion written over it. They'd got their man. But Leonard had got something else. The photographer and his girl had seen to that. They were now tucked up under police guard in their flat. The investigation wasn't tucked up. It was vulnerable. It needed something.

Lane was struggling through the transcript of Norman Philips's confession. It made sense, even in the tidied way it was presented when they went back and got him to put it on tape to make doubly sure. Philips had made a clumsy pass at Lynda

Elström because he thought she was giving him the come-on and when she'd screamed he'd tried to shut her up and he'd strangled her. Then in a fit of spite he'd hung her on stage for everyone to see. He was warped. But there was something that didn't make sense. Something odd there. Lane was re-reading the statement when Leweson arrived. He sat back in his chair, hands clasped behind his neck. He was getting too old for this. He looked at the self-assurance on Leweson's face. The confidence that his background and education had given him. In Lane's early days, most of the coppers hadn't been much smarter than the villains. DI Ray Lane's nose told him that a smart young officer like Leweson was about to get into the major league.

'Give us it here. What have we got?'

Leweson opened the plastic box. He took two bundles and a double A4 typewritten sheet.

'The DI asked me to check when all these theatre people had worked with each other, particularly with her.'

He handed over the list.

'That's it, sir. Everything I could find including drama school, commercials, rep, television, videos, films, the lot. There are also a couple of columns of personal appearances, but it's not that accurate.'

He put the two bundles on either side of Lane's desk book.

'Pictures in the blue one, sir. Newspaper cuttings in the brown one.'

Lane started to sift. It could take all day. He patted his pocket for a cigarette packet then remembered that he'd given up six months ago.

'Okay, *dottore*, what's hot?'

Leweson opened a white envelope from the blue folder and laid a whole plate black and white photograph in front of Lane. Then from the cuttings file he took the front page of an old tabloid daily and matched it to the photograph. A very wet blonde being groped by two unidentified young men – and apparently enjoying it. The small insert of a man in collar and tie, looked anything but happy. The newspaper headline was corny, suggestive and had sold newspapers.

His Wife in Their Hands

Lane read the copy, winced, then laughed. Picked up the glossy picture and whistled.

'She really was something, wasn't she?'

Leweson was a very serious young officer. He allowed the DI three seconds' further drooling.

'Well, yes, sir, I suppose so.'

'You what? Suppose so? In my day this was known as crumpet. Very tasty.'

'Yes, sir, well, for our purposes, I mean for the DI's purpose, I think you'll find the two men in the picture, um, tasty.'

Lane turned over the photograph. Leweson's neat fist had written their names in circles. Held up to the light, each name was written across the forehead. This time Lane's whistle was unmistakably in a major key. He picked up his phone and tapped a double digit.

'DI Lane here. Put out a call for DI Leonard will you – like now?'

He looked up, smiled.

'Well, Bernard. Well, well, well, what a clever little bunny you are.'

Forty-Five

Tiggy Jones, sinner maybe, but no law-breaker he, put his arm out to stop Leonard and Jack at the side of the stage. They watched as the twins rehearsed another routine with the new dame. Leonard had never seen Rudi Sharpe working, but there was something quite alien about his stand-in. He was a well-known television comic. Great with one-liners. Not so great with slapstick. It was hard-going. The Rostows were helping all they could. But it wasn't the same. On the night, the name would carry the act. The comic would foul up once a scene and the audience would love it. Playing it for laughs, they'd think. Playing it for lemons? Of course not. And when it went right, then that would prove that the famous funny man could do it for real whenever he wished. Now, out there on the stage, he was desperately trying to make it so. For the moment there were too many bumps and too few daisies. Leonard stood back and to one side of Tiggy Jones and watched in silence as the act came together. But he didn't see two famous twin dames and a highly professional stage manager. He saw sweating bellies, too-old nakedness, chained ankles and wrists, tatty imitation leather and real weals of red flesh from flaying thongs.

This was Bath. This was family entertainment. This was the livelihood for the Rostows. Weston, Minehead, Bristol, Chippenham, Bath. Big in panto and nowhere else. Bath, dirty beneath, clean on top, liked to think that the dank side of life was kept at arm's length and appeared in the theatre only if written thoughtfully and intellectually by near unpronounceable names. On the top shelf it was porn. On the stage it was culture. But if it became public that the wicked sisters, were into whips and bondage, then local management would drop them – for good. Local charities who hired them to appear, to open and to sign, thus bringing in money for the charities and good publicity for the Rostows, would strike them off the personal appearance lists. When the audience of kiddies shouted 'Behind You!' then Management didn't want to see Cinders holding up A3 colour pictures.

Time to send in the beaters.

'Where's Jason Williams?'

Tiggy Jones smiled. Not at Leonard's question. The routine. He answered without turning.

'Could be anywhere. Didn't get a call today.'

'What's that mean?'

'Wasn't needed. Probably Christmas shopping with his simply wonderful and much loved mum.'

'What for? Children's clothes? Or something more exotic? Leather goods, for example.'

Now the stage manager did turn.

'How's that, m'lud?'

'Cut the shit, Jones. Where's Williams?'

'So brusque. So ill-tempered. Why so?'

Leonard remembered Marsh's contempt.

'Holiday snaps. Yours and theirs.'

He nodded at the stage. Jones was losing his colour.

'I, eh – I, eh, don't think I follow.'

'Dare say you don't. You do like lying there and taking it rather than following, don't you?'

'What does – does that mean, Inspector?'

'It means I've got the pictures that Lynda Elström had.'

'I don't understand.'

'You're about to – m'lud.'

On stage there was a crash of zinc bath and back scrubber, a screech of whoopee cushion and a cackling of mechanical hen. It looked dreadful, but on the night the whole thing would end on a big *Ooooops!* There'd be a roll on the snare drum, a clang on the cow-bell and they'd be taking their bows before the first hands came together in the traditional applause for the Ugly Sisters' first routine which would be a highlight of all three acts. For now they just sweated a lot and went off stage left to see if they could get the director to tickle the script. On the way off, one of the twins looked back. The smile wasn't big. The flickering hand was effeminate and not feminine. Leonard was certain it wasn't for him. The lights dropped power and seconds of almost silence descended as the chattering Uglies disappeared downstairs to their dressing room.

Jack came up the steps from the stage-door entrance. Following her was DC Leweson. Leonard blinked at him, wondering why he was there. Then he saw the folder and turned his back on Tiggy Jones who was scribbling lighting instructions in his notebook and looked at the open folder. The picture. The cutting. The circled names on the reverse of the print. He didn't say anything, but Leweson was pleased, very pleased with the slow nod of understanding.

Tiggy Jones had finished his notes and tried one of his better hooded brown-eyed smiles. The stage manager may have recovered his style but certainly not his ground. The hand went up the forehead. The eyes angled to the heavens. Not at all SM, too luvvy for Leonard. Jones fussed with his green spotted neckerchief. Leonard's contempt was open. He too would play the thespian game and he would win.

'Look, Inspector, we must talk.'

'We just did.'

'Let's be reasonable.'

'Listen to me, Mr Jones, and listen well. Your consenting adults thing is no business of mine. If you want a couple of old tarts to whip seven different types of shit out of you, then that's your problem. Okay?'

Leonard looked across the stage. An unreal place of temptation as if some mighty wurlitzer had been left unattended. Leonard went on. Head down. Then stopped, firmly centre stage. Jones stood to stage left and waited to see if Leonard would speak. Strangely uncertain of his lines, the policeman looked about him at the larger-than-life panto palette of candy blues and lemons, greens and pinks, sparkles and stars. Cinderella's three-legged stool where she sat to hug her tears away. The black and white besom for her to sweep the cobwebs and dust to the Ugly Sisters' orders. The red and white brick hearth she scrubbed morning and night. The rickety black stove on which she cooked and cooked and cooked to fill their greed. Three centuries of fantasy. Pure panto and all now silent and dully lit by half-power lanterns hanging high above on crude, galvanized gantries.

Leonard took one hand from his pocket and waved it slowly about him.

'For the kids. Yes?'

Jones nodded.

'Yes, indeed. For them.'

Leonard looked at him. Jerked his chin in approval. Chewed at imaginary crumbs.

'Excellent. Good Christmas fun. Look behind you stuff. That's what you called it. Yes?'

'Yes.'

The voice was quiet. Uncertain.

'Hundreds of years they've been doing it. That right,

Mr Jones? Hundreds of years. *Recueil des pièces crieuses et nobles.*
Isn't that right?'

'I don't know, I'm sorry.'

'You don't know? But you're the expert. The one with the
notebook. The one who knows everything. A luvvy-in-chief.
Now me, who am I to cry God for Harry? Mm? Go on, tell
me. I'm just the thick copper. Perrault. Cendrillon. Surely you
know that.'

The brown eyes looked down. Troubled eyes. Leonard
stalked a pace. Turned and pointed at the bright scenery.

'You see, Mr Jones, you're as phony as this stuff. Worse. You
pretend you're not. Right?'

'What do you have in mind, Inspector?'

'In mind? I have in mind what I have in an envelope. An
envelope of pictures, your pictures.'

'You'll have to explain.'

'No. Maybe you'll wish to explain. Not to the law, of course.
After all, this place has seen worse – for art's sake, of course.
But what you can explain to me, Mr Jones, is when was it our
late Cinders tried to blackmail you?'

Tiggy Jones came a step closer, but observing some protocol
of stage direction, not too close.

'This may sound like the worst line in the worst play, but
truly, Inspector, I don't know what you're talking about. In all
my life I've never been blackmailed. You may have some silly
pictures, but as you say yourself, so what? A scene from *Donatien
Alphonse*. A rehearsal, nothing more.'

Leonard leaned back on one heel and very slowly, clapped.

'Good, very good.'

'It happens to be true. Ask the twins.'

'Presumably they're word perfect. Tell me, Mr Jones, why
don't I ask the audience?'

He turned to the empty auditorium.

'Let's see what the people think, mm? Good people of Bath,
would you like your pantomime performed by perverts?'

'For Chrissakes, this is crazy.'

Leonard looked up at the silent, darkened dress circle.

'Let's see what the management thinks. Does it really want

the risk of keeping you on. SMs are two a penny, Ugly Sisters are at the end of every pier.'

He turned to the boxes.

'And what of the critics? Let's see who can remember this production of Sade – so meticulously dressed in rehearsal. Let's see who believes you.'

Jones wrapped his arms about himself. His body sagged beneath the cosy cardigan.

'Okay. Your point is taken. No production, just a private matter.'

'Just a private matter, he told the *News of the World*. Then let's see who employs you. You'd be finished, even in this business. You're not big enough to ride. You've made your home in the provincial theatre and the provinces are unforgiving.'

'I love it here.'

'Mm, but they won't love you when the tabloids have this lot all over the front pages. This place is about bums on seats not whips on bums. The Bathian morality is unforgiving, Mr Jones. You're going to drop more, much more than your trousers by the time I've finished with those pictures.'

'That's unfair.'

'It's what she threatened, wasn't it?'

'It's not as simple as that.'

'Murder.'

'Nothing to do with me. You know that.'

'I know it was.'

'You can't.'

'Really?'

'What I mean . . .'

'Yes?'

Leonard looked down his nose. He found cruelty as easy as compassion and he felt no compassion whatsoever for the stage manager.

'And there are other pictures—'

'What pictures? Nothing to do with me.'

'I didn't ask you to speak.'

'I'm sorry.'

'My lord? No? No, "m'lud?"'

'I'm sorry. An affectation. We all have them.'

Leonard removed his spectacles and rubbed gently with yet another silk handkerchief.

'There are pictures of other people. Part of a wonderful pornographic collection. You're hardly the star performer. Not even top of the bill.'

'She was a bitch.'

'Hardly unique. Hardly an excuse for murder. Or was it?'

'She wouldn't listen. Just kept saying the same thing over and over again.'

'Blackmailers do.'

Jones went to the edge of the stage, leaned against the marbled pillar. He rubbed at his eyes with podgy fingers.

'She was wicked.'

'Oh yes? I bet you longed to punish her.'

'She said she'd tell everyone. I said she was crazy.'

'You offered to buy her off.'

Jones dropped his head. His voice was deep and tired.

'Please, Inspector. You've had your fun. Just listen will you? She wanted recognition. She wanted a big part, a lead. Something really big. Hedda. That big. I told her she was mad. Anyway, I'm just the SM. But she said fix it or she'd fix me.'

'You can do better than that.'

'Listen, m'lud – I'm sorry. Listen, she was mad. She'd lived for thirty years with her mirror image. She believed it. Totally barking mad.'

Leonard raised his hands. Let them drop with a slap against his thighs in mock exasperation.

'So she had to be put down.'

Jones was still fearful of this policeman. He was fearful of all policemen and he was of the generation who understood what the sinister authority of accusation could hold.

'No and no again. What is it with you? Norman blew a fuse. Norman throttled her. Everything else that you're grubbing around is sad in your script, Okay, maybe sad in mine, but that's all. No one set out to kill Lynda. It – it, just happened.'

'People don't just happen to get murdered, Mr Jones.'

'Yes they do. But murderers don't just *happen* to murder. There's always a deeper reason for extreme behaviour.'

'And what's yours? Love, pain, guilt?'

'All three, if you want the truth. But that doesn't make me a murderer. Okay, you think you can destroy me and anyone else you wish to finger. I can't stop you. But there's no grand conspiracy. You won't find some cabal in this place, where everyone took it in turns to throttle her.'

Leonard tapped at the milking stool with his boot and squatted. He looked out into the stalls.

'Why should I believe that? You've been lying since the day I walked in here. You said you didn't know her, but you did.'

'Not really.'

Leonard got up, walked into the wings and took the glossy print from Leweson. The original disco party picture from all those years back. Two very young bare-chested men, each with a hand cupped beneath Lynda Elström's barely covered breasts. Leonard handed the print to Jones and went back to his stool.

'Not exactly the sort of thing to forget.'

'Just a wrap party. Happens at the end of every shoot. Just fun.'

'Page One fun.'

'Didn't hurt anyone, certainly not her. She got two magazine offers and a new film because of it. She wasn't complaining, nor was her agent. Ten per cent of the deal she cut was worth a roll of film.'

'I don't follow. Why her agent?'

'Cassie? She took the pictures. Course she wasn't an agent in those days. Unit stills photographer. You know? Publicity? That's how she made her name. Once she'd done that she made her money. Lynda was her first client. They made each other.'

Tiggy Jones looked at the picture again. He tapped the face of the third person in the photograph.

'You wouldn't think it there, but Maurice is ten years older than me. We were at drama school together. Sort of been around each other ever since. He got some work after that movie, but not much. Lynda made sure of that. Anyway it was a dog. Everyone remembers this picture. Everyone remembers

Lynda. No one remembers the movie and they certainly don't remember Maurice and me. I was running for donuts. He was trying to make something out of a nothing part. But he wasn't really an actor. The difference was I knew I wasn't going to make it in that side of the business. Maurice didn't. Or if he did he wouldn't accept it. Never has.'

'Angry.'

Tiggy Jones rubbed his mouth with the ends of the green neckerchief.

'Inside. Maurice never forgets, never compromises. Actors hate him until the notices. But if they let him down, or worse, if they do him down, they'll live to regret it.'

'Or die?'

The stage manager had said enough. He'd moved the fire. He was out of the heat. Leonard looked into the wings. Jack and Leweson hadn't moved. They were watching Jones's face. There had to be more. Leonard gave a huge sigh.

'Who took the pictures?'

'You really don't know?'

Leonard waited.

'You really *don't*, do you? You stupid policeman. You really are. Isn't it obvious?'

It was coming.

'I thought you knew.'

Jones shook his head. Slow sideways rocks of disbelief.

'Rudi, of course. Rudi Sharpe.'

The story of Rudi and his cameras, according to Tiggy Jones, was complex yet hardly surprising. In his early days, Rudi Sharpe had been a good actor, handsome as a matinée idol who could juggle and joke in four languages. But then he had a bad patch. Maybe there were too many east Europeans with thick accents who wanted to do more than three-line waiters. So Rudi did what a lot of young actors had done; he earned his rent money performing in alternative films. They weren't pornographic movies, but the post-war rave of so-called art films which claimed to be exploring unfulfilled dreams. Whatever their artistic talents, most of the film-makers became typecast, bitter and obscure. Most of the actors disappeared. It was then that Rudi started his photography. In those days, anyone with more than a box Brownie, would be taken seriously. Rudi did a few art magazine jobs and then met up with an art editor who wasn't too good. The art editor started an arts magazine which was nothing much more than soft porn and Rudi did the pictures.

Leonard sat on his milking stool realizing how little he knew about the characters in this murder. Now he was trying hard, just as Angela Billings had said he should have from the beginning. He looked up at Tiggy Jones.

'So Rudi became a porn photographer.'

Jones shrugged.

'It's deeper than that, but if you like, yes. The irony was that he had started getting acting jobs again. Rep mostly. Some television when they wanted a good looking Russian spy.'

'But he didn't sell his camera.'

'You still don't get it, do you? Rudi was mentally an exile. Stateless. His state was that bizarre apartment of his in London. Two rooms in Holland Park. Ever been there?'

Leonard said nothing. They hadn't. They should have. It was a bad miss.

'Amazing. It's a relic from some pre-World-War-Two life. Ugly furniture. Drapes. Lace. Antimacassars.'

'Pornography.'

'He didn't see it that way. Erotica. He loved it. Go and see for yourself. The apartment is wall-to-wall. Okay, one man's erotica is another's porn, but Rudi had one of the best catalogued private collections of Gill in London.'

Leonard was fascinated but he felt uncomfortable with his fascination.

'We're talking about murder. We're talking about suicide. There are no excuses for either.'

'I didn't offer you an excuse, Inspector. I'm trying to give you an insight – but then that's all beyond you. You're only interested in a conviction.'

Leonard scrubbed his hands through his curly hair. He was fed up with being tired. Fed up with being sick of what he did for a living. Fed up with low life like Jones being right.

'I just don't need this art house shit. You're telling me Rudi Sharpe was a porn photographer. No one calls the pictures we've seen erotica. No one. They're not even good pictures. Where did he take them?'

'I think the term is house calls, Inspector.'

Jack turned a new page and wrote herself a note. Why hadn't she thought of it herself?

Leonard was still looking puzzled. He'd lost his track. He was now interested. He had to drag himself back to his loathing.

'What I still don't understand is how Lynda got hold of the stuff.'

'She stole them.'

'How? When?'

'Last summer.'

'How?'

Jones shrugged.

'Simply took them when he wasn't looking. That's when the, eh, interest—'

'Panic.'

'The interest began. Rudi told me she had them. He said she'd been to his apartment. He'd gone out to get wine or something and when he got back she'd gone. It wasn't until later that he realized so had the negatives. So, yes, panic I suppose.'

'Including you.'

'Yes, Inspector. Including me. Including a lot of us. Until then, it was just good dirty fun. Private consumption, if you'll excuse the innuendo.'

'Including Jason Williams?'

Jones said nothing. Leonard scrubbed at his hands. Rubbed them together with such force they hurt. All very thorough, but it made no sense.

'Okay, okay, okay. But still I don't understand why. Why would anyone, why did *you*, let someone take pictures that after all, well could show up anywhere?'

'Because until now, they hadn't.'

'But tell me why the pictures were taken in the first place. To sell? To show each other? Christmas cards? What in hell were they for?'

Tiggy Jones closed his eyes, humphed his shoulders in a slow, inoffensive sigh. When he spoke, his voice was soft again, quiet, careful, almost kindly. Counsellor to mix-up.

'Ever take a picture of your girlfriend, Inspector?'

Leonard said nothing. Jack didn't move. She remembered Leonard's flat. Not a single photograph. Never before? She didn't know.

'Most natural thing in the world, Inspector. It starts as a photograph for the mantelpiece. It gets a little private. Then sexy. It gets to be fantasy. You know you can buy magazines with hardcore porn taken by husbands? So why? So the truth is there's a buzz. Maybe sad, as you said. Maybe a little sick, as you said. But life's full of fucking maybes, m'lud. I thought even policemen had one or two.'

'You mean you liked the pictures of yourself.'

'I mean maybe I got something that's legal and private and, yes, maybe I buzz. It was all very private – until now and no one hurt.'

'That's a crock of phony crap.'

'Inspector, you of all people should know about being phony. Look in the mirror – or perhaps you spend too much time doing that. Me? I don't pretend to be anything else. Try it. You'll get closer to people. But maybe you don't want that.'

Tiggy Jones had had enough and he'd seen through Leonard. He turned and walked off with more dignity than he'd walked on. He didn't care what Leonard thought or did. He was too old to care a damn.

Leonard sat where he'd been left, on his milking stool. Jack was scratching in her tiny writing in her tiny notebook. Leweson had gone. The long pause was broken with the quiet bell of Jack's mobile. She listened for fifteen seconds, said okay, and switched off. For reasons she didn't understand, she wanted Leonard to say something. He looked up, worn out and ridiculous, squatting nine inches above the boards.

'Mm?'

'That was DI Lane, sir. He's with Philips. He says he thinks you'd better get over there.'

Forty-Six

Philips sat in the interview room with his clasped hands resting on the thin table. By his side, the slip of a lawyer Marsh so detested. Leonard sat across from them with DI Lane to one side and Jack standing in the corner. Philips wanted to look at her. But he wouldn't, couldn't lift his bowed head. The film was running.

'You want to tell Inspector Leonard what you told me, Norman?'

Philips said nothing. His eyes never left his tightly gripped hands.

'Okay, Norman. From the top.'

Still nothing. Philips's breathing was uneven. He was confused. Lane had come to him in the prison and talked to him as a friend. Philips didn't feel angry now. Lane had calmed him, told him that he believed him and said that all they wanted was to find the truth, the whole truth. Philips liked Lane because this policeman was unhurried, older than the others, quiet.

Lane sat back, hands behind his neck, belly out, the button still missing. Lane had understood. Lane had spotted something odd while everyone else was riding with the confession. It was Lane who'd been left to read and re-read and re-read again. He'd asked Philips the right question – not *why*, but *how* did he kill her? There was no absolution for Philips, but the confession was simply his, and Lane had understood that. Now, Philips looked at him again, for the reassurance he needed.

Lane gave a half-smile, which was enough and Leonard leaned forward. He knew what was coming. Knew what Philips would say, but he wanted to hear the words and ask his own questions. Get the full implication for himself. This time the

246

lawyer would keep quiet. All different now. Lane nodded in quiet encouragement and Philips wet his lips.

'Like I said, she was outside when I saw her. Looking for a cab. Most of them won't pick up on the street nowadays, will they? I mean not nowadays. Not that late. I told her that. Like I said, she was all nervous, like. Talked a lot. Thought she was on something. Knew she wasn't. I mean, she didn't, did she? Then a couple of blokes came by. Give her the eye. I mean, you could see everything. No coat, you know. See the lot. Any rate, these two stop, didn't they? On the corner. One of them starts coming back. Slow. I knew there was trouble. I mean, there had to be.'

He took a breath.

'What did you do?'

Philips looked up at him. Forgotten he was there. Looked at Lane. Another quiet nod for his word-perfect pupil.

'Well, I says to her, "You better come with me. I'll phone you a cab," I says. Put it on the account. She just looks at me at first, she's still shivering and that. Then she sees this bloke coming so she grabs me arm. Real tight. We go down the side and I unlocks the place and lets us in. But she's screwed up. I says she can have me anorak. So I takes it off and goes to give it her. But she says no. Then she's really shivering. But I reckoned she's scared of something. Then she starts rubbing herself.'

'What sort of rubbing?'

'To get warm. She's rubbing herself all over. Crazy it was. Then she's really frightened. "What about those men," she says. Wants to know if the doors are locked.'

'Which doors?'

'Outside and the one up to the stage.'

'Go on.'

'I says I'll go and do it. She says no, I'm to stay. Next thing she's got her arms round me. Well . . .'

Leonard kept quite still. This was the moment he wanted.

'And?'

'Well, she starts moving against me. It's not just hugging or anything. Real moving. And I got a bit scared. I mean, I know

247

who she is, but I can't help it. I starts touching her. Just not much, you know. And I thinks she doesn't mind, like. So I try to kiss her. That's when she starts screaming and calling something rotten. She's right demented. This funny noise of hers. Sounds like some animal. First she runs at the door up to the stage. But of course it's locked. That makes her madder. She says I've trapped her. She's now real screaming. So I grab her as she goes for the main door—'

'Why?'

''Cos the bitch is crazy. She's going to say things.'

'What happened?'

Philips raised his arms in a grabbing motion.

'I've got her from behind. Nearly lifting her off the ground, I am. But I've got her. And she starts that screaming again. And so I've got to stop her, haven't I? I mean I can't let it go on. She'll have me. No one will believe me. And so I does it.'

Only Lane had thought it through. Only Lane, who remembered her as crumpet, had imagined Lynda was in front of him, had put his arms about her and then worked out what he would have done if she'd screamed rape. The one thing he wouldn't have done to a woman in a struggling frenzy, was strangle her. Too difficult. Lane had guessed the obvious and Philips had done the obvious.

'I put me hand over her mouth. But she's still screaming and she bites me. So – so – well – I've still got me anorak somehow, so I puts it over her face and then – and then – well – I just holds on until she stops.'

Philips let his head drop forward. Slowly. Until it touched his hands. He was very still.

'Did you at any time put your hands around Miss Elström's throat?'

'No.'

'Are you sure?'

'No.'

'You mean no you're not sure?'

The lawyer moved in.

'Mr Philips has made it perfectly clear what he means. He means no, he did not put his hands about the deceased's throat and no he did not attempt to strangle her nor did he strangle her.'

'No. I don't think so.'

'Tell me, Norman, what don't you think?'

'I don't think I did.'

'But you're not certain?'

'I don't know. But you see, don't you? She stops her screaming because, well, because she couldn't breathe. Then she just collapses and I'm still holding her.'

'Then what did you do?'

'Like I told you before. I left her by the red couch thing and goes outside to see if I could see someone. Someone to help.'

'Why didn't you use the telephone?'

'I didn't think. I just wanted someone quick. I thought maybe there'd be someone. So I went round into the square. But there wasn't anyone. No one I could ask, anyway.'

'What happened when you came back?'

Philips was now visibly frightened. He'd rehearsed it with Lane, he thought Lane knew it anyway. This one wasn't the same. Those flaming specs of his.

'Tell me. Norman, what did you see?'

He looked at Lane again. Lane wouldn't let him down.

'Mr Poulson and Jason.'

'Where were they?'

'They were with her.'

'Was she alive?'

The lawyer sprang. She spoke, looking at the camera. Wanted to make certain it was working.

'My client is not qualified to give a medical opinion of the condition of Miss Elström at that or at any other time.'

Philips carried on as if she weren't in the room.

'Mr Poulson looks up and he says I've killed her. I just stands there. Then Jason says don't worry. Tells me that I've got to go home just as normal and come in tomorrow just as normal and they'll take care of things. I says what are they going to do and they says don't worry, they'll do what's got to be done.'

'Who said that?'

'Mr Poulson. He said they'll handle it. Then he gives me me

anorak, only I didn't want it, but he says I've got to have it and I've got to wear it in the morning like I always do, so everything's normal.'

'What did you do then?'

'I went.'

'What did they do?'

Again, the lawyer was leaning across the table.

'My client left the building and therefore can have no knowledge of what happened after his departure.'

Leonard wondered. Removed his spectacles and then asked the three questions Lane had forgotten to ask.

'Did you go *straight* home, Norman?'

Long, long pause. Lane woke up. The lawyer looked at her client. The answer was just audible.

'No. No, I didn't.'

'You hung around.'

'I must object. The question makes an assumption. My client does not have to answer.'

But Norman understood the question. Had the answer.

'Yes. Over by the deli doorway.'

Then the second question.

'Did you see Mr Poulson and Mr Williams again that night?'

'When they came out.'

'What time?'

'About two.'

The third.

'What did they do?'

'There was a car waiting for them. It turned up about five minutes before they came out.'

'Did you recognize it, Norman?'

'Oh, yes. Blue BMW convertible. I saw her. Easy in the street light where she was parked. Her all right.'

'Her?'

'That agent woman. Cassie Whatshername.'

Forty-Seven

Lane's car was an adventure playground for a bad-tempered environmental health officer. Sandwich wrappings, hamburger boxes, toffee papers and a stale stench of small-cigar smoke said a great deal about Lane's innards and future. Now he drove with one hand on the wheel, the other tugging at a sweet foil clenched between his red-gummed teeth. Jack sat in the back, the window lowered a fraction for fresh air – any air. Leonard slumped in the front seat, his head barely visible to any passer-by. They hadn't said much since the interrogation. Philips, pathetic in his blue prison garb had shaken hands with all three and thanked them for coming before limping away to be locked up for the rest of the day.

'Could be lying. But I can't see why. Can you?'

Leonard didn't answer. He believed every word. Knew that he shouldn't. Jack gazed from the window as they stopped at traffic lights on the outskirts of the city.

'But why now?'

The lights changed and Lane glanced at her in his mirror.

'Screwed up. Emotionally unbalanced. Perhaps he even believed it all first time round. He wouldn't be the first to confess to half a story. After all, he's not saying he didn't kill her. And his lawyer's not saying that. So we've still got a case.'

'No.'

Leonard's voice came from deep in his chest. He sounded weary. Sad. Overwhelmed. Lane poked at toffee stuck to a right molar and glanced down.

'But he's not backing off.'

'We've only his word that he killed her. But he didn't strangle her. The medical report says she was strangled.'

'Hang a tic, Jimbo, he didn't say that. He says he smothered her—'

'As you spotted—'

'Right. But then you pressed him and he admitted that he could have strangled her as well. Afterwards.'

The traffic was almost at a standstill. Jack opened another knuckle's width of window.

'One thing we do know, sir. Philips didn't string her up.'

Lane sucked hard and the last bit of stuck toffee gave way. The car phone shrilled and Lane wiped his fingers on his lapel before answering.

'Lane.'

He listened for a few moments.

'Wait one, Bernard. Better have a word with DI Leonard.'

Leonard took the receiver. It was sticky with toffee and sweat. He listened for a couple of seconds.

'Okay, Leverson. DI Lane'll meet you at the theatre in ten minutes. Keep him there – and the rest of them. Have the warrant with you and then come on to the Williams place. You'll need a search doc. But no noise. No bother. Wait at the corner until I call you in.'

He clicked off the phone and let it dangle to the floor where Lane normally stowed it and pointed to the cab rank.

'Pull over, will you, Ray? We're going up to the bungalow. You talk to Poulson. At this stage it's nothing more than further questioning. Wait until we see what Williams says. Perhaps we need a confrontation.'

The car crossed the lane and came to a halt on the other side of the road behind the only cab and Jack and Leonard got out. He leaned back through the open driver's window.

'Just a thought. Ask Poulson who else was with them.'

'Apart from Williams?'

Leonard nodded.

'Cast of thousands. Maybe I'm wrong. But Philips couldn't have seen the stage door from the deli. Only the road. So what if there were others there and they went the other way?'

Lane drove off with a blip on his hooter and Leonard turned to where Jack stood at an empty bay. The cab had gone.

'Shit.'

'Yes, sir. Oh, and by the way, it's Leweson, not Leverson.'

He was looking at the ground. Buzzing.

'What is?'

She turned away with half a smile. Bernard's mother would never know.

'Never mind, sir. Never mind.

Forty-Eight

The lights were already on. The curtains all closed except for the sitting room where a gap was left to show off the silver and gold twinkling Christmas tree. In the kitchen a digi-disc was playing carols from King's College. Mrs Williams bent over the cake she had made in early November and hummed 'Ding Dong Merrily' as she smoothed the icing with a warm spatula.

'Nearly finished, Mum, just this to do.'

Mrs Williams smiled fondly at her son as he stood by the long work surface, slim in his father's blue-and-white striped apron. His hands protected by white cotton polishing gloves. The teapot was Georgian. Jason had bought it for them. They'd never used it, of course. It only came out of the display cabinet to be cleaned, along with the hot water jug, tongs and sugar bowl and those dangerous round clippers for beheading boiled eggs, or as the late Mr Williams had once joked, for beheading more private parts. He'd only made the remark once. Mrs Williams did not approve and told him so. Told him to wash his mouth out with carbolic. He could leave his smutty talk on his ship where it belonged. Mrs Williams was washing the bowl and spatula and thinking about a nice cup of tea and a chocolate digestive or a ginger nut when the door chimes rang the first bar of 'Wonderful You', Jason's biggest hit, which he'd dedicated to her.

Mrs Williams and Leonard blinked at each other. Jack smiled.

'We've come to see Jason, Mrs Williams.'

She said nothing and her son, curious at the silence, came into the wide square hall. He stood, a silver-polish stained yellow duster in one hand and a two-hundred-year-old sugar bowl in the other. Mrs Williams stood aside and her son led them into the kitchen. Leonard and Jack said no to tea, no to ginger nuts. Heavy in their winter street clothes, they stood as intruders in the spotless kitchen where the glittering pom-poms and paper sticky-tape and scissors ready for present wrapping presented a scene of clean, ordinary, loving family life alien to the two police officers.

'I wonder if we may have a private word, sir.'

The formality stuck in Leonard's throat. But it was enough. As they'd arranged, Jack stayed with Mrs Williams and said yes after all to tea while Jason Williams led the detective into a large oval room with a Victorian library desk in front of the triple-glazed aluminium French windows and two soft sofas either side of the white marble fireplace. On a Georgian Pembroke with a brass green-shaded lamp stood a gallery of signed pictures of honour in crinkly silver frames. Jason with the past Prime Minister, Jason with the Queen, Jason with the UN High Commissioner for Refugees, Jason with the US president before last. Jason with his decoration and his mother at Buckingham Palace. Jason flopped into one of the sofas and flicked back his hair. Leonard remained standing, conscious of his dirty boots on the spotless carpet, scruffy in his old coat made shabbier by the white Adam-styling behind him backlit by the flame-effect log fire.

'Okay, Inspector, what this time?'

'Do you mind telling me, sir, where you were at approximately midnight on the night Miss Elström died?'

Williams shook his head in disbelief. He recrossed one exquisitely tailored soft green trouser leg over the other and fiddled with the pearl button of his silk midnight blue polo shirt. The effect was as elegant as it was meant to be. He wore his disguise as one who has long-forgotten old clothes.

'My God, I'm not hearing this, Inspector. I mean, my God, you get the Best Supporting Lemon Oscar, yes? Tell me something, do your superiors know you're here?'

'Do you mind telling me, sir, where you were at approximately midnight on the night Miss Elström died?'

'It's stuck or something. My God, I mean, oh my God, this

is too much, really, too much. You know, Inspector, I have a whole organization that does nothing else but keep pests out of my life. But you pest officially. My God, I mean, you want to go now before I call my lawyers and then a real policeman?'

'Do you mind telling me, sir where you were at approximately midnight on the night Miss Elström died?'

'That's it. That, Inspector, is it. Okay?'

He grabbed the portable phone lying on the sofa arm.

'You know what I'm going to do, Inspector, I'm going to call the police and have them come over here and arrest you. Harassment? Invasion of privacy? Persecution? It's a pity there's no law against stupidity or they'd throw the key away.'

He looked at the key pad. Finger poised, but with no number to dial. Leonard had taken a pencil stub from his waistcoat pocket and was scribbling on the back of an unpaid Woods restaurant bill. He handed it to a surprised Williams.

'If I may suggest, sir, you call either of these numbers. Detective Superintendent Marsh at Manvers Street, or Assistant Chief Constable Heng at Portishead and I also suggest, sir, that one of your lawyers, or even all of them may be a good idea. While you're doing so, I wonder if you'd mind telling me where you were at approximately midnight on the night Miss Elström died?'

Williams looked at the two numbers.

'How do I know these are real?'

'Try them, sir.'

Williams bounced the slim phone in his thin hand. His mouth twisted in indecision.

'Okay, just for a minute, let's play games. You know perfectly well where I was, Inspector. I've told you before and I'll tell you just one more time. I was here in this very house. I was here all evening and all night. You have my word and my mum's word. She saw me and she heard me.'

'Miss Elström died in the theatre at approximately twelve thirty. Would you like to tell me where you were at that time?'

'Here.'

'You're perfectly sure?'

'Yes. Perfectly sure. So is my mum.'

'Could you be mistaken?'

'Absolutely not. Nor is my mum.'

'We shall, of course, ask her ourselves.'

'Inspector, I'm trying very hard to keep my temper, but I guess you are trying harder. I think, Inspector, you are winning. I am getting mega mad.'

He rubbed at his temples.

'I now have a headache. I think maybe it's time to try these numbers.'

'As you wish.'

'What?'

'Go ahead. Dial.'

'Okay.'

Williams stabbed at the phone. The dialling was obvious.

'Engaged.'

'No, sir. Never engaged. All calls are automatically answered after the first ring, you get tone options and then you're stacked. Infuriating, but true. The music's the police band. You want to try again?'

Williams, sitting among the folds of the comfy sofa, didn't bring off his attempt at being above Leonard's irony. The hair bounced with the toss of the head, but it didn't come to much more than a shampoo ad. He tried staring. Hard stare. Leonard ignored him. Instead, the policeman picked up the photograph of the pop star with Mrs Williams holding the flat, padded box and the gaudy insignia. Leonard weighed it and looked at Williams for likeness. He put it back on the table in its original position where Williams could see it from where he sat. Leonard took out an envelope from his duffle coat pocket and removed a photograph.

'And while you're on to Superintendent Marsh, sir, or even the ACC, you might ask them what they thought of this.'

He tossed the picture on to the sofa.

In one moment the bombast was gone. He dropped the phone back on the scarlet cushion and tried clearing his throat. Something else that didn't quite come off. His hand stretched towards the glossy photograph, but he didn't touch.

'Where did you—'

'I think you know where.'

Williams looked at the picture, then away. Suddenly the door opened. Mrs Williams, smiling eyes behind her granny glasses, popped her head around the door. Williams flopped a cushion over the print.

'Anyone for tea in here?'

Leonard said nothing. Williams twisted in the deep sofa, his hand firmly on the cushion.

'No thanks, Mum. Not just yet.'

'But you haven't had your tea yet, Jason. That's not like you.'

'We've – we've things to talk about. We'll be out.'

She looked at Leonard who had once more picked up the Palace photograph. Instead of leaving, she came over to where he was standing.

'Don't you think that's lovely? A lovely, lovely day. I'll never forget it. Everyone was so nice. Weren't they, Jason?'

He nodded. Trying hard to look at her but couldn't.

'Lovely, Mum. Really excellent.'

'And the Queen—'

She turned beaming to Leonard.

'Has Jason told you what she said?'

'No, Mrs Williams, I'm afraid he hasn't.'

'Oh, Jason, you should have. She said that she knew all his songs and she had all his records. Records! I ask you. Those were the days, weren't they?'

Neither man spoke.

'What is it, darling? You look a bit queer. Have some tea.'

The easy nature slipped away.

'Mum, please? Really, please.'

She started for the sofa, but in panic he put up his hand to fend her away.

'Mum! I'm sorry, but, my God, this is important, okay?'

She looked shocked, looked to where his hand remained firmly over the cushion. Her mouth set in a tight line. Her eyes glinted. The smile had gone and she hurried from the room, pulling a tiny handkerchief from her sleeve as she did so. Leonard followed, closed the open door then returned to the fireplace. Williams hadn't moved.

'Where shall we start, Williams? Paedophilia or murder? I don't mind. Entirely up to you.'

Williams closed his eyes and lay back with his hands limp in his lap.

'You, of course, have a right to call your lawyers. But you might wish to get the preliminaries done in a less formal manner. We have evidence that you were in the theatre, that you were with Lynda.'

Leonard paused and took a chance.

'We have evidence that you were with her when she was lying on the floor *while* she was still alive.'

'Maurice.'

Leonard waited. There'd be more, always was. The waiting game, someone had called it. Hanging around was Leonard's version. He said nothing. Williams wanted to talk.

'Maurice told you this.'

Williams's voice was flat. But he wasn't finished – not yet.

'Course he did. He hated her, always had.'

'What did you see?'

'Maurice killed her.'

'You saw him?'

'Oh yes. Everyone saw him.'

The voice was in a dream.

'Who was everyone?'

'Just everyone. But she had to die. You see that don't you?'

The eyes that turned to Leonard were empty. Clean. But no longer of any world Leonard inhabited. Afterwards, Leonard would remember those eyes. Eyes detached from a decision already made deep down.

'Bastards, you see.'

There was a noise from the hallway, but the door remained closed. Williams gazed at nothing. The same voice talked to nobody.

'Mum. She won't understand, you know. Never in a million years.'

He moved the cushion aside and looked at the photograph. His face twisted in something deeper than agony. But no shame. There should have been a ticking clock on the library desk. The golden silence of the quartz carriage didn't inspire much in the way of tranquil reflection. Perhaps it was enough for the singer. Suddenly, Williams stood with both hands cupped over his mouth. He was crying a muffled, animal, whimper.

'I'm going to be sick.'

There was a gulping sound from deep in his throat and he rushed from the room. Leonard took his time, but followed as the other man with short, almost mincing steps trying to control his bowels as well as his stomach, scurried across the hallway into the open bathroom and slid the bolt behind him. Leonard stood outside. Waited. Listened to the the sound of lunch going into the lavatory pan. Across the way, Mrs Williams watched with a solemn childish expression. Jack hovered protectively at her shoulder. Leonard opened his hands. One of those things. His attempted reassuring smile was no more successful than any other he'd rehearsed. Instead he ushered them into the kitchen.

'Better get a car up here. Let's have a WPC to stay with Mrs Williams for the moment. And get Leverson in. Tell them quiet. No fuss. After all, it's Mrs Williams's home, okay?'

Jack went out to the hall, closing the kitchen door as she did so. No need for Mrs Williams to be frightened. With any luck, they could get her son out, into the car and down to Manvers Street before she knew what was going on. Leonard could explain that at least.

Mrs Williams poured tea. She was born of a generation and caste for whom pouring tea was the means of reducing any crisis to a problem. Her parents had fought what her father had called the Second German War, in the hope that a good brew-up would show a nation unruffled rather than ignorant of what exactly was going on and what exactly it was supposed to do. Mrs Williams felt that now. She remained unruffled because she was ignorant of what had happened although something "was up", as her father would have said. She pushed the cup and saucer across the table to Leonard. She'd not asked if he wanted tea. She didn't like him, but for Jason's sake she felt that she was going to have to appear to like him. She sat down crossing her neat, fluffy slippered feat beneath the chair.

'It's all very difficult, isn't it?'

'Your son's going to come to Manvers Street with us and help us sort a few things.'

'What's Manvers Street?'

Leonard looked up from his untouched cup. But there was only innocence in the old eyes. To them all, Manvers Street had become jargon. To anyone outside the force, the street was simply that traffic-packed, fume-filled throughway to Bath Spa station.

'The police station.'

'But Jason's not been arrested or anything. I mean, he hasn't done anything wrong, has he?'

'We believe so, Mrs Williams. I'm sorry.'

He sipped his tea. It was weak. Scented. Horrid. He scraped his chair closer to the table.

'Tell me, when you said that Jason was in all that night, are you sure?'

'Yes, of course I am. I mean, I heard him.'

'But did you see him?'

'Oh, yes.'

'Certain?'

'Oh, yes. Very certain. You see he came in to say goodnight, just as I said, and then I had a little doze and then the naughty boy woke me up, you see, with his radio.'

'In your room?'

'No. In here. This one.'

Leonard flicked a glance to the neat, perfectly balanced Bose on the fitted cherrywood dresser. He picked up the thin remote control and touched the play button. The music was low, sweet, inoffensive. It would never have frightened anyone in a lift. He brushed another button. The station changed to more songs for aging swingers.

'Very nice.'

'Jason bought it for me. Of course it's too complicated for me. I just press the bit that makes it turn on.'

She sipped her tea and touched her mouth with her handkerchief.

'He's going to be all right, isn't he?'

Leonard was only half-listening. The murmur of voices in the hall told him that the young DC had arrived with the search team. He hoped the WPC wouldn't be long.

'I'm sorry, Mrs Williams, what was that?'

'I said he is—'

She stopped. They both did. From the hall came a heavy banging. He could hear Madelaine Jack shouting Williams's name. He waved Mrs Williams down with a flutter of his hands and reached the hall to see the big Bristolian boot of constable Bradley belting the bathroom door at handle level. The bolt took one kick and gave way. Madelaine Jack was first in and first out.

'Shit! Get an ambulance up here now. Very now. And the doc. Oh shit! Shit! Shit! Shit! Shit!'

Leonard could now see into the bathroom. Bradley was on his knees, slipping on blood. Leonard didn't have to ask. Jack looked by him and nodded to Mrs Williams. DC Leweson took the old lady by the elbow and led her back into the kitchen. But she knew. They all knew. No need for the siren.

Forty-Nine

Marsh had the air of solemn calm amidst dreadful blasphemy. In his corner first-floor office, he sat stiffly in his high-backed chair. Black suit buttoned, dark blue tie tightly knotted into his starched white collar. He glared at the single sheet of paper that lay on his otherwise clear desk and ran his silver pencil down the eighteen lines of terse explanation. That done, he breathed sharply out through his nostrils and then placed his pencil parallel to the report and looked across to where Leonard, legs straight, hands in jacket pockets, slumped chin on chest in the only other comfortable chair in the office.

'This will be going to the ACC tonight. You've nothing to add?'

Leonard shook his head without looking up.

'No, sir. He said he was going to be sick. He went into the bathroom. He was sick. I heard him. DS Jack waited in the hall. I talked to Mrs Williams. DS Jack heard the shower running, then banged on the door. At about that time, the search group arrived. That delayed action while she let them in. She asked Constable Bradley to effect entry to the bathroom. Constable Bradley's boot obliged. They found Williams on the bathroom floor. He had slit his jugular, apparently with a cut-throat razor, which, sir, we understand had been the property of his late father, Hubert Williams.'

That was as near Leonard could get to a formal presentation.

'Why was he being sick – if he was?'

'I heard him, sir.'

'You heard the sound of someone being sick. A trick. The man was a thespian. Illusionists. All of them. You were tricked. Now tell me, what prompted him?'

'I had confronted—'

'Confronted?'

Leonard's stomach grumbled. He couldn't remember the last time he'd eaten. Certainly not that day. He could taste his dirty breath. His teeth felt caked and his gums bloody. He was tired, dirty, disappointed and his thoughts and temper confused. He didn't need Marsh. He needed time to himself.

'Look, sir, three hours earlier we'd got it from Philips that Williams was with Poulson. One of them, both of them maybe, hoisted her on the wire until it half cut her head off. Maybe she wasn't even dead when they strung her up. There's that whole bag of pictures downstairs. Williams screwing children. Yes, sir. I confronted him all right. I showed him one of the pictures. He crashed.'

'And you let him get away.'

'I had no idea. I couldn't have.'

'You could have and you failed. It is carelessness of the most obvious order to allow a suspect to commit suicide. We shall now be accused of causing his death. Williams remains a man

262

of considerable public standing. He has millions, perhaps even billions, of followers.'

'It'll do wonders for his sales.'

'We have the world's media descending on this city. Descending on this force. This will not be the moment for No Comment.'

'Then show them the pictures.'

'What!'

The exclamation rode on a hiss of non-conformist wrath.

'Show them, sir. Show them what we've got. After all, he's not coming to trial. Tell them what he was. A nasty, corrupt bastard of the lowest form. Tell them that he loved his mother and screwed nine-year-olds. That'll divert their attention from everyone's promotion prospects.'

'I believe you're over tired. You judge badly, Leonard. You judge badly. We live in an age of instant litigation. His agents, music company, probably even the person who makes Jason's T-shirts, would sue us for defamation, loss of earnings, character assassination by association, or anything else their lawyers could think of. Not to mention the way we handled his mother. We're going to have everyone from Liberty to the WI on our backs. Where is she now? Not in some ICU, one hopes.'

'No, sir. Sergeant Jack organized things. She's in the Rivers Hotel with the Rosses. Cassie Ross, or Makins as she still calls herself, was Williams's agent. They're old friends.'

'Did she not . . .?'

'Makins? Yes, sir. But we've a WPC with her and two men outside the door. But I thought it was best to let Mrs Williams be with a friendly face.'

'Let's hope we have some when the time comes. Somehow I doubt it.'

Leonard stood. Circled the room with his fists rubbing his aching spinal cord. He stretched as high as he could. He felt all in. Marsh was right. He shouldn't have left Williams alone. Now they'd want someone for it. He'd do. He'd had enough, anyway. He'd had enough all those years ago but hadn't done anything about it. This time he would.

'Look, sir, I can either clear out my desk, or go into the MIR and make coffee for everyone or—'

'And when the media hear that, it'll be seen as an admission of wrong-doing by us, not just you, us. Oh no, you will tie this up in a reef knot. Not a granny, mind you. A nice flat reef knot. You and that sergeant of yours will get along to the theatre and sort that sanctimonious pouch of charlatans and whores. But let me tell you, if any one of them so much hints that he or she wishes to use the facilities you are to stick to them whatever their sex and whatever the function they wish to perform. Is that understood?'

Leonard nodded. Didn't speak. Left the door open as he headed down the corridor to collect 'that sergeant' of his.

Fifty

The news of Williams's death was out. In front of the theatre, metal barriers and twenty-two special constables kept the press on the other side of the road. Enough camera crews to record the aftermath of a monarch were stacked along the kerbs. Photographers perched on high ladders. Above them, a television news crew had promised half a year's income to a civil rights lawyer who worked from one room and two windows overlooking the theatre. His desk had been shoved into one corner while cameras appeared from his legal turret and the lawyer was sent out for rolls and fresh coffee. He'd been gone for some time. Behind the press, the public had gathered and the crowd was growing. The narrow roads and lanes as far back as the station, the abbey, Queen Square, Quiet Street and the Upper Bristol Road had come to a standstill. No one seemed to know what was going on, but it was enough to know something was. There was no fear of anyone in the theatre doing a runner. They couldn't get out unless the Fairy God-mother's wand really did work. It had taken Leonard and Jack, using three uniformed officers as battering rams, twenty minutes to get from Manvers Street and into the theatre by the Beauford Square side door.

The constable who let them in pointed up to the auditorium. There weren't many stone steps to climb, but his legs ached. Jack kept respectful pace with him. He kept his eyes on her shoes. He was puffing. She wasn't.

'D'you work out?'

'Ride.'

'Didn't know that.'

'Between me and the pony, sir.'

She held the door open for him and he felt even older.

The theatre was brightly lit. The house lights were up and the iron down. The ones he'd asked for were there. Angela Billings with yet another nearly finished crossword. Joanna Cunliffe and Tiggy Jones side by side in the third row, heads bent in whispers. The twins crunching cachous. Perfectly set. Perfectly arranged. Beneath each green Exit sign stood a hatless, uniformed constable. Leonard paused at the side aisle.

'Poulson?'

The constable looked around.

'The guy in black, sir?'

'Right.'

'DI Lane said to keep him in his office, sir. It's down the back somewhere, I think.'

Leonard nodded his thanks. He knew exactly where. He could wait. Even if he had a lavatory en-suite, Poulson had no problems with himself.

Leonard walked between the first and second rows, tapping the backs of the front seats as he went. He stopped in the centre and leaned back. Everyone was waiting. Angela Billings pulled her scarlet and black shawl closer. The Rostows brushed their puffed and flowing frocks and giggled in unison. Tiggy Jones sunk deeper into his woolly mustard scarf and Joanna Cunliffe stretched in her green silk shirt to little effect. To Leonard, they all looked very ordinary. He thought about them for a moment. Hell, why be subtle? They were, after all, children – and very nasty ones.

'A few hours ago Jason Williams killed himself. He bled to death.'

The Rostows fluttered their ancient lashes at each other. Joanna Cunliffe scratched at her thighs and dropped her head. Tiggy Jones rolled his head side to side as if the whole thing was just too much. Angela Billings smiled contentedly. Now what? Hell. Why not? If Marsh wouldn't tell the press, this lot would do it for him.

'Shortly before he killed himself, Williams had been shown a photograph of himself screwing a small girl. I repeat, screwing a small girl.'

Now he had their attention. This was better than make-believe.

'He'd also been told that we now have evidence that he was with Lynda Elström at the time of her death. We also know that he was not alone – and I do not mean Norman Philips. Okay?'

No movement. Nothing except fear. Which was exactly what Leonard wanted. God, how he hated them.

'Jason Williams was a nasty, cruel shit who fucked small children and made them satisfy his perversions. He was, at the very least, an accomplice to murder. Understand?'

Nothing. Total silence. No movement at all.

'I *said*, do you understand?'

Slight nods. They understood.

'Good. Some of you here understand more than most. For example, we also have photographs of three of you performing a sadistic sex act.'

The false eyelashes were still. Tiggy Jones looked straight ahead.

'These pictures were once held by Lynda Elström and were being used as blackmail. So forget Norman Philips, we're now going to put together what happened *after* he attacked her and – and – who was there. Okay?'

Again nothing.

'I *said*, okay?'

Again a few nods. Now was the time to take his chances.

'Questions. I have the answers. I want them confirmed. If

any of you lies or evades the question I shall take you in, throw you in the slammer and take my fucking time about opening the door again. *Forget* police procedures. *Forget* your legal positions. So *forget* any idea of fucking me about.'

Madelaine Jack stared. Bewildered. *Forget* your career in this or any other police force. But the effect was what he wanted.

Tiggy Jones opened his mouth to speak. The Twins held hands. Angela Billings looked interested. Joanna Cunliffe looked anxious. This was exactly what Leonard wanted. He needed to make them all think he knew more than he did – which wasn't much beyond guesswork. Make them dump on each other.

'Let's start. First question is the original question: where were you? Don't lie. Don't hold back. I'll rip out the truth if I have to. Miss Cunliffe. You were here, in the Vaults. Until when?'

She huffed some breath into her lungs. She of all people believed him.

'Twelve, almost exactly.'

'How do you know?'

'I set the alarm when I let everyone out. It was reading zero. At first I thought it was broken. Then it clicked to one minute.'

'Not 2400?'

'You can check.'

'I will. Who was left?'

'No one.'

'Sure?'

'Certain. Just as I told you before.'

'You said you got a cab. True?'

'Yes. You can check with Triple A. It was on the theatre's account. It, eh, shouldn't have been, but it was.'

'I'll check. Where to?'

She looked down. He was still pissed off.

'Where to, Miss Cunliffe?'

'Is it necessary?'

'Speak!'

Jack was fascinated. She remembered the mongoose. His voice was sharp. Cruel. Hideously antagonistic.

'Nathan's. It's – it's a club in, eh, Bristol. Clifton.'

'I'll check.'

He looked across to Jack. She made a note. She knew Nathan's. Run by a Frenchwoman who understood the needs of very private women, especially wives. Private was a nice understatement. There'd be no alibi. Joanna Cunliffe was either very clever or very frightened, or both.

Leonard stabbed a finger at the twins.

'Which one had flu?'

One podgy arm was raised. A smile was not.

'Bollocks!'

Angela Billings smiled. She was beginning to enjoy this. Jack did not. One of the twins popped a cachou. The other didn't. The spell was broken.

'Which one came down here?'

The beginnings of giggles didn't get far. Leonard was going too fast. He switched to Tiggy Jones.

'Which one?'

'I, um, well m'lud, I um—'

Leonard was back on the Rostows.

'You were both up and down here together and going through your routine within twenty-four hours. Someone hit with 102 degrees doesn't do that. You had rooms on the ground floor. The going for a walk thing was nothing more than setting up an alibi. One of you went out by the garden window.'

Jack remembered the de-briefing in the Incident Room. Remembered the new constable being told to think about it. Leonard had, even then. He should have told her. Maybe everyone was right. Leonard was the only one on his team. Now he didn't wait for an answer.

'Okay, tell. What happened?'

Leonard thought it was probably Hilda who started to speak.

'My loverlee little dearie, you're quite wrong, you know. Isn't he just so jungly?'

The other didn't so much nod as bounce her head on her chins. Leonard bounced them together.

'Don't give me shit. We've done that bit.'

He turned to the whole group and pointed at the Rostows.

'Okay, for everyone who doesn't know, the twins were part of the blackmail. We've now got the pictures Lynda Elström had. They include a set of prints showing these two in leathers chains and mask whipping shit out of—'

He paused, watching Jones sweat.

'Out of a so-far unidentified naked man.'

He bored into Hilda Rostow who stuffed her mouth with two cachou pastilles.

'You came down to meet her.'

The voice was high, squeaky, a stuck piglet.

'She was very naughty.'

The other Rostow nodded.

'She was very, very, very naughty. She had silly pictures and she said she was going to show everyone.'

'She told you that?'

They looked at each other. Shook their heads. In unison. Tiggy Jones gave himself a big, reassuring hug and spoke into his puffed chest.

'She told me.'

'She said?'

'You know what she said. I told the twinnies because, well, because it involved them. We all agreed to meet her. Talk it through.'

'Where?'

'Here.'

Leonard pointed to the floor.

'You mean in here?'

Jones nodded towards the safety curtain.

'Yes, up there.'

Leonard waved a hand at Joanna Cunliffe.

'So she's lying when she says she let everyone out.'

Jones shook his head.

'No. Jonah had a cab waiting. I simply came back in. Hillie came down and I let her in.'

'When was that?'

'Twelve twenty.'

'Why that time?'

'She said not before. Not after. She said she'd be by the stage door.'

'That's when you met her.'

'No. She didn't show. We waited.'

'Who else was here?'

'Maurice.'

'She was blackmailing him as well?'

Jones tried a laugh that did quite well.

'No one would dare blackmail Maurice. No. You see, I'd told him what was going on.'

'Why?'

He shrugged.

'I always have. I've always told him everything. He's my oldest, maybe my only friend.'

Leonard didn't say 'Ah'.

'And Williams? He was here?'

'Naturally, he had most to lose.'

'What happened?'

The twins were looking at Jones. Jones was looking at his jumbling podgy hands in his lap.

'I don't know. We stayed up here.'

'You're lying.'

'Maurice and Jay heard her. She was screaming. They went down to the stage door. Next thing we knew she was dead. Ask him, he'll tell you. He was there. We weren't.'

So much for his oldest and closest friend, thought Leonard. But he was right. According to Philips only two of them had been there. Poulson and Williams. Williams was in the morgue. Poulson was alive. They still needed to check times. To find out how Lynda Elström, or her body, had got from the stage door to the wire. Leave that to young Leweson who'd just come in. The man who had the answers was the man who'd always had the answers.

Fifty-One

Maurice Poulson sat at his desk in the subterranean office at the back of the theatre. There was a smell of damp that a mortgage surveyor would have given an eye tooth for. The director had been waiting for Leonard for four hours. If the wait irritated him he gave no sign. Leonard thought Poulson had never given any sign of any emotion, except, of course, as the second groper in the Spanish disco. But that was a long time ago. The third person in the picture was now dead. That wasn't so long ago, but maybe the motive was.

Jack sat, as ever, in the furthest corner. It was always best to be out of direct sight when you were writing it all down. Leonard was back on The Chair of Chairs. It would never be repaired. Never be discarded until it collapsed. Ever faithful to the text. Like Poulson. Like Leonard.

'Tell me, Mr Poulson, who strung up Lynda?'

The eyes were still as the black cotton of his shirt. Not a heartbeat out of time.

'Does it matter? She was dead.'

'You're a doctor?'

'She was dead. It's the only time I've ever been sure about her.'

'What you see, what you think, and what is, are rarely the same.'

'The conclusion is.'

'You should know that Norman Philips saw you and Williams with her when he returned. You should also know that he says you sent him home and said that you'd take care of everything.'

'And that she was dead.'

'Like you, Mr Poulson, Norman Philips holds no medical qualification.'

Poulson leaned his elbows on the desk and rubbed at his eyes with the heels of his hands. He looked up. Mouth open as if about to speak. Held it there. Looked away and then back.

'As I said, Inspector, she's dead. So it doesn't matter a toss.'

'If it's true, it matters a toss. If it's untrue, it matters a toss why you're lying. So try me.'

'We heard her screaming. We were right above. We'd been waiting for her.'

'You did what?'

'We ran down to the stage door.'

'All of you?'

'No. Just me and Jason. She was lying on the floor. She was still alive. And before you ask, I could see her breathing. Lynda had a lot to breathe. But she was out. The stage door was open. I ran out. I assumed that whoever had attacked her couldn't be far. I didn't see anyone.'

'How long were you out?'

'Couple of minutes at the most.'

'Then?'

'Then, then I came back and—'

Poulson was not overcome. Poulson looked hard at Leonard. His expression said he really couldn't see why he was bothering to tell him anything.

'Mr Poulson, please. Three dead, hopefully none to go. Act's over. Then what?'

'Okay. He had his hands round her throat—'

'Who had?'

'Jason. He was strangling the life out of her, literally. I shouted at him and tried to pull him off. That was unfortunate. All he did was grip her tighter. When I got him off, she was dead. Her tongue was out. She was the wrong colour. She was dead.'

'Philips saw this?'

'No. He came back, maybe a minute later. He was somewhat excited. Shouting at the top of his voice that he'd killed her.'

'You claim he hadn't.'

'He didn't. Jason did.'

'Then why didn't you say so in the beginning?'

'And be in jail? No thank you. I have no need of twenty years of distance-learning Serbo-Croat.'

'Because it was you and not Jason.'

'Easier than that. It was complicated. Norman attacked her.

Jason strangled her. Who was responsible for her death? I would, Inspector, have got one third equal share. Don't try telling me anything else.'

'So you'd let Philips swing?'

'We don't any more, no matter how much you'd prefer we did.'

'You know what I mean.'

'Look, Inspector, Norman is a pathetic creature. He has been mocked and rocked by women all his life. His girlfriends demanded money when he screwed them. His wife was screwed every day by his best friend, even on the biggest night of his life – his famous crash. He hates his mother, his mother-in-law and any woman who reminds him of anyone he's ever loved. Why? Because they've all mocked him. At last he's done something about it. He gets his hands round Cinderella's tits, which he's been longing to do for twenty years, she screams rape and so he kills her, or so he thinks. The big punishment. He's done something other than falling off motor bikes. He's getting back at whatever or whoever made him an ugly, tongue-tied cripple with an incurable body-odour problem. Why be noble? He's happier in jail. At least he'll go down as the man who killed Linda Elström. Probably sell his story for a couple of million and be out in five. So why risk my freedom for his miserable neck?'

Leonard sucked at his tongue tasting the contempt he felt for Poulson.

'Didn't you work it out that he would change his story? Any half-way good lawyer would see to that when it all came back to him.'

'You think anyone would have believed him? Jason Williams, whiter than white. Loves his mother to distraction. Mr Clean. C'mon, Inspector. Until sweet baby Jason admitted it to you, he was safe.'

'He told us that you killed her.'

The slow shake of the head.

'No way. There's no way I'd risk a breath of my life for hers. The bitch wasn't worth anything I've ever owned.'

'Why hate her so much?'

'I always have.'

'It started in a bar in Spain.'

The laugh was short. A snort more than a laugh.

'Tiggy tell you that?'

'No. Newspaper cuttings.'

'You really want to know? I'll tell you. That movie was a dog. But the pedigree was good. What they used to call the big break. I needed that film. You won't remember, because no one does, that the sequel was *Morning Sunshine*. Really good thing. I could, I was, set to direct that. I was wild. I had ideas. Isaac Goldman liked me. Told me it was mine. Then I get the telephone call. Sorry. Gone to some gook who'd made commercials and two nominations for a festival in somewhere no one had heard about.'

'Why?'

'Because she had the hots for him. And if that wasn't enough, she was being screwed by Goldman. Because she promised lover boy that she'd fix it. She did. In twenty-four hours I was yesterday's news. She destroyed me.'

'Other jobs?'

'Not then. Not how the industry worked then. You know what she told Goldman? She told him I was screwing Jewish kids from some orphanage.'

'Were you?'

'She'd read something, or seen some story on the TV, or heard about it. She knew that Goldman, of all people, the great movie mogul and – wait for it – the great philanthropist, the one-man Diaspora conscience, would make sure I never worked again.'

'Why did she? Had to be more than getting her stud your job.'

'Oh no it didn't. That's what made her different. Anyone could play the politics. She had to play the bitch. She didn't want anyone to believe my version. It took a long time. I've never worked in a movie since.'

'So you hated her.'

'An understatement, but, let me tell you, I hated her so much that I would never give her rotting soul the satisfaction of seeing me done for her murder.'

Williams had been just as convincing.

'You wouldn't be if you could pin it, conveniently, on Williams.'

'Try to make it stick, Inspector. No chance.'

'And the public hanging?'

'He thought it was wonderful.'

'He wasn't strong enough to do it. Anyway, he wouldn't know how to operate the high fly.'

'He didn't have to. He had plenty of help from his friends. Once, remember, she was dead.'

'If she was.'

'She was. Ask your own doctor. It was in the papers. Didn't you see it? Quite a hero.'

Leonard got up. The chair squeaked its thanks. He stretched and leaned against the closed door.

'Accessory.'

'I'll deny it. Listen, Inspector. You've got a murder and you've got a murderer. You've got one whose character will be torn about on the basis of a couple of pictures. And you can release that poor sod Norman. Justice will be done and Jason's tape sales will double. Everyone wins.'

'Including you.'

'No. She cheated me twice. The first time was that movie. The second time was about to happen.'

'Her memory? You wanted her to fail, didn't you?'

'She was crumbling.'

'Which is why you brought her to Bath.'

'Why not? Full houses to see her body. Full houses to see her fail. She'd never work again.'

'And then you worked on her. Telephone calls?'

'Simply asking after her welfare.'

'Threatening her welfare.'

'No. Biology was doing that for me. I'd waited a long time. It was my turn to gloat and, yes, if you wish, help with the destruction of a bitch.'

'Nemesis.'

'Wrong gender, Inspector. I would say simple revenge long overdue.'

'After all this time?'

'It seems like yesterday.'

'Sick.'

'I wanted to be there and watch. I wanted to see her rot in public until all she had left were those silicone tits of hers. Then *I* would have been the one with the camera. That's what I wanted. Williams cheated me out of that. They both did. I'll never forgive them.'

Fifty-Two

It was Christmas Eve. Present-wrapping time. It was Jack, flipping through her notebook, who remembered the gift Tiggy Jones had offered just twenty-four hours earlier. She walked into Leonard's room and dropped a photograph from the Detained Property Store on his desk. The same child. The same obscenity. Leonard looked up. Puzzled through his red-rimmed eyes.

'The bungalow, sir.'

'What is?'

'That is, sir. Jones said something about Sharpe making house calls to do these pictures. I've just shown this to DC Leweson.'

Leonard looked again at the picture. He'd never been through the bungalow and the lighting wasn't that good. The shadows were grotesque. But he supposed that the search team could identify the setting. The closed blue silk drapes with their motif of Chinese dragons were obvious if not exclusive.

'Bernard says he thinks it was taken in Williams's bungalow.'

Leonard shook his head.

'No. *Mrs* Williams's bungalow.'

She hadn't thought of it that way. Now she did.

'Yes, sir.'

'She still at the Rivers?'

'Sir.'

He looked from the window. The sun was shining. It was cold. But for the moment it was clean. As good as any time for a stroll up the hill.

Mrs Williams sat on the tall chair in the corner of the square Georgian room. Cassie Makins and her husband sat together on the long regency-striped bench. Leonard sat facing them on the only rickety chair in the hotel. Jack stood in the corner. No one spoke. The maid, seemingly caught in the tension, fussed with the coffee tray, stumbled over her promise to get anything else they needed and beat her retreat closing the door with too much clatter. The chocolate box came to life.

'We have a couple of points to clear up and then, well, and then we will leave you to get on with whatever you have planned for—'

Leonard was going to say Christmas. He felt as clumsy as the maid.

'Well you know what I mean.'

Mrs Williams had insisted that she should stay to hear what the Rosses had to say about her son. After all, they were all friends, especially now. Cassie Ross held out her hand and her husband half-knelt to pour coffee. Leonard shook his head at the surgeon's inquiring glance and offered cup. He wanted to get on with it. Manners and niceties were best left to another time.

'Tell me, Mrs Ross, why did you fetch Jason and Maurice Poulson that night?'

As he spoke, Leonard had half an eye on Mrs Williams. Not a flicker. The sad smile was set as evenly as her dentures.

'Maurice asked me to.'

'You were waiting?'

'I was in bed. He called. Problem. Jason. Come quickly. I did.'

'Why?'

'I owned him. Getting out in the middle of the night comes with the territory. Maurice said it was A-1 serious. I believed him.'

'Why?'

'Maurice never, but never, asks for help. It had to be.'

'He told you what had happened?'

'Maurice said Lynda had had an accident, said it was bad. Said the ambulance had been called, and that Jason had to be got out of there. Don't forget I owned fifteen per cent of both of them.'

She reached out for coffee. Her husband didn't move. He was looking at her in apparent complete astonishment. She turned to look at him, seemingly surprised that he hadn't poured.

'Well?'

'You mean to tell me, darling, that you knew all the time?'

'Don't be pathetic, of course I did.'

'But—'

She turned back to Leonard.

'Anything else?'

'When did you know she was dead?'

'Then. I drove Jason home. We had to sit outside for twenty minutes before he could get out of the car. On the way back, Maurice told me what had happened.'

'Told you what?'

'I imagine you know by now. He and Jason went down to the stage door. Found her there. Jason lost his head.'

There was a long silence. Chris Ross was quite pale.

'Lost his head? Lost his head? What does that mean?'

Leonard looked at Mrs Williams. She hadn't moved. Same position. Same sad smile. Same teeth.

'According to Maurice Poulson, Mr Ross, according to him—'

Again he looked at the old lady. Nothing had changed.

'I'm sorry about this, Mrs Williams. Would you like us to leave this?'

Still the smile.

'According to Poulson, Jason strangled Lynda.'

'My God.'

Leonard remembered Williams's frequent blasphemy. From Ross, it sounded heartfelt. He turned back to Cassie Makins.

'And so you went to Cornwall.'

'Easy. Low profile when the sniping starts. My great-grandfather died ignoring that.'

Ross sipped noisily at his coffee. The coffee cup remained at his lips even when he'd finished drinking. His wife didn't bother looking at him. She knew how weak he was. But he didn't slink away.

'Why? Will someone tell me why?'

His wife looked at her nails. Leonard closed his eyes. He wanted this day to end.

'We believe, sir, that your ex-wife was blackmailing a number of people including Jason. She had—'

Mr Williams stared straight ahead.

'She had, sir, um, compromising pictures.'

'I had no idea.'

'Oh shut up, will you? Don't wet yourself. No one's arresting you.'

He looked from Leonard to Jack. A weak smile.

'I can assure you, Inspector—'

He tailed away. Helpless. Out of depth. Leonard wanted to tell him to shut up. Not to be so wet. Cassie Makins held out her hand for coffee. Her husband had had enough. He ignored her. Her lip tightened and bent in its contempt for her husband.

'You knew about these pictures, Mrs Ross?'

'I knew she was a crazy bitch.'

'The pictures?'

''Course I didn't. I'd have stamped on her heart if I'd known.'

'Disapproval or investment?'

'I disapprove of anything that threatens my investment.'

'Fifteen per cent of Jason represented a big investment.'

''Course.'

'Enough to kill for?'

Cassie Makins lit a cigarette and forgot about the holder.

'How many murderers d'you want, Inspector?'

'How many were there?'

'Don't be a smartarse. You're only the arse bit.'

He was beginning to believe her. About everything. Another long silence and then Mrs Williams pushed on the arms of the elegant chair and stood.

'I think I'd like to go home now, dear. Better that way don't you think? Things to be done. It's Christmas tomorrow, you know.'

Jack was standing near the old lady. She put a gentle hand on her arm.

'Perhaps it might be a good idea if you stayed for a little while, Mrs Williams. Don't you? We'll find you a room of your own. Yes?'

Mrs Williams looked confused. Confused? Leonard didn't think so. Not for one second. He was suddenly on his feet. He picked up long woollen coat from the arm of the sofa.

'Perhaps Mrs Williams is right, Sergeant. Perhaps a visit home is just what she needs right now. What we all need. Yes? Get a car downstairs, will you? Maybe we'll see her home.'

Mrs Williams allowed Leonard to help her on with her coat and smiled as he buttoned the top two buttons and handed her her sheepskin gloves and cashmere scarf Jason had given her in her bright red stocking just twelve months ago to the day.

Fifty-Three

They sat in the kitchen with the inevitable pot of tea on a tray and a tin of ginger nuts between them. Outside the watch of cameras and scribes kept vigil. Leonard's outburst in the theatre had already hit the newsreels and tapes.

'He's a good boy. You know that, don't you? He really is. And so many friends. Everyone knows him and of course they all love him. Well, we all know that. And the Queen, you know, God bless her, well dear, had all his records, you know.'

Leonard said nothing and dipped a fresh ginger nut into his tea. Mrs Williams smiled.

'That's how Jason likes them. Dunkin' nutties, he calls them.'

Leonard put the soggy biscuit in his saucer.

'You must have been very proud, Mrs. Williams.'

'Oh, I am. Go anywhere in the world and everyone says nice things about him, everyone.'

'He was very fond of you.'

'Oh, he is. I'm not just his mum you know. Oh no. We're friends, real friends. Takes me to all the best places, he does. Oh yes, sounds silly, but my Jason says, "Mum," he says, "Mum, we're the ideal couple." Isn't that lovely?'

She looked from Leonard to where Jack sat on a high stool against the breakfast bar. Jack managed a smile. Leonard didn't even attempt one.

'Yes, Mrs Williams, very nice. Friends.'

'Oh, yes.'

'No secrets.'

'Of course not. Not my Jason. We don't have secrets.'

'About anything.'

'No, why should we? We wouldn't be proper friends then. He tells me everything. Well, almost everything. The only thing he never tells me is gossip. Jason's not a gossip. Nothing good comes from it, that's what he says. So he doesn't.'

'You knew, then.'

Mrs Williams worried her bottom lip. They eyes didn't twinkle anymore. She reached for the teapot.

'More tea, dear?'

'Did you?'

She looked to Madelaine Jack.

'What about you, dear? Another cup? Come on, there's plenty in the pot.'

'Did you, Mrs Williams?'

She put down the teapot and tugged the knitted cosy back into place.

'Did I what, dear?'

'You knew. No secrets, remember?'

'Knew what?'

The lip was wobbling. But just for a moment.

'Mrs Williams, please. You see, it's better if you tell us. Better for Jason.'

'Jason?'

The name came softly from her lips. Wondering where she'd once heard that name.

'You see, Mrs Williams, we need to know. We need you to help us. Your Jason is accused of something that perhaps he didn't do. You can help him.'

'He's a very good boy. Heart of gold.'

'The children. They came here, didn't they?'

'Oh lots of people come here. All the time. He loves to see them. Gives them presents and things.'

'Tell me about the children. Tell me about them, and Jason.'

'Which children, dear?'

'Tell me about the ones who came here. The very young ones. The ones who came to – the ones who came to play with Jason.'

She sat still except for a tugging at a small nerve at the corner of her mouth. He could smell the lavender water. He could see the distance in her wet eyes. With effort she stood.

'Would you excuse me a moment, dear?'

Leonard didn't move. Jack did. She followed the little woman from the kitchen and across the square hall to a short corridor. At an open bedroom doorway she watched as Mrs Williams took a blue photo album from the top drawer of a mahogany chest and then followed her back across the hall, without a glance at the sealed bathroom door.

Leonard was fiddling with the remote-control card. Switching stations from carol to carol. Clicked off. Then on. Then off.

She sat down clutching the album.

'It's the timer, isn't it?'

She didn't understand. Jack did. She did it every night. Programme the bedside radio to come on in the morning. Six. Seven. If she were lucky, eight. Just as easy to make it one o'clock.

Mrs Williams smiled and pushed the dark mock leather album across the table to him. Large gold Gothic script proclaimed the Azir-Armenia Adoption Society. Leonard opened the album. On light blue leaves, young faces smiled at him.

She stretched a wrinkled hand across and traced the outline of a child's face with her dull-gold ringed wedding finger.

'Lovely children. So pretty. Jason loves them you know.'

'They came here?'

'Oh, yes. They love it. You see, they haven't anything. Just waiting for proper families. So they come for a little while. I always make fairy cakes. Jason's favourite, of course.'

Leonard's sigh was sad enough. No frustration now. Just deep sadness. He tried to put as much gentleness into his voice as possible.

'Tell me, Mrs Williams, do you know what happened when the children were here?'

She nodded, happily enough.

'Oh, yes. He gives them so many presents, you know. And they play games and things and they have a clown.'

'A what?'

'You know, a clown.'

'Where from?'

'My Jason arranges it. Actually, it's that nice Mr Sharpe, but the children don't know that. They just love all the games.'

'Mrs Williams, I'm sorry to have to ask you this, but do you know about those games? What they did?'

'Oh yes. We all played.'

'I don't think you understand. You see—'

'Lovely games. Well, sometimes a little naughty. But he gives them so many things and they truly love him. They really do. I know they do. Some of them cry when it's time to go. They really don't want to.'

'But – let me ask you something else then. Do you know how they come here? Do you know who Jason speaks to?'

'Jason?'

'Yes, Mrs Williams. Your Jason. He must have known someone who arranged for the children to come here.'

'Oh no. Not Jason.'

'I'm sorry, Mrs Williams, I really am. But he must have done.'

'It's always a special treat for him. We play surprises. I love giving him surprises. He gives me so much. A mother couldn't wish for a kinder more thoughtful son.'

'But there must be someone, or a telephone number, or someone he knew.'

'No dear, you don't understand. Not Jason. I do it for him. It's my treat.'

Fifty-Four

The lights blazed along corridors, through open-doored offices, in the depths of store rooms and across the holly and paper chains in the canteen. But not much moved. Even at Manvers Street, it was the eve of Christ's Mass. Those who could be spared had long gone to their homes. In the first-floor corner office, Marsh sat rock still behind his L-shaped desk, his expression grim enough to reap. Leonard slumped and tasted his aching gums. Jack sat straight backed, still clean, still fresh, still weary.

'Bizarre. Utterly bizarre. But she must have had someone to start the whole hideous arrangement.'

Leonard said nothing. He no longer cared. Jack gave her diplomatic cough.

'Well, sir, as you say, bizarre. As far as we can make out, the guy who runs this is a former roadie. Forget the Azir-Armenia thing. He's from Liverpool and operates out of smart offices in Amsterdam and God knows where else. As far as I can make out from E-21, this sort of thing's been running all over Europe for twenty years. Started with the big refugee thing in the seventies and hasn't stopped. Europol know all about it. Can't stop it. They close one down and another opens up.'

'But why his mother?'

'Seemingly she was, well, being mumsy. She found out by chance and rather than have her darling Jason nipping off to dubious premises in Amsterdam, she took charge. Don't roam the streets, darling, bring your friends home.'

'James? Where does this leave us?'

Leonard stirred himself. He wanted it to leave him alone. It wouldn't. He knew that. It was the beginning, not the end.

'At a guess, sir, the old lady's untouchable. We'd never get anything on her. She's apple pie. I'm more concerned with Lynda Elström. The way this is running, we've got Philips for nothing more than assault and a dead pop star down for murder and maybe a couple of actors for – well, nothing much we can prove other than spitefulness. All very neat.'

'But you don't believe Philips? Poulson?'

Leonard's mouth twisted sideways. He blew a long sigh from a deep undrainable reservoir of exasperation.

'Philips, maybe. Poulson? No, sir. Convenient. Poulson had more reason to murder her.'

'I'd have thought Williams and his pictures was reason enough.'

'Perhaps. But Poulson had longed for something like this. I know he said he wanted her public humiliation. Well, they strung her up. He got it. But there's something else and I don't know what it is.'

'Prejudice, James?'

'Am I?'

'Indeed. And within these walls, you understand, a commendable prejudice. They do not represent a very healthy part of our society. But then, I suppose we should be used to that.'

Leonard struggled upright. Crossed an ankle on to his knee and tugged at his sock. Marsh tapped the tip of his nose with his silver pencil.

'Maddy?'

It was Christmas.

'Well, sir, we've got Ike so that's the motive tied up. We've got Poulson as eye witness but accessory. Philips and Ross as circumstantials. Not much, is it, sir?'

'What about this Sharpe fellow? Hit and run or part of all this?'

'We don't know, sir. For the moment it seems hit and run. Coincidence. Mrs Potts said Sharpe was a bit deaf – might not have even heard anything coming.'

'At that time of night? And his hearing was good enough for his work.'

'Maybe, sir. Anyway, there's nothing to prove it wasn't a straightforward RTA. As I say, sir, there isn't much to go on.'

It wasn't.

'So?'

Leonard stood. Stretched. Crackled his spine.

'Okay, sir. Then what do we do? Go the easy way and get a result or go for Poulson?'

Marsh turned to the wall chart of duties, shortages, targets, shortfalls.

'We'd never get him, James. Never in a thousand years.'

He swivelled his chair and reached for the private line. Time to tell Mrs Marsh that he would be home in good time for the midnight service.

Outside it was raining, but the air felt fresh. They stood for a moment on the long steps without saying a word. He buzzed then gave that up.

'Wonder where the original negatives are.'

'Presumably Ike's got them.'

They wouldn't take long to surface. They'd be worth a fortune, or a ransom.

'It's a bastard, isn't it?'

'Yes, sir.'

He squinted at his pocket watch. He wondered if Con was in Shades.

'Tell me, you fancy—?'

'Sir?'

They walked slowly towards the abbey and the hill. No hurry. She might have taken his arm, but she didn't. It wasn't that sort of Christmas.